ALSO BY DAVID L. GOLEMON

THE
SUPERNATURALS

David L. Golemon

St. Martin's Paperbacks

This is a work of fiction. All of the characters, organizations, and events portrayed in this novel are either products of the author's imagination or are used fictitiously.

THE SUPERNATURALS

Copyright © 2016 by David L. Golemon.

All rights reserved.

For information address St. Martin's Press, 175 Fifth Avenue, New York, NY 10010.

ISBN: 978-1-250-19101-4

Our books may be purchased in bulk for promotional, educational, or business use. Please contact your local bookseller or the Macmillan Corporate and Premium Sales Department at 1-800-221-7945, ext. 5442, or by e-mail at MacmillanSpecialMarkets@macmillan.com.

Printed in the United States of America

St. Martin's Press hardcover edition / October 2016
St. Martin's Paperbacks edition / November 2018

St. Martin's Paperbacks are published by St. Martin's Press, 175 Fifth Avenue, New York, NY 10010.

10 9 8 7 6 5 4 3 2 1

For Buck, Eunice, Steve, Scott, and Valisa, and also for our little boy lost, Ric. This novel is far more than a ghost story, it's more wishful thinking about what is to come after we finish with this life . . . until we see each other again, my thoughts are forever with my family.

AUTHOR'S NOTE

More than four years ago I ran a story on my blog at Event-GroupFiles.com asking my readership to send me examples of a real haunted house that I could possibly use in a story. Needless to say, the response was overwhelming. I received so many letters that I decided not to print any of them, as it would have taken most of my time to do so. I thanked everyone, then placed the project on hold, trying to put my thoughts about ghosts into perspective.

However, there was one particular letter that that caught my attention and became a thorn in my side. It was from a family in upstate New York who wished to remain anonymous. They told me of the beauty of a house nestled quietly in the mountains. Confused as to the subject matter of this note and suspecting that the author of the letter had misread my blog, I read on nonetheless. They explained that this house, although beautiful, had something wrong with it. It was the summer home to a very wealthy and famous family with a sordid history of sorts. The family had not lived in the summer retreat since the fall of 1940. They described the house as a three-story gothic structure that sat alone in a valley of immense beauty, built in the years leading up to World War I, yet again they reiterated that there was something wrong with this gorgeous estate. Curious beyond belief, I pestered the writer until I received via snail mail the address of this estate in the mountains, on the lone condition that I not use their name or the actual house in my story, if indeed I did write one. I agreed.

A month later I went to see this house and the hundred-acre estate surrounding it. When I arrived, expecting nothing more than a run-down shanty of a house, I was amazed to see a three-storied, yellow-and-white-painted gabled mansion that looked as if it could have been built the week before. After seeing a FOR SALE sign on the main gate, I called the real estate broker and asked if I could see the interior. My request was granted and the agent met me later that afternoon.

Although the agent unlocked the front door for me, she informed me that she would wait for me on the porch. Thinking this odd, I entered the house on my own.

I spent a grand total of two minutes inside the most beautiful foyer I have ever seen before I turned on my heel and left the summer mansion. I am not a believer in things that go bump in the night—I write about them, talk about them, and in the end I laugh about them. But in those two minutes, standing in that foyer and looking up at the immense staircase that seemed to travel up to the sky, I realized through my feelings alone that there was indeed something wrong with the house. I got a chill as I looked around, at the way everything in the living room looked freshly dusted, and the way the Persian rug looked as if it had just been carpet-swept, and the wood of the wall paneling looked just oiled.

Standing there I felt, and this may sound ridiculous, that the house was aware; aware I was intruding. With a final chill, I turned and left that house in the mountains and never returned. Now, I must remind you that I don't believe in ghosts, or any other agent of the night that you cannot see, cannot study, and cannot feel with your hands. But I do believe one thing: that house in the mountains wants to be left alone. I am convinced of that.

So, here we are. I made several inquiries about this house, and yes, it was once and still is owned by a very famous and wealthy family. Although the summer home has not been lived in since the forties, its upkeep is maintained through a private contractor and the estate is kept immaculate. That brings us to this story. I have written this tale with the elements of the supernatural as just a figment of my rather tormented imagination, but there is one thing I must stress. I attempted to bring the feeling alive from my memory of walking into that house four years ago—to pass along the feeling of dread in such a supposedly inanimate object. As I said, most elements that make up this fictional story are from the author's imagination, but the house almost described to a T in the story is real. I have been there, and I will never go back after my two-minute stay. The reader—that is, you—can travel to this small valley in the mountains if you're good enough to find it, because I will keep my word to the people who guided me there and never reveal it. Then you can judge for yourself just what makes you want to run from that beautiful home and its property and never look back.

So, just this one warning: The account you are about to read is, as I said, fiction, made up, maybe overblown possibly, but there is one immutable fact that you can take to bed with you. The house depicted as Summer Place in this story—*is real*.

Oh, very gloomy is the house of woe,
where tears are falling while the bell is knelling,
with all the dark solemnities that show
that death is in the dwelling!

—THOMAS HOOD, "The Haunted House"

Whatever walked there, walked alone.

—SHIRLEY JACKSON, *The Haunting of Hill House*

PROLOGUE

Jessica and Warren stood like sentinels—or at the very least, like guard dogs—next to the master's third-floor chambers, only feet from the master bedroom suite and the sewing room. It had been three hours since the professor had ordered lights out and allowed the experiment to truly begin. Warren Atkinson placed the digital recording device in the center of the Persian rug. The twenty-five-year-old grad student slapped Jessica's hand away again. She kept grabbing for him every time the old house creaked or settled in some far-off place. At the rate they were going they would never place all the sensitive equipment in time. The young girl wasn't exactly ghost-hunting material, and he felt sure that Professor Kennedy would end up regretting having chosen Jessica for the team to investigate the old, rambling house.

"Look, you're going to have to quit pulling on me every time you hear a noise or feel a draft," Warren said. The girl was terrified. He knew asking a psychology major to join the experiment had been a mistake, but the professor wanted objective opinions; not just from the "extreme nature point of view," but also from the human mind also—thus Jessica. "Listen." He tried to speak calmly to the girl. "The house is a hundred years old. Boards have loosened up. It's not ghosts and it's not supernatural at all . . . it's just house noises."

"We've been to a lot of places with Professor Kennedy on this study, but this house is *not* just a house. If there is one place in the world that's haunted, it's this house, these grounds. I can feel it."

Warren was amazed that the psych major had worked herself up into such a fear-induced frame of mind—something she of all people should have recognized.

He shook his head. She was now an uncontrolled part of the experiment, and he knew he was going to have to report her status to the professor. Jessica could no longer conduct herself as an observer of the house. Instead of lambasting her— or teasing her at the very least, as he normally would have done—Warren nodded and placed a hand on her shoulder. The girl was shaking. He patted her shoulder and then smiled.

"Look, I just have to place the last thermal imager down by the sewing room, and then we're done. Why don't you go wait on the third-floor landing? That way you can still see me down the hallway, but you'll be closer to an escape route."

Jessica shook off his hand and glared at his bearded features. "Just because I'm hearing things that are definitely not house-settling noises doesn't mean I'm too scared to do what Professor Kennedy has asked of me. Go ahead and get on with what you have to do, so we can meet the others in the ballroom. We're running behind schedule."

Warren smiled again, then pushed his wire-rimmed glasses back up the bridge of his nose.

"Okay, that's the stuff. Shall we place the last imager?"

She finally smiled in return and then gestured for Warren to proceed. As he turned away, Jessica heard the creak of a door. She stopped and once more reached out for Warren. "Listen! I just heard a door open up here." She tried desperately to peer into the darkness of the hallway.

"Enough is enough. You know as well as I that all of these doors are locked. The owner of the property saw to that. We don't have access to the rooms on the third floor."

"Okay, they're locked." She grabbed his hand and directed his penlight down the hallway. Its weak beam settled on the two sets of large doors at the end. One set, on the right side, was the master suite; the door on the left was the sewing room. That door was standing wide open. "So why isn't that door shut, like it was just a second ago?"

The door was not only open, it was pinned back against the wall, as if someone were holding it there as wide as they could get it.

"That door was triple-locked, with two dead bolts and a knob lock. And the damn thing *was* closed, just a moment ago."

"That's what I just said, smart-ass. I suppose that's the sewing room settling because it's so old?"

Warren shook his head. "Knock it off." He reached for his radio with his free hand. "Professor, this is Warren up on three," he said into the small radio.

They heard a crackle and hiss, and then silence.

"Professor, are you reading me?"

Jessica and Warren watched the open doorway of the sewing room. They jumped when they heard the poundings. They echoed out of the sewing room, as if some giant had started walking toward them. Jessica's fingernails dug into Warren's arm and her grip was iron. They both felt the poundings through their feet. Then as quickly as they started, the pounding footsteps stopped.

"What the hell was that?" Warren asked, not really caring if Jessica answered him at all.

"They had to have heard that downstairs—right?" she asked. Warren shined the light around the hallway.

A door creaked, but it wasn't a sound one would associate with a door opening. It was more like someone was placing a stupendous amount of pressure against the wood. They could hear the cracking of the grain. Warren moved the penlight to his right, where the door to one of the larger bedrooms only feet away was bent outward. It seemed the wood of the thick door couldn't withstand the pressure being placed on it. Then it rebounded, as if whoever was on the other side relinquished their assault.

"We have to leave," Jessica said as she tried to pull Warren away.

He shook her off and raised the radio to his lips. "We have to get the professor up here," he said and pushed the transmit button.

"Pretty boy."

The voice that came from the radio made Warren freeze. He swallowed the lump that had formed in his throat the best he could, but the strange statement hung in the dark, cold air of the hallway.

"Get on there and tell whoever is screwing around to knock it off," Jessica said angrily.

"Pretty girl," said the feminine voice over the radio.

Warren looked down at the radio. The bedroom door next to them rattled in its frame, and then something on the other side hit it hard enough to shake the cut crystal doorknob. Once more, the door bulged, and this time the impact was so fierce that Warren and Jessica backed away, half expecting the wood to explode outward. Then once more, the door relaxed and went back to its normal shape, only this time with something akin to a deep breath, as if the exertion of bending the door outward had taken too much energy. A voice, different from the one they had just heard, came over the radio.

"Run," came the whispered order. *"Run, NOW!"*

Warren started to turn, but his eyes fell on the sewing room at the far end of the hallway. A large area to the left side of the door bulged outward, sending plaster and wallpaper snapping off in small chips to fall to the Persian rug down the center of the hallway. The bulge moved a foot, stopped. It looked like a chest, inhaling and exhaling as it moved. It came on again, this time surging three feet before it stopped.

Warren backed away, pushing Jessica as he went.

"Get out of here," he said as loudly as he dared. All thoughts of contacting Professor Kennedy in the ballroom had vanished.

"Go!" came the whispered voice from the closest bedroom.

"Pretty boy, pretty girl, babies, babies, please come

home." This time the voice wasn't coming from the radio, but the large pulsing bulge in the wall. It was only ten feet away now. *"You're mine!"*

That was all Warren could take. He turned and pushed Jessica down the hallway just as the plaster on the wall bulged once more and came on like a shark cutting through water. Just as Warren neared the third-floor landing, something grabbed him. It was as if an iron giant had grabbed his shoulder. His arms flailed and the penlight and radio went flying. The light spun crazily in the air and then hit the carpeted runner. Jessica stopped. The light had aligned perfectly with Warren's legs. She screamed when she saw a large, dark, smoke-encased hand reach out from the bulging wall, shearing the wallpaper away as it grabbed hold of Warren.

"Help!" he screamed.

Jessica couldn't move; she looked to the right, toward the bedroom door. It was still and silent, as if its warning earlier had never been. She looked at Warren and his fear-filled eyes and knew that she couldn't stay. She had to run.

Warren was yanked hard into the wall. Half of his body was embedded in the plaster and wood. Then he was yanked again. This time his body went rigid and then he almost vanished completely. His eyes were pleading for Jessica to help him. His arms reached for her. She slowly reached out and her fingertips touched Warren's, but with another sharp jerk Warren was pulled completely into the wall, his glasses flying free. Jessica heard the crunch of bone and the shattering of his arms. She collapsed to the floor, unable to move.

She didn't know how long she remained on the floor. She was aware of the smell of plaster and mildew, even the dust as it formed and then scattered in the dark around her. She finally reached for the penlight on the Persian runner and then slowly raised it to the spot where Warren had been. The papered wall was intact. Not one mark showed; not one bit of evidence that Warren had ever been there. Jessica started shaking.

The sewing room door swung closed. Slowly, with the

same penetrating squeak she had heard a few minutes before the house had turned on them. Jessica knew she was starting to lose consciousness, but through her daze she heard the softer, far gentler voice come once more through the bedroom door. This time it seemed as if the voice were tired, exhausted, but persistent nonetheless.

"Get out, NOW!"

The men and women sitting around the large conference table watched as she slowly placed her files and large case on the table before her. The movements seemed deliberately slow, and everyone knew the man sitting at the head of the conference table was the object of those deliberate actions. The man himself sat stoically. His eyes never left Kelly Delaphoy—everyone in the company knew the young woman was after his job. That in and of itself wasn't too surprising. After all, when you swim with sharks, there's bound to be at least one in the water with designs on biting your ass. As everyone summoned to this meeting knew, there were no waters more shark-infested in the world than Hollywood.

There were sixteen people in the room, all of them with a hand in television programming. Kelly Delaphoy had notified everyone a week in advance of the meeting, and they all knew she had to have some backing. She had not only lured them, but also had the power to summon the president of the entertainment division to an afternoon production conference. That was unheard of. The power of the number one show in all of television gave Kelly that right. It also meant that she had backing that went far beyond the entertainment division.

Kelly punched a button on her laptop and waited. As for the president of entertainment, his eyes never strayed to the screen. They all could feel his gaze on her, and they also knew Kelly could feel the man's eyes burn into her. He didn't show the slightest interest in her presentation—his mind was on how much he despised the young woman from Cincinnati.

"First off, I would like to thank each and every one of you for attending," Kelly said. "What I have to show you is this."

The first slide was replaced by what could have been an advertisement in a Realtor's book. The house was beautiful and sat on manicured grounds. With one look toward the head of the conference table, the young producer started the meeting in earnest by nodding toward her executive producer—the only man who knew what this particular meeting was about.

Jason Sanborn stood and walked toward the screen. With his empty pipe, he tapped the gorgeous house and grounds.

"Ladies and gentlemen, I give you the vacation retreat Summer Place." He turned to face the others around the table. As he spoke, the grounds in the picture played across Jason's face, making them blend together with his beard and soft features. "As you will come to know through Ms. Delaphoy's presentation, this is a house that needs attention."

Out of the corner of her eye, Kelly Delaphoy watched the man she was about to go to war with over her project.

"The famous American author Shirley Jackson," Kelly began, "was reputed to have vacationed at Summer Place a very long time ago. At least, that is the rumor. Like the strange stories surrounding the vacation retreat itself, it is hard to confirm. Ghost stories always seem to be that way: everyone knows, but they don't remember who told them, or how the stories originated."

Kelly walked a circuit around the conference table as she spoke, delivering every word as clearly and precisely as possible. The only area she avoided was the head of the table.

"After I came upon the tale—or rumor, if you will—of Ms. Jackson's stay, I since learned that no one has been an official guest in the house since 1940. Ms. Jackson didn't achieve her fame until 1959, so one would have to eliminate the author as a possible invitee to Summer Place—at least, by the owner's invitation."

Jason Sanborn cleared his throat. He removed his cold pipe once more from his mouth and looked around the table.

"The original rumor of Ms. Jackson's stay began circulating in 1957, just two summers before she published her famous novel *The Haunting of Hill House*. Nineteen years after the closing of the summer house, that book became a critical, literary, and financial success. Still, the anonymous gossips and storytellers persist that Ms. Jackson's famous tale was based on her visit to Summer Place."

There were more than a few chuckles around the table, but not from the man watching with interest from behind a studiously bored demeanor. His eyes only moved to Kelly as she stopped at Jason's chair and placed a hand on his shoulder.

"Unlike Ms. Jackson's description of the stone monstrosity called Hill House, Summer Place—at least outwardly—has a feeling of peace and tranquillity when you look down upon it from one of the many surrounding hills and privately maintained roads."

Jason added, "For more of a description of the house and grounds, Kelly and I have commissioned the former news anchor John Wesley to narrate and take us through the rest of this presentation."

Everyone seemed impressed that Jason and Kelly had coerced one of the most important men in the history of the network to narrate the story. His deep and booming grandfatherly voice would lend much power to the tale, and their ability to bring him out of his retirement suggested powerful backing for the project. This point wasn't lost on the most important man in the room. His eyes finally moved to the screen as the voice of the retired anchorman began.

"To view the fifteen carved wooden gables lining the edge of the steep roof to the house itself, you believe that Summer Place could be a scene borrowed from a wondrous fairy tale of gingerbread houses."

The voice of the former anchorman was comforting, as it had comforted all of America when he'd told the world each night, "We are still here, so here's the news."

"The sewing machine magnate F. E. Lindemann built Summer Place in 1892 as a family getaway deep in the Pocono Mountains of Pennsylvania—a relatively short commute from New York City even in those days of washboard roads and dirt drives. New York was home to Lindemann's industrial empire. His was the first family not only of the modern sewing machine, but of New York's garment industry as well."

The view on the screen switched to a large family portrait.

"Ten family members, including Lindemann's eight children, dominated the grounds in the summer months, and the children and parents were not alone. After years of hunting vacations in the area, Lindemann cut loose with ninety thousand dollars for the property's eight hundred and thirty-two acres.

"F. E. Lindemann loved the location so much," the anchorman's voice continued, "that he erected Summer Place for his wife and soon-to-be large family. Elena Lindemann was a beautiful woman, and part of the extended royal family of Czar Nicholas the Second of Russia. Very little is known about her. However, it is known that she dearly loved each of her eight children. She insisted on giving birth at Summer Place, even in the dead of winter. She would dote on those children until they were all, one by one, consumed by tragedy or illness."

The view on the screen switched to show close-ups of each of the eight children.

"Still, she worshipped them with every ounce of her soul until the day she died in 1951. Every one of her children were brought back to Summer Place for burial after their deaths. As she put it, 'to be brought back to the place they were born and lived the happiest years of their lives.'"

The slide changed to a painting of a beautiful woman who smiled at the artist as if she knew she would be viewed for hundreds of years.

"The tranquillity and demeanor of Summer Place changed in the summer of 1925. Gwyneth Gerhardt, a German opera star and acquaintance of the Austrian-born Lindemann, visited Summer Place as a prized guest. Miss Gerhardt came up missing on the evening of her own official grand reception. Among the guests that week were silent-film stars from Hollywood and the royalty of Broadway theater. Although no guests were ever directly quoted, it was whispered inside closed circles that Miss Gerhardt had been troubled by noises, voices emanating from the walls in her suite, in the days leading up to her reception."

The next slide showed the grainy official photograph of guests mingling in the ballroom inside Summer Place.

"The night of her official introduction to American high society and theater circles, Miss Gerhardt never came down from her room. First, Frederic Ernst Lindermann himself searched every one of the twenty-five bedrooms and suites of Summer Place."

There were curious nods and a few comments not fully heard from the table.

"A local girl, Leanne Cummings, a shy seventeen-year-old from the nearby village of Bright Waters, trained by the Lindemanns for serving at social functions, claimed she had left Miss Gerhardt in her suite after laying out a beautiful sequined gown upon her bed. That was the last anyone ever saw of the famous German opera star Gwyneth Gerhardt."

Kelly allowed her eyes to fall on the entertainment president. He was watching the presentation, but every now and then would write something on the notepad before him.

The slide changed to a festive scene of Christmastime at Summer Place.

"There were other strange instances at the house, to be sure. The Christmas party of 1927 is one of these. The Lindemanns very rarely spent Christmas outside of New York City unless Mrs. Lindemann was there for the birth of one of her children."

Another slide. This one was of a woman most in the room recognized, but most failed to come up with her name.

"The incident in the winter of 1927 involved Vidora Samuels, a silent-film star of some renown. She retired from acting at the height of her popularity, after claiming she had been attacked at Summer Place during Lindemann's Christmas gathering."

A paragraph from a magazine filled the screen.

"When questioned about the incident several years later by *Variety* magazine, Vidora denied ever claiming to have been attacked. Follow-up with the immediate family after her death in 1998 revealed that Ms. Samuels actually lived in terror from that night in 1927."

The slide changed to a gorgeous view of the mansion in summer.

"The most famous incident occurred in the very next turn of the seasons. In the summer of 1928, gossip columnist Henrietta Batiste, eminent in her literary slashing of the world's most popular authors, was invited to visit for a short weekend getaway. Miss Batiste, an accomplished rider and renowned horse lover, was out riding alone one sunny Saturday morning before breakfast.

"The next anyone saw of the columnist was at five thirty that evening. Lindemann had just returned with an unsuccessful search party to find the woman sprawled on the Persian rug in the entryway. She was bleeding from her mouth, and one arm was almost completely ripped free of her body. The same police report states that the thirty-six-year old was in a state of shock from loss of blood—but I must note here that there was more than one quote from the house staff after their dismissal a few years later, stating that it wasn't only loss of blood that precipitated the shock, but sheer fright.

"A local physician removed the torn remnants of her left arm and stayed through the night to keep an eye on his famous patient. When she awakened, still in a state of shock, she was able to relate her experience to the good doctor. In the woods at the back of the estate, her horse had stumbled upon what looked like an unearthed human skull. There had been other remains—an old tattered gray dress, a woman's shoe—but before she could discern more, she had been pulled from her horse by the sharp tug that had injured her arm. She was thrown to the ground, where someone—or something—pulled her hair, ripping free her riding hat, then showered open-handed slaps to her face. She had felt horrid fingernails rip down her cheeks and exposed neck. Miss Batiste claimed that if it weren't for the horse, she would have been beaten to death. But the horse went wild, attacking her attacker with flying, flailing hooves. When the doctor and Lindemann attempted to question the woman further, her screaming fit started. She said it was a man, and then screamed it was a woman. The story switched back and forth until the only course of action was to discount her memory of the event altogether."

Kelly looked around the meeting. The slide show and its powerful narration, the results of months of research and planning, were doing their job.

"As for her claim that her horse had unearthed the skeletal remains of a woman long dead, searchers returned to the scene and found no trace. Our producers attempted to gather more information, but sources in the small town refused to talk to us. It may seem ridiculous to us now, but thoroughly understandable when you see the faces of the locals. They are still haunted by the mention of Summer Place."

The slide changed to the winding roads and forested slopes of the Pocono Mountains.

"Several weary travelers have reported eerie happenings on the roads surrounding the estate. Blood-curdling screams in the night, deer and other animals lying dead along a roadway that no one travels. There are even rumors of missing cross-country skiers who may have happened upon Summer Place in the season that sees the grounds shrouded in a white veil of snow. Ski tracks lead up to the property, but no tracks ever leave."

The portrait of the sewing machine magnate again flashed upon the screen.

"With the death of F. E. Lindemann in 1940, Summer Place closed its doors. The only other time it received guests, save for the Lindemann children's burials, was during the

lease in 2003 to the now famous—or, *infamous*—Professor
Gabriel Kennedy. The state of Pennsylvania reports in tripli-
cate that the professor walked into Summer Place one spring
night with six students. A day later, he and only five others
walked out alive."

Kelly finally looked directly at the head of entertainment.
His brow was furrowed, and she knew that he had just figured out what the meeting was about.

"Since 2003 and the Professor Kennedy incident, the
house has truly remained empty except for the Johanssons—a
local family hired as caretakers in 1940 and paid handsomely
by the Lindemann estate. The house continues to sit in the
peaceful valley, and anyone traveling the lonely roads in the
Poconos may still happen upon Summer Place. Eunice Johansson still changes the bed linens in the twenty-five bedrooms
and suites religiously every other week. She polishes the wood
floors every month. The felt on the billiard table is brushed,
and the table itself is leveled. The pool is drained every fall
and refilled promptly the second week of spring. Though
there are no horses at Summer Place these days, the straw
inside the stables is still tossed bimonthly. Fresh water is
still changed out daily for animals that will never drink it."

Kelly started to gather a few items from her case, unno-
ticed. The presentation continued under the deep, soothing
voice of the narrator.

"Summer Place stands and waits, still looking like a home
from a fairy tale. It pays no mind to the ghostly rumors that
permeate the valley, but those wishing to test the myths find
Summer Place as well guarded as the castles of olden days.
From the road, the upright lines and warm glowing windows
of Summer Place and its benign atmosphere lend no credence
to the ghost stories. It is a beautiful estate, with a foundation
strong and sound, the walls and doors upright and tight, and
always sensibly shut, just like Ms. Jackson's story says they
should be. And when you look at Summer Place, always from
a distance, a line from *The Haunting of Hill House* may come

to mind: "Whatever walked there, *walked alone*." This was the heart of her terrifying story, and it may also be true of Summer Place—the resemblance is just too strong to ignore.

"*Whatever walked there, walked alone.*"

Jason Sanborn raised the lights and paused to survey the faces around the table. They looked confused, but also interested. He moved to his seat as Kelly passed sheaves of paper around the conference table, saving the last for the silent man at its head.

"The following transcript is the last journal entry of Professor Gabriel Kennedy, head of behavioral sciences at the University of Southern California. It was found on June 19, 2003, by the Pennsylvania State Police, and entered as evidence in the official state report."

Each person studied the paper before them.

Note: The enclosed memo is for Entertainment Network Management only.

June 19, 2003—3:35 A.M.
The search for Jessica and Warren was halted fifteen minutes ago on my orders. Sarah Newman and John Kowalski were the only two students to return from the third floor. Pete Halliburton and Francis Dial are here with me in the ballroom.

Three witnesses reported that Warren was pulled into the third-floor wall, but as a rational man, I cannot accept this version of events. I checked the plaster underneath the wallpaper and found it to be sound. I admit to chills when I found his glasses and class ring at the wooden baseboard, at the very spot where this event is said to have occurred. And there was something else that I shoved in my coat pocket before any of my students could see it. At first, the small pieces of metal confounded me. But when I examined them outside later, they looked like fillings, quite possibly from Warren's teeth. Regardless of what I think, this house—or my students' perception of it—has become dangerous to the point that we must leave. We will return with qualified people to search for my student. I will make an entry once we have left Summer Place.

"The second page of the memo is of most importance," Kelly said. She found she couldn't even face the people around the room now. Instead she focused on the large window.

The man at the head of the table watched Kelly's back for a moment and then looked at his people around the table. His left brow rose. They were interested in the strange tale Kelly had related to them. He watched them as they read the addendum to the memo.

Addendum to memo for network eyes only.

Note: Pennsylvania State Police sergeant Andrew Monahan recovered the notebook inside the ballroom that had been left by Kennedy the night before. After the last entry by Professor Kennedy, and scribbled on the lower half of the same page, was a cryptic note that has since proven not to be in Kennedy's handwriting. The same message was written on the wall where the student vanished. The message had not been there when the police conducted their search, but was discovered after the house had been vacated and taped off for the night. In effect, someone had written the passage and the wall graffiti while the police were still present but posted outside the house. It is worthy of note that Kennedy was under observation by two state troopers at that time. Two days later, the Pennsylvania State Crime Lab examined the substance used to write both entries and declared it "an unknown material."

A facsimile of the entry depicted in Kennedy's journal was obtained by a network contact inside the

Pennsylvania judicial system. (Name withheld for security purposes.)

The message written in the journal and on the wall was:

THEY ARE MINE

PART I

THE PITCH

1 Burbank, California

Kelly Delaphoy waited for her presentation, and the accompanying memo, to set in.

"As you can see in the folders before you, I was sent a copy of the investigation by a network contact at the Pennsylvania State Police. It was verified by a court clerk, who filed several injunctions after rulings in the Kennedy case."

The men and women sat around the large conference table and eyed the beautiful young woman with suspicion as she stood smiling an arrogant smile. Only her executive producer, Jason Sanborn, pretended to read the package she had painstakingly pieced together and placed before them, although he knew the contents almost as well as Kelly did.

"I assume you know that possessing this report is a criminal offense, since the case hasn't been closed yet."

"It's nothing I haven't done fifty times for this show, as far back as when we were a mere half-hour throwaway on basic cable in Cincinnati. I never use these types of items in our case studies, so no one is ever the wiser. And you have never once questioned my research, as long as the advertising money comes in." She continued to challenge Lionel Peterson, staring directly at him. "Should I have also not accepted the notebook and police entries?"

"Okay, let's put the legalities aside for the moment." Jason stood and moved to the small refrigerator, removed a bottle of sparkling water, and then returned to the conference table. "Did you get a chance to talk with this Harvard-educated"—he leaned over and looked at his notes for the show as he opened the bottle—"Professor Kennedy?"

For the first time in a production meeting of this nature, Kelly lowered her head, looking defeated just minutes into the expected confrontation. She would corner Jason later about embarrassing her with his question.

"He won't see me. He wants nothing to do with us," Kelly finally said.

"You mean you've finally come across someone with a little dignity?" Peterson smirked.

"We don't need him." Kelly smiled broadly, and then looked around the room for effect while biting her lower lip. It was the best *little girl being attacked* face she could muster. "I have the sole owner of the estate, the great-grandnephew, Wallace Lindemann."

That created the buzz she was hoping for. People started talking all at once. Her show, *Hunters of the Paranormal*, would indeed air live in two months on Halloween night from the Pocono Mountains in Pennsylvania; she knew it by the excitement in the room. They had already forgotten about her not being able to obtain the reclusive psychiatrist Gabriel Kennedy.

As she looked from person to person, her eyes finally fell on Lionel Peterson. He was looking at her with his left eyebrow raised once more, in that *maybe you have us hooked, and maybe you don't* way of his. Peterson had been overruled two years before by the man who had previously sat in the entertainment president's chair, and so a small cable series that had shown promise in the ratings had become a network franchise that was now a juggernaut according to the television god Nielsen. The man just would not, could not, let go of his failure and embarrassment at the way Kelly had out-maneuvered him years ago.

Peterson slapped the table twice. His entertainment people quieted, returning to some semblance of a professional group.

"I can't help but think we'll look like Johnny-come-latelies on this, Kelly. I mean, so many ghost-hunter shows have investigated the Lindemann summer house and found absolutely nothing since this Kennedy fiasco—they couldn't even air the footage they had in the can."

Kelly was actually stunned that Peterson knew of the summer house and its television history. She tried not to show her surprise.

Peterson looked down at the conference table, thumbed the thick pages Kelly had placed before him, and then looked up with a smirk.

"Kennedy won't see you because he probably made a deal with his missing student to take it on the lam so that Kennedy could get a book deal out of his disappearance." He again thumbed through her proposal and pulled a sheet of paper from the binding. "In addition, devoting four prime-time live hours, and another four live hours into late night, well, that may cost us too much. The advertisers would run for cover. As you said, there's not much of an 'evil owner' angle here. Even I've heard about the philanthropic Lindemanns."

Kelly pulled out her chair and sat down. She had done the interviews herself, everyone from Philadelphia television news reporters who had covered the Kennedy story, to a few of the canceled ghost-hunter shows that couldn't keep up with hers in the ratings. They all claimed the same thing: the place was so beautiful and charming and so very much *not* haunted. After listening to them all, she even started having her own doubts. Then she'd heard what happened there in 2003. It was something the other shows never touched on because of legalities, or they claimed never to have even heard of the Kennedy incident. Her research had taken her from USC to the Poconos; from Beaumont, Texas—where either USC or the Pennsylvania authorities tried to hide Kennedy from the rest of the world—to this very boardroom, pitching the greatest live event since Orson Welles and his *War of the Worlds* broadcast in the thirties. The one difference that emerged from her research was the one thing the other shows lacked, *her* imagination.

"That's true, those shoddy shows and news reporters didn't find anything, but they don't have our experience. Even if the place is benign, which I know it isn't, we have the official Kennedy account from the great-grandnephew of F. E. Lindemann himself, that says something horrible *did* happen there in the summer of 2003, contradicting the official state police report. We tell *that* story along with the others we have related to you in the slide show, and then, if we have to, we'll *make* our audience believe. And there's one thing the other shows refused to touch on: whatever is in that house was triggered into action by Kennedy and his team. He awoke something in that house that had lain dormant for more than three quarters of a century. With a cast of 'experts,' I can get the house to awaken once more. Only this time, it will be on my cue and on live television."

"Am I hearing you right?" Peterson asked, staring straight at Kelly. "You want to fake events at that house if it proves not to be haunted? I want to hear you say it, Kelly. I want everyone here to understand it clearly."

"That's a rather hard turn of phrase, Lionel. All I mean is that since we don't have Kennedy, we push the boundaries a little. That's all."

"And your aboveboard hosts, writers, and other producers are good with this?"

"They will be, yes. They're troupers. They've been through thick and thin on this show for five years and they'll do anything to keep *Hunters of the Paranormal* on top of the ratings. I have a line on two of the students that walked out of that house with Professor Kennedy."

"What of the other three?" Peterson asked.

"They have never spoken to anyone about Summer Place. Their parents wouldn't even tell me where they were currently living. It's like they dropped off the face of the earth."

"How much?" he asked.

"The largest expense is the house rental itself. That will run one million dollars."

"For just one night?" Peterson asked, loud enough to startle a few of the more timid people around the table. His eyes bore into Kelly's and she could tell that this time he wasn't putting on a front.

"The nephew, Wallace Lindemann, is rich beyond measure, but is also a cutthroat little bastard. He won't take a penny less than the one million for the two weeks we need the house. That's one week for signal testing and setup two weeks before, and one week for the actual broadcast on Halloween night."

"You're bordering on blowing a quarter of a season's budget on an eight-hour special? The network brass would go ballistic. No way am I approving this."

Kelly smiled with as much fabricated embarrassment as she could muster. "I, uh . . . already broached the subject to Mr. Feuerstein in New York when we attended the Emmys a month ago. He said corporate would be on board, on one condition."

Peterson frowned. Kelly was sure he thought her an arrogant bitch for going over his head and making him look like a moron, or at the very least a dupe. However, she watched as he looked around the table at his very own people. Their enthusiasm for the project was obvious. He forced himself to smile and nod his head. He knew the game she was playing very well; after all, he had almost invented it.

"Okay, I'm all jittery inside with expectation and anticipation," he said sourly. "What's Mr. Feuerstein's condition?"

"They want Julie Reilly of the *Nightly News* to go along, for window dressing and legitimacy."

Peterson didn't say a word at first. He stared at her and then lowered his head with a shake.

"You want the best investigative reporter at the network to tag along? And what if she sees through your little scam?" He finally looked up. "Some people in that money-losing division are actually good at their jobs."

"Lionel, she works for the network. She'll do as she's told. Besides, it will never come to that. We can trick the house out days before—and don't give me that look. It won't be people dressed in bedsheets being caught on camera, or things moving by a string the audience can see. I think I know a few things, after all these years, about how to scare people. Small stuff, it doesn't have to be much, just enough to get viewers' eyebrows to raise and their hearts to race a little. We'll fine-tune it during the test broadcast two weeks before."

She could see the gears turn in his head. If corporate wanted their star reporter in on this, it was so that entertainment could help prop up the sagging ratings of the news division. Ultimately, it would help those people he just mentioned—the ones who were good at their jobs.

"You're taking an awful big risk," he said. "Correct me if I'm wrong here, but wasn't it Julie Reilly who made her bones by hanging Professor Kennedy, asserting that he was a publicity-seeking opportunist who wanted nothing more than to sell books? I believe she reported that an unnamed source claimed that the only way he could do that would be to have at least one of his students vanish into thin air. She cost him his career, and now corporate wants her to tag along? Ms. Reilly is another person who climbed to power by not naming her sources. This is quite a cast of characters you'll be pulling together, Kelly."

"Look, there have been other deaths at the estate. And if it was a hoax, why hasn't this student ever turned up? I'm willing to cut Julie Reilly loose and see her investigate *that,* regardless of the outcome—it would make just as good a story if we could prove Kennedy is a nutcase and a murderer, or at the very least, the opportunist you claim he is. The angle here is the missing student and the stories about the house's past."

"What other deaths? I thought the only incidents were a disappearance, a horse riding accident, and a supposed assault."

"Several prominent families have died on their way home from weekend stays at the retreat in the twenties and thirties . . . maybe not right at Summer Place, but on the roads leading from it. It's everything rolled into one ball. And one very important bit of information you're overlooking, Lionel, is the small fact that Kennedy has refused to write or discuss a word of that night, even though one publishing house offered him a flat two million dollars in advance money. And that, Lionel, *is* documented and quotable."

The conference room grew quiet.

"This house sits on land that has some of the most treacherous roads in Pennsylvania. Let me venture further: most of these accidents occurred long before there were paved roads in the area. Am I correct?"

"I really haven't checked the—"

"In addition, the fact is that the longer Professor Kennedy waits, the more money he will get when he finally does write his book. Am I right?"

Kelly Delaphoy raised her eyes from the table and looked into Peterson's. She knew he was attacking her because of her discussion with corporate. She had a good guess he also knew she was after *his* job, just as he was after the CEO's.

"Yes on one, but not on the other two points. Kennedy was frightened by something in that house. In order for him to write about it, he would have to relive it. He doesn't want to do that." She looked at the faces around the table that were silent, waiting for her last push. "I believe there is something here that goes far beyond the accidents. This Halloween special will bring viewership to an all-time high. And here's something for you to chew on: The reason Professor Kennedy chose this house above all others when he sought his research grant from USC was the fact that it supposedly scared the holy shit out of one of America's literary giants, Shirley Jackson."

"You have to admit, Lionel, that coupled with these tales, this whole thing is pretty creepy stuff," Sanborn said. He pulled his pipe from his pocket and placed it in his mouth.

All eyes turned to Peterson, whose jaw muscles were

working as he looked at Kelly. She could see the hatred in his eyes at what she had done, but she knew with this latest bit of information out in the open, others would now bring pressure to bear on the entertainment president.

"I'll let you know in twenty-four hours," Peterson said.

"But we need to get—"

"Kelly, I said twenty-four hours, and not one minute before. And leave the Kennedy file here with me. I want to look it over."

Kelly slid the thick file down the long table, passing it from one person to another until it reached Peterson's girlish hands. A few executives nodded their supposed support as they left the room. Her eyes went to the four-inch-thick file on Professor Kennedy sitting under Peterson's hand. She bit her lower lip, hesitated, and then turned and left.

Once he was alone in the conference room, Peterson opened the file to the eight-by-ten color glossy of the house in question.

Peterson shook his head and wondered what a joint like that would cost to build in today's dollars. All of this opulence from money provided by the sewing machine— well, that, and ten thousand sweat-factory workers in New York City. He perked up at that thought, and then just as quickly deflated. It had been a well-known fact that the Lindemanns, at least the founding branch, had been the least likely candidates for scandal. It was Kelly's slant or nothing. Anyway, since it had already been brought to the attention of the president of the network and the board of directors, he could do little about it.

Peterson lay the folder aside and looked at the facsimile of Kennedy's notebook entry, the one also supposedly found on the wall that the boy had disappeared into. He furrowed his brow as he read the harshly written words once more.

"They are mine."

The entertainment president repeated the three words

from the fax aloud repeatedly, expecting them to lose meaning the way repeated words usually do. These did not.

"They are mine. *They are mine.*"

Kelly Delaphoy sat with her show's two hosts inside her large study in her Studio City home. Greg Larsen and Paul Lowell stared at her, wanting desperately not to believe what she had just told them.

"You mean we have a chance to finally get into that house, and instead of really investigating it, you want us to fake it if something doesn't happen?"

Kelly had known the two men since they were nothing but freelance photojournalists eight years before. They had been her closest friends during good times and bad. She smiled. "Listen, Paul, we'll have too much invested in the live show. We won't be able to explain away a flop to the sponsors and our viewers. Sometimes, as you know, ghosts don't show up on cue."

"But Kelly, we've always been on the up-and-up."

"We need this," she said. Her eyes could not hold his, so she looked away.

"Kelly, we've never faked anything that—" Greg started, but was cut short.

"Camera angles, tripping by clumsy soundmen, house settling noises? Come on, we've faked a lot. *It's all in the editing.* Remember that statement, Greg?"

Greg Larsen shook his head. He had said that to Kelly years before—that scaring people on film or videotape was just a case of creative editing—and now it had come back to haunt him.

"Come on, at the very least we have an opportunity to go to a place we've always wanted to investigate. I promise we won't go overboard on tricks."

The two hosts sat quietly for a moment. It was Greg, just who she thought it would be, that spoke first.

"We only use outside people, a technician whom Paul and I trust to trick out the house, and only sound gags. No material props that can be caught by the investigative team. That's the only way we'll do it."

"Deal! We'll test-sound gags during the test broadcast. That's a full two weeks before Halloween. I'm going to make another attempt at seeing Professor Kennedy. I know I can make this work—for *all* of us."

2 Lamar University, Beaumont, Texas

Professor Gabriel Kennedy's fall from grace almost broke him, spiritually as well as monetarily.

The long, difficult fall had taken Kennedy from the well-funded psychology department of USC to a moderate behavioral psych position at Lamar University in Beaumont, Texas. He was there only because he had gone to school with Lamar's science chair, Harrison Lumley, a million years before. An old dorm room pal, Lumley used to sell methamphetamine for spending money and take speed to assist with his finals. Harrison Lumley was everyone's pal at one time or another.

Kennedy was hiding from the world; hiding from the questions that he couldn't answer without going back in his mind to that night at Summer Place. He had come to this place to hide and have his nightmares about a house that transcended the realities of the physical world.

He had even tried to explain the night in question once. When Harrison Lumley offered him the position at Lamar, Kennedy felt the need to tell his friend what had happened, to explain he wasn't what the newspapers and television shows said he was. He had failed miserably in his attempt to explain the unexplainable, just as he had failed to explain it properly to the police in Pennsylvania. Just reliving that night with his friend, he nearly had a mental breakdown. Gabriel thanked God every day that Harrison had known him when he had been considered a brilliant—if a little misguided—clinical psychologist on his way to the top.

"So, where do we stand to this point?" Kennedy asked with his back to his large class. "Freud never said that most issues of the human consciousness could be traced to a mean daddy or unloving mama. What he did say was, everything we read, see, and experience is placed into that human mind, but how it is processed, stored, maintained, and then acted upon is the real work of clinical psychology."

The buzzer sounded and the students started to rise and leave for the weekend. He almost didn't see the woman sitting at the rear of the class, hidden well in the theater-style seating. He reached down to his desktop, picked up his wire-rimmed glasses, put them on, and then looked again. The woman was blond and had her hair cut short. Kennedy didn't recognize her, so he continued to put his papers away.

"I'm not doing any outside tutoring this semester, sorry."

The woman did not respond. She sat quietly and watched the professor until he looked up once more. He studied her a moment and then frowned.

"No," he said as he closed his briefcase and secured its latches. "I don't speak with newspapers, television people, or ladies' sewing circles."

"Well, I don't work for a newspaper, and I haven't sewn anything since summer camp twenty years ago. So I guess that leaves me guilty of television," the blond woman said. She stood and slowly made her way down the slight incline of rowed seating.

Kennedy looked at his watch. "Listen, I don't even have the time it would take to say no again. I have to—"

"Go home to your apartment, eat a Hungry Man frozen dinner, and stare at the walls?" She placed her case on his desk.

"Actually, it's a Marie Callender's Salisbury Steak frozen dinner. I have distinguishing taste." He lifted his briefcase and turned away. "And it's not the walls I stare at, it's *Jeopardy!* This week is Tournament of Champions week, so I gotta go."

"You may not remember, but I wrote to you, and called. Boy, did I call."

Kennedy took a few steps away and then stopped. His head dipped in exasperation.

"I just want"—he paused, turning so the woman could see his face—"to be left alone. I have nothing to offer anyone, and I will never allow someone like you to make money from me saying anything about Summer Place. I owe it to my kids—to one of them in particular."

"We're going back into Summer Place, Professor. We're going on Halloween night for a live broadcast."

Kennedy closed his eyes and turned away, walking toward the door at the side of his teaching podium. His knuckles were white from his tight grasp on the briefcase handle.

"Halloween ... . that's a selling point for sponsors," he said, not even affording her a look. "I wish you luck, miss. Now, as I particularly like Salisbury Steak, I'll be saying good-bye."

"This is your chance, Professor. A chance to let the world know what happened."

Kennedy continued walking without looking back. The door opened and then closed.

"Damn it!" she said, and slapped her hand on her case.

Kennedy watched the microwave dinner rotate through the double-paned glass, his eyes fixed but not at all focused. Kelly Delaphoy had guessed correctly—a Hungry Man frozen chicken fried steak twirled in front of him. He couldn't afford the luxury of Marie Callender's. Though he stared at the spinning dinner, his eyes were seeing the bright yellow house.

He was so intent on his memories that he jumped when the bell went off. He shook his head and popped the small door open, but when the smell of the meal hit his nostrils, he frowned and slammed the door again without removing the dinner. He rummaged in the cabinet above the sink until he found the small bottle of Tennessee whiskey. He spun the cap and let it fall to the floor, and then poured a small shot.

He lifted it to his mouth and then hesitated. He let the small glass crash back into the sink.

He turned and took two quick steps to the small kitchen table and its one orphaned chair. He sat and pressed his palms to his eyes as hard as he could.

It was only then he realized that he had not thought of Summer Place in more than two months. He had mentally blocked it from seeking its strong handhold on his mind, and he had done so without any psychology tricks learned in practice or school.

Kennedy fell into a deep sleep at the table. Unlike most nights, tonight he had cried himself to sleep without the need for alcohol.

At three in the morning, he came awake just long enough to stumble to his fold-out couch—it had not been made up from the day before, or even the day before that—and collapsed. Gabriel was well on his way to reliving that night long ago when he tried desperately to save his lost boy and the sanity of his remaining students from an entity, an enemy, that could not be defended against.

As he drifted back to sleep with that night surrounding him once more, he knew that Summer Place was a live thing, a hungry thing, and somehow he also knew that dinner service was once more being offered at the Pennsylvania retreat.

The house was once again awake, and very hungry.

Bright River, Pennsylvania
October 13

Greg drove the van over the uneven blacktop that wound around the farthest reaches of the estate. He had turned off the state-maintained highway and onto the private road that led to Summer Place.

Kelly sat in the front seat with a road map and her cell phone—and the phone's GPS, which was telling her that the road map was mostly wrong. Paul Lowell sat in the backseat with Jason Sanborn, who had his ever-present water bottle in his right hand and his pipe clenched in his teeth. Every once in a while he would give his goatee a fatherly swipe of his hand.

"With all the money this damn family has, they could fix these roads!" Greg said angrily as he swerved to miss a large pothole in the macadam.

"I'm not really convinced that Lindemann has that much money."

Greg looked over at Kelly and then quickly back to the road.

"You mean he went through the family fortune in less than twenty years? That had to be something in the range of a billion dollars."

"Bad investments, four wives, and the collapse of the base company back in the seventies helped drain most of it away. At one point, right around the time of the Kennedy fiasco, Wallace was flat broke. Only the death of the original Lindemann's brother's granddaughter bailed him out of his financial straits. She left him her small fortune of twenty million. He's been scraping by ever since," Kelly said facetiously. "The real fortune was left to the Lindemann philanthropic foundations in New York and Philadelphia— more than a billion dollars, untouchable to Wallace. That must kill him, to have that much money being doled out to the poor, museums, and art galleries."

"Jesus Christ," Sanborn said, almost to himself.

Greg looked in the mirror and Kelly glanced at Jason in the backseat.

"Did you see that?" Jason asked, pointing up ahead, "Through the trees?"

All of them strained to see what Jason was pointing at. As the van slowly came around a bend in the road, they saw it. There, through the thick pine trees, was Summer Place.

"My lord, it's gorgeous!" Kelly said.

Greg slowed the van to a stop. The house sat in a large cleared valley below them like some turn-of-the-century countryside painting.

"I have never seen a private residence this large look this gorgeous and homey," Jason mumbled. He glanced worriedly at the back of Kelly's head.

"This looks like a resort, not someplace where people have come to die," Paul said, leaning over Kelly's seat.

Greg placed both arms on the steering wheel and looked at the house sitting two miles distant. "It looks like something from a Walt Disney movie."

"Yeah, just as scary, too," Jason said.

Kelly didn't answer them. She was looking at the numerous windows that lined the second and third floors of the house. The house had twenty-five bedrooms, but at this moment with their high vantage point above the property, it seemed so small. Her eyes roamed to the windowless fourth floor and the upper reaches of the gabled roof. The many angles caught the sun and she crooked her head and smiled.

"You're not getting the same vibes I am, boys." She rolled her head and then closed her eyes. "This is the place where dreams come true."

Greg looked over at the blond woman who had carried them from Cincinnati to LA—a woman who had never missed a beat as far as the show's creativity went. Now he looked at the creator of *Hunters of the Paranormal* as if she had gone off the deep end.

"We don't need dreams here, Kelly, we need nightmares."

She opened her eyes and looked over at him with her perfect left eyebrow raised. "The sweetest of dreams can turn into nightmares, Greg, far more often than you realize."

Thirty minutes later, the van sat idling at the fifteen-foot-high wooden front gate. The crisscrossed beams of hewn wood were thick and looked as effective as steel. A small guard shack sat empty on their right.

Greg honked the van's horn several times and succeeded only in startling birds from the green hedges and trees that had yet to taste the first real frost of fall. The hedges lined the front gates and the long, high fence that encompassed the main drive. Fancily trimmed, they were sculpted to look like the parapets of a castle.

The sound of an approaching tractor stopped Greg from honking again. As they watched, it slowly wound its way around the large barn and onto the main paved drive. Kelly's eyes went from the young man sitting atop the tractor to the main doors of the house that sat underneath the largest portico she had ever seen outside of a grand hotel.

The tractor pulled up and the driver shut the loud diesel engine off, then blithely hopped from the large machine while wiping his hands on an old red rag.

"Property's shut down for the season," the young man said as he stepped up to the thick wooden gate. "Hell, we're shut down every season." The boy brushed a lock of long, oily blond hair from his face.

Kelly rolled her window down and stuck her head through the opening. "Are you one of the Johansson boys?" she asked.

The teenager stopped wiping his hands on the filthy rag. He appraised Kelly as if she had been a delivery and it was up to him to inspect the shipment. Greg got out and walked around the front of the van to get between Kelly and the kid, who acted as though he were lord of the estate.

"Yeah, Jim Johansson. Now, who are you?" He seemed to take offense at Greg's attempt to block his view.

"We're supposed to meet the owner here at noon," Greg answered before Kelly could.

The boy tilted his head to the side and smiled at Kelly from around her guardian. Facing Greg, still smiling, he spat on the ground.

"Mom and Dad never said nothin' to me, and they would have, seeing our family's been caretakin' here for the past sixty-two years."

"Well, regardless of that fact, we—"

"Jimmy, what in the Sam Hill you doin'?"

The voice that cut Greg off came from the shed on the other side of the guard shack. As they watched, the boy looked down at his shoes and then tossed the rag from hand to hand.

"Don't you have to finish mowing? I have to winterize that damn tractor early tomorrow morning, now get to it."

The voice belonged to an older man who stepped onto the drive from behind one of the hedges. Kelly had the strangest feeling he had been watching them from his hidden shed the whole time they had been sitting there.

The man stood about six feet, five inches and was heavy around the middle. His denim work shirt was clean but wrinkled and his green John Deere hat was crooked at a jaunty angle on his head.

"Sorry, we didn't tell the boy that there would be comp'ny today," the man said. The tractor engine fired up and his son drove off with one last look back at Kelly. "Wife's up to the house with your lunch on the table. Mr. Lindemann hasn't shown yet."

As Greg climbed back into the van, the man unlocked the chain holding the two halves of the wooden gate, and pulled the left side open.

Kelly, in the front seat, took the opportunity to examine Summer Place as they approached on the circular drive.

The long drive led to massive front steps, covered by a roof that sent a high gable climbing toward the sky. A large old-fashioned wood-carved chandelier hung low as the van drove under the portico and parked.

"I have to admit, this place is something. I could see why the rich and famous would come here to get away from the grind of counting money," Paul sniped as he stood and stretched. He turned and looked up the large stone staircase leading to the massive double doors and suddenly went rigid. A woman was standing at the top of the stone stairs, staring down at them.

Kelly had to smile. "Some ghost hunter you are." Quickly, and with her best smile, she turned and bounded up the stone steps two at a time. "You must be Mrs. Johansson?"

"Yes, name's Eunice. I was told you were fourteen?"

"We're it for now. The other two vans will be along shortly."

"Mr. Lindemann hasn't arrived yet. I have instructions for you to start your lunch without him."

"Thank you," Kelly said as the tall woman started to turn away. She was dressed in regular denim jeans with a bright red blouse, and Kelly thought she looked nothing like a housekeeper of a mansion was supposed to look. She had been expecting an old woman in a black dress who would issue dire warnings about the dark. "Uh, would you mind if I ask you just a question or two?"

"Not at all, ask away," she said. Her hand paused above the large door handle on the left.

The three men joined them at the front doors. Greg raised a brow as he took in Eunice Johansson and nodded his approval.

"I know you two," she said, looking at the show's two hosts. "We watch your show religiously, right after *Wife Swap*."

"Do you and your family live on the property?" Kelly asked, getting the woman back on track.

"Yes, we live five miles down the road, in a house that was built especially for our family by the Lindemanns."

"So you've been in their employ for—"

"My family, along with my husband's folk, have been in this valley since Revolutionary times. That's my husband, Charles, who let you in. You'll also run into my four daughters and three boys around here. It takes all of us to cover the grounds and house full time during the summer months. The girls take turns going to school in the fall and winter."

"Must be hell." Kelly caught herself. "I mean, it must be hard to get the kids to school, living way out here."

"My oldest girl is going to Penn State, thanks to the Lindemann Foundation. My children, like myself and their father, and my parents before, are homeschooled. We don't take to the townspeople around here much, just as they don't take to us. Never have."

"Why is that?" Kelly asked.

"When our family was chosen long ago to caretake this place, others around here didn't take too kindly to old man Lindemann's choice: steady income, and all that."

"I see," Kelly said.

"I'm sure you do, miss. Now, if you'd like to follow me, I've set your lunch out in the formal dining room."

"Thank you."

Kelly, Greg, Jason, and Paul entered the house for the first time.

They passed through the grand living room. Every piece of furniture was impeccably cleaned and dusted. The massive stone fireplace—twenty feet wide and twelve feet high—was cold and empty, but looked as if it would have been very warm and inviting in the early spring and late summer. Kelly could picture guests congregating here, drinking brandy and smoking cigars.

They followed the housekeeper through the arched doorway and into the formal dining room. They all had to stop as they took in the fifty-foot cherry table centered in the room. The ceiling that hung over it was forty feet above them and had etched flowers in the plaster. Down at the far end of this expansive table was their lunch.

"I hope you like brook trout; I also have a nice Chicken Kiev for anyone who doesn't like fish. Please keep to the main floor until Mr. Lindemann arrives." She looked at her wristwatch. "He should be along anytime now. I have to excuse myself, my family and I must be—"

"Leaving before it gets dark?" Greg asked with a mysterious air to his voice.

The woman smiled at Greg as if he were just an obstinate child.

"Not at all. We still have chores to do before three, and tonight *is American Idol* night."

"Thank you, Mrs. Johansson, we appreciate it," Kelly said with a smile. "Mrs. Johansson, can I ask one more question?"

Kelly could tell that the housekeeper had anticipated her

question and put on her happy face for the answer that was to come.

"To us this is just a house. We have from time to time had some excitement out here, and have had to clean up some god-awful messes by vandals and such—and that man, Professor Kennedy. However, if you're going to ask me if this place bothers us, or if we have ever experienced anything like what your show investigates, the answer is no. We love this house and the property. It provides for my family, so how could that be bad?"

Kelly smiled and nodded. "Thank you."

The four of them watched her leave. Jason slapped his hands together and started for the table. He stopped when Kelly placed her manicured fingers on his shoulder.

"Do you for one minute think we're going to eat when we have this place to ourselves?"

"But the food—"

"The housekeeper said to stay put until Mr. Lindemann—" Greg started to say but stopped when he saw the mischievous look on Kelly's face.

She smiled and started pulling at Jason's sleeve, tugging him away from the food and cutting off Greg's concern.

"I checked. Wallace Lindemann has already cashed the check from the network. What's he going to do, give back the money because we went exploring?"

The men exchanged uneasy looks.

"Okay, guys. It's time to introduce ourselves to Summer Place."

Los Angeles, California

Lionel Peterson listened to the voices of the chairman of the board, Abe Feuerstein, and CEO Garth Timberline, who had initiated the conference call from corporate headquarters in New York. He had to assume Kelly Delaphoy had called them to say she had received grief from him in the production meeting, and that they had waited a few days to call in order to cover the fact that she had done so.

"I understand you've given her a blank check for this Halloween special. That doesn't alleviate the fact that we have concerns about covering the cost through sponsorship."

"Yes," he answered, "I understand the company's position on how this will cement viewership for years to come. My main concern here, Mr. Timberline, is that Ms. Delaphoy's inexperience makes this a risky proposition at best. My sentiments will not change, despite the faith the board has placed in her."

Lionel sipped his drink with a scowl.

"Yes, sir, her advance team arrived onsite this afternoon Eastern time. They're going to set up camera angles and . . . well . . . *other* things at the house, and they'll be running a line and air test from the valley to be sure we can go out live from the location on Halloween. I'll be monitoring the test from here."

Peterson avoided mentioning the fact that Kelly and her technical team, along with the show's two hosts, were there to explore the areas of the house that would best serve the faked part of her risky business. He was saving that small tidbit. A few days before the show, he would announce to the board in New York that Kelly had done the planning for her little con on her own. That might get the special stopped, and Kelly out of his hair for good. Then New York would look to him as their savior from this eight-hour live fiasco.

The CEO informed him that all of corporate in New York would also be watching the live test feed from the house in Pennsylvania this evening. Lionel frowned. He hated it when New York looked over his shoulder for any reason.

"Well, it should be pretty boring, but the test is a must. So if you want to doze off, please feel free to watch."

Peterson hung up the phone with a bad taste in his mouth.

Bright River, Pennsylvania

The four of them stood before the grand staircase. It was impressively wide—at least fifty feet at the bottom, and tapering to about thirty feet at the top. The broad risers were covered in an expensive Persian rug. To the right of the grand staircase on the first floor was the expansive ballroom, complete with sixty-foot bar and raised stage for a band. To their left was the entertainment room with one of the old-fashioned silver movie screens. The small, ornate room was outfitted with fifty theater-style red velvet seats, and even boasted a small half-round concession stand with popcorn popper.

As they slowly climbed the beautiful staircase, they examined the portraits of the Lindemann family lining the wood paneling that faced the stairs.

"The interesting thing about the old family line after Frederic and his wife, and one that we have to stress in the script, is that their eight children all died before the age of twenty-two."

Jason Sanborn pulled a folded packet of papers from inside his jacket.

"Well, according to your research, four of them died in the influenza epidemic of 1937. Then another two in 1939 from a measles outbreak at their boarding school in upstate New York. Again, tragic, but explainable. The last two—the oldest, a boy and a girl—died together in a house fire in Orono, Maine, where they had gone to university. The house was leased by the Lindemanns for the kids' privacy. Something we can touch on and maybe even elaborate upon"—he looked up as he slid the papers back into his jacket—"you know, for some creepy innuendo."

"There is one thing that stands out. Since the attacks here began, the Lindemann family luck kind of went to hell, didn't it?"

Each of the men looked at Kelly. Indeed, losing that many children to accidents was on the impossible odds side, even if they had lived in a time that tried especially hard to kill kids. They had to catch up with Kelly, who was already moving again.

Soon they found themselves at the very top of the stairs on the second-floor landing, looking at the patriarch and matriarch of the family; F. E. and Elena were facing them from on high at the uppermost landing. The great ten-by-eight portrait was one of the most impressive any of them had ever seen outside a museum.

"Well, he doesn't look like I thought he would," Greg said. "Maybe we could get that portrait changed out for something that looks a tad more evil. He looks like someone's kindly grandfather."

Kelly saw just what Greg meant. The portrait was done in soft tones and bright hues of paint, unlike most paintings from the turn of the century.

"We'll avoid showing these. We need something out of an Edgar Allan Poe poem, not people out of a Dick and Jane children's book," Kelly agreed. "Come on, let's check out the master suite before Lindemann arrives." She hurried forward, deeper into the house. The others quickly followed.

The bedrooms were hidden behind thick, rich cherrywood doors and were passed by without any concern by the four. The doors were closed soundly against the intrusion of the visitors, except for one. It opened a crack as the padded footsteps moved farther into the long hallway. The eyes that moved behind the door watched Kelly as she walked jauntily toward the huge master bedroom at the end of the hall.

"Look at those doors," she said. "They look like they belong in a church."

They all came to a stop. The double doors rose to a height of twenty feet. Carved into the wood was a scene from the Nativity. Christ was depicted lying in Mary's arms, The soft features and eyes seemed to be looking down at them from over his mother's loving arm.

"We'll have to have an infrared camera angled down the hallway and aimed right at these doors. This we can definitely work with," Kelly said as she ran her small hand over the polished wood. "Just by using a handheld, we can get these shadows in the crevices on the carvings to literally move."

"I agree. I want close-ups of these doors, maybe from one of the rooms nearby," Jason said.

Kelly tried the left-side door of the master suite and found it locked. The large and ornate cut-glass handles gleamed under her touch as she transferred her hand to the opposite handle. It, too, was unmovable.

"Damn," she muttered, frowning. She looked to the top of the door and the etched window perched there. She thought she saw a shadow pass by beneath the gilded glass on the other side. "Did you—"

"That door is locked for a reason, Ms. Delaphoy."

Kelly jumped and Jason let out a girlish yelp, spilling his water on his blue shirt.

Standing five feet away, making Greg and Paul wonder how he had approached without any of them aware of his presence, stood Wallace Lindemann. He wore a black suit with a scarlet tie over a silken white shirt. His blond hair was combed straight back and cruelly parted on the right side. He stood only five-foot-six, but commanded a presence of a man much larger. He looked directly into Kelly's eyes. One hand was in his coat pocket and the other twirled a set of keys.

"You scared us. We were just—"

"Snooping on your own?" he asked, though he clearly had no expectation that they might answer truthfully. He stepped forward with the large set of keys and unlocked the large doors of the master suite. "As I said, this room is locked for good reason." He swung both doors open and gestured inside. "There are many valuable pieces of furniture and paintings in this room, of which my family is very fond."

As Kelly and the others stepped inside, they could see the truth of his words. Kelly saw several paintings, one of them an original Rembrandt. The furniture was antique, with names she had never heard of, but just by looking at the rich polished wood she knew them to be Old World and expensive. The large twin beds were spaced ten feet apart, and the Persian rugs were worth more than the combined salaries of Kelly and her crew.

"We didn't mean to—"

"Yes, you did. You come with a reputation, Ms. Delaphoy, and even before you signed the papers for the rental of

Summer Place, I had you checked out. You're used to following your own rules. But here, I call the shots and make *all* the rules."

"Well, I just—"

"Just follow the parameters of our agreement and this little transaction should go off without a hitch." He waited for them to vacate his great-great-uncle and aunt's room, and then locked the doors again. "The only reason I am allowing you in Summer Place is that I can't get rid of this property, thanks to the reputation it garnered after I rented it to Professor Kennedy and his students. Therefore, I may as well try to make the best of a bad situation and get what I can out of this place. Who knows? When you find nothing here, maybe I will be able to clear up some of the misconceptions surrounding this property and get it sold.

"Your technical crew is here. I directed them to the main foyer." He faced Kelly once again. "We do understand each other? There will be no damage inflicted upon the house; I stress again: *no damage.*"

"No damage to the house. Will you be staying for the test feed?" Kelly asked with her best and most condescending smile.

"If I may. Maybe from your control van, if that's all right?"

"Yes, of course," Kelly answered.

"And you should be safe here, Ms. Delaphoy, as I'm afraid everything that you've heard about Summer Place is a blatant lie."

"How many times have you personally stayed at Summer Place, Mr. Lindemann?" Kelly asked, watching his face.

"I've never spent one night in the house," he said finally. "I'm more what you would call a city boy. As I said to you in New York, you have the complete run of the place, except for those locked rooms where family keepsakes are stored."

"Wait. You mean we're denied total access to the house? We never agreed to that," Paul said. He turned to Greg for support.

"That's right, we—"

"This is not your normal house, gentlemen. Summer Place is *my* house, and certain private areas will not be exposed to the public." He looked at his wristwatch. "The day grows short. If you have any questions, I'll be in the bar until dark."

Before they could look back at each other, a man with long hair and a beard bounded up the steps, nodded at Lindemann, and then smiled when he saw Kelly, Paul, Greg, and Jason.

"What a great place, huh?" Kyle asked as he bounced to a stop.

Kyle Pritchard was one of the best gagmen in the industry. He would be laying some of the sound effects for the EVP segments on the live broadcast. He would also lay hidden speakers for the Electronic Voice Phenomenon wherever he could, for some of the more blatant scares they had in store for their unsuspecting investigative team and the viewing public.

With the exception of the technicians in the control van and the electricians, the test group was now complete. The only staffers at Summer Place who knew that the house wasn't actually haunted—or at least, who doubted that it was—were the five conspirators now gathered on the second floor.

"Hey, Kyle," Greg said.

"Kelly, you or Jason better get downstairs and get the broadcast crew out of the house as soon as they've eaten. They're making the owner a little nervous."

"I'll go," Jason said. "Kelly, you take the guys on a setup run for camera, audio, and still-photog placements. I'll get the tech boys situated outside in the production van. The electricians will need someone to guide them through their setup. Besides, I'm starving."

Greg had already produced a roll of white medical tape, placing a small "X" on the fourth door down from the master suite. "We'll have to use a stand for the camera, but I think this is a good angle."

"Professor Kennedy said in his testimony that the elemental—or, stronger—force manifested on the third floor.

I want cameras covering every angle. If we need to adjust, we can do it after the test. This is the time to make sure our placements for cameras, digital recorders, and electromagnetic monitors are where we want them for the show."

Greg and Paul were used to Kelly's habit of micromanaging every aspect of setup, but that didn't make listening to her orders any easier.

"Kyle, where do you think we can best disguise the speakers?" She took the long-haired man by the arm and led him toward the staircase opposite them.

"Hey, remember, the rest of our team isn't as dumb as you may think. Don't make this too blatant," Paul called out to Kelly.

Kelly stopped and turned. Her smile was genuine, but that didn't make it any less creepy.

"What will sell the gag is *your* reaction. Genuine is the key. If you buy it, your team and thirty million viewers will also. You're trusted, so get used to it."

As she turned her back with Kyle in tow, Greg shot her the bird.

Kyle and Kelly had been on the third floor for the past twenty minutes discussing possible placement positions for the audio test.

"What do you think?" she asked Kyle as he climbed down from the stepladder.

"These old heating ducts are way too obvious for speakers." A thoughtful look crossed his face.

"What is it?"

"Actually, obvious may be what we want here. Look at the size of the iron vents. They're large enough for me to slip my entire body inside. If the speakers were placed far enough back where the team couldn't see them, we could have a real nice effect here. I'll trick out the speakers to run on batteries, with remote wireless to initiate the sounds. By the way, what sort of phenomenon you looking at?"

"For tonight, just voice. No, wait . . . a jumbled, very deep voice. No actual words for the network guys to keep looping to figure out what's being said. Can you manage that for the test?"

"Yeah, no problem.

"Okay. Install it, but don't let Greg or Paul see you do it. I want their reaction to be as believable as possible. They may figure it out later, but they won't say anything while we're streaming a live feed."

"You got it, boss."

Kelly, Greg, and Paul stepped into the well-appointed bar-room and found Lindemann sitting on a high-backed bar stool, talking on his cell phone.

Lindemann took another swallow of his drink and watched them over the rim of his glass. He then placed both of his elbows on the bar as if he were examining three strange bugs.

"We were hoping for the rest of the tour from our gracious host," Kelly said. She advanced into the room with what she thought was her best smile in place.

Lindemann watched Kelly as she moved. Her figure was impeccable and her clothes clung to her as if painted on. He decided that she would be worthy of his company after this joke of a show was wrapped up. He smiled at her as his eyes moved to her chest and not her smiling face.

"Although I normally don't do the tour guide thing myself, I'll be more than happy to show you how mundane this joint truly is."

"We thank the gallant gentleman for his time," Kelly said. She turned and rolled her eyes at Greg and Paul.

As the four went through the expansive kitchen, which would have made any top chef envious, Kelly saw the large door that led to the basement. A large lock secured it. Lindemann produced his keys and slid one of them into the dead bolt. The tumblers moved to accommodate the key with a loud thump, which echoed on the other side of the thick door.

Lindemann turned and smiled. "The stairs are very steep and I don't want one of the Johansson kids taking a spill. Besides, nothing is stored in the lowest root cellar any longer."

"But of course."

"If you don't mind, I would rather not exert myself at this late hour for some cobwebs and dampness, so I'll only warn you to be careful on the stairs and stay away from the root cellar. It's the only area of the house that isn't inspected or maintained."

Kelly nodded and moved past Lindemann as he turned the old-fashioned light switch on the wall. Looking down, she could see that the stairs descended into darkness about fifty feet below them, and then turned away to the right. Standing at the top, she could not see the bottom. Greg and Paul followed.

As they took the old wooden steps slowly, they heard Lindemann's footsteps lead away from the door. Kelly figured he was returning to the barroom. They finally made the turn and saw the concrete floor beneath them. Lindemann was right—the musty smell smacked Kelly hard and produced a grip that held on to her face like a hand.

As they gained the floor, Kelly could see the history of the kitchen. Many of the original appliances, including the two original wood-burning stoves and three iceboxes, were lined up against the wall like a domestic museum.

"Seems like it would have been easier to get this stuff out the front doors than to negotiate those stairs to get them down here, wouldn't you think?" Greg asked.

"Lindemann probably thought they would be worth something if he kept them, and he's probably right," Kelly answered. "But they're not what I'm interested in. Basements can be a nice feel, very visual for ghost hunting. We should think about getting an infrared camera down here."

Greg slapped his hand against one of the concrete walls.

"It will have to be recorded; these walls would never allow a live signal out. Maybe a handheld would do. We'll definitely get down here, though."

"Hey, look at this." Paul stomped his foot down on a flip-up door. A hollow sound reverberated through the basement.

"That must be the root cellar," Kelly said.

"Damn, how deep does Summer Place go?" Paul asked. He reached down and opened the door, holding it in place as he stared into the darkness. "Doesn't seem to be a light switch. How the hell are you supposed to see anything?"

"Jesus. Close that up," Greg said, pinching his nose at the earthy smell.

Paul let the door fall back into place just as Kelly turned and made her way to the stairs. The two cohosts quickly followed. As they did, pressure from somewhere below in the root cellar made the door jump. Then it settled and lay still.

Lindemann was waiting inside the giant kitchen when they were finished down below, this time with a drink in hand, ready to conduct the rest of the tour. The house was, as expected, gorgeous. They covered the ballroom and the family room,

Then they climbed the grand staircase once more and examined the bedrooms and suites on the second floor. When they stopped again at the second-floor landing, Lindemann started heading down.

"Aren't you forgetting something?" Kelly asked.

Lindemann drained his glass and eyed her for a moment.

"The third-floor bedrooms?" Kelly reminded him. "The famous wall of the third-floor hallway, and the suite where our opera star disappeared."

"And also the room where that supposed assault occurred," Greg added.

Lindemann dipped his chin to his chest and held it there a brief moment.

"I guess I forgot, didn't I?" He abruptly stepped back onto the landing and made his way back down the hallway, toward the upward-leading stairs on the opposite side of the second floor.

Lindemann paused at the stairwell after their long walk

to the opposite side of the house. Then, after it seemed he had built the courage to do so, he bounded up the stairs.

When they reached the third-floor landing, Kelly looked both ways down the hallway.

"Corner suite, outside wall is where that crazy bastard said his student disappeared. The opera star's room is directly across the hall, opposite corner. The one with the double doors. As for the silent film star's suite, I have no idea. That was one of the blatant lies I'd never heard before. The large suite at the end of the hallway was my great-grandaunt's sewing room. Be respectful, please. She loved it there, so the stories go, and never really went anywhere else in the house when there weren't any guests," Lindemann said. He turned, and was already on the second riser before Kelly halted him.

"You're leaving us?" she asked. It was curious that she had never heard mention of any sewing room, especially one so high up in the house. *A tad inconvenient,* she thought.

"I have calls to make, Ms. Delaphoy."

Paul and Greg followed, examining the papered wall as they went. The bright yellow floral pattern, while meant to be cheery, felt very much out of place.

"Does the wallpaper look new to you guys?" Kelly asked.

"Hadn't noticed," Greg said. The look he gave Paul warned him not to encourage her with a positive answer.

Kelly paused with her hand resting on the cut-glass doorknob. "I would like more input from you two. I saw you looking at the wallpaper and I know you also think it's out of place. The other floors have solid colors, so why does this have a floral print?" She turned her head and looked at the two hosts. "Lindemann tried to add a false cheeriness to this floor, and failed miserably when it was cleaned up after Professor Kennedy's visit." Kelly turned the knob and opened the door. "Get with it; I can't do this on my own."

Greg shrugged his shoulders and then stepped up behind Kelly to look into the large suite.

The room was huge. The main bedroom was occupied by one of the largest beds any of the three had ever seen. It was at least sixteenth-century, and was complete with a canopy and a bedspread that looked as if it were made of mink. The walls were papered in a satin-type rose-colored print with fine stripes, the type seen in boudoirs at the turn of the century. There were three very large cherrywood wardrobes, with three Japanese silk screens at the side of each.

Kelly walked to the opposite wall, where a large window looked out and down onto the pool and the grounds beyond.

"So far the only creepy thing around this place is the damn owner, and I very seriously doubt if we could fill eight hours with just him," Greg said as he opened up one of the ornate wardrobes. He suddenly jumped back from the black sequined evening gown hanging in front of him. For a moment, he thought it was an apparition.

"What?" Kelly and Paul asked at the same moment.

"Jesus. Ah . . . it's only a dress."

"Yeah, I suppose it's a sequined evening gown?" she asked mockingly.

"As a matter of fact, yeah, it's black and it's sequined. It's also the only thing hanging in here."

Kelly lost her smile as she stepped in front of Greg and peered inside. Her brows rose as she pulled the dress out of the closet and looked at it in the light. Years of dust fell free of the gown and a small piece fell to the rug at her feet. Moths had had their way with the old dress for nearly a century.

"Why would they leave that here? This can't be the opera diva's dress, that's just a little too far-fetched," Paul said.

"I doubt it," Kelly answered him under her breath, and then quickly hung the gown back up. "If it is or isn't, I want shots of this thing on Halloween. That's got creep factor."

She pushed the silk-screened door closed, checked her watch, and moved out into the hallway.

"Look at this," Paul said. He was kneeling on one knee and probing the wallpaper with his fingertips. He slid his hand up the wall until he had to straighten. Then he ran his fingers down the wall again.

"What are you doing?" Kelly asked.

Paul finally straightened, then stepped back from the wall and tilted his head. He was still staring when Greg touched his shoulder.

"Are you going to let us in on it?"

"The glue for the wallpaper didn't adhere in some spots. Look." He pushed with his index finger, and Kelly and Greg both heard the soft crackle and saw the bulge dimple inward.

"Okay, shoddy paperhanging, I'll call the union," Greg said.

Kelly stepped back against the opposite wall and looked at the spot more closely.

"I see it," she said.

"See what?" Greg asked in frustration as he stepped backward to join her.

"The place where the glue didn't stick to the plaster? It's in the shape of a man," Paul said. He stepped out of the way so that they could see it better.

Kelly could see the torso, arms, and legs. The head was slightly too large for the body, but it was there also.

"Okay, now that is creepy." Greg swallowed.

"We need to get one of the cameras on this and make it look like an accidental finding during the show. We'll test it tonight."

Paul turned and looked at Kelly.

"This isn't where that student disappeared, Kelly. Hell, come on; this is just a fluke. Bad workmanship, that's all."

"Okay, I'll buy that, but this is something we can use, damn it. I sure as hell wouldn't have thought of something like that."

"Okay, point taken," Paul said. Kelly jotted it down on her notepad.

"Now, let's check out the sewing room," Kelly said. When there was no immediate answer, she looked up with her pen poised above the paper. "What?" she asked. She was starting to get annoyed at her team's hesitation. Then she saw both men looking to their left. Her eyes followed theirs. The door to the sewing room was standing wide open. It looked as if the room were welcoming them.

"That door wasn't open a moment ago." Paul stepped back and brushed against the wall with the outline in its paper. He took two quick steps forward, away from the outline.

"Lindemann must have opened it on his way back down," Kelly said.

"Lindemann went the opposite way back to the stairs," Greg said. "We need to get downstairs; we'll check that room out . . . later. Maybe during the test."

She scribbled another hasty note and then underlined it. The 132nd entry on her notepad read, *Check out the sewing room after the test!!!*

Paul also looked one last time at the flaw in the wallpaper. He decided he would give the stand-up shot to Greg and one of the assistants. He didn't want to be too near the strange outline.

As Kelly stepped up next to her partners, she glanced back and her eyes widened. The sewing room door was closed.

3

Kelly, Greg, and Paul stepped into the large broadcast trailer. They sat in various chairs around Jason Sanborn, who was huddled with the director, Harris Dalton, watching the sixteen screens arrayed on the wall of the trailer—one for each of the cameras throughout the house. For Kelly, this was a reward of sorts, a standard none of the *Hunters of the Paranormal* production team was used to. Usually they ran control from the back of a Ford van with just enough small computer monitors to cover the live action cameras. Almost everything on their show was run from a small laptop. This van had enough equipment to rival a NASA remote station.

The lead audio technician, a woman Dalton had worked with before, pushed a large red button and sent a signal out—just five beeps and three dashes in electronic language.

"Bright River, this is New York. We have a hundred percent audio signal from the satellite. It is bouncing well to New York and LA. Thank you—we show audio test complete and A-okay."

"Thank you, New York. We are on schedule for nine o'clock sharp," Dalton said, looking at the digital readout on the large monitor in front of him.

"Okay. If our hosts will get to their places, we can start," Kelly said, stepping in to give her team direction before Dalton could have a chance to do so.

Dalton shot Kelly a harsh look. "Take note that all camera angles are subject to change. Handheld number one, are you ready?" he said. It was a not-so-subtle barb, and Kelly caught it. He was reminding her that her placement sucked.

"Mobile camera one, up and ready," a voice answered over his headphones.

"Billy, are you ready?" Dalton asked, again shooting Kelly a look. She supposed he wanted her to have covered the silver screen in the theater with a blanket or something.

"Camera two, on the second floor. Ready," came the late reply.

"Then say so, goddamn it. Third floor, John, camera three?"

"Handheld three, ready for the fun."

Satisfied that all of his handheld cameras and their accompanying sound techs were ready, Dalton nodded. "Soundboard, how are you reading your soundmen?"

"Loud and clear, strong signal," the audio technician answered three chairs down.

"Okay, boys and girls, we queue with the standard *Hunters of the Paranormal* opening narrative and credits, and then Kelly will take the test over, and then we'll follow Greg and Paul on the tour. Let's keep chatter to a minimum during the test and only talk when we have a technical issue. I want the recorders started now for detailed tech review later. Let's do this thing."

Greg and Paul exited the large van. Summer Place stood

before them. With all the interior lights on and the exterior landscape lights burning brightly, the house and grounds looked warm and inviting. They were going to have a hard time selling this thing as haunted.

Upstairs, in a second-floor bedroom that overlooked the front yard, Jimmy Johansson watched the van below through a space in the ornate drapes. He had almost been caught looking at Kelly earlier on their brief tour, when the door had creaked and one of the men had turned and looked his way, but he had managed to close the door just in time. Jimmy had snuck into the house after telling his parents he would be late for supper. He loved the way the woman's ass moved and was excited to see her panty line through her black slacks. Now it looked as if she was going to stay in that big van and not come back out. *Bummer,* he thought.

Jimmy turned away from the large window, narrowly avoiding the large bed in the semidarkness. As he felt his way toward the door, the hairs on the back of his neck began to stand on end. He shook it off as he reached out for the glass doorknob and glanced back at the window and the soft night-time light coming through the space between the two curtain halves. He suddenly felt as if he were not alone in the room.

He had been in the second-floor bedrooms a thousand times before and had never felt uncomfortable. He swallowed and turned the knob. He felt his heart skip—the door was locked. He jiggled it and then turned it harder. Still locked. He closed his eyes and calmed himself, then reached down and turned the ancient key in the plate beneath the handle. He let out a relieved sigh. He must have accidentally turned the key when he closed the door.

"Idiot," he whispered to himself. The old-fashioned key protruded a good five inches from the lock. He was happy to hear the heavy release of the lock inside. When he tried the handle again, his smile and self-rebuke faded. It still would not turn.

The large walk-in closet doors slowly swung open with a crawling, squeaky noise. Jimmy could not make himself turn around to investigate—he knew for sure that if he did, he would see something dark and scary. Instead, he started shaking the handle and pounding on the door. The thoughts of Kelly's ass and of getting caught in the house after dark by his parents were no longer much of a concern.

Outside in the hallway and only eight feet away from the room where Jimmy was frantically calling out and pounding on the door, Kyle, the effects man, had placed the large cast-iron grate back in the wall and screwed it back into place. He hopped down from the stepladder and slapped some of the dust from his clothes. He thought he heard a sound, but decided it was just the old house settling.

Almost directly across from where he was standing in the hallway, Jimmy Johansson was pounding and screaming for someone to let him out of the room. Kyle could hear none of this. He picked up his toolbox, folded the stepladder, and walked away, passing inches from the room where Jimmy Johansson was learning the meaning of stark terror.

Kelly opened the van's large door and allowed Wallace Lindemann inside, pulling the curtain back to usher him into the control area. She introduced him to Harris Dalton, who just held out his hand without turning from the bank of monitors.

"No, goddamn it, I want Paul on the outside standing in front of the ornate doors and Greg in front of the damn staircase, then he'll greet Paul when he comes inside the house for the first time. How fucking hard is that?"

Kelly grimaced, and then nodded at an empty seat for Lindemann. On the broadcast monitor, Greg finally stepped through the front door and then stood with his soundman. He waved, showing Dalton he indeed could follow instructions.

"Yeah, we know you're there, numb-nuts," Dalton

mumbled. "Okay, send the picture test signal out and see if New York can see these dumb-asses."

"Test pattern is up and New York is receiving," Kelly said. She placed a set of headphones on her head.

"Cue intro."

Los Angeles

Peterson watched the test pattern from Pennsylvania go from the old Indian head to the *Hunters of the Paranormal* ghostly logo. Peterson shook his head. He had never understood why people—viewers *or* sponsors—would waste their time on this sort of programming.

"Peterson, are you watching this?" a voice said over his phone's open speaker.

"Yes, sir, we have a crystal clear picture here," he answered CEO Feuerstein in New York.

"Good, looks like everything's up and running. It is a beautiful house."

"Up, running, and beautiful," Peterson mumbled. He sipped his drink. "Terrific."

Summer Place

Jimmy Johansson became still. There was a presence in the room—it was behind him. His breath came in sharp, short gasps of air that he could clearly see in front of him. The temperature in the room dropped below freezing. The glass knob had frosted over.

Light peeked through the drapes from the floodlights outside. The television people were starting their test. But the light didn't reach him—he saw it being absorbed by a swirling blackness that appeared before the window. The glow in the break between the curtains was dispersing, bending, and then darkening, and something large seemed to be assembling before him. It resembled smoke being sucked out of a powerful vent. His body felt limp and he slowly slid down the door to the floor, the skin of his back making squeaking noises as his shirt hitched upward.

The black mass formed into a shape, and then just as quickly spread apart, only to re-form. The light from the window was completely gone, but Jimmy was seeing the impossible in front of him. A tendril of inky blackness reached out and tentatively caressed his face. Everywhere that the tendril touched, frost formed, producing long streaks of ice across the boy's cheek and jaw. The mass silently dispersed, blowing apart softly as a dandelion, and then it slammed into the floor almost as if it had become liquid. Then the darkness curled past Jimmy and slithered under the door frame.

"Hold it, Greg, we have a malfunction on infrared number five on the second floor," Dalton said. He ordered camera six to take its place.

"What was that?" one of his people asked, watching the monitor at his station.

"What was what?" Dalton shifted angles. "Greg, hold the intro a sec, we have—"

The color monitor showed the multicolored view from the forward-looking infrared camera, or FLIR. The screen flared bright blue and green, as if the air in the hallway suddenly froze, and then it flashed quickly back to its normal hue.

A garbled, deep sound reverberated through the speakers mounted on the van's interior walls. The crew listened, and watched the gauges on all the sound monitors peg out in the red. Kelly leaned back and smiled at Kyle, who was looking up at the speaker. Then Kyle looked Kelly's way, and she didn't like the expression on his face at all. He slowly shook his head and mouthed *that's not us.* He held out the small device that was meant to trigger his sound effect remotely, and she could see the instrument was dark. He had not even turned it on. She slowly turned away and backed toward the bank of monitors and the angry director. The sound still droned, halfway between a moan and garbled speech.

Harris Dalton angrily pushed his right headphone into his ear. "What the hell is that? Latin?"

"New York is picking it up also," his assistant said.

"No, not Latin . . . something . . . wait. It's English, but it's being spoken so deep that we can't understand it," the audio technician said.

"Harris, are the recorders working?" Kelly asked. She stood and brushed past Wallace Lindemann, who was sitting wide-eyed and listening to the eerie sounds coming from inside his house.

Dalton looked over at the video feed from the second floor. "I can't tell from here. Now, what's wrong with that camera? What kind of equipment are you people using?"

"The FLIR has returned to normal function on the second floor, normal heat signature. The flare-up was more than likely electronic," the assistant director called out.

The infrared camera poised next to the low-light stationary camera suddenly went fuzzy around the edges.

"There it is again, the same thing as before," Dalton's assistant said, pointing to the monitor.

It looked as if part of the viewing angle went inky black while the rest stayed normal green.

"We have a serious degradation problem on that damn floor. Jesus Christ, turn that noise down!"

"New York wants to know what the problem is," the assistant director called from her workstation.

"Tell New York that when I know, they'll know."

Kelly looked back at Kyle, who was watching with bemusement. She nodded toward the house and raised her eyebrows—a gesture that ordered him to find the problem with his equipment before the whole test was blown. He stood and leaned toward her.

"I'll go check it out, but that's not the recording I used. Mine is just incoherent mumbling. This crap is actually saying something," he whispered to her. He parted the black curtain and left.

Kelly watched on the monitor as he bounded up the steps and into the house, carrying his toolbox and ladder. An astonished Greg quickly stepped out of his way. Then he held his hands up in the air in a *what the hell is happening?* gesture.

Before the audio engineer inside the van could turn the incoherent noise down, the sounds stopped just as suddenly as they had started. Harris looked from monitor to monitor but could no longer see any malfunctions. He shook his head just as Kyle came into the grainy picture on the second floor.

"What is he doing?" Dalton asked as he ran his hand through his hair. "Paul, you're on the main floor. Get your ass up there and pull that asshole out so we can get these kinks worked out."

On camera two, which had the benefit of bright lighting, they saw Paul shake his head as he turned and ran up the staircase, his sound and camera people close behind.

"No, damn it, just Paul!" Dalton yelled, but the camera and soundman bounding up the large staircase ignored him. "These people better start using some freaking common sense!" he said through clenched teeth as he watched the three men continue on their way.

Kelly closed her eyes, knowing that every single word was going out live to New York and LA. She could picture the brimming smirk on Lionel Peterson's face.

New York
At New York corporate headquarters, Abraham Feuerstein watched the test. The other executives stared at the large screen where the fiasco in the Pocono Mountains was unfolding. However, Feuerstein was seeing something very different from the rest of them. He was watching a lot of network money being spent, for sure, but he could also smell even more money coming in. Advertisers—after a little creative editing of these test sequences—would see the potential of this special.

The CEO pulled up his coat sleeve. He had goose bumps. He didn't even believe in this crap, but that beautiful old house scared the shit out of him for some reason.

The door opened and Julie Reilly, the news division's number one field reporter, walked in. She kneeled in the dark beside the CEO.

"So, has our intrepid producer produced?"

Feuerstein reached over and touched Julie's cheek softly.

"Right now, it's in doubt. They seem to be having trouble with the electronics, but we'll see. You just may be off the hook if it keeps going the way it is."

"Thank God," she whispered. The testing droned on around them.

Feuerstein gave Julie a closer look. He wasn't sure if she was relieved that she might not have to do the show, or relieved that she wouldn't have to relive ruining the career of Professor Gabriel Kennedy. He suspected some of both. He also suspected that old tough Julie regretted her reports on Kennedy, even though they had bought her the fame she needed as a small-time reporter back in the day.

The other executives, when they snuck glances toward their boss, saw that he was actually watching the debacle with interest. They sat quietly in the darkened screening room, watching the man who signed their paychecks.

Summer Place

As Paul reached the second-floor landing, he saw that Kyle was on the stepladder looking into the large ornate iron heating vent midway down the long hallway.

"Hey, Harris is pissed. He said to get the hell off this floor. Remember, you're not even supposed to be here."

Kyle turned and looked at Paul and his two-man camera and sound unit. His face didn't look all that healthy.

"The sound isn't coming from here, it's—"

Suddenly all the power went out, including the battery-operated sound equipment and camera. The static video camera at the entrance to the long hallway went out and the four men were cast into darkness.

"Oh, shit." Paul inched closer to his large camera operator. Suddenly the still camera, which was battery-operated and equipped with a bright flash and attached motion sensor, started popping off bright flashes of light, creating a strobe effect. Then it stopped as suddenly as it started.

Harris Dalton lowered his head in frustration. He couldn't believe they had lost all power.

"Do these people ever check their batteries? And please tell me the electrical for this house has been upgraded since the turn of the *GODDAMN CENTURY!*"

"Damn it, Harris, everything was charged before the test began. We're not amateurs here!" Kelly said angrily. "Now, you tell me what the statistical odds are that when the power goes out, our battery backup also goes on every piece of equipment. Huh, smart-ass?"

Dalton backed off when he realized Kelly was right.

Paul was breathing heavily. There were sounds ahead of them in the hallway.

"Kyle, I suggest you take it easy coming down that ladder," he said. He felt the comforting shoulder of his ex-marine camera operator.

"Man, I can't move. I swear to God there is something right on the other side of this grate. I can feel hot breath on my face and I smell roses. Jesus—"

The camera operator looked over at Paul's dark outline. The cohost was actually grabbing his arm for some sort of comfort.

Inside the production van, they heard snatches of conversation from the recorders on the second floor—it was as if the battery packs were being shorted out by something, and they could only hear when they connected.

"We have battery power on some of our equipment coming back online. We have something—not much—but it's definitely our people's voices," the sound technician said from his stool.

"Bring it up as high as you can get it, full gain!" Dalton

switched out his headphones for another set. "Paul, get your team closer to whoever it was that was talking just a moment ago. Or was that just you?"

There was no answer, just a mewling sort of crying.

"Paul, goddamn it, what the hell is that?" He then turned to face Kelly. "For the live feed, if there is one after this technical nightmare, I want stationary, parabolic microphones placed throughout the damn house!"

"There's something—Kyle—on the ladder. . . . Jesus, he says—right—front—him."

"You're breaking up, Paul, goddamn it! This tech was your and Kelly's idea. Now get in there and pull his ass out. We have a power problem to fix!"

Paul closed his eyes and tried to adjust his sight to the pitch blackness before him. He had never in his life seen such utter and total darkness. It was like looking into a bottle of India ink. Even his hearing was faulty—he could swear he could hear whispering coming from all around him.

"Look, guys, batteries are working now. I'm picking up noise on every microphone in the house. It's like this place has just come alive." The soundman pressed his headphones harder into his skull and held the mic boom farther into out the hallway. His faintly illuminated gauge told him he was at full gain. "This is a closed system. I shouldn't be picking up the microphones on other floors."

"Kyle, you still with us?" Paul asked nervously.

"Shit, man, I can't move. This thing is right in front of me and it smells to high heaven. It's not roses anymore, it's a rotten smell. God, please. . . . You guys have to pull me off of this ladder."

"We can't even see you," Paul said. He hoped beyond hope that Kyle was doing some sort of act that he and Kelly had cooked up.

"Why?" Kyle asked from the darkness.

"Wake up, open your eyes. The power is out, damn it. Even our camera light is dead."

"Oh, man. The goddamn lights are blazing in here. I can see you—you guys are only about five feet away. Oh, God, the screws are coming out of the damn grate—turning by themselves!"

"All right. If you're screwing with us, that's enough. You get—"

There was a loud crash, followed by a bloodcurdling scream that Paul had only heard in the movies. It was a sound he thought no man was capable of producing.

That was it—the three men turned and ran for the stairs. Paul caught his right foot on the camera strap and tripped. His voice caught in his throat as he heard the two others pounding down the staircase. They were gone, and he was alone on the floor, sprawled on the expensive Persian carpet runner.

"Damn, you guys, get back up—"

He heard the footfalls behind him. Kyle's ladder hit the floor near his head and then rebounded into the wall, knocking wallpaper and plaster into his face. Paul tried to get to his feet, but stumbled and fell. The footsteps sounded as if whatever was in the hallway with him was walking on hollow planks. They reverberated, shaking the landscape pictures on the wall. It was as if a giant were pursuing him. The pounding footfalls were beginning to sound more and more like the beat of a heart.

Shaking, he tried once more to push ahead with his feet, actually bunching up the Persian runner. He rose to his knees, ready for a sprint into the dark, when something closed around his ankle so hard that he heard the bone snap. Screaming in pain and terror, he was yanked backward so hard he found himself airborne.

On the first floor, the sound and camera operators heard Paul's scream of pain. Then something slammed into a wall upstairs and the house shook under their feet. The two men screamed. Every light in the house suddenly switched on, even though the power to each individual floor was under the control of the electricians standing by at the breaker box outside.

As Kelly stumbled from the van, she saw the house illuminate so brightly she thought there had been an explosion. Then, as her eyes adjusted, she thought they were failing her. The house expanded, as if taking a deep breath, and then all went quiet and the lights went out one by one, floor by floor. A loud sigh echoed in the valley around her, just as Paul's sound and camera operators came running from the house and down the steps. The soundman took a misstep and tumbled onto the drive, with his mic boom flying into the air. There seemed to be another sigh and then a sudden wind sprang up, swirling around the house for mere moments before it vanished. Then the sound of terrifyingly loud footsteps resonated from the interior, as if whatever it was began retreating to where it came from.

Inside the van, Harris Dalton sat so hard into his chair that the headphones fell from his head and went crashing onto the control panel. The rest of the production crew stared silently at their monitors.

"Someone . . ." Dalton cleared his throat. "Someone . . ." He patted his jacket, looking somewhat lost. "Does someone have a cell phone?"

The assistant director held her phone up. At the same time, Wallace Lindemann's cell phone fell from his hand. He was staring at the monitors in shock.

"Call nine-one-one and get someone, anyone—out here."

4

In the hour it took for the Pennsylvania State Police to arrive, Harris Dalton took it upon himself to search the house. Kelly was sitting on the porch questioning the soundman and camera operator but not getting anything useful. These two had been part of countless incursions into houses and situations far more menacing than Summer Place, yet they were still shaking from their experience on the second floor. The only thing Kelly was getting from them was that they had not actually witnessed a thing.

Wallace Lindemann had been furious at Harris Dalton for calling the state police before they knew what was happening. He paced on the large covered porch, smoking a cigarette as he spoke to one of his high-priced attorneys in New York. He evidently didn't like the advice he was receiving. Angrily, he tossed his cigarette off the porch.

Harris Dalton and his assistant Nancy Teague stepped from the open double front doors just as the first unmarked police cruiser honked at the front gate. Mr. Johansson was there—Lindemann had called him—and he allowed the first of four cars through. Soon, red and blue lights colored the landscape and the front façade of Summer Place, just as they had after the Kennedy debacle years before.

Kelly stood when she saw the large black man step from the unmarked car. He examined the house as if he were seeing a scourge upon the streets of Philadelphia. He shook his head, buttoning his coat as he came around his car.

Kelly recognized the officer from her file on Gabriel Kennedy. Lieutenant Damian Jackson was the man who wanted to pin murder on Gabriel's lapel so badly that he had knocked UBC star reporter Julie Reilly on her ass, bumping her as he passed her during the grand jury hearing. Even though they both had fought for the same cause and had supplied most of the rope to hang Professor Kennedy with, they still hated each other.

"All right, is someone going to explain to me why I was pulled from my bedtime glass of milk?" The man's eyes were locked on the soundman, who wiped his face and lowered his head.

"Lieutenant Jackson, these people are with me. It seems we've had . . . had some trouble."

The state detective looked up at the man bounding down the stairs, taking in his three-thousand-dollar suit. His brows rose.

"Mr. Lindemann, I would have thought you'd learned your lesson after the last time."

"I assure you, I thought I was dealing with professionals this time around. They are, after all, a major network." Lindemann held his hand out to Jackson in greeting.

Jackson stepped past Wallace Lindemann without shaking his hand. He looked at Kelly Delaphoy, studying her for a moment as the bearded Harris Dalton and his assistant approached.

"I take it you're the man in charge here?" Jackson asked him. "Maybe you can explain why I'm not in my robe and slippers right now."

"Actually, I'm only the director. The producer is right there," he said, pointing at Kelly.

"I'm Lieutenant Jackson; it seems I can make a living coming out to this place. Now, miss, please enlighten me." Several more uniformed state troopers joined the group at the foot of the stairs.

"It's Ms., Detective, and if I may ask, aren't you part of the state police barracks in Philadelphia? I would've thought they would just send us local troopers."

Jackson watched the woman. She gave the soundman a comforting pat on the back.

"You may ask."

From the look he gave her, Kelly knew she could indeed ask as many times as she wanted, but she wouldn't get an answer. The man must have been close by, perhaps at one of the two motels in Bright Waters. The word had spread quickly that the "television people" were here in force, and she figured the detective still had a stake in Summer Place. More than likely, he had assumed Professor Kennedy would be mixed up with the production, and had decided to spend the night nearby. The man was watching her, no doubt waiting to see if she had anything else to say so that he could show her how in charge he was.

An old station wagon pulled into the driveway, but it had not come from the main gate. Mr. Johansson was there to meet it as all of them watched Eunice Johansson step out. She was agitated, and it looked as though she were arguing with her husband about something. She turned toward the house and pointed a finger directly at them. When she started toward them, Mr. Johansson reached out and tried to take her arm, but she shook him off and strode determinedly to the base of the front porch.

"Is he with you? Please tell me if he is. He won't be in trouble, I just want him to come home," she said to Kelly.

Kelly shook her head, then looked at Greg. He had finally joined them after taking some time in the production van to settle himself down. From the smell, Kelly suspected he had accomplished this with a hefty shot of bourbon—or two.

"Is who with us, Eunice?"

The woman was clearly struggling to keep calm. She twisted the bottom hem of her red blouse, which had worked its way out of her jeans. Her husband, with worry written on his face, looked from the production group to the large police officer.

"Our boy, Jimmy. He never came home this afternoon. My wife, we . . . well, we figured he would be here. You know, all the excitement . . ."

Kelly looked from the worried couple to the faces of her team. They all shook their heads.

"We seem to have misplaced two of our own at the moment, so we're probably not the best people to ask. But this man, that's what he's here for," Dalton said, gesturing to the state trooper.

Damian Jackson had met the Johanssons before, during the Kennedy investigation. He shook his head. *The cast is almost complete,* he thought.

"The last place you saw him was on the property? He

couldn't be in town, whooping it up with the other kids?" Jackson asked the couple.

"Our kids aren't welcome there, and you know it. No, he would be drawn to something like this. He has to be here." Eunice looked at him with pleading eyes.

"We'll look for him. Take it easy. Why don't you head home, and I'll send a man over to you as soon as we get in there and check things out."

"I'll wait right here," Eunice said. She shrugged off her husband's hand once again and started for the steps. "I'll be puttin' on some coffee."

"Ma'am, stay out here until we have a chance—" Jackson started, but stopped with an exasperated sigh. Eunice took the steps at a pace that said she would brook no interference.

Jackson looked at one of his men and then his dark eyes fell on Mr. Johansson. "Well, get after her and make sure she stays in the kitchen." He watched one of the uniforms and the large Johansson take the steps two at a time to catch up with Eunice. "Damn hicks," Jackson muttered under his breath. "Now you," he said, pointing at Kelly, "I assume you were taping . . . recording, whatever it is you do?"

"Both, yes. We have the camera and video footage queued up for you when you're ready, but the cameras won't be much good. The batteries were drained. The audio may help. It's in bad shape, but there's something on it."

"That can wait. Right now, we'd better start at the top floor and work our way down, in case one of your people broke a leg or something." He looked first at Kelly and then Dalton. "My bet would be on someone pulling your leg. If this is a joke, that someone is going to spend the night in jail. Is that understood?"

"If it's a joke, I'll turn the key in the lock," Dalton said. He stepped aside to allow Jackson and three of the state officers by.

"That'll be hard to do from the side of the cell door you'll be on," Jackson retorted. He pushed by the director and started up the steps with the officers. Dalton sneered at Detective Lieutenant Jackson's back.

"What a dick," he said.

"That dick, along with our intrepid reporter Julie Reilly, ruined a man's life because they got it into their heads that he was lying about this house. He's not a nice man, from all accounts."

"Yeah, well he better watch it. I think there's something in that house that's equal to the challenge of Lieutenant Jackson."

Kelly turned and looked at Dalton, watching the man's eyes roam over the brightly lit house.

"So you're a believer now?"

"I guess we'll find that out if they don't turn up our two people." He finally looked at her. "Won't we?"

"Harris, Mr. Peterson is on the line from Los Angeles. He's not a very happy camper," one of the technicians called from the van.

"What are you going to tell him?" Kelly asked.

Dalton took a deep breath and started walking away, but then stopped. Without turning, he said, "That we no longer have a show, and that corporate may have one hell of a legal mess to clean up."

"Shit," Kelly said under her breath. She hurried to catch up with the director.

Kelly entered the van in time to hear Dalton answer the call from Peterson. She was about to sit down when Nancy, the assistant director, tugged at her shoulder.

"You have to see the—"

"Not now," Kelly snapped. Hearing this call was more important than anything else right now. The fate of the show hinged on it.

"This is Harris," the director said angrily into the phone. "Yes, I recognize your voice; you don't have to be so melodramatic about it, for Christ's sake. The plug *is* pulled, so get your blood pressure under control. Yes, yes, she's right here. Damn . . . all right."

Kelly watched as Dalton placed his large hand over the phone.

"Get me an intercom working so Kelly can talk and I can hear. NOW, goddamn it!"

The technicians piped the call from Los Angeles into the van.

"Okay, you're on," Dalton said into the phone.

"Kelly, are you there?"

"Yes, Mr. Peterson, I am most certainly here."

"You screwed the pooch out there, huh? I mean, if you're going to pull stunts like this, we expect you to keep police involvement to a minimum."

"This is not a prank! It's as real as—"

"All right, knock it the fuck off, Kelly. Wait until the state police leave, and then get your two missing people the hell out of there and back to LA. Whose bright idea was it to call the state police anyway, damn it?"

"Mine," Dalton said, rolling his eyes. "Look, we have two missing—"

"Don't do it, Harris. Don't start thinking again. I'll do that from now on. Kelly, get your ass back here."

"Mr. Peterson, I have CEO Feuerstein on the line. He wants to sit in on the conference call," Peterson's secretary said in the background in LA.

"Very well. Patch him through."

"Peterson, that you?" came the voice of the CEO from the East Coast.

"Yes, sir, I was just trying to straighten out this god-awful mess."

"I guess you have a big one on your hands. Look, I don't want this to leak out until you can get another show to back up *Hunters,* and try to keep the sponsors intact in case we have to go with an alternate show. I would hate to lose them."

Kelly listened as the two-sided conversation droned on. The assistant director tugged at her shoulder again. Frustrated, she turned and mouthed the word "What?"

"You better see this before everyone hangs up," she whispered, pointing toward a monitor with a green-tinted piece of film framed up. She pushed a button on her remote. "Seriously, you've got to see this. It's from Paul's cameraman and the FLIR."

"The cameras were dead and there was no power. How could they have recorded anything?"

"I don't know. It's only a few frames. I think I've wet my pants!" the assistant director hissed, low enough that no one else could hear.

Kelly watched the frames slip by on the monitor. She could see Kyle standing on the ladder with his head half turned toward the camera. It was dark, and she couldn't see all of Kyle because the camera wasn't centered right on him. The special-effects man was talking and looking into the grill in front of him. Then suddenly the grill fell from the wall and a dark cloud-like shape emerged from the vent. It looked like a large hand to Kelly, with tendrils, finger-like, that wrapped around Kyle's head. And then he was pulled inside the vent, just that simple and just that quickly. Kelly looked over at the FLIR footage that was looped at the same time speed as the nightvision camera. This time the hand-shaped blur was blue, meaning the image framed up was cold—possibly freezing. It wrapped around Kyle and squeezed, pulling him into the vent.

"Jesus Christ!" Kelly said. Dalton's tap to her shoulder made her yelp and jump. She spun in the air with her hand to her mouth.

"Well? Are you going to answer the CEO?"

"Excuse me, I'm sorry—what?" It was a moment before she could get her eyes to focus on Dalton.

"Ms. Delaphoy, my question was: Is there anything you should be telling us about any hidden agendas for the test, before Mr. Peterson proceeds with what he has to do?" Feuerstein asked from New York.

Kelly made the "rewind" gesture to the assistant director, twirling her fingers. The woman caught the meaning at once and went to work.

"Admit . . . well, yes, sir, there is." She smiled and looked at Dalton. "We're sending some footage to New York and LA. I will abide by whatever punishment you want to give me, or resign at your pleasure, if after seeing this you still believe that I've faked it."

Kelly nodded toward the assistant, then closed her eyes. The tape started again, and exactly one minute and eleven seconds later, Harris Dalton sat heavily into his chair.

"I'll be goddamned," the CEO said from New York.

"Ms. Delaphoy, this is Julie Reilly. Mr. Feuerstein allowed me to sit in on the test tonight. Is what I just witnessed real, or are you bullshitting all of us?"

"I'm not about to sit here and be grilled. If you think I faked the footage, fire me now. And as for *you* asking me about credibility? This footage should be one more knot in your hanging rope, Ms. Reilly. After all, aren't you the one who hung Professor Kennedy for not being able to produce one shred of evidence about Summer Place?"

"Well, I—"

"That's a profound denial, Julie. You'll have to excuse me now, I believe Mr. Peterson was just about to fire me. I think I'll take this footage to CNN, and fuck the Halloween special."

"Now, now, let's all calm down," Feuerstein said.

"Calm down, hell, sir," Kelly said. "Keep her on a chain. I have lost two very close friends, at least for the moment, and we have a missing teenage boy, and now the president of entertainment programming is sharpening his teeth so he can sink them into my neck."

"Now, Kelly, Mr. Peterson is a smart man. He must realize we were all jumping to conclusions. We weren't given all the information to make a logical decision, were we?"

"No, sir, but—"

"Mr. Peterson, we are going to hold off on any rash decisions until we know what's happening. I'm sure our young lady here is just anxious about her crew, and I think it would be in bad taste for anyone to act prematurely upon anything."

Peterson, near to three thousand miles away, kicked the

desk drawer closed where he had his foot propped, making his assistant jump.

"Yes, sir," he said with all the grace he could muster.

"Now, get Kelly our best legal team in case the state police want a pissing contest over this. I also want you, Kelly—and you, Harris—in my office for lunch the day after tomorrow. We'll all have a nice chat and get to the bottom of this thing."

The connection from New York was terminated, but Peterson didn't bother to wait on the line for further insult to his authority. He also slammed the phone down.

Kelly bolted from the control van and fell to her knees, scraping them on the gravel driveway. Then she heaved and threw up violently onto the ground. After a few minutes, Dalton helped her struggle to her feet.

"You okay?" he asked.

Kelly wiped her mouth once more and looked at the looming visage of Summer Place. She shivered.

"I can't go back in there tonight, Harris." That was the realization that had sent her stomach into a fit. She was terrified of going back inside.

"Well, it looks like we have to."

"We need help with this thing. A lot of it." Kelly tasted blood in her mouth and realized she had nervously bitten through her lower lip.

Kelly and Dalton looked at the glowing house. It looked so welcoming now. Then they turned away, as if they didn't want Summer Place to know it had succeeded in scaring the hell out of both of them.

5

Detective Jackson waited for Wallace Lindemann on the second-floor landing. With the ornate hallway fully illuminated, the detective could see that Lindemann wanted to be anywhere but here—even with the six armed Pennsylvania State Police escorting him.

Jackson looked down at the fallen stationary camera. It looked intact. Then he saw, at the midpoint of the hallway, the fallen stepladder and an open toolbox against the wall. He walked slowly down the hallway, looking the scene over. Reaching up, he felt the cast-iron grating that covered the heating vent. When he brought his hand away, there was no dust. Then he knelt down to one knee and touched the hardwood floor between the Persian runner and the wall. He rubbed the old plaster between his fingers and then stood and looked at the grill again.

"Look in that toolbox and get me a flathead screwdriver." He gestured, and one of the troopers handed him the screwdriver. The five troopers and Lindemann watched as Jackson set the stepladder upright, then climbed up and started unscrewing the grill from the wall.

"What are you doing?" Lindemann asked. "You don't actually believe that guy was pulled into the vent, do you?"

"This grill has been removed in the past few hours, that plaster is pretty fresh, and Eunice isn't the kind of housekeeper that would skip vacuuming this hallway—not the way she keeps this place," he said as he removed the last large screw. "Besides, our friend had to go somewhere. We may as well start checking here."

Lindemann cleared his throat and shifted nervously but didn't answer. He didn't want to be standing here if the lights went out again.

Lieutenant Jackson pulled the heavy grate off the wall and handed it down to one of his men. Then he looked inside and frowned.

"I hate to ask, but who's the smallest man we have?"

The five troopers looked from Jackson, who still had his head in the vent, to each other. The smallest of the five grimaced, shook his head, and silently mouthed the word *fuck*.

"I guess I am . . . sir." He removed his Smokey Bear hat and handed it to the trooper standing next to him, who was smiling from ear to ear.

"Okay. Get in there and see what you can see. There's no dust inside, so someone has been in here recently." Jackson pulled his head out and climbed down from the ladder.

The small trooper grimaced and then went up the ladder. With one last look back at the others, a few of whom were trying to hide their snickering behind their hands, he pulled himself up and inside. Once in, he clicked on his heavy-duty flashlight and started crawling. When he thought he was far enough away from the opening and prying eyes, he silently and carefully pulled his service weapon from its holster and then continued down the steel vent, feeling a little better with the weight of his nine-millimeter.

Jackson turned to the four remaining troopers. "While we wait for our tunnel rat, let's start checking these rooms."

"All of these rooms were locked and I have the only key," Lindemann said. He looked like he was about to bolt from the hallway—his eyes refused to leave the vent's opening. To him, it had looked like the trooper had willingly climbed into an open maw of an animal. He didn't want to be there when that darkened mouth closed.

"Mr. Lindemann, I have a worried mother and a pissed-off television crew down there. Now, you say you have the only set of keys?" Jackson asked.

"I do."

"Well, we happen to have a missing boy. Do you think he may have had access to a set of keys, considering that he's one of the caretakers?"

Lindemann lowered his head but didn't answer.

"Start unlocking doors, Mr. Lindemann. This is a big house and we don't have that many men to cover it." He looked at his watch. "Now. Someone may be hurt in this mon-strosity, and I would like to find them before they decom-pose." The large black man leaned closer to Wallace.

Lindemann produced his keys. Anything to stop the large man from looming over him, making him feel smaller than he actually was.

As the first door was unlocked, Jackson glanced back at

the vent for a few moments. He gestured one of the troopers to stand by in the hallway.

"This room is clear, Lieutenant," one of the men said as the three of them stepped out of the first bedroom.

"Keep going. We have a lot to check." He turned to one of the troopers. "The trooper in the vent—his name is Thomas?"

"Yes, sir. Andy Thomas," the man replied.

"Thomas, are you all right in there?" Jackson called out toward the vent.

"Hell, no, it's hot as hell in here, and—wait, wait. What the hell is this?" His voice echoed inside the vent. "Oh, God—what the—?"

Jackson brushed by the officer standing beside the stepladder.

"Are you going to tell us what the hell you're doing?" he called out angrily.

"It looks like a speaker or something, and uh . . . a little box with an antenna on it. But it's covered in, I don't know, puke or something."

"All right. Gather it up and keep going."

"No can do, Lieutenant. The vent drops—oh, shit, it drops straight down and then up from here. I guess I'm at the junction where the vent peels—"

"I don't need a description. Get that speaker, or whatever it is, and get the hell out of there."

As Lindemann turned the key in the next door along the hallway, a piercing scream emerged from the room, and the door flew open toward him. Wallace was so shocked that he screamed as well, and fell backward into the three state policemen standing ready to enter the room.

Jackson turned around, his nine-millimeter automatic drawn. A blur of motion shot through the door and into the mass of stunned men. The state trooper standing next to Jackson knocked over the ladder getting his nine-millimeter out. He aimed it at the blur, wide-eyed.

"No!" Jackson yelled and slammed his hand down on the trooper's gun.

Damian Jackson stared, shocked, at the boy who was trying desperately to crawl down the hallway. His hair was ghostly white and he was jabbering in incoherent words.

"Jimmy—Jimmy Johansson!" he called out, but the boy kept up his gibberish and started crawling even faster.

Jackson stepped around the stunned troopers and Wallace Lindemann. In a few long strides he reached the boy, grabbing the back of his jeans to pull him to a stop. When the boy screamed again, it froze the blood of every man in the hallway. When Jackson turned Jimmy over, he saw that the boy's eyes were wide and the whites were bloodred. He was shaking uncontrollably and he smelled as if he had soiled himself. His fingers were broken, twisted, and bloody, and scraps of flesh from his knuckles. All of his fingernails with the exception of the thumbs were curled back like banana peels. Yet despite all his injuries, it was the color of his hair that had the men standing over him staring in rapt fascination.

"My God." Wallace Lindemann choked. He turned away from the boy and shoved through the line of police to vomit against the baseboard.

A loud crash sounded. The police turned with their guns drawn and pointed at the heating vent. Thomas was on the floor behind them, having fallen out with his hands full of speaker and receiver.

"Who moved the goddamn ladder—" The sight of four guns pointed at him made him close his mouth. He swallowed, staring down the barrel of the nearest weapon. "I take it I missed something?"

It was close to 2:30 A.M. The crew of *Hunters of the Paranormal* watched the ambulance carrying Jimmy Johansson drive away from the estate, with a Pennsylvania State Police car for escort. Kelly could see Eunice and Charles through the ambulance's back windows, trying desperately to get their son to respond to them.

"Jesus Christ." Harris Dalton rubbed his forehead. "What happened to that kid?"

"His hair . . . what the hell could do that?" Jason Sanborn asked. He stared wide-eyed after the red and white ambulance lights as they went through the main gate. He tried to light his empty pipe with shaking hands.

"Whatever took Paul and Kyle, the kid must have seen it," Kelly said. "He was in the room right across from where they were. He had to have seen something."

Dalton was tired of Kelly speculating without as much as a thread of evidence. She was taking this disaster far too calmly for his comfort, considering that she had two people missing and a teenager who seemed to have gone insane. Before Harris could say anything to her, a trooper approached them.

"The lieutenant is in the main dining room. He wants to see you—all three of you."

Kelly, Jason, and Dalton slowly followed the trooper inside, each of them with their own personal reservations about going into the brightly lit, cheerful-looking Summer Place.

"The fucking house almost—well, it feels sated, doesn't it? I mean, it's not as bad as it was earlier."

"Kelly, I'll tell you one time only: cut that crap out. Stop writing script for the goddamn show."

Kelly looked at Dalton but decided to let it go.

As they entered the main dining salon, past two troopers standing on either side of the double doors, they saw Damian Jackson with his coat removed. Wallace Lindemann was pacing not far away.

"Come on in. I have a couple of questions for you."

Kelly turned on a small tape recorder and made sure that the lieutenant saw her do it.

"First," Jackson said, "I want the tape that reportedly shows this . . . this incident." The falsity of his smile was clear, and its intent also.

"Well, we—" Dalton started.

"The tape was accidentally erased when we tried to show it to New York, sorry," Kelly cut in smoothly. She matched Jackson's glare.

"Is that right?" the lieutenant asked Jason Sanborn, and then turned to Harris Dalton.

"I never saw it and I don't know anything about it," Jason answered truthfully.

Dalton tried not to shift his eyes toward Kelly, who was standing her ground like the greatest liar in the world. He tried with every effort to hold his temper in check. Then he reminded himself that he was a television man—regardless of what he thought of Kelly, that tape was great television.

"I'm afraid she's telling the truth," he said. "However, we will supply you with it, nonetheless. We are going to make a copy of the erased tape and send it to New York. Maybe our technicians will be able to get something off of it. If we do, we'll shoot you down a copy."

Jackson didn't respond, but Kelly and Dalton both saw the man's jaw muscles clinch under his smile.

"Okay, you can play it like that, if that's the way you want it. But let me warn you, if I see that damn thing on television and I don't have a copy of it sitting in my crime lab, I'll get arrest warrants for all three of you for withholding evidence from the commonwealth of Pennsylvania."

Kelly tilted her head, waiting for the other shoe to drop. Dalton suspected she knew exactly what size shoe it was going to be.

"Now, maybe you can explain what this is." Jackson reached behind him, and with a handkerchief, picked up the small speaker and the miniature transmitter.

"It looks like a remote sound unit," Kelly said before Dalton could. Jason rolled his eyes and Kelly could only hope that was all he would do.

"Can you tell me what this was doing in the vent your crewman supposedly disappeared from? Call me suspicious, but it doesn't look like it's original to the house."

"We were conducting a sound test for the Halloween show, in case we wanted to place microphones in the heating vents for coverage." She looked at Harris Dalton. "I forgot to mention that Kyle had placed it—that was why he was in here."

Dalton frowned. He now had his evidence that Kelly had been using a gag—and a bad gag, at that. He now knew she was desperate enough to have engineered this whole stunt. He was tempted to come clean right then about the tape and his suspicions, but decided he would just report it to corporate and let them handle it.

"I don't see what this has to do with our missing people," he said instead.

"Is that right, 'Detective' Dalton?" Jackson said snidely. He placed the speaker and remote on the tabletop. "Right now, everything has to do with your missing people and that traumatized boy." He raised his eyebrow and pulled a sheet of paper from his inside suit jacket.

Kelly looked from the paper to Dalton. He refused to look her way. She knew he was going to explode directly in New York's direction the first chance he got.

"We ran a check on this gagman of yours. It seems Kyle Pritchard did time in prison—three years in Chino, to be exact, for sexually assaulting a child."

"Look, we didn't—"

"It was just a boy, not much younger than Jimmy Johansson," he said. "Now, we have a boy that's obviously been traumatized severely, and we discover that one of your crew has a lurid criminal history and is capable of inflicting such trauma. And then, amazingly, he comes up missing."

"As I was trying to say, we—"

Again, Jackson didn't allow Kelly to speak. "If we don't find your men, I'm going to charge you and your entire production crew with criminal endangerment of a minor for having this man on your crew."

"That's bullshit and you know it," Kelly said. "Is this what you did to Professor Kennedy, railroad him like you're trying to do to us?"

"You've already lost one host—he's probably out in the woods, hiding your child molester." He stood. "I want to speak with the other host."

"Answer my question. Is this the way you treated Professor Kennedy?"

Jackson glared at Kelly. He was just starting to respond angrily when two men walked in through the double doors.

"Ms. Delaphoy, please, I advise you to not say anything more, other than what you directly witnessed."

The two men wore brand-new jeans and cotton shirts. One had a briefcase; the other, older man, a scowl.

"My name is Harvey Dresser, attorney-at-law. My partner and I have been retained by the UBC television network to represent your interests."

"Were you hiding in one of their vans?" Jackson asked.

"No, Lieutenant, we were actually staying about ten miles from here on a fishing vacation. I received a call from Abraham Feuerstein, the chairman of the board of General Television and Electronics. I don't know him personally, but someone I do know does, who also knew I was up here."

"Now, that's what I call pull," Jackson said, shaking his head. "Another coincidence."

"Not pull, Detective Jackson, we'll call it fortuitous, since I believe you were about to cast an awful lot of circumstantial perversions of this strange situation at the people I now represent. Any other questions can be asked after you conclude your immediate investigation. My clients will, of course, be amenable to further interview at any time. But until then, I have instructions for them to return to New York posthaste."

Jackson reached out and removed his trench coat from the back of a chair. He put it on, following it slowly with his brown hat.

"You bet, Counselor. We'll be in touch," he said. His smile didn't reach his dark eyes.

The attorney and his associate continued into the room, toward Wallace Lindemann. The estate's heir had stopped pacing and was watching the exchange.

"Mr. Lindemann, I was instructed to pass on to you the network's sincere apology for what has transpired on your property this evening."

Wallace nodded and puffed out his chest, looking from the attorney to the other faces watching him.

"Well, that's the least of your worries, my friend. I plan to—"

"Also, I am to pass on to you that if you attempt to break the lease for the dates and times specified in your contract with UBC, we will sue you for the price of said lease, in a breach of said contract. It is my understanding that would be almost all the remaining liquid funds available to you."

Wallace suddenly lost the bravado he had been feeling just a moment before.

"By the way, sir, I was a great admirer of your family."

The attorneys turned away and gestured for Jason, Dalton, and Kelly to follow them out of the salon.

"Detective, the network and their legal department will be eagerly awaiting your findings," Dresser said to Jackson as they left.

"I'll be sure to get your bosses everything, Counselor. You can count on that."

On her way past the large gate, Kelly leaned out of the van and looked back at the brightly illuminated house. If and when she returned, she needed to be armed with the best people money could buy. She had a distinct, inexplicable feeling that the house wanted her next.

She desperately needed one man—a man who knew Summer Place better than anyone alive. She needed him to come trick or treating with the rest of America on Halloween night.

She needed Professor Gabriel Kennedy.

PART II

CASTING CALL

6 Lamar University, Beaumont, Texas

Harrison Lumley had known Gabriel Kennedy since their graduate studies at Cal Berkeley. Harrison knew that television producer had visited Kennedy, and had a hunch her visit was what was occupying Gabriel's mind. After reading this morning's *Houston Chronicle*, he thought he better check on Gabriel.

"You know, October in East Texas isn't like October in LA, my friend," Lumley said as he looked down on Gabriel. "It's hot as hell out here. It'll make your peanut butter melt."

Kennedy looked up, shielding his eyes, and held out the sandwich.

"With what you pay me, all I can afford is cheese."

Harrison tossed the Houston paper down upon the grass next to Kennedy.

"I already know. It was on *Good Morning America*. Nice way to start the morning information, losing your toast and coffee."

"This vindicates what you told the police seven years ago, wouldn't you say?"

Kennedy shook his head.

"Vindication for me, or vindication for my lost student?" he asked, looking away toward the science building.

"You. If you're cleared of this mess, that means they have to reopen the case and try again to find that kid."

"Just because a network television show will go to any

lengths to promote a Halloween special doesn't mean any-one has been vindicated."

"Gabriel," Harrison said uneasily, "I took the liberty of calling the hospital where this caretaker's boy is. Of course they wouldn't tell me anything at the nurses' station, so I used an old trick. I spoke with one of the elderly volunteers at the reception desk. She said that the boy is comatose—and then she told me he'd been scared nearly to death. Of course there is no such thing as being scared almost to death, clinically speaking, but we all know what shock can do to higher and lower brain function."

"I met that boy, you know. I really liked his mother and father."

"From what I'm hearing, this helps your story."

"No, Harrison, it just adds to it," Kennedy answered sharply. He stood and tossed his lunch bag into a nearby re-ceptacle.

"Did *Good Morning America* inform the public that this crazy producer is going on with the Halloween special?" Lumley reached down and picked up the newspaper.

Kennedy slowly took the paper from his friend's hand, looking him in the eyes as he unfolded it.

"What do the police have to say about that?"

"Doesn't say."

"If they keep fucking around with that house, it will kill them all." He scanned the paper for the article.

Harrison turned away and started walking back to his of-fice. "Then if I were you, I'd make sure they understand just what they're getting into." He stopped and looked back at Kennedy. "For your own peace of mind."

Kennedy closed the paper. "I will never in my life go back to Summer Place, Harrison."

His friend smiled at him sadly and walked away. Open-ing the paper once more, Kennedy quickly found the head-line.

OLD NIGHTMARES CHURN ONCE MORE IN POCONO MOUN-TAINS

Kennedy stood riveted to his lunchtime spot, and read. As he lowered the paper and let it slip from his hands, an old familiar chill coursed through his body, defying the heat of the Texas sun.

UBC Network Headquarters, New York City

Kelly Delaphoy had been expecting a boardroom full of suits, but instead she found herself facing only two men.

Abraham Feuerstein looked at Kelly calmly and silently. On the other side of the table, sitting and smiling like a Cheshire cat, was Lionel Peterson, fresh from his morning shower at the Waldorf-Astoria.

"Let's open this little get-together with a few numbers," he said, looking from Kelly to Feuerstein. "There's only one good number here. It's says that Kelly and her crew actually stayed within budget for the broadcast test. In fact, she came in under budget. Probably only because the test was terminated thirty-five minutes in."

"Were we supposed to keep going after—?"

Peterson held up his hand, cutting her protest short.

"We have two people missing, and after two full days it seems the Pennsylvania State Police cannot locate them. The house, Summer Place, has been searched with the proverbial fine-tooth comb. The network is being accused of hiring a known child molester and exposing a teenager to that danger—a teenager who, by the way, is in a near comatose state. I say 'near' because every few hours he awakens and screams for a solid thirty minutes. Then, when he can't continue, he passes back out."

"You've seen the tape. What—"

"One of the hosts of the show is missing, probably with the child molester Kelly brought to the house without network knowledge. Now your other cohost has resigned."

"The show will—"

"There is no show, Kelly," Peterson said, closing the file.

"Mr. Feuerstein, am I going to be allowed to talk, or am I to be cut off by Mr. Peterson every time I open my mouth?"

"I believe Lionel has said what he came here to say," the chairman said. He stood up and poured a cup of coffee at the large credenza, then turned and slowly paced back to Kelly's chair at the table. He placed the china cup and saucer in front of her. "You may now have the floor, Ms. Delaphoy," he said, returning to his large chair.

"No matter what the state police are saying, you saw the tape, the eight frames of footage. Something came out of that vent and took Kyle. I know the same thing took Paul. It's the same thing Professor Kennedy claimed happened to his lost student."

Peterson cleared his throat. "Our best, most experienced technicians don't know what they're looking at on that tape. They say the image was recorded at such a slow speed, due to the loss of battery power, that the image may have been created by dust caught up in the night-vision and infrared optics." He smiled at Kelly, and then looked at the chairman and shrugged his shoulders.

"You have got to be fucking kidding me!" Kelly stared a hole through Peterson. "The goddamn image was blue, which according to the infrared scan means it was cold! Loss of battery power or not, the FLIR camera *was* operating. It was drawing power from a source other than the batteries or the outside power grid. Fucking dust? Is that the best you can do?"

"Ms. Delaphoy—Kelly—please. I think we can get through this without resorting to profanity. Mr. Peterson proves the point that everyone who sees the images will interpret this thing differently. Now, we also had to turn the tape over to the Pennsylvania State Police, who—I may add—are threatening charges against you, Mr. Dalton, and Mr. Sanborn for withholding evidence."

"If we don't capitalize on this free publicity for the special, it would be unforgivable to the stockholders."

The chairman let his face drop for a brief moment before looking up at Kelly. "Young lady, I and I alone answer to those stockholders. You do not."

"You see what I have to deal with here, sir?" Peterson asked.

Feuerstein held up his hand for Peterson to be silent.

"However, I am a businessman, and did not rise up to be the head of this corporation by being blind to opportunity."

Kelly closed her eyes and allowed her heart to settle back into its normal position in her chest.

"Now, we have a mess on our hands. Wallace Lindemann has recovered some of the bravado he lost in front of our attorney, and has filed an injunction to have our lease canceled before Halloween."

"I'm sure we have legal recourse to—"

"Kelly, you have a bad habit of jumping the gun before people have finished."

Peterson looked away.

"Now," Feuerstein continued, "as I was trying to say, our friend Lindemann has many unpaid obligations to other people, most notable of which are right here in our fair city. I think he can be persuaded to cancel the injunction and allow the special to go forward."

Kelly let out the breath she had been holding with relief. Peterson, still tense, did not.

"So, I am inclined, at least for the moment, to start the final preparations for October thirty-first."

"Thank you, sir. Thank you so—"

"There is one caveat, Kelly." Feuerstein looked at her intently through his thick glasses.

Kelly waited for the ax to fall and sever her head from her neck.

"Professor Gabriel Kennedy has to be a part of the show. Not just part of the show—he has to host it."

Kelly's mind was churning at the speed of light. "Do I have a blank check for hiring Gabriel Kennedy?" she asked.

"Let's just say you have a free hand to do what you do best."

"I need Julie Reilly also," she said. "You said she was to

be a part of the show, anyway. She may be useful in getting Kennedy to cooperate."

"What can I say? You have her. She goes on official assignment as of today. She answers to me alone, not to you. Use her any way you wish, but I want her face on that television screen forty percent of the time, preferably right alongside Kennedy."

"Fair enough," she said, and then thought a moment. "There is one more thing." She looked back at Peterson.

"You're just full of demands, aren't you?" This time, Feuerstein was smiling.

"I want a free hand. No interference from programming, and no budget arguments. Of course, that is, if the president of entertainment can fulfill his side of the bargain and land those high-rolling corporate sponsors he brags about so much."

"You must learn to curb your tongue, Ms. Delaphoy. I'm sure Lionel will do as he is told. Isn't that so?"

"Kelly, I'm going to get you so much advertising revenue that you'll drown yourself in budget money." Peterson stood and buttoned his coat. "And with all due respect, sir, I'm also going to get the proper length of rope at the same time, so that Kelly will have no trouble hanging herself when this thing flops."

"Well, if it does, you'll be ringside to see it."

"Sir?" Peterson asked.

"I believe you started out as a producer, yourself. Am I correct?"

"Yes," he answered, sinking hesitantly back into his chair.

"I think Kelly and Harris Dalton would be more comfortable having your expertise onsite during the live broadcast." He looked up thoughtfully, and then fixed Peterson with a wry smile. "As a consultant."

"But sir, I—"

"Pack your bags, both of you. You're going to the Poconos." He nodded, enjoying his private little joke, then rose and walked to the door.

Kelly and Peterson did not see the old man pause at the open door, and his final thoughts on the subject caught them both off guard.

"I expect this to be better than the live broadcast of *War of the Worlds*. I want everyone in this country talking about it the next day. If they aren't, changes might be in order over at the entertainment division."

With those words, the door closed. Kelly's and Peterson's fates had just been tied together into a knot—a knot that was not only tied around their necks, but also firmly connected to the rafters of the most dangerous house in the world.

Bright River, Pennsylvania

The hired security guards kept the press outside of the massive wooden front gate of Summer Place. Three network news trucks and several print journalists waited for Lieutenant Damian Jackson to give a statement about the progress of his investigation. The news crews were perpetuating the rumors that the two missing men had never left the property, in stark contrast to the Pennsylvania State Police "off the record" statements that suggested the two men were part of an elaborate hoax aimed at capitalizing on the UBC television special only two weeks away.

Julie Reilly wasn't with the news van that had been dispatched from the local UBC affiliate in Philadelphia, or the one from Pittsburgh. Instead, she parked her rental car a quarter of a mile away from the crush at the front gate. She looked at her watch and frowned.

Julie had fought against the stereotype of the dumb blond field reporter most of her career. She rose through the ranks with solid filings to the network from Iraq and Somalia, earning the right to call her own shots at UBC. She knew the anchor chair for the evening news was going to be up for grabs within the next year, and she wanted it. Julie knew she was now irrevocably linked to Kelly Delaphoy's disaster in the making; she also was aware that this stunt would do nothing for her credibility with the news division unless she could get an angle. She had to prove either a real haunting, or an elaborate hoax. Since she didn't believe any of the crap Kennedy or Delaphoy spouted about ghosts and mysterious happenings, she was aiming for the hoax angle.

Julie had her hair in a simple ponytail and she wore little makeup. She was here to take notes and ask questions of two men she had interviewed many times before: Lieutenant Damian Jackson, and the owner of Summer Place, Wallace Lindemann.

She looked at her watch one more time, then she glanced out her window. To her right, several state policemen and their bloodhounds left the barn and entered the stables, the dogs pulling hard on their leashes. She shook her head. She knew the two missing employees were holed up somewhere off the property, waiting until such a time as Kelly Delaphoy could stage a dramatic return—live, before the eyes of forty million people, more than likely. Julie was not going to be a part of that kind of deception.

She yawned, and noticed the limousine coming up the road. It slowed down to pull in behind her rented compact.

She took a deep breath, setting her jaw as she always did when she braced herself for confrontation. Opening the door, she put on her best smile. She reached the rear door just as it opened, and climbed in.

Wallace Lindemann looked haggard and tired. He wasn't wearing his customary tie and he was unshaven. He instructed the driver to continue on to the house, and paid no attention to the gathered reporters screaming for the limo to stop as they slowly pulled up to the front gate.

"Mr. Lindemann, it was good of you to allow—"

"You people have more gall than I could ever have. First your bosses in New York sic your legal dogs on me, and then they resort to strong-arm tactics, and now here's their ace reporter come to ask her questions, knowing I have to cooperate. Un-fucking-believable."

Julie saw that the owner of Summer Place was going to be hostile.

"Number one: I cannot be held accountable for the actions of our legal department, nor the influence my network has with your creditors, although a man as smart and savvy as yourself should have seen this coming. Two: I suggest you take advantage of whatever opportunity is presented to you. This can be a godsend for you, if you play your cards right."

"Lectured by a talking head," Lindemann grumbled. Then he looked over at Julie. "Although . . . a beautiful talking head."

"I won't even comment on your opinion, Mr. Lindemann. I never do when people take that tack with me."

"Okay. What do your masters in New York want?"

"I need more background. The last time I was here, you were far more in control of things and wouldn't let me near you. I need to know what you really think about—"

"Look, Ms. Reilly, I was in the production van that night and I didn't see anything. If you want—"

"Professor Gabriel Kennedy," she finished.

If Lindemann was shocked by the question, he covered it up well, only raising his right eyebrow.

"He's a crackpot. Of all the people in the world, you should know that."

The limo pulled through the gate. Reporters smashed their faces against the tinted windows to view the long black car's interior. They slapped at the glass and shouted questions that were muffled and unidentifiable.

"Score one for you. I assume you've been thinking about that the whole way here." Julie closed her eyes and then opened them. "I don't care what you've heard or what you believe." She removed a notepad from her bag just as the limo stopped under the massive portico's overhang. "I just want to know about the cleanup after that night in 2003."

Wallace Lindemann was taken aback by the question. Julie could see it.

"Cleanup?"

"Yes. You obviously had to hire someone to repair the physical damage to the house. It's described in the official police report." She made a pretense of looking at her notes, though she knew the details by heart. "Plaster was damaged in the second-floor hallway, several heavy doors had to be rehung—the police confirmed those parts of Kennedy's story. So, what was the damage and what did your contractors have to say?"

"They came and fixed several items. I don't exactly recall—"

"Why didn't you use local contractors? You hired a company out of Altoona—almost two hundred miles away."

Lindemann looked away as the chauffeur opened his door. He stepped out quickly. "I'll have to check my records. I don't remember what was done exactly."

"Who said you could bring in a reporter?" a booming voice called from the top of the steps.

Julie looked up and saw the large figure of Damian Jackson, replete with his tan raincoat, standing with his right hand in his pocket and looking down on them—his favorite position in life. *Probably sexual in nature,* Julie thought.

"Nice to see you again, Lieutenant," Julie said as she climbed out of the backseat. "I see you're still trying to convince the world that you're Colombo and Superfly all rolled into one."

Jackson didn't respond, he just watched as Lindemann and Julie climbed the steps. He eyed Wallace as he passed.

"I'll be in the bar," Lindemann said. He slithered by the detective.

"This crime scene is off-limits to the press for the time being. Your network may have enough on Lindemann to get him to sneak you in here, but they have nothing on me."

Julie eased up to Jackson and leaned closer to his large frame. He didn't look down at her, but stared straight ahead.

"Let me clue you into something, Damian. You and I are linked to this place, and this case." She continued past him, up the stone steps. "After all, many people think that it was you and I who railroaded an innocent man. And now here we are all over again. Only this time there's not just Kennedy, but a whole network team of Emmy winners saying some-thing's wrong with this place. And that, Detective, has bite."

Jackson took a deep breath, waiting until the front doors had opened and closed before he turned around. The moment he had first heard about the network broadcast test, he had known that the past would be coming back to bite him right in the ass. Now the first piranha had arrived to start the feeding.

When Jackson entered the barroom, he saw Lindemann at his usual bar stool and Julie helping herself to a cup of coffee.

"Look, before you start with your crap, I can bring any-one in my house that I want to," Wallace said like a petulant child. He stared into his glass of whiskey.

"So, what is the state of your investigation?" Julie asked, removing her coat and leaning against the bar.

"What, no note taking?" Damian advanced into the large ballroom.

"No, this is more of a personal interview. After all, Lieu-tenant, I think both of our career advancement opportunities are on the line."

"Yours maybe, but I see my career advancement as still viable. After all, I based my report on facts, unlike you. As I see it, you have to prove Kennedy guilty all over again, while I only have to prove another party guilty of the same crime. A fresh start, you might say."

"Still smug as hell, aren't you?" Julie asked, studying Jackson.

"Not smug, just right. I know this house didn't take those people. There are no ghosts and there's no such a thing as a bad house, just bad and very stupid people who prey on the gullible."

"Look, I'm here to call a truce with both you and Linde-mann. I'm going to report the same facts that I did before. I need to prove that people are the real evil here, just as you say. If I don't, and if Kelly Delaphoy proves that there's an otherworldly problem here, then our careers are both fin-ished." She took a sip of the hot coffee. "Public opinion is a strange thing, Damian. Its power has even been known to stop unpopular wars."

Jackson knew Julie was right. His harshness with Gabriel Kennedy in 2003 was on record. Jackson removed his hat and tossed it on the bar next to Lindemann. His bald head gleamed in the overhead lights. "You're willing to go against your network and actually say this Halloween special is a put-on job?"

"I'm going to do far more than that," Julie said. "I'm going to be here for all eight hours, and I intend to prove that this haunted house crap is just that. And there is one more thing, Lieutenant." Julie locked her green eyes onto Jackson's.

He raised his eyebrows, waiting for the piranha to take its last bite.

"The network is trying to get Gabriel Kennedy to host the special."

Lindemann and Jackson both stared at Julie. The big detective glanced around the ballroom, a curious look on his face.

"What is it?" Julie asked, placing her coffee down.

"Didn't you hear that?" Jackson said, looking at the two of them with eyes wide.

"What?" Lindemann asked, standing from his stool, spilling his drink on his hand in his haste.

"Why, the house, of course."

"What . . . what do you m-m-mean?" Lindemann looked around.

Julie hid her grin at Wallace's obvious discomfort.

"It's laughing its shingles off—Kennedy is coming home."

Every door on the second and third floors suddenly slammed closed, making all three of them jump.

Julie swallowed and looked at Jackson. "Draft must have closed all the doors up there."

"How in hell would a draft close doors that were already closed and locked?" Lindemann emptied his glass and slammed it down.

Damian Jackson smiled as Lindemann stormed past him. He looked at Julie, who had also lost her brief sense of humor.

"Maybe the house isn't happy that Kennedy is coming back."

Jackson looked at her, then looked around him at the ostentatious ballroom.

"Maybe not." He smiled again. "But I surely am."

7 Lamar University, Beaumont, Texas

The sun had set and the heat of the day had finally drained from the air in the classroom. It was now cool enough that the windows could be opened and Kennedy could catch some of the breeze that found its way between the old buildings.

He turned and walked with purpose to his desk, producing his set of keys as he went. There were only four keys on his key ring—one to his studio apartment, one to his classroom, one to his mailbox, and the last and smallest opened the bottom drawer of his desk. He sat heavily into his chair and took a deep breath.

The drawer and its contents had eaten at him all day. He stayed after everyone had left, finally deciding to breach the vault that held the combination to that night in Pennsylvania. He inserted the key and opened the lock, and then he pulled open the largest drawer. Before he could lose his nerve, close the damn thing, and once more hide the truth, he reached in and removed the five journals and ten file folders.

The journals chronicled the experiment he had been conducting that night, long ago. He wasn't interested in rehashing what happened to him and his students; he was concerned with the research that had led him originally to Summer Place. The interviews, the research on the property, the numerous face-to-face talks with what living Lindemann relatives were left. The answer, the very key to what the house was about, was here in his research files—somewhere.

He was responsible for that night. He knew that and never denied it, not even to himself. Before that night, he had been a skeptic himself. His fascination had been with how static objects could instill such inherent fear into one's psyche. How the influences of rumor and innuendo had the power to change the reality of perception, thus creating the human ability to literally scare oneself into a state of unrest. A person could end up with a broken mind merely because the mind had believed in the impossible and thus made it real to them.

Kennedy had to smile at the memory of the theory. He pulled on his beard. *Yeah, scare yourself into a state of unrest and broken mind—that was what I surely did.*

The following day, Gabriel Kennedy entered his classroom and placed his briefcase on the desk. The Summer Place materials he had removed from the desk drawer were still sitting out. He rubbed his face. He had shaved his beard off for the first time in years. Now he didn't recognize the man who faced him in the mirror.

The door at the topmost tier of the classroom opened, admitting Harrison Lumley. His friend stood there looking down at him, amazed. "Well, the iceman cometh," he said as he started down the aisle. "Why the sudden change in personal imagery?"

"What change? You mean being early? Well, the simple answer in our field is always best: I never went to sleep."

"I want to discuss something with you, if you have a moment."

Gabriel pulled up the cuff of his blue shirt and looked at his watch. "It's your dime for the next eight minutes."

"What would you say to tenure here at Lamar?"

"I know that I've only been here for four years. It should take considerably longer. Especially with my, let's say, sordid past."

"Well, having the chairman of your department as a friend can be beneficial."

"The one benefit of being a clinical psychologist, Harrison, as I'm sure you know, is the ability to smell a rat." His smile didn't reach his blue eyes. "Have anything to say to that, Mickey?"

"I should have known you would smell me out," Lumley said, slapping the desktop lightly. "There is a catch. What would you say if you were responsible for the psychology department receiving a one-and-a-half-million-dollar grant?"

"I'd say I gave you too much. I want at least one million, four hundred thousand of it back. Now explain your fantastic statement." He picked out a piece of chalk and started to write the day's lecture topic on the blackboard.

"I received two visitors to my home late last night."

"Who offered you the money, Harrison?"

Lumley took a few steps back from Gabriel's desk and gestured toward the door at the top of the classroom. Two figures stepped in and looked down.

Gabriel Kennedy recognized the woman from a few days before, the young producer from UBC. With her was a face he had never wanted to see again. Julie Reilly still had an arrogance about her that only seemed to have intensified over the years, and its aura traveled from above to inflict itself upon Gabriel.

"Ladies, will you join us please?" Lumley called out. "Gabe, listen, they have an offer for you to consider. I wouldn't ask if it was only for the grant, you know that. I'm asking it of you because you're a friend, and this is your one chance to redeem your credibility."

Kennedy looked from the two women walking slowly down the steps to Lumley.

"I'm sure Judas had something similar to say—that he only did it because he was a friend, and it was all for the best. That makes your betrayal justified in your mind?"

"That's a little harsh, isn't it?"

"No—but this may be." He pulled out his keys and opened the bottom desk drawer. Out came all his research on Summer Place. He grabbed his briefcase and, with everything under his arms, walked past Lumley.

"What are you doing?" Lumley asked.

"Harrison, you can kiss my ass, and shove your tenure up your own." He brushed past Kelly Delaphoy and Julie Reilly.

"What about your class? What about my offer?"

"I already told you what to do with your offer. The lesson plan is by the blackboard."

With that, Gabriel Kennedy left his classroom for the last time.

"I'll give him at least that much credit," Julie Reilly said. "He does have his standards. Which is far more than I can say for you," she added to Kelly, "or the professor, here." Frowning, she started back up the risers and left the classroom.

"Fucking great!" Kelly said, glaring at Lumley.

Gabriel Kennedy chose not to return to the studio-size prison he called home. Instead, he found the nearest sports bar.

"Can I join you for a minute?"

Gabriel looked up and could not believe the woman had actually followed him. It wasn't every day that you could look into the beautiful face that had ruined, or helped to ruin, your professional life—twice. For him, that face was Julie Reilly's. He had hoped never to see it in person again.

"Once wasn't enough for you? You had to track me down to zap me one more time?" He snatched his drink from the server's tray. He took half the glass down in one swallow.

"I'll have the same as the professor," Julie said. She removed her bag and squeezed in beside Gabriel. "And bring my friend another."

"Friend . . . is that what they call victims nowadays?" he asked.

"That's what they call someone who's in the same boat, which we are."

"I don't follow, Ms. Reilly," he said, stringing her name out.

"You lost your job over Summer Place, and now my career is hanging on that same damnable house."

"I don't see how one connects with the other, especially since I don't give a flying fuck about your career. Here's to your health." He finished his drink and then, again, grabbed the next before the server could place it on the table. Julie did the same and downed hers without hesitation.

"One more, please. I have a rather long and disheartening plane ride back to New York with company I really don't care for."

"Where's your little friend—being punished for failing to land the big one?"

"Professor, don't give yourself too much credit. No matter what you may think of yourself, Summer Place will always be the star of your story."

Kennedy was taken aback by the strange comment.

"So you actually believe the house is at the center of it all?"

"Of course. Now ask me if I've changed my view about you being guilty of negligent homicide."

Gabriel didn't say anything; he just waited.

"Why am I to blame for you losing your student, Professor? Can't you admit that you took them into that house, and then afterward there was one less than before?"

"I was always able to admit that. However, I will never admit to being a part of his disappearance. As I remember, the other participants backed me on that. Hell, it was they who reported it to me. There is a difference between being responsible for a thing, and being *the* cause of it."

"From a man who, before he went into that house, didn't really believe the bullshit he was researching, you just can't get past that story about the house taking him and ruining you, can you?"

Kennedy downed half of his second drink and looked into Julie's green eyes.

"That's your problem, Ms. Reilly. I always believed in what I taught. The lesson of Summer Place was a lesson of the mind—how one inanimate object, and how it's perceived, can influence the thinking pattern of a viable and otherwise intelligent person. It was never about haunted houses. But then again, my ancestors never thought the world was round, either."

"One million dollars, Professor," she said, swirling the ice in her glass.

"Excuse me?"

"Eight hours of your time. I host, and you are, well . . . the color, so to speak." She didn't smile at her obvious joke.

"I know you're not asking me to return to Pennsylvania."

"No, I'm asking you to fight for what you believe in—or once did, anyway. And I'm offering you one million dollars to do it. You get what the university was offered, plus a chance to show the world on live television what you couldn't show them years ago."

"You are out of your fucking mind!" He stood suddenly, almost knocking Julie out of the booth. He dug in his pocket and threw two twenties on the table, then thought a moment, reached out, and took the money back. "You can use part of that million to pay for the drinks—I'm unemployed."

Julie opened the passenger door and climbed into the rental car. The air-conditioning felt like heaven as the morning gave way to the early afternoon.

"Well, I saw Kennedy leave in a huff, so I guess your charms failed to sway him," Kelly stated flatly as she buckled her seat belt.

"My charms, as you put it, had nothing to do with it. I planted a seed and now we'll see if anything grows. Let's head over to Kennedy's apartment building. This is the part where he figures out he's in deep trouble. Fertile ground will encourage the seed and make my offer a little more attractive."

"Offer?" Kelly asked, putting the car in gear.

"One million dollars to a man with six hundred twenty-five dollars in his savings account can be very good fertilizer, don't you think?"

"Does the network know about this offer?"

"Unlike you, Ms. Delaphoy, I have the power of negotiation."

* * *

Kennedy sat in his apartment, staring at the chipped top of his rickety table. He opened his personal journal from that night at Summer Place—the one with the evidence tag still stuck to its cover—and turned to the last page. One student had been taken from him, and the others were now lost in a world that no longer made sense to them, because of an entity the likes of which was unprecedented in the field of . . . here, Kennedy always laughed. It was hard to find the words for what he was dealing with. Everything sounded too fantastic to be true.

His doorbell rang, making him blink. He realized he had been transfixed for the span of several minutes. Worse, he couldn't remember a single thought he'd had while he stared at the journal's last page.

Kennedy slammed the journal closed and stood. He knew who was at the door, but he opened it anyway, returning to the kitchen without a word.

"I only have one chair to offer," he said over his shoulder.

Kelly and Julie looked around the small but tidy apartment. Kelly started to speak, but Julie placed a hand on her arm, silencing her question before it could be spoken. She watched the professor sit down at the table and pick up a journal.

"Tell me, has either one of you ever seen this?" He slid the book across the table.

There was a Pennsylvania State Police evidence tag still stuck to its cover and a larger plastic bag sticking out of the back pages somewhere. Gabriel opened it and turned the journal upside down so they could read the three words below the last entry through the plastic.

They Are Mine.

"I've never seen the actual journal, no. Only photographs," Julie said. She placed her bag on the kitchen counter and took the only available chair.

"I only saw a copy, too," Kelly seconded. Finding nothing to sit on, she leaned against the kitchen wall.

Kennedy pulled the journal back toward him and closed it.

"I have read and touched those words so many times. Do you know what happens when you touch the letters that make up those three words?"

Julie and Kelly waited. Kennedy had the reins now. They were there just to witness his turn of faith, and fate.

"Not a fucking thing. No insight into who—or what—wrote them. No magical epiphany that explains the mockery or the malice. It was a statement of fact. Whatever wrote it was in complete control."

Julie wondered now if Kennedy really was in control. His deep blue eyes looked haunted as he lowered them to the closed journal.

"Now you want to go back into a place controlled by something that can kill?"

Kelly again started to speak, but Kennedy's eyes said that the question had been rhetorical.

"This house"—he tapped the pile of research before him on the table—"is *the* haunted house. The one house that inspired *every* horror writer in the country to write about haunting, and the funny thing is, most never knew it even existed. Most still might not know. It's like Summer Place travels through people's minds and then they magically forget all about it, even though most of the literature on the subject of ghosts may be based upon this property, and this property alone."

"You're speaking of Shirley Jackson?" Kelly asked.

"Before her, there were ghost stories, but none that truly grabbed the reader and said, yes, there *are* things that go bump in the night. There *is* an unknown thing under your bed, and most definitely a horror in your closet. It preys on your mind and it knows exactly what scares you. It knows because whatever it is, it was once one of us."

"Ghosts?" Julie asked.

"Ghosts, spirits, whatever you want to call them," Kennedy said. "They protect something, maybe a dark secret. I think what makes this entity in Summer Place so evil, so insane, is the fact that it's hiding a secret from the world that it will kill to keep."

"Is that why anyone who goes in there runs a risk of encountering—it?" Kelly asked, mesmerized by Gabriel Kennedy's intense gaze.

"It's in here somewhere," he said, tapping the pile of research. "It's in the house's past."

"Can you find it?" Julie asked.

"I don't know if I want to. Probing around has already cost one boy his life, and it's cost five others, including myself, a life that makes sense. And now, as I understand it, two of your people are missing, and one young man may have lost his mind. The gamble is too great, I think." Kennedy placed both hands on the table, as if he were done with a lecture. The gesture seemed to say, *I hope you wrote that down, because that's all you're going to get.*

"But can we—"

"One million dollars and the right to choose my investigative team, and they get two hundred thousand dollars for their services—each," he said firmly.

"Done," Julie said. Her eyes held his as if she were challenging a bluff in a card game.

"The people I need, well, some will be hard to find; others, not so hard. However, I'll warn you now, there is one thing they'll have in common with me: they won't like the two of you one bit. They won't like who you work for, and they most assuredly won't tolerate any interference."

"You got it," Julie said.

"Wait, Ms. Reilly, this part concerns you directly." A small smile creased his lips.

She arched her eyebrows, waiting for the drama to end.

"Lieutenant Damian Jackson will have to be on the team. There will be no negotiation. Without him, the deal is off."

"We can't guarantee his cooperation," Kelly said. "He hates and despises you."

"Not my problem," he answered, still staring at Julie.

"He's your"—he smiled without humor—"coconspirator in the ruining of my career. So get him."

"Despite the undeniable desire to tell you to go fuck yourself, Kennedy, I'll just say instead, somehow I'll get Lieutenant Jackson, if only for the reason that Kelly already stated. He'll want the opportunity to finish tying the knot in the rope he placed around your neck seven years ago."

"Also, have that weasel Wallace Lindemann handy during the show. He may be useful," he said, ignoring Julie's threat.

"Is that all?" Kelly asked. She looked up from the list she'd made of Kennedy's requests, grimacing at each written word.

"It's still not enough," Gabriel said. He started writing a list of names. "If one person on my list doesn't enter the fight, the deal is off."

The word "fight" wasn't lost on them.

"Okay, Professor. I can give you what you ask for, but I need an answer to a question that our principals back at the network will be certain to ask."

"Why I changed my mind?"

Julie Reilly's silence told him he was correct.

"When I look at you two, I see the world for what it really is. Or at least, what it's become. I figure, why not join the rest of the human race and become as big an asshole as both of you?"

"Not buying it." Julie smirked.

Kennedy leaned forward. "Then how about this: I'm going to destroy whatever it is that walks inside that house. If I have to use you and every one of the people backing you to do it, I will."

8 United Broadcasting Corporation, Burbank, California

Lionel Peterson signed the payroll outlay for Gabriel Kennedy and the four names on Kennedy's list without batting an eye. It was just another silver bullet in the chamber to eventually use against Kelly Delaphoy. He knew the same silver bullet could take him down too, but that was a fact he was almost willing to live with as long as she hit the ground before he did.

He knew he had to find a way to distance himself from Kelly's destiny. All he could do for now was make sure the production side went off without a hitch. He and Harris Dalton would make sure that Kelly's downfall was live, in color, and technically perfect, for the entire country to see.

He smiled as he looked over the list Kelly had faxed him. The people Kennedy wanted for his team had, according to network security, all fallen from grace. Just like Kennedy himself.

"This is going to be something," he said to himself. "If I wasn't tied directly to this suicide attempt, I would be laughing my ass off."

Ogunquit, Maine

The first name on Gabriel Kennedy's list was a man well known to the local constabulary of the seaside resort of Ogunquit. He was one of the broken people, homeless, seeking the comfort of the ocean that drew so many. He was a man in hiding, almost a twin of circumstance to Gabriel himself.

On any other day of the week he could be found down by the beach, dragging along the one possession that was his constant companion: a Halcyon A-260 metal detector. However, today he was in the local jail. He sat not on the steel cot but on the cold concrete floor, with his legs crossed and his eyes closed. Instead of digging for the lost treasures that had belonged to vacationers, he was a guest of the local community. That, in and of itself, was a small blessing to the islanders, who despised people like George Henry Cordero.

The private detective hired by UBC had a hard time tracking Cordero down. Then he came across his name on the Internet, listed by the night desk of the Ogunquit police department. One of the four officers on duty escorted the detective through the booking area and into the holding cell, exactly twenty-four hours after Cordero's name had been placed on Kennedy's list.

The tall man looked at the vagrant's unkempt beard and long hair, and winced. This was the creep he'd been sent to round up for a television special?

"What's the charge against him?" the detective asked.

"Charge—you mean charges?" the policeman said. "That's plural, buddy. Some kids were, you know, playing around with him. Things got out of hand, as things sometimes do." He looked at the filthy man on the floor. "One of the teenagers accidentally broke his metal detector, and Grizzly Adams here took offense."

"I see. They destroyed his property?"

"It was accidental."

"And these kids . . . they're locals? You call them islanders?"

"Yes."

"So, what are the specific charges against Mr. Cordero?"

"He manhandled one of the boys. He, well, spanked one."

"Spanked?"

The cop looked uneasy.

"How much to set Mr. Cordero free?" The tall detective removed a cell phone from his pocket and held it to his ear.

"That's for Judge Bennett to decide tomorrow morning, but it won't be cheap. The judge doesn't take too kindly to vagrants."

"Yes, I have Cordero," the detective said into the phone. "The judge's name is Bennett, and the charges are bullshit. Right, right . . . okay, I'll be here, just let me know."

The detective returned the phone to his pocket and turned to the man sitting on the floor, ignoring the officer.

"Mr. Cordero, you'll be out of here by ten o'clock in the morning. I've made arrangements for you to come to New York."

"I don't want to go to New York," the man said with a thick Spanish accent.

"A man you may know said to tell you"—the detective pulled out a small notebook and referenced Cordero's page—"that he's going back into the house, and that he needs your expertise. You'll be paid two hundred thousand dollars for the four days leading up to and including Halloween."

The police officer momentarily lost control of his jaw as it fell open.

"House?" the shaggy-haired man asked, his eyes still closed. "Just who is this man?"

"Professor Gabriel Kennedy." The detective closed his notebook.

Cordero's eyes opened. His demeanor seemed instantly more alert and aware, as though he had just awakened after a long sleep.

"Summer Place, isn't it?" Cordero said with a growing smile. "That stupid bastard is slapping that bitch again? What can I say? Count me in." He stood and felt at his beard.

The detective looked at the cop. "I don't think he'll be seeing your local magistrate after my bosses make their calls to your Town Council—which they should be doing right about now. Mr. Cordero, if I may ask, what is it that makes you important to Professor Kennedy?"

The man in the cell thought a moment, pulling on his long beard.

"I'm a clairvoyant."

Loveland, Colorado

The dinner party was proceeding far better than Leonard Sickles would have ever thought possible. The young man from Los Angeles had held his own with intellectuals from both Hewlett-Packard *and* IBM. Every once in a while his language would revert to the streets from which he sprang, but more times than not, he would mentally corral the harsh words that were boiling over to get out.

Leonard Sickles, former gangbanger, was famous for rising from the front ranks of the Crips in East Los Angeles to become one of the most gifted software designers in the world. His talent had been discovered by accident by a former professor at USC. It took two years for the professor to gain the trust of Lenny "Too Smart" Sickles and then another year for the kid to recognize his own genius. Leonard was a prodigy. He had just graduated at the top of his class, completing six years of instruction in only four. It had taken the death of his younger brother in a drive-by shooting to make him focus on bettering himself. He knew his mother could not take another death in their small, struggling family.

The dinner party was an excuse for Electro-Light Design Incorporated of Fort Collins, Colorado, to thumb their noses at the people from IBM and Hewlett-Packard, who had not been able to land the brilliant former gang member for their own.

His new boss and the owner of Electro-Light Design, Thomas Reynolds, pulled Leonard away from one of the hired kitchen helpers—to whom he was telling a very sordid joke—and smiled his way into the hallway with his arm around the boy.

"Leonard, you have visitors at the front door. A couple of men from New York."

"Really?" he asked.

"How did anyone know you were here?" Reynolds asked. He nodded his head to one of the guests in passing. "Is there something you'd like to tell me? I mean, we *do* have a deal in principle, right?"

"Sure, my word is righteous."

"I mean, you wouldn't hang me out to dry by talking with another company, would you? Computer Associates in New York, or some other East Coast outfit?"

"Look, Mr. Reynolds, I said I would sign the contract. What's the matter, my word ain't good 'nough?"

Reynolds placed his arm around the smaller black man. Leonard got very uncomfortable every time his new boss performed that particular gesture. It was as if he were trying to act like his father. The clothes Reynolds had purchased for him for the dinner party were starting to feel just a little tight.

"Okay, son, just checking. Maybe you better go and see who your visitors are. I'll make nice with the sharks in the dining room."

"Sure," Leonard said. He returned to the kitchen worker he had been speaking to earlier.

"Hey, baby, where's the front door to this funeral parlor?"

She pointed to the left and Leonard treated her to his once-famous slumped-over walk, winking at her before he rounded the corner.

When he was out of sight, he straightened up into the practiced calm and confident stride that made white society take him seriously. He approached two men in dark suits, who stood just inside the door. His mind was racing, but on the outside he remained cool.

"I didn't do it, number one. And number two, I was actually invited here."

"Sir?" the larger man on the left asked.

"It's obvious you're cops. Come on, man, I really was invited."

"No, sir, we're private security from the UBC Television Network in New York." The two men looked at each other, and then at a file photo that the shorter one held. Leonard shifted. He'd jacked some cars from the UBC lot in LA once, but that had been a long time ago.

"Mr. Leonard Sickles?"

"Come on, man, just say you're cops."

"Sir, we are here to offer you a job for seven days and one night—Halloween night. The offer is for—"

"Get the fuck outta here, man," Sickles said. He slapped at the air and started to turn away.

"Two hundred thousand dollars," the man finished.

Sickles tuned back around and looked at the two men.

"Two hundred large?" He smiled. "What's the catch?"

"No catch. You'll have to spend the week before Halloween in New York doing some technical work."

Leonard looked the smaller of the two over and then eyed the larger.

"Get the fuck outta here," he repeated. "This is a fuckin' joke, right?"

The two men exchanged looks. "No joke, Mr. Sickles, Professor Gabriel Kennedy asked for you personally."

"Professor Gabe? Where's he at?"

"We don't know," the large one said. "We are to retain your services and get you to New York within the next twenty-four hours."

"Is he in trouble again?" He fidgeted, shifting his weight from one foot to the other.

"We don't know, sir." The smaller man pulled a sheet of paper out of the file he was holding. "There is this." He handed the paper over to Sickles.

He eyed the man and then slowly reached for the paper.

"Bring your Infra-Spectroscope design—I found you the money to build it." He read down the page, looking for a signature, but there was none. In its place was one word that he read aloud. "*Punk!* That's Professor Gabe, all right—the asshole."

"Hey, hey, what's going on here? You're taking a hike on me and my company for New York?"

The three men at the door turned to see Thomas Reynolds standing angrily in the outer entranceway.

"Spying, Mr. Reynolds?" Leonard asked, his right eyebrow rising. "Is this the kind of trust I can expect from you and your company, man?"

"I'm paying you enough to buy your trust. Now what's this about?"

"What this is about, is the man who saved my life. My shrink from a long time ago. He needs me, and I'm going to help him. I'll be back . . ." He looked questioningly toward the two men.

"The day after Halloween, sir."

"Yeah, the day after Halloween. Then I'm yours. And don't think I'm not going. I owe this man everything I am, and all that I *will* become."

Reynolds's posture eased. He reached into his inside

jacket pocket and withdrew his wallet. He handed a card to Leonard.

"Use this. It's a company credit card. Try and keep it reasonable, okay?"

Leonard smiled and nodded. "You bet. The big-city hookers can wait until I have an expense account," he joked. Reynolds shifted uncomfortably, and so did the two network security men. Leonard stuck out his hand, and when Reynolds took hold of it, he turned his hand upside down and grasped Reynolds's hand with both of his in a hoodshake.

"Thanks, Mr. R, I'll be cool with it." He let go of his hand and then smiled again. "Give my regards to the pukes inside; tell them my main man needs me."

"Leonard, do you even know what you're getting into?"

"No, not really."

"Do you know what this man does now?" Reynolds asked.

"What does he do now?" Leonard asked the two men.

"Sir, all we know is that he is working for the producers of a reality television show."

"Yeah, what's it about?" Leonard asked.

The two men looked at each other, and the larger one opened the door and turned.

"Ghosts, I believe. A haunted house type of thing. Shall we go, sir?"

Leonard's smile faded. He started to wonder what the hell he had just agreed to.

"Ghosts, huh?" he asked as he cautiously stepped forward.

"Yes, sir," the small man said. He gestured for Leonard to leave first.

"Haunted house?"

"From the rumors and gossip we've heard at the network, sir, it's very, very, haunted."

Leonard felt a sudden chill. He reached out and snapped on the front porch light before stepping out into the darkness. "I thought Professor Gabe was a full-time shrink," he mumbled to himself. "Ain't there enough live people around, he's gotta go after dead ones?"

Kennedy's team had its second member for the live broadcast from Summer Place.

Browning, Montana

John Smith—at least, that was how he had signed in—sat alone inside the coroner's examination room. The lights were low, with only a single spotlight illuminating the sheet-covered body on the stainless steel table before him. He knew the sheriff and coroner of Glacier County would be coming along soon, so he waited. That sheriff would know him as John Lonetree, headman, activist, and also the chief of police of the Blackfeet reservation, near the border with Canada. He had used the fake name and ID to gain entrance to the county offices when the sheriff and coroner went to dinner. He had made his prayers, his examination, and had done all the right things his people traditionally called for, for the young woman laid out on the cold steel table.

The girl's name was Betty Youngblood. John had known her from the day she came into the world, and now on this dark day he performed her death rites. As he lowered his head, he removed his cowboy hat and tossed it on the chair next to him, freeing his long black hair to cascade around his shoulders. Betty hadn't been important enough for the coroner to delay his dinner. Her wounds were unattended and had been unexamined when John had arrived. He swallowed hard to keep his emotions in check. The world would never change for his people, it seemed.

The girl had been born, like most Indians on the Blackfeet reservation, into abject poverty. She had endured a life of abuse by a single mother who had tended toward the bottle and who had taken out every one of life's failures on her oldest child. At fifteen, Betty had left the rez and escaped into the white world. John had heard she had taken to prostitution and other forms of criminal life to keep from going home again.

John heard their voices long before the examination room door opened. As the overhead lights came on, he kept his head lowered and his hands clasped in front of him. The voices ceased suddenly when the two men saw they weren't alone.

"Just who the hell are you?"

Lonetree finally looked up. He saw the small, balding fat man who called himself the county coroner, standing with his hands at his sides. Beside him was Sheriff Van Kimble. They had been friends since they were kids, but now the sheriff had his hand on the butt of his nine-millimeter, looking at him in anger.

"What are you doing here, John?" the sheriff asked.

"Who is this man?" the coroner asked.

"He's the police chief over at the Blackfeet reservation. You two haven't met yet. John, this is Dr. Fleming, our county coro—"

"I know who he is, Van," Lonetree said, standing. He towered over both men at six feet, five inches. "Doctor, do you usually leave a body to sit while you go and eat, without taking the decedent's vital stats?"

"I, uh—"

"This girl was raped; there may be seminal fluids that are at this moment deteriorating. Have you even fixed the time of death through body temperature?"

"Now wait a minute, John, we already have the killer in custody," the sheriff said. He stepped forward and let the door close behind him.

"Yes, I've heard that also. Randy Yellowgrass, that right?"

"Your Harvard education hasn't failed you. Yeah, that's right. My deputy found the drunken, stupid bastard still standing over the girl in the alley at Eighth and Monroe."

"And you believe Randy, harmless Randy Yellowgrass, could do something like this?" Lonetree pulled the white sheet away from the body and let it fall to the floor.

On the table, Betty lay with her eyes open. The left one was half shaded by her eyelid, the other dilated to almost pure black. Her throat had been savagely cut from ear to ear. Her left breast had been completely removed, and her vaginal area was wrecked. John stepped forward and placed his hand on her hair. It had been tinted with tiny streaks of blond dye. He shook his head.

"Please don't touch her until—"

"Until what? Until you examine her, Doctor?" John turned and faced the much smaller coroner. His own nine-millimeter handgun was temptingly heavy at his right hip.

The sheriff looked at the gun and the man wearing it.

"Why are you armed, John? You're not on the rez; you're in my bailiwick now."

Instead of answering the sheriff, Lonetree walked to the other side of the table and looked down at Betty.

"John, why are you here?"

"I had a dream the other night."

"Do your dreamwalking on the rez, John. Not here."

"The dream was of falling stars, a meteor shower. Then a smiling girl came into the dream. It was the young Betty, coming over to my ma's house after a beating. The stars in my dream circled her, colliding as she smiled at me. Then the stars stopped, and all but one fell. That lone, single star stayed floating around her heart, and then it, too, finally vanished, and as I looked up in my dream, Betty wasn't smiling anymore."

"And?" the coroner asked.

John shook his head and smiled briefly. "Then . . . nothing. I woke up. Didn't think a thing about it until this evening. I received a call from Randy Yellowgrass's mother, telling me about Betty and of her son's arrest.

"Tell me, Doctor, what you make of this." He pointed to a small red line, a mere impression to the right of center on Betty's chest, not far from the breast that had been removed. It was shaped like a tilted, backward L.

The coroner leaned in close, and then lowered the large light and magnifying glass.

"Seems like a compression wound."

"That's what I see, Doctor. Obviously postmortem, wouldn't you agree?"

The coroner nodded. "Yes, there was no blood pumping through her system when this was made."

"And the vaginal wounds, I see the same. Postmortem. Oh, there was blood, but not as much as should be present in a wound such as this."

The coroner examined the vaginal area and then looked up. "I concur, Chief, but—"

"Now, the removal of the breast was obviously done while she was still alive. The wound would have eventually been fatal if she hadn't had her throat cut, correct?"

This time the coroner didn't have to look at the body. With the amount of blood that had been expelled through the chest wound, the large Indian was obviously correct. He nodded his agreement.

John swallowed and then raised his right hand and gently touched the cold flesh at the side of the young woman's face. Then he slowly pulled her lips apart. The girl's front teeth were broken all the way to the gum. John looked from the table to the coroner, waiting.

"Well, from first impressions, I would say the killer held her mouth closed while he tortured her. Maybe even struck her with a fist."

"Close, Doctor. But notice the bruising around the mouth, the redness, the breaking of small capillaries in the lips and the lower cheek area, all the way up to the orbital bones of the face?"

"Yes, I see that now. Not a blow to the mouth, but a constant pressure, yes. Her mouth was being kept closed with some considerable force."

"Not only that, but with enough force not just to loosen her teeth, but to snap them off. Quite a feat for little Randy Yellowgrass, all one hundred and forty-five pounds of him."

"There could be any number of expl—" the sheriff started to say, but John cut him off.

"Yes, any number of explanations for it, I'm sure." John patted Betty's face lightly, closing her destroyed mouth. "Sheriff, it's not the wound itself, but the size of the impressions left on the skin. Randy would have had to use both of his hands to cover that much area with that much force. Not only that, but he would have to have fingers of steel. Mere pressure would not have been enough to shear those teeth off like that. The hand that did this was not only a larger one, but one that wore at least one ring, possibly two. Metal needs very little help to cause damage to teeth. I suspect if you check Betty's throat, you'll find a few of the broken teeth, chipped by metal."

The coroner nodded his head, conceding that John was possibly right.

"So?" the sheriff asked.

"Randy Yellowgrass wears no jewelry, except for a small cross around his neck. But you know that, because you took his personal effects when he was booked."

"Jesus Christ," the sheriff mumbled.

"You agree with this so far?" he asked the coroner, who merely nodded once.

The sheriff's radio crackled to life. "Sheriff, this is Jennings. We just had a message dropped off at the station from the reservation. I was told to deliver a telegram to John Lonetree over at the coroner's office. Is he there with you?"

Sheriff Kimble reached for the microphone clipped to his brown jacket, but stopped when John raised his eyebrows and then held his hand up.

"Your deputy, Jennings, he was the one who discovered the body?"

The sheriff's silence was answer enough for John.

"Ask the deputy to bring the message to me here."

After the sheriff relayed the order, the answer came.

"It'll only be a minute, Sheriff; I'm right outside the county building."

John picked up his cowboy hat and put it on.

"What now?" Kimble asked.

"We wait."

Five minutes later, a knock came at the door. The sheriff opened it and took the small yellow piece of paper from the young deputy and invited him inside. Spotting the exposed body on the table, the deputy quickly turned away. He started to leave, but John stepped forward and closed the door, effectively blocking it with his large frame. The sheriff looked up from the message, then at the closed door, and then at John. He handed the telegram to Lonetree.

"From New York, of all places," he said. Lonetree pocketed the paper, ignoring it and the sheriff. Instead he looked at the deputy.

"Hard thing to look at, isn't it?" he said to the young man, who removed his hat and then turned and looked at John, carefully keeping his gaze away from the examination table.

The sheriff stepped away from the door and walked around the table to watch the two men. He was tempted to stop whatever it was Lonetree was up to, but his instincts held him back.

"She had most of her clothing on when I found her. It made me sick."

Lonetree nodded and patted the deputy on the back. "Deputy Jennings, isn't it?"

"Yes, sir."

"You did good work tonight. I wish I had dependable men like you on the rez." He smiled and looked at the sheriff. "Hell, we wouldn't have any crime at all."

"Just lucky, coming across that Indian like I did."

"That Indian?"

"The suspect, I mean. No offense to you, sir."

"No offense taken, Deputy. That was a stroke of luck, coming across a murder and rape in that alley. Do you always check the alleys on that side of town?"

"As often as I can, yes, sir."

John lightly pinched the deputy's shoulder, then patted it again. "Say, that's a nice set of rings."

Jennings looked down and nervously switched his wide-brimmed hat to his other hand. John wasn't looking at the deputy's hand any longer, but at the embroidered badge on the man's jacket.

The sheriff slowly unsnapped the holstered weapon at his side.

"We've had some disagreement here, Deputy. Maybe another set of trained law enforcement eyes can sort it out for us." John held his hand out, gesturing for Jennings to face the girl's body. He kept his large hand on the boy as he led him over to the midpoint of the stainless steel table. "This impression right here . . . do you have any idea what that could be?"

The deputy leaned in and looked at the backward L indentation on the girl's chest. He cleared his throat.

"No, sir . . . I uh . . . no, I don't know."

"Falling stars," John said. He looked away from the body and released the boy's shoulder.

"Sir?" The deputy looked up.

"Nothing. Just a dream I had a few nights ago." John smiled. He looked at the sheriff and let the smile fade. "Deputy, you say Randy Yellowgrass was leaning over the body when you found him?"

"Yes, sir."

"There's no doubt in my mind Randy was intoxicated. You know, drunken Indian and all that. But I find it hard to believe Randy was capable of doing this. Especially since Betty was his very own cousin."

"I didn't know that, John," Kimble said, staring at his deputy.

"Yeah, well, in all honesty, that's neither here nor there, Sheriff. Cousins have killed cousins long before this. However, there is one thing—that damn dream I had, falling stars. Well, they were falling around Betty, of all people."

"There's some who say John here has certain"—the sheriff looked from the deputy to Lonetree—"abilities. We laugh it off most times down at the station. 'Dreamwalking,' they call it."

"Indians—what are you going to do?" John asked jokingly. But he quickly advanced on the deputy, reaching inside Jennings's uniform jacket, past the embroidered star, and ripped free the metal badge pinned to the officer's shirt. He took Jennings by the arm and threw him toward Betty Young-blood's body. The deputy turned in indignation as he slammed into the autopsy table, shaking the dead girl's body violently. John Lonetree placed the star-shaped badge on Betty's chest—right into the imprint of the backward L. "Falling stars, Deputy Jennings."

"Goddamn!" the sheriff said. He pulled his nine-millimeter out of its holster.

For a split second, John didn't know who the sheriff was going to point the weapon at. He was relieved when he saw it was Jennings who was being covered.

"When you held her mouth closed, you broke her teeth off with your rings. And then after you cut her breast off, you cut her throat." John grabbed the deputy by the jacket and deftly removed Jennings's own weapon. He tossed it to the shaking coroner, who juggled it and finally caught it. "After that, you thought it was safe enough to fuck this little girl—after she was dead!" he said through clenched teeth.

"You fuckin' . . ." the sheriff said, taking very close aim at his own man.

"Then you cut her up some more, didn't you? But you didn't count on the badge you were wearing—the star. It made that backward L shape. Add three more of those L's and you have a five-pointed star."

"Jesus," the coroner said. He looked like he was close to going into shock.

"I think if you look in the back of his cruiser, or search his house, you'll find the uniform he was wearing when he murdered this little girl. The knife he used on her is more than likely in the sewer or a lake. The doc here will be able to extract his DNA from Betty's body." He shook Jennings one last time, tossed the deputy aside like a rag doll, and stormed out of the examination room.

An hour after Jennings was taken into custody for the rape and murder of Betty Youngblood, Sheriff Kimble found

John Lonetree sitting on the curb, leaning against a parking meter.

"I've never in my life seen or heard anything like that."

Lonetree looked past the sheriff, up toward the night sky. The nights held a chill that was getting ready to morph into outright cold as the middle of October approached.

"Cursed is what I am," John said. He took a shuddering breath. "The curse of dreamwalking has always been with me, my mother, and grandmother." He finally looked at the sheriff. "It really sucks." He pulled his gun, and then his own badge from his Levi's jacket and handed them to the sheriff.

"What's this?"

"I want you to give them to the tribal council for me. I can't go back and face them."

"Why? You have nothing to hide. You did good, John—real good. You made me look like a fool."

"Van, making a redneck like you look like a fool isn't that difficult a task, and not something I aspire to do very often." He shook his head. "I had the dream of Betty and the falling stars and didn't act on it. I'm not tired of my red blood, but I'm tired of being numb inside and not recognizing things for what they are." John rose slowly to his feet.

"Where will you go?"

Lonetree pulled the telegram from his jacket pocket.

"New York, and then Pennsylvania—a house called Summer Place. An old classmate of mine from Harvard, we used to play football together. Anyway, he needs my help. I figure this is a good time for a vacation and a hard case study on what it is that I am. He needs help, and I need to get the hell out of here."

"Help with what? What is Summer Place?" Kimble asked.

John had turned and started to walk away, but he stopped. When he turned back, he had a crooked grin on his face.

"It ate his grad student a few years ago. Leave it to Gabriel Kennedy to make my guilt seem small."

John walked off into the darkness of the Montana night, his black hair gleaming in the moonlight. His cowboy boots clicked down the road leading away from the reservation, possibly forever.

The third member of Gabriel Kennedy's team was on his way to New York.

Seattle, Washington

The man tilted the faculty ID so the heavyset bartender could see it clearly in the dim light of the filthy, smelly dive someone had the gall to name *Nirvana*. The bartender looked it over and eyed the man at the bar. The man wore a brown suit and a white shirt. His collar was open, and he wore no tie.

Instead of answering his question, the bartender poured a tap beer and walked away. The man in the suit sighed and placed the photo of Jennifer Tilden back in his coat pocket. He turned to leave.

"Let me see that again," the bartender said. He had returned, and was wiping his hand on a wet towel.

The man in the brown suit reached into his pocket once more and produced the photo.

"You say she's a what?" the burly bartender asked.

"She's a professor of paleontology from the University of Oklahoma."

"Get the fuck outta here," the bartender said. He handed the picture back to the network's detective.

"By your reaction, I assume you know her?"

"Look, I can tell a cop when I see one. As much as I like doing my civic duty, I don't want to hurt someone I know."

"I'm not a cop. If you point her out, you'll be doing her a big favor."

"That right? Look, she may be down and out, but everyone in downtown pretty much likes—?" The bartender paused and looked expectantly at the detective.

"Jennifer," he supplied.

"We know her as Pinky—you know, her red hair."

The man waited. He knew enough not to push the bartender.

"She's right over there, in the corner booth." He placed the beer down in front of the man, spilling the foam over the rim of the glass. "The one that looks like she's passed out."

The man turned toward the booth in question. The small-ish woman sitting there was slumped over the table with her head in the crook of her elbow.

The detective started through the dingy bar toward the booth, dodging people who looked his way with indifference or mild hostility. He sat his beer down and the thump made the small woman jump, but she still didn't look up from where her head rested on her arm.

"Dr. Tilden, may I have a moment?" When she didn't respond, he sat down in the rickety seat across from her. He raised his voice and repeated the question.

Finally, she looked up. Dr. Jennifer Tilden had startling green eyes, ringed in red. She was clearly exhausted and could barely focus on his face.

"I don't know you," was all she said. Her voice was hoarse and raspy, as if she hadn't had a drink of water for years. She looked at him more closely and then closed her eyes. She had fallen asleep.

"Doctor, I've been sent by—"

"Sorry, buddy," the bartender said. He took the smallish woman by the shoulders and shook her. "She's on, and if I let her miss her spot, well . . . we don't want to see her lose her temper."

"Wha—what?" She came awake, if only barely.

"You mean she's actually going to—"

"Yeah, she's going to sing." The bartender helped her to her feet. "Come on, Pinky, wake up."

The detective forgot about his beer as the woman was lifted from her seat in the booth. She wore faded blue cordu-roy pants, a small white shirt that had seen better days, and a green sweater. Her short red hair looked as if it hadn't been introduced to a hairbrush in weeks.

As she was helped to the small stage, the crowd became restless and started making catcalls. Several of the women and a few of the men called names at the small woman as she stumbled onto the stage. The bartender waved his bar towel to shoo several of the patrons out of his way and hopped down from the small raised platform.

Jennifer Tilden held the tall microphone with both hands as if it were a lifeguard and she were a victim of the rising and angry seas around her. Her head tilted forward and struck the microphone, producing a loud and piercing screech. That brought most of the patrons to their feet with even more boos and curses.

The bartender waited until the small woman pulled her short, red hair back slowly and deliberately. Then he pressed the button. Without looking up, she started to sing as the slow piano music from the karaoke machine filled the room.

"It's almost heaven—being here with you—the first time I saw you—I knew it to be true—but after all, dear, I love you—I do—angel baby—my angel baby . . ."

She sang the first verse in slow, hauntingly soft words, and then the karaoke machine chimed in with more instrumentation at the start of the chorus. The barroom became quiet as a church, all the patrons enraptured by the sweetness of the voice coming from the woman on the small stage.

The man recognized the old song "Angel Baby," originally recorded by Rosie and the Originals. As Tilden sang, her eyes remained closed and she gently swayed with the song—as if she were feeling it from somewhere deep in her soul.

The notes, both high and low, were perfectly struck. When the song came to an end, the crowd was mute.

Jennifer Tilden once more grabbed the microphone for balance, but this time she went over, dragging the instrument with her.

That broke the spell. The barroom erupted in applause and shouts for more. The detective ran forward and assisted the doctor to her feet, then helped her from the stage. When she gained her balance, she glared at him.

"Leave me the fuck alone!" she shouted. Her voice was once more ragged and burned out.

She shrugged his hand away and stumbled through the crowd toward the front doors.

He quickly followed her outside into the cold night air, where he found her sitting on the curb. She had no coat, just the light sweater she had been wearing inside. The woman was hugging herself and crying.

The man removed his suit jacket and placed it over her shoulders. She shrugged out of it and bent at the waist, then straightened. She rocked forward again, hugging her knees.

"Go away," she moaned through her tears.

"Dr. Tilden, that was an amazing song. Your voice, it just—"

She turned on him with her red and angry eyes. "It's what—what?!" she shouted.

"Ma'am, I've been hired to find you and give you a message. Professor Kennedy said to tell you he needs you."

The woman opened her eyes and turned her head slowly toward the detective. "Who the hell are you?" she asked.

"Two hundred thousand dollars, ma'am, for a week's worth of work in Pennsylvania."

Slowly, she wiped a hand over her wet eyes.

"Gab . . . Gabriel Kennedy?"

"The UBC network has sent out a private jet for you. It's at SeaTac right now."

"I may as well; I can't sleep as it is."

The man ignored her strange behavior. "As I said, you have the most amazing voice."

For the first time, the detective heard her laugh.

"I take it Professor Kennedy didn't enlighten you as to my . . . malady?"

"I've never met the man. I was hired out of the Seattle office to find you."

"Well, let me explain something to you." She took the man's arm with her hands. "That wasn't my voice." She laughed again.

"Kennedy should have warned you that I have some baggage. Actually, another person has to come along, so you'll be traveling with two of us. Me, and the ghost you just heard sing. His name is Bobby Lee McKinnon."

The detective stopped in the middle of the street. "What?"

"For a man working with Kennedy, you're not very informed." She turned and continued toward the parking lot. "I'm possessed by the ghost of a songwriter, murdered in 1959 in New York. The motherfucker won't let me sleep. He thinks his penance is to sing forever, and he does it through me."

The man stared after her.

She turned, waiting on him. For the first time this evening, Dr. Jennifer Tilden seemed present behind her own eyes. She smiled and batted her eyelashes, looking almost relieved to be going somewhere.

The final game piece had been found. The real game could soon begin.

9 Bright Waters, Pennsylvania

Gabriel Kennedy sat outside the hospital room and watched the occasional nurse stroll by and eye him with suspicion.

He heard the click of heels approach, and knew who they belonged to before he saw her.

"I had a feeling this would be your first move." Julie Reilly stopped before Gabriel.

"Ace reporter, always vigilant," Kennedy answered. He tried not to look the woman in the face.

"Professor, since you agreed to take the network's money, that makes us partners. Do you think for the next eight days we can be civil?"

Kennedy smiled faintly. "No."

"I did my job. I asked the questions everyone was thinking. Because you couldn't answer them, Professor, to any degree of believability, I'm the bad guy?"

"A reporter's job is to report the truth, not to speculate on what she thinks might have happened. Not to offer alternative solutions to a question that has but one answer. You lynched me in the public's opinion and gave the state police what they needed to open the trapdoor underneath me." He finally looked her directly in the eyes. "And the fall *hurt*, Ace Reporter."

"What happened that night, Professor? Did your student really vanish into thin air, or was he part of a broader conspiracy for your financial freedom?"

"You just never quit, do you?" Gabriel stood and looked down at Julie. "Have you contacted Detective Jackson?"

"Not yet. I expect he'll be around soon enough. I don't have to hunt him down—he's hunting for us."

"What do you want?" a deep voice asked from behind them.

Julie and Gabriel turned. Charles Johansson stood just outside his son's room. He glanced behind him and made sure the door was closed.

"Sir, my name is—" Gabriel started.

"I know who you are, Kennedy. I remember the mess you made at the house—a mess me and my missus had to clean up. What do you want?"

"Mr. Johansson, I would like to speak with your son," Kennedy said. Julie stepped up beside Gabriel and smiled, taking his arm. He flinched.

"He's not speaking with anyone, haven't you heard?"

"I understand he's nonresponsive. I'm a psychologist. I think I may be able to help him."

Charles looked from his wife to Kennedy. He lowered his head and walked away. Eunice watched his back retreat down the hall.

"Mrs. Johansson, perhaps you remember me. I'm Professor Gabriel—"

"Kennedy. Yes, I remember. I remember both of you."

Julie untwined her arm from Gabriel's with an embarrassed look.

"Tell me, Professor, why would you want to see my boy?"

"I think I may be able to—"

"Too late in the day for lies, Professor," she said sadly.

Gabriel looked from Eunice to the closed door. "I'm going back into the house."

Eunice Johansson shook her head. She thought a moment and then slowly pushed open her son's door, behind her. Her tired eyes remained on the two visitors.

"You just won't learn, will you? Your students, those TV folks, and now my boy . . . well, look and see what that house did to my son. I never really believed in things before, but something took part of our boy. He was wayward sometimes, but he didn't deserve this."

Kennedy cautiously stepped around Eunice and through the door she held open. Julie followed.

Gabriel was shocked. It was as though he were looking at a young child with white hair, not a strapping teenage boy, strong from working for a living with his father. He was curled in a fetal position on the hospital bed, wide-eyed and staring at nothing. A small puddle of drool had accumulated just below his mouth and had run onto the small pillow. Eunice moved to her son's side, wiped his mouth, and then dabbed at the pillowcase.

"Five minutes, ma'am. I'll do your son no harm."

Eunice's eyes went blank for a moment. She allowed Kennedy to lead her to a chair and sit her down. "What more harm can be done?" she asked sadly.

Kennedy patted her hand and then turned back to the boy, and his demeanor changed. He was in his element now.

Kennedy eased himself toward the bed. He reached out with one hand and brushed the long white hair back from the boy's eyes. He tilted his head and looked deeply into Jimmy's vacant, bloodshot eyes. Straightening, he reached into his sport coat and pulled out a small notebook. Thumbing through the pages until he found the one he wanted, he looked up at Jimmy again, then sat down on the edge of the bed.

Eunice had stopped crying and was watching the professor. He leaned close and said something into Jimmy's ear. There was no reaction. Kennedy looked into his notebook once more.

Julie Reilly leaned forward in her chair, also watching as

Kennedy confidently read a page and then closed the note-book once more. Again he whispered something to the boy. Still no reaction. Again, Kennedy checked his notes.

The door opened and Charles Johansson stepped into the room, carrying a cardboard tray that bore three cups of machine-brewed coffee. He gave one to his wife, and then placed the tray on the table. Standing over Eunice, they both watched Kennedy. When his eyes shifted to Julie, she couldn't hold the man's accusatory stare.

Kennedy put the notebook away and leaned over the boy once more, again whispering into his ear. Suddenly the boy sat straight up in bed, almost knocking Kennedy over. Jimmy's vacant eyes stared at nothing and he started to shake. Kennedy was strangely calm. Eunice stood with a start, her Styro-foam cup of hot coffee spilling to the floor, forgotten. It was the first time since her son had been brought to the hospital that he had made a voluntary movement of his own. Charles Johansson took his wife by the shoulders and held her, not allowing her to go to their boy.

Gabriel Kennedy leaned over and said something else to the boy, and this time they heard it.

"It's gone, Jimmy. It didn't want you."

Jimmy Johansson seemed to relax for a brief moment, and then he pointed insistently at nothing. His arm stretched out so tautly that they could see the muscles working under the skin. Kennedy gently pulled the boy's arm down.

"No! It's gone now. She will never bother you again. She wasn't after you . . . she wasn't after anybody. She was lost and she felt you in her room. She only wanted to be close to you. She didn't mean to scare you."

Jimmy's eyes blinked, as though he were waking up. He looked over at Kennedy and blinked more rapidly. Kennedy gestured for Julie to shut off the lights; he stood and pulled the curtains closed. When he went back to Jimmy's bedside, he suddenly lashed out and struck Jimmy in the face, mak-ing his head snap back. This time it was Charles who started forward and Eunice who held him in place.

The slap produced the desired effect. Jimmy started to cry. Looking around the room, his eyes fell on his mother, and then he really let loose. Gabriel stepped back and nodded for Eunice to go to her son. She threw herself on the bed and took the boy to her chest. She was soon joined by Charles, and they hugged their son together. Kennedy stepped away from the three and pulled a handkerchief from his jacket to wipe the sweat that had covered his forehead. He was soon joined by Julie, who was wide-eyed.

"What did you say to him? What's in that notebook?"

Kennedy glanced toward the Johanssons, then turned and slipped out of the room, Julie following close behind. They soon saw a doctor and two nurses go into Jimmy's room; as they passed Kennedy, they both gave him strange looks.

Kennedy sat down in a chair in the hallway, leaning forward to catch his breath.

"Well, what did you say?" Julie persisted, standing over him.

He finally looked up. "I spoke some words to him."

"What words?"

"It's not the words, but the language. I played a hunch."

"Goddamn it, Kennedy—"

"German. I spoke German to him."

"What did you say?"

Kennedy stood and walked a few steps. Then he turned and looked at Julie.

"You're a nonbeliever, but you'll have to agree, the boy woke up."

"Yes, I agree with at least that. Now, what did you say?"

"The German opera star, the missing diva from the third floor, from the 1920s."

"What about her?"

"She was taken by whatever is in that house. I don't think Jimmy came across the real entity at Summer Place, because he wasn't taken—he's still alive."

"So, what did you say to get him to wake up?"

"As I said, I played a hunch. I said something in German.

I don't know if it was the words themselves, or if he just recognized the language and it brought him back."

"What were the words?"

"*Helfen Sie mir,*" he answered.

Kennedy turned his back on her.

"Just what the hell does that mean, damn it?"

Gabriel turned back and smiled. His small breakthrough with the boy had made his day, but frustrating Julie Reilly was the icing.

"It means 'Help me.'"

Julie said nothing.

"This means, I suspect, that we may have more than one ghost at Summer Place. Possibly several. But one thing is for sure: that boy didn't meet the real entity that's walking those halls. He wouldn't be in there with his parents right now—he'd be missing, or dead."

Julie climbed in behind the wheel of the rental car and glanced at Kennedy. He sat quietly, looking through the windshield at the crystal blue sky overhead. As she snapped her seat belt, she blurted the question before she knew she was going to ask it.

"Feel like seeing Summer Place?"

He sat quietly, long enough that she began to think he hadn't heard her question.

"Yes, I think it's time. I'm ready to see it." He looked over to her. "From the outside."

"You don't want to go in?"

"We'll save that for your big night. It would be better for your cameras. Suspense, I guess you'd call it?"

"Yes, that's what we call it."

She put the car in gear and drove away from the hospital.

Kennedy was silent for most of the forty-five-minute drive to the house. Julie took her time, watching Kennedy for any kind of reaction as they made their way closer to the property. Gabriel kept his eyes closed most of the way. It wasn't until they were almost right above Summer Place, near the spot from which the UBC crew and Kelly Delaphoy had first caught sight of the house a week before, that Kennedy's eyes suddenly popped open. It was like watching a small animal sense the shadow of a predator flying over its hiding place.

"May I ask, off the record, what are you feeling?"

Gabriel looked over at Julie. He was feeling that anything was preferable to looking into the small valley below where the beast waited patiently.

"I don't know. It's not fear, though I am fearful. It's not confidence that I'm right about what that house is, because I am not confident. And it's not the overwhelming feeling that it's expecting me back, because how could it?" He shook his head. "I am afraid, but not of the house. I'm afraid I won't be able to kill whatever is in there."

The conviction of Gabriel's beliefs burned brightly in those few words. Julie was beginning to see that she would have more than a hard time proving Kennedy was a nut, or a stone-cold liar. Years ago, he had been like an eyewitness to a tragedy, expected to give a full and complete statement immediately. She never realized that his perspective would have changed and developed confidence once he'd had time to absorb what had happened; she and Detective Jackson had never allowed him up for air. As she drew around the corner and the house became visible through the trees, she found cold chills running the length of her arms. Gabriel's fervor had been convincing, even to her. It was like he was capable of pulling back a curtain to allow you to see what the possibilities really were.

"Jesus," he whispered to himself.

The property looked quiet. The Johanssons were still in Bright Waters, attending to Jimmy. The house was brilliant in the dazzling sunlight, and the sparkles coming off the pool dappled the awnings and deck chairs with a beautiful, otherworldly glimmer.

As the car crept down the long hill toward the house, Julie was kicking herself for not taping what Kennedy had said. Not for the television show, but as some sort of record for her personal use—maybe as a talisman that would later prove just how right she had been about Gabriel's mental makeup and his capacity for doing what she and Damian Jackson had accused him of: the glorification of an event for later celebrity.

As the house grew in the windshield, Julie saw a large car parked off the road just outside the gates. A large man was leaning on the hood. State police lieutenant Damian Jackson watched the house from a distance. Julie started to pull into the entrance.

"We can avoid this if you want," Julie said. "I'll just turn right around and head back to town."

"Why?" Kennedy asked, placing his wire-rimmed glasses back on. "Neither you nor he has ever intimidated me. Honestly, I would much rather have you both where I can see you."

As the car pulled to a stop, Kennedy opened his door and stepped out without hesitation. Ignoring the police detective, he walked straight to the gates. Julie stepped out, too, watching Kennedy bypass any greeting to Jackson. Then she watched the black state policeman as his dark eyes followed the professor.

"So, have you transferred permanently to the thriving metropolis of Bright River, forgoing the small-city challenges of Philadelphia, Lieutenant?" Julie called.

Damian Jackson removed his hat and tossed it onto the hood of his car.

"No, no transfer. Vacation time. Halloween has always been a favorite of mine."

Jackson spoke to Julie, but his eyes remained on Gabriel Kennedy's back. The professor studied Summer Place quietly through the large beams that made up the front gate.

"Did you receive the invitation to the big event here on Halloween?" Julie stepped casually between Jackson and Kennedy, allowing Gabriel the time he needed.

The large state policeman reached into his coat and retrieved a large envelope. Then he pulled out the check that had come inside it.

"Handsome reward to give someone who just wants to do his duty, wouldn't you say?"

Jackson smiled, watching her face as he slowly, deliberately ripped the two-hundred-thousand-dollar certified check in two.

"Does that mean we won't have the pleasure of your company on the thirty-first of October?"

Jackson stepped around Julie and made his way to the silent Kennedy. He stood beside him and, like Gabriel, took in the view of Summer Place.

"Tell me, Professor, how it feels coming back," he said, gazing out at the house.

"You mean, how does it feel returning to the scene of the crime?" Gabriel asked, looking over at Jackson with a smile.

"Something like that."

"I think it's the same for both of us." He half turned, acknowledging Julie. "Excuse me, all three of us."

"The lieutenant just tore up his compensation for attending on Halloween, Professor," Julie said. This visit wasn't turning out at all like she expected. Gabriel was just too cool and collected, seeing the house for the first time in so many years.

"Is that right?" He smiled. "Well, that's about what I expected. The lieutenant's always been more of a 'wait until they hang themselves' kind of guy. Watch from the sidelines and then piece it all together later—no matter if the puzzle pieces fit or not."

Jackson chuckled. "Just because I can't accept your money doesn't mean my investigation won't continue. I'll be there on the thirty-first, on two conditions."

"Okay, I'm waiting," Julie said. Kennedy turned and looked at Jackson, too. Now he seemed interested.

"One: There will be no camera shots of me. I am officially

not there that night. No mention of me in your script and no mention of my name on any electronic media. Two: I want ten minutes with Kennedy alone on the third floor before the night is done. You see"—he held the professor's gaze—"I believe the good Professor Gabriel here is going to give up far more than the ghost that night. He's going to make my case all by himself, and I'm going to take him into custody for murder. And that, you can film all you want."

Jackson turned his gaze toward the house once more. "Now, that's pretty good, Miss Reilly. If your network can pull off the small stuff like that, then we may be in for quite a fun house ride on Halloween."

Julie and Kennedy turned back toward the house in silence. Both of the large front doors were standing wide open, and every windowblind in the house had been raised. It was as if the house were welcoming them all back, inviting them inside so the party could start early.

Lieutenant Damian Jackson turned away, laughing at what seemed to be a clever prank. He picked up his hat from the hood and placed it on his head at a jaunty angle.

"Yes, ma'am, I wouldn't miss it for the world." He opened the car door and then looked back at the house. "Yes, ma'am . . . nice touch, with the doors and windows."

"Well, I guess that makes the guest list complete," Julie mused.

Gabriel said nothing. His eyes were still glued to the open front doors of Summer Place.

10   UBC Building, New York, New York

The next day, the large conference room at UBC headquarters played host to Professor Gabriel Kennedy's invitees. George Cordero, at the wet bar in the corner of the large room, tried mentally to size up the others.

The large Indian sat quietly at the center of the table. John Lonetree was dressed in black slacks, a white shirt with string tie, black sport coat, and black cowboy boots; his black cowboy hat sat on the table in front of him.

Cordero next surveyed the small black man sitting beside the Indian. He had introduced himself as Leonard Sickles, and then quickly told them all to call him "Too Smart" instead. Leonard was not as well dressed as the big man next to him. Every once in a while the black kid would look up suddenly, as if he expected the police to break in at any moment.

Cordero poured the expensive whiskey, then considered the small woman at the window, who seemed even more out of place than the rest of the menagerie at the table.

George moved to his chair across from John Lonetree, and smiled as he sat. Lonetree looked Cordero in the eyes for the briefest of moments and then looked away. He sat up a little straighter and then glanced at the door. The Indian raised his index finger and pointed to the conference room's large double doors. At that very moment, the doors opened. Lonetree's smile grew and he winked at Cordero.

Julie Reilly, Kelly Delaphoy, and Lionel Peterson entered the room, followed by the man who had been introduced to them earlier as Harris Dalton, dressed in a blue shirt and tan sport jacket. Behind the mysterious project's director, Professor Gabriel Kennedy entered, clean-shaven and carrying a small briefcase. He stood rooted just inside the door for a moment, looking at each of his friends in turn. Then he smiled and came forward, laying his briefcase on the table as the others settled in around it.

"John, I hoped you would come," he said, taking the larger man's hand in his own.

Lonetree slapped the hand away and took Kennedy into an embrace, patting his back so hard that Gabriel thought it would knock the wind out of him.

"What can I say? Rez life ain't what it used to be—figured I needed some crazy shit to lighten my burden."

Leonard Sickles waited patiently until John released Kennedy. Gabriel smiled and took Sickles by the shoulder. "Hello, you little shit. How are things in the 'hood?"

Too Smart smiled and slapped Kennedy's outstretched hand.

"Man, the 'hood don't have nothin' on those vultures in the business world. Those cats are dangerous!"

"I told you when we last spoke, watch out what you ask for—"

"Yeah, yeah—I just may get it. Well, I got it."

Kennedy gave Sickles a low five and then turned his attention to Cordero, who stood on the far side of the table. He was admiring Kelly Delaphoy's ass as she leaned over to place her own case by her chair. He looked up and raised his eyebrows twice. The last time Kennedy had seen George, he had been performing on Sunset Boulevard in Hollywood to sold-out crowds. He hadn't spoken to him since his arrests on several embezzlement and fraud charges. Kennedy just smiled and pointed a finger at Cordero, who held up his hands in a mock surrender.

Jennifer Tilden hadn't even seemed to notice that the others had filed into the room. Kennedy approached her slowly while the others took their seats around the table.

She had been cleaned up nicely and dressed well.

"Hi, Jenny," he said, smiling into her tired face.

A slow-moving smile started to brighten her face.

"Hello, Gabriel. I see you're trying to get back into business again."

Kennedy touched her cheek.

"How's Bobby Lee?" he asked.

Jennifer looked away, out the window once again. "Oh, he's been pointing out all the changes down on Seventh Street."

Gabriel frowned gently. "I think Bobby Lee needs to lay off for a while, Jenny. It's nice that he's taking you on a tour of memory lane, but it wasn't you who had him killed, and it wasn't you who led him to deal with the worst elements of the music industry." Kennedy took her hand. "Why don't you join us at the table, and I'll explain what it is we need you for—what we need you *and* Bobby Lee for."

Jennifer Tilden tried to smile, but failed miserably. Still, she allowed Gabriel to assist her from her chair and lead her toward the conference table.

Lionel Peterson rubbed the bridge of his nose. "Professor, I have a busy day planned. There's more to my job than seeing to Kelly's wants and wishes."

Kennedy's dislike for Peterson had been instant, the moment they had been introduced at a breakfast meeting that morning. The man was a schemer, and was not to be trusted any more than Delaphoy or Reilly.

Gabriel walked to the head of the long conference table. He looked at the faces of the only people he trusted—his old friends.

"John, I'll start with you."

Lonetree eyed Gabriel. He already knew what was wanted of him. He knew he could deliver, but wondered if Kennedy remembered the toll it would take on him to do so.

"Ms. Delaphoy, we will need you to contact Mr. Lindemann to request several items from Summer Place for Mr. Lonetree's use."

Kelly started writing on her notepad. "Such as?"

"A family portrait, a dish or two, a piece of the drywall, water from the pool, hay from the stables, silverware—"

"What is this for, Professor?" Peterson asked, raising his right brow as if that alone were enough to show Kennedy that he was still in charge.

"I'll explain when I'm done."

Peterson bit his lower lip, stopping the demand that was about to burst out of his mouth. He dipped his head forward in a brief, sharp nod.

"Thank you. John needs a sampling of the house. In particular, anything from the upstairs. Bed linen, a swatch of wallpaper, a piece of drywall, anything. You'll see to that, please?"

Kelly finished writing, then looked up as if to ask if there was anything else.

"Can you add to the list, John?" Kennedy asked.

"That may be a good start. But with less than four days until Halloween, I need the items overnighted if possible." He smiled at Gabriel. "I'll only have two nights in which to travel."

Kennedy returned the smile and then looked at the curious faces around him. "Dreamwalking runs in John's family. By keeping items from the house close around him, John may be able to feel something that may help us in the long run, and it may help him key in on something during your broadcast."

Julie glanced over at Lionel Peterson, who closed his eyes and shook his head.

"I hope you'll let us in on whatever Mr. Lonetree comes up with so it can be used on the air?" Peterson said.

Kennedy again didn't answer Peterson; he turned back to Kelly instead.

"Do you foresee a problem with acquiring those items, or similar ones?"

"When you deal with Wallace Lindemann, you don't foresee. You know. Yes, he will bitch and complain, but he'll do what's asked."

"Good, because if he doesn't, I'll need you to get out there and steal the items I have asked for—it's key to the overall assault plan on Summer Place."

"Assault?" Peterson asked.

"Yes, that's the only word that fits. We have to assault that house. Its defenses will be up, and I already know its offensive capabilities."

Peterson smiled and shook his head again. "I hope you're writing down everything Professor Kennedy is saying, Kelly. It should make for one hell of a script."

Kelly looked up from her notepad. Before she could retort, Peterson nodded to Kennedy. "Continue, Professor."

Gabriel walked around the table to Leonard Sickles, who was still doodling on the notepad in front of him.

"Leonard, we come to you. The Infra-Spectroscope—how's it coming?"

Leonard felt the pressure of Gabriel's hands on his shoulders—still the only man alive whom Leonard trusted enough to touch him. The young man ripped the first four pages from his notebook and lifted them into the air. Gabriel took them and glanced over them. While they had thought the small black man was doodling, he had actually been working.

"Looks like these parts may be expensive," Gabriel said.

"Nah." Leonard looked toward Harris Dalton. "The network techs may have everything we need right here in this building. I might have to contact Sperry Rand, or maybe GE, for a few things, but nah . . . it should be no problem."

"May I ask just what Mr. Sickles is going to be building?" Peterson asked. When Gabriel looked his way, he quickly held up his hand. "I have budget concerns here, Professor—and I will ask whatever I want to ask regarding this show."

"The Infra-Spectroscope is a device Mr. Sickles started developing when he heard about my rather curious investigation."

"What kind of device is this, kid?" John Lonetree asked, visibly curious.

Leonard "Too Smart" Sickles looked absolutely delighted to be asked a direct question. He didn't care about the network people but was pleased to be accepted by Kennedy's friends.

"Well, Mr. Lonetree, it's a cross between a night-vision scope and an air density accelerator. I can use it in several different ways. If it's ghosts we're looking for, I may be able to see them. I made a cheap version once and was able to catch a few things that Dr. K didn't even believe."

"They scared the hell out of me. I still don't know what he caught on that damn thing." Kennedy smiled at his young friend.

"Can this device be hooked into one of our remote cameras?" Harris Dalton asked, leaning forward in his chair.

"Yeah, man, I think so . . . if you can spare a few of your guys to do some experimenting."

"You'll have a team assigned to you from any division you

want, if it means we might catch a ghost on camera," Dalton said with a smile.

"Well, failing that, I know I can at least track the bastards."

"You're kidding?" Julie asked, looking from Leonard to Gabriel.

"Air density," Leonard said. He grinned appreciatively at Julie, eyeing her up and down and not caring who saw him do it. "Anything that moves—I don't give a damn if it's invisible and weighs nothing—even a ghost has to push aside air in order to move from place to place. No matter what, it has to change its environment—air temperature, dust in the air, or even light refraction. And when it does, old Too Smart will have its ass."

Leonard looked around the room with an *I just ate the canary* smile on his face. Lonetree nodded appreciatively.

The double doors opened and Jason Sanborn came through them, holding a giant roll of paper. He laid the sheets on the conference table, almost burying George Cordero. George politely smiled and removed half of them from his lap, then shook spilled whiskey from his hand.

"Sorry, old man," Jason said, removing his pipe from his mouth. "And you must be Gabriel Kennedy." He came around the table and took Gabriel's hand in his own.

"And you must be the producer."

"Yes, Jason Sanborn . . . and I have something for you, Professor." He released Kennedy's hand and walked back around the table. "Excuse me, young man, can you hand me that schematic at your feet, please?"

Cordero looked from Sanborn to Kennedy. He smiled without moving. "Let me guess . . . you found the diagrams of the original specs to Summer Place?" he asked Sanborn.

"Yes, that is correct," the producer answered. He replaced his pipe between his teeth and pushed his glasses up on his nose.

"That's not really a stretch, is it, Mr. Cordero?" Lionel Peterson asked with a small smirk. "I mean, it's quite obvious that Mr. Sanborn was carrying architectural drawings."

"That's not the something he was talking about," George said. Kelly and Julie were watching him, as if they both suspected that another of Kennedy's prodigies was about to show off. George smiled at them, then closed his eyes and held up his right hand. With a mysterious hum, he shook the hand over the table. "He's going to tell you that the original architect was none other than F. E. Lindemann himself."

"That is correct," Jason said. "How could you know that? These drawings weren't listed with the county, but in the family wing at the Philadelphia museum."

"I'm sure we're impressed with this gentleman's prowess at guessing games. Can we move on?" Peterson said, frowning.

"Well, George here just demonstrated his ability to feel things," Kennedy said. "The same with Mr. Lonetree. Now we'll use them to—"

"Professor, we get the gist. You can set up the details with Mr. Dalton later."

Kennedy stared at Peterson for the longest time. Then he turned and sat in his chair. He looked from Kelly Delaphoy to Julie Reilly and fixed them with his blue eyes.

"This man is going to get people hurt," he said.

Peterson didn't say anything; he only smiled and raised his brows at Kennedy's statement.

"If we rush in there without a plan, that house will literally chew us to pieces. This asshole doesn't even believe the damn place is haunted. He thinks it's nothing more than a pretty summer retreat for rich idiots like himself."

"Lionel, it seems you're upsetting a man we have just paid an awful lot of money to. May I suggest a little leeway here?" Julie said. She tapped her cell phone, on the table in front of her. Peterson didn't begin to fathom the power she herself wielded at the network.

"When you have concrete plans, I'll go over them with Harris. Until then, I'll be in my office." Peterson stood, buttoned his suit jacket, and strode from the conference room.

"Thank you," Gabriel said as he stood. "He didn't need to

be here for this, anyway. George, could you close the blinds, please? Ms. Reilly, will you do the same on your side?"

They drew the blinds and Kennedy turned off the overhead lights. He walked over to Jennifer, who sat quietly at the window, even though her view of the outside world had been cut off by the closing of the blinds. Her eyes were still fixed on the same spot. "Let me say this to you, and you may research it if you wish, but Dr. Tilden is the most brilliant anthropologist in the United States, if not the entire world."

All eyes sought out Jennifer in the semidarkness. She lowered her head, turning her gaze to her hands where they rested in her lap. When Kennedy placed a gentle hand on her small shoulder, she looked up for the first time.

"Jennifer Tilden is why I sought out paranormal research. She came to me as a patient, and I'll be betraying no confidential aspects of her case that she would not care to share. As a matter of fact, she really doesn't care one way or another."

"What is wrong with her, Professor Gabe?" Leonard asked.

Kennedy kneeled beside her and pried one of her hands free, holding it in his own. In the darkness, none of the others could see the gentleness that came to Gabriel's face as he touched her.

"Jenny is quite insane."

"Really?" Cordero said mockingly.

Kennedy glanced over. "And I would expect anyone but you to have something smart to say about her circumstance, George."

Cordero tried to smile, shifting to cover his embarrassment.

"How are you doing in there, Jenny?" Kennedy asked.

Jennifer didn't answer, but she did use her free hand to brush away some hair that had fallen into her face. She also squeezed Gabriel's hand a little tighter.

"We need Jenny for what we have to do in Summer Place. She will be invaluable as we try to seek out what we're dealing with." He looked up at the men and women sitting around the table. "Jennifer and her special friend will be able to talk to that house and what inhabits it."

"You'll have to explain that, Gabe," Lonetree said.

Kennedy turned back to the anthropologist. "Jenny, I want you to relax. You're here with me, so *he* won't be mean to you."

Cordero, perhaps thinking Gabriel was referring to him, scrunched down in his seat just a little more.

"He's not angry, he just wants to know why I'm not singing," she said without looking up.

Jason and Harris stood so that they could hear better. Julie was watching Kennedy more than the small woman he knelt with, and Kelly Delaphoy was writing furiously on her notepad.

"If you sing, will he let you speak to us without interfering?"

Jennifer looked up at Kennedy and tilted her head to the left, as if she were listening to a far-off voice. She almost smiled, and then she looked over at Leonard Sickles, who sat farther back in his chair.

"Hey, boy, whiskey and water with lots of ice."

Jason Sanborn's pipe fell from his mouth. Kelly's pencil snapped its point off against the paper. Julie Reilly stared in stunned silence, and the others—Harris Dalton included—stood suddenly.

The voice that had come out of Jennifer Tilden's small mouth was male.

Leonard looked just as shocked, but infuriated even more.

"Who you callin' 'boy,' bitch?" The words didn't come out with as much bravado as he would have liked.

"That's not her, Leonard, and you will damn well apologize when she wakes up," Kennedy said. He looked sternly at Sickles, who only stared wide-eyed at Jennifer.

"We don't call a black man 'boy.' Not here, not anymore, Bobby Lee."

"Ah, you know I didn't mean nothin' by it," the male voice said. This time Jenny looked directly at Sickles. The male voice had a thick New York accent. "Hell, most of my friends are Negroes, you know that."

"Forget it. I can see you've backed out of our deal," Kennedy said. He released Jenny's hand and stood, then lifted her chin up toward him.

"Look, man, you left this poor girl alone for years. What was I supposed to do, abandon her like you did?"

"We'll get into that later, Bobby Lee. If Jenny sings for you, will you let her be for the next few hours, maybe even let her have a full night's sleep?"

"She's gonna sing, Kennedy, you can bet your ass on that. And as far as leaving her alone, well, you can just kiss my—"

Gabriel reached into his coat pocket with his free hand and brought out a small syringe, holding it where she could see it. He still held Jenny's chin.

"What the hell you gonna' do with that?" Jenny's male voice was starting to sound strained.

"I'm going to put her out for more days than you would care to know about. Now, if she sings, will you leave her be for the next twenty-four hours so she can rest?"

"She sings first—that's the deal."

"She sings first."

Kennedy stood over Jenny and waited, keeping the syringe in the woman's sight.

"Professor, is this dangerous to the girl?" Harris Dalton asked. He slowly lowered himself into his chair at the head of the conference table.

Kennedy shrugged. "Jennifer has nothing to lose here. She's bordering on exhaustion and her system is close to shutting down. As it stands, we may not be able to use her—and her friend—if she can't rest. Without Jennifer, this project will be for nothing. I need her, and to put it frankly, she needs Summer Place."

Before Harris could voice further concerns, the anthropology professor slowly stood. With her eyes closed, she walked over to where John Lonetree was sitting and eased onto his lap. If he was surprised by her actions, he didn't show it. The temperature in the room felt like it dropped at least ten degrees. Julie folded her arms across her chest for warmth.

The rest of them stared, watching Jennifer as she looked deep into John Lonetree's eyes. Jason glanced over at Kelly, and she exhaled a breath that produced vapor—the temperature in the conference room was dropping even more than they had realized.

Gabriel swallowed. He had seen all of this before. He had seen it just three weeks before the incident at Summer Place, and his guilt at not helping Jennifer was something he regretted even more than the disaster of that night seven years before. He had left her after she had sought out his help, and he was miserable for it. Still, the fact of what he was about to witness never failed to scare the hell out of him. A case study would show that Jenny exhibited a classic case of split personality, but he knew that diagnosis to be the easy way out. She had a split personality, all right, but it was because she had someone else inside her. Not unlike a haunted house, Jenny herself was being haunted, by Bobby Lee McKinnon.

As they all watched with rapt fascination, Jenny slowly placed her arms around the big man's neck and stared deeply into his eyes, as if she were begging John's forgiveness for something she was about to do. John would never see it that way; when Jenny opened her mouth, John Lonetree's world changed forever.

In 1958, the prodigious record producer Phil Spector, before his more powerful days behind the glass directing the talents of most of the early rock 'n' roll stars of the fifties and early sixties, had been a part of a singing group, The Teddy Bears. This small group had one song that went straight to the top of the *Billboard* Top 100: "To Know Him Is to Love Him." It was this slow and melodic song that came out of Jenny's mouth as she stared into Lonetree's brown eyes. Phil Spector, Gabriel would later explain, had been a writing partner of one Bobby Lee McKinnon.

"To know, know, know him . . ." Jenny took a breath and

leaned closer, her eyes never leaving John's. It was as i
everyone in the room were seeing Jennifer relax for the
first time, as if she were safe for the first time in years. She
took a small breath, her voice beautiful and haunted at the
same time.

"My God," Jason Sanborn said aloud.

John Lonetree was lost in the moment, staring into Jennifer's eyes and feeling like he was drowning, and no
minding it one bit. His left hand slowly rose and slid up her
back, caressing her as she sang.

For exactly two minutes and twenty-two seconds, she sang
only to John Lonetree and no one moved. Then she smiled
at him with eyes that finally had her own light shining through
them, and she slowly lay her head upon John's chest. She
sobbed a moment and then passed out.

Kennedy leaned over and smiled at his old friend, and then
nodded and mouthed the word "thanks." Then he straightened and stood over John, who still held Jennifer while she
slept.

"Bobby Lee McKinnon, are you there?" Gabriel asked.
Leonard Sickles edged farther away from the haunted woman.

Suddenly the blinds shifted as an internal wind hit the
room, raising the temperature as if someone had opened a
door to a summer Arizona day. There was a loud moan that
seemed to sound from every corner of the room. Then as suddenly as it started, the wind died and the room's temperature
returned to normal. A gunshot fired loudly, and they all
jumped as one. Then there was nothing.

"He's gone," George Cordero said from his seat directly
across from Lonetree. He hadn't moved since the show had
started. Unlike the others, he hadn't been transported down
memory lane. He had been living the last minute of Bobby
Lee McKinnon's life as he was dragged from his bed and shot
in the back of the head by the Mafioso he had been in financial debt to. It had been a horrible vision and George had even
felt the bullet penetrate his head. He wasn't frightened; it was
something he lived with most every day of his life. But it

was never easy living the final, terrifying moments leading up to someone's death, and Bobby Lee's had not been a good way to go.

"Jesus Christ, man!" Leonard said from his standing position. "What the fuck!"

"Gabriel, you know for a fact this woman is insane, don't you?" George said, ignoring Sickles's protests. The others around the table slowly realized that perhaps they hadn't witnessed the haunting of an individual, but the torn and fractured mind of a woman lost to the real world.

"Obviously, she has to be," Harris Dalton added. He slowly sank back into his seat.

No one saw the angry look that came into John Lonetree's face as he slowly stood, Jennifer's limp, light body cradled in his massive arms. He walked over to a couch and gently laid her down. Her hand wouldn't let him go until he eased it from his neck. He removed his jacket and laid it over her still form.

"I don't mean she's insane alone," George said. "I mean whatever is inside her head, he's also insane, and he made this woman that way. He's angry he was murdered." He looked at Gabriel. "How did Bobby Lee latch on to her, Gabe?"

"She went to study a small case of an apartment haunting in 1999. She went thinking it was routine, but when she left that small place in New York, she didn't leave alone. This trip to Summer Place is not only for our benefit, but also hers. Bobby Lee, whether he knows it or not, is going to be a link."

"A link?" Jason asked.

Kennedy smiled and looked from face to face. "Yes, Mr. Sanborn, Jennifer and Bobby are our link to the other side."

For the first time, Harris Dalton and the others realized this trip to Summer Place might not have been the joke everyone outside of this room was thinking it would be.

Professor Gabriel Kennedy looked at the team he had assembled and realized it was a small army indeed preparing for battle in a house he knew to be a gateway to something few people on earth understood. All he knew was that the force the house held inside of its rotten bowels was something from a place that scared the hell out of him. And worse . . .

Kennedy mumbled under his breath as he gathered his papers.

"What was that, Professor?" Dalton asked.

Gabriel smiled and then shook his head. He slowly wiped his brow of the sweat that had formed there as he thought about the days ahead.

"I was just saying to myself that the advantage of this fight still goes to Summer Place."

"And why is that?" Kelly Delaphoy asked.

"Because that goddamned house knows exactly what scares the hell out of us."

The conference room fell silent. The live broadcast was only days away.

The planning for the Battle of Summer Place was about to begin.

11

After the fantastic and terrifying scene in the conference room an hour before, the group was slow to respond when Lionel Peterson walked back into the meeting, with the CEO of UBS following close behind. Peterson sat at his usual place at the head of the table and Abe Feuerstein took a seat in the far corner, his smile and ever-present bow tie impeccable as always.

"We seem to be missing someone—two someones, to be exact," Peterson said as he looked from face to face, finally settling on Kelly Delaphoy.

"Mr. Lonetree is sitting with Jennifer Tilden in my office," Kelly answered. "She felt a little ill. We had a rather—"

"—strained session a little while ago, and Ms. Tilden felt ill, that's all," Kennedy said. He didn't like Peterson and felt he need not explain anything to him.

"If the young lady is ill, I would think a doctor—a real

doctor, and not a medicine man—would be of a more practical use than Mr. Lonetree," Peterson said. It was clear that they were keeping something from him, but it didn't matter. He would eventually know everything about what had happened, anyway.

"Now, now, no need to disparage anyone's background here, Mr. Peterson," Feuerstein said. "Let's move on."

"We were just getting ready to go over the schematics for Summer Place," Kennedy said, cutting the conversation short. "It seems Mr. Sanborn has something interesting he's been dying to tell us since he came across the plans. Mr. Sanborn?"

Jason stood on shaky legs. He still had not recovered fully from the experience with Professor Tilden. He was wondering after that if he was up to the tasks that lay ahead of him. For a man who was accustomed to random sounds on a digital recorder or a mere cold spot in a house, he was wondering about the real side of parapsychology for the first time.

"Uh, the plans . . ." He moved the diagrams over to a large easel. "The originals as drawn up by Mr. Lindemann himself back in 1890 were at best crude. However, I did come across something that was not in the later specs for the house." He rifled through the large schematics until he came to a hand-drawn depiction of the lower levels of Summer Place. "Right here," he said, pointing at the lowest part of the page. The drawing was in old-fashioned lead pencil and was hard to read. "You see Lindemann's drawing of the basement, and below that, on this side view of the diagram, is the root cellar."

"Your meaning, Jason?" Kelly asked.

"The root cellar is not depicted on the original architectural drawings. It was as if the root cellar were eliminated from the plans but was built anyway."

"So?" Peterson said.

"So," Kelly said for Jason, "we saw the root cellar; it's there. Why would the cellar be eliminated from the final drawings?"

"Oh, come on, there's no big mystery there. It's a root cellar, for Christ's sake."

Kennedy looked at Peterson. He was right, of course; on

the surface it didn't seem all that important. But as he thought about it . . . most architects were very deliberate in their drawings for legality's sake. He himself had never explored the lower reaches of Summer Place seven years ago, due to their short-term lease of the property.

"Ms. Delaphoy, I think we need to make time in the schedule for a trip down to the root cellar. Maybe Mr. Sanborn has something here."

"We will have trouble broadcasting from there," Harris Dalton said.

"That shouldn't be a problem, my man. I could rig up a relay system."

All eyes went to Leonard Sickles. He pushed forward a quickly drawn schematic of a series of relay antennas he had sketched on his notepad. He looked at Kennedy, the only person he was really trying his best to impress. The professor smiled.

"Okay, that takes care of that."

Peterson even smiled, but it was an alligator's smile. Control was slipping even farther away from him.

Jennifer Tilden opened her eyes. The brightness of the office lights made her blink and roll over on the couch.

"The lights, please. I can't see," she said to the presence she felt beside her. Her voice was harsh and barely audible.

John Lonetree stood quickly and shut off the overhead fluorescents, then closed the drapes halfway.

"You had a rough go of it about an hour ago. How are you feeling now?" John eased himself back into the chair next to the couch.

"Like shit." She slowly rolled over, keeping her arm over her eyes. "Who are you?"

"My name's John."

"I didn't ask you that, I asked who you were."

"I'm a friend of Gabriel Kennedy's."

Jennifer slowly moved her arm away from her face and blinked several times.

"Do you know how long it's been since I saw sunlight that wasn't through the lenses of dark glasses?"

John didn't answer; he just watched her facial features as her eyes took in the office and then, finally, him.

"Well, neither do I," she said with a smile as she sat up. She looked at the clothes she was wearing and then at John. "May I assume you didn't change my clothes for me?"

Lonetree was taken aback for the first time in many years. He prided himself on knowing what people were going to say or do within a few seconds of meeting them. However, this question took him off guard.

"Why . . . uh . . . no, I didn't—"

"Easy does it, big fella. I wasn't accusing you of peeking at my underwear." She placed her small feet on the floor. "But someone did get my bra size wrong; I'm afraid I am the victim of someone's wishful thinking." She smiled at Lonetree and adjusted her blouse and bra.

"You're—in—New—York," John said, very slowly and deliberately.

Jenny looked at the large man and smiled, then leaned closer to him like she was conveying a conspiracy.

"I—know. I—have—been—in—here," she said, tapping her temple, "and—I—remember—most—everything."

"Everything?" John asked, becoming a little concerned. But he was even more embarrassed at the dumb way he'd handled things thus far.

"Yes, everything. Bobby Lee isn't as bad as he tries to make out. He doesn't torture me all that much. He allows me to control a few things—by the way, I love your aftershave."

Again John Lonetree was taken aback.

"Don't look so shocked; I smelled it when I was sitting on your lap."

"You have a beautiful voice," he said, to hide his further embarrassment.

She looked at John for the longest moment of his life, and then she smiled.

"Thank you, but you have to give the credit to Bobby Lee,

not me. Listen to me . . . I'm not exactly capable of singing like that. I sound like Janice Joplin with her vocal chords cut."

John smiled for the first time since bringing her into Kelly's office. "Is he . . . is he—?"

"He kept his word. He's going to let me sleep." She stood, wobbled, and allowed John to steady her. "I'll tell you right now, he's not too happy with what Gabriel has in mind." She took John's strong arm and leaned into him.

"You'll have to take that up with Gabe; I don't think he'll let Mr. McKinnon off the hook that easily."

"Well, where is he? I would like to see him before I sleep forever."

"He's right down the hall." John started leading her to the door but stopped. "Can I ask you something?"

"Since you have the advantage of brute masculinity and I don't have the strength to swat a fly, I think you can brave your question."

"Why did you choose me to sing to?"

Jennifer looked up and into John's dark eyes. Then she swallowed and stepped toward the door.

"Because I thought you were safe, and you were thinking good thoughts about me. That's why I sang to you."

"Oh."

Abe Feuerstein was the first to notice the door slowly opening, and Jennifer Tilden's entrance. She pulled her sweater close to her body and crossed her arms over her chest. John Lonetree followed and gestured toward Kennedy.

"She wanted to see you, Gabe." He steered the small, exhausted-looking woman toward the professor.

Kennedy went immediately to her, and she took him in her arms. He could feel Jennifer sobbing while he held on to her closely.

"Where have you been?" she said low enough that only he and Lonetree could hear.

"Oh, Jenny, I've been hiding away from the world. I'm so sorry I left you out there." Gabriel finally broke the embrace and looked her over. "Do you forgive me?" he asked with a sad smile.

"Fuck no," she said through a sob.

Gabriel smiled and led Jenny to a chair. The rest of the room watched them with curiosity.

"John, Dr. Tilden has a suite at the Waldorf-Astoria, as do all of you. Would you take her to her room when this is over?"

Lonetree looked from Kennedy to the others around the table.

"I'll take her," Julie Reilly said before John could answer.

Kennedy looked into the reporter's eyes, his accusation clear. She swallowed, and then lightly shook her head. She wouldn't question the professor on her ghostly experiences—at least not yet.

"All right. Everyone, aside from the team I have invited, has their doubts as to the validity of the power of Summer Place," Kennedy continued. "Let me tell you, there is no rationality as far as that house goes. I didn't believe it at first. I sought out explanations, too. I looked for anything from underground waterways to old mining operations. I'll say this— while you're taking this as a joke that could possibly bring you ratings, I have learned through my research that Summer Place is insanity personified. Whatever lives in that house is real, and it is angry. It drove the wood, the plaster, the foundation of that house insane, and now the pretty yellow home is just as culpable as its unwanted guest."

The room was silent, watching the conviction grow in Kennedy's eyes.

"It devours people, and there has to be a reason for it. As I said before, those it doesn't want, it will scare. Those that it does want, those whom it likes, or those who may cause it harm, or those who get a little too close to its secret . . . it will eat them alive." Gabriel moved slowly around the table, looking off toward the distant Pocono Mountains. "But whatever walks there, it wants mayhem and death. It's as if it uses these to cover a purpose. Our job, before the thirty-first, is to find out what that purpose is."

"Researching the family, the house?" Peterson asked. He pulled his notepad forward with a small roll of his eyes.

"Everything about the family, the house, and the grounds, all the way up to and through the live broadcast. Anyone who isn't on assignment or going out live will report to the ballroom, where they will continue going over all the research that I have gathered about Summer Place. They will be connected to mainframes at NYU and Columbia here in the city. They will have computing power. They'll be able to dig all the way past curtain time." Gabriel finally smiled down on Feuerstein, who returned it most uneasily.

"I assume that doesn't mean you want technical people in the ballroom, Professor," Peterson said with a smile.

Kennedy returned the smug look. "As far as I am concerned, Mr. Peterson, you do not exist. Anything outside of Summer Place is not my problem. My job will be to make sure those people inside the belly of the beast remain alive for the fourteen hours they are there. The control van, the producers, you'll all be on your own, with the warning that Summer Place may not be able to be controlled."

"We'll risk it, Professor. Now, you say fourteen hours inside the house?"

Gabriel held Peterson's glare and then smiled.

"That's right, fourteen hours. Everyone needs to get a feel for the physicality of the house. Remember, we'll be mostly in the dark for the broadcast hours."

"How many camera teams will there be altogether?" Jason Sanborn asked, looking from Kennedy and Peterson to Kelly and Harris Dalton.

"We'll have six teams, fifteen static cameras, and the entire house rigged for viewing. Nothing will be able to move in that house without us knowing about it," Kelly said proudly.

"It's not you that will be watching the house; it will be the house watching us."

Kennedy turned toward Jennifer.

"What was that, honey?" he asked.

Professor Tilden placed her coffee cup down upon the table and then tried to smile.

"The house already knows you're coming, Gabriel. It has a connection with more than you in this room. This little meeting has been observed from the moment it began."

"What are you saying, young lady?" CEO Feuerstein asked from his chair in the corner, leaning forward and placing his elbows on his aging knees.

"It's like Gabriel's Summer Place has been waiting for this moment since its existence began, long after it was built."

"She's right, Gabriel. I have been getting vibes ever since the professor's performance this afternoon," George Cordero said, looking very much concerned. "It's like Miss Tilden's presence has given me a boost of some kind, like I'm a battery that was once drained but is now connected by jumper cables to a fresh one."

"Oh, come on, enough with the mysticism. Say what you mean," Lionel Peterson interrupted.

"What I mean to say, Mr. Producer Man, is that Summer Place, or whatever is trapped there, is here right now, in this room." George stood and moved around the table. "It's like a tiger examining its prey, and let me tell you this: it's not afraid of what it's seeing. It's anticipatory. I get the feeling that it believes we are there to harm it, to stop it from doing what it does best, what it feels it has the right to do." He stopped and looked at Gabriel. "It's there to protect something, just like the professor has surmised. Whether it's the house itself, or a secret, it's not afraid of us. It figures it has that right—at least that's the way I figure it."

"And that is?" Feuerstein asked, leaning forward in his chair. "I mean, what right is that?"

Kelly watched the old man. He was taking this in hook, line, and sinker. She could have kissed Cordero and Tilden for their performances.

"Why, the same as any living entity—the right to defend itself," Jennifer answered for Cordero.

They all looked at Jenny, and a chill filled the room.

"Do you feel it?" John Lonetree asked Gabriel.

Indeed he did. The room temperature had fallen by twenty degrees, just as it had before. Feuerstein watched his breath fog in the air in front of him.

"I think this is one little trip that you'll have to make without old George, Gabe," Cordero said as he moved away from the table.

At that moment, the double doors of the conference room creaked. They all looked that way as the sound repeated. Then came the cracking of wood. The doors were actually bending inward.

Peterson stood, angry at being toyed with. He started toward the doors, but the air became almost impossible to breathe—it was as if something were sitting upon the chests of everyone in the room.

"No!" Harris Dalton reached out and grabbed Peterson's arm. "Leave it!" he hissed.

Abe Feuerstein, closest to the double wooden doors, stood and backed away. The smile he wore was a mask to try to cover the fear he was really feeling. He bumped into the long table between Kelly and Julie.

The door handles started rattling and the doors bent farther in.

Kennedy looked at Jennifer. She wasn't watching what was happening. She saw with eyes closed as whatever was outside of the room continued to put pressure on the doors.

Finally, the left-side door cracked down the middle from the pressure exerted upon it. Then, as quickly as the phenomenon had started, it ceased. The room temperature immediately rose back to normal and the air was clear of the suffocating atmosphere from a moment before.

Peterson threw off Harris's restraining hand and went to the double doors. He examined the crack and then suddenly threw the door open. Outside, all was normal in the news division. People went from desk to desk sharing assignment reports, and the soft clacks of typing filled the air. Not one person outside the conference room had heard a thing.

"Who the hell is fucking around out here?" he demanded from the doorway.

The few people closest to the conference room stopped what they were doing and looked at Peterson as if the man had lost his mind.

"Close the door, Lionel," Feuerstein said. He gently pulled the entertainment president back inside.

Everyone in the room was shaken. Kennedy didn't even know how to proceed.

"It knows what scares us."

"What was that, Jenny?" Kennedy asked Tilden.

She looked up, and her eyes went from face to face.

"It knows what scares us, and has the power to project that over time and space." She finally looked back at Kennedy and then lowered her head.

"Are you all right, Jenny?" he asked, placing a hand on her shoulder. She seemed to be listening to something—she tilted her head first left and then to the right.

"It's laughing at you, Gabriel. It's laughing at all of us." She looked at Kennedy. "It hates."

"What?" Peterson asked by the door. "What did she say?"

"I said, 'it hates.'"

After the chills had departed and everyone settled back in, Kennedy sat silently by the large easel at the front of the room. He swallowed and then looked up. He was afraid he was showing his emotions on his face. John Lonetree, who had pulled his chair closer to Jennifer's, finally looked up at him and shook his head slightly.

Kelly Delaphoy didn't like the way Professor Kennedy had been looking at the members of the broadcast team since the assault on the conference room doors. He was once more feeling the effects of Summer Place. She needed to boost his confidence and get him back on track, make him defend his right to find out what happened to his student and himself.

"So, Mr. Peterson," Kelly said. "Do you think that was a gag concocted by me and my team?"

Peterson didn't hesitate to attack even this most obvious of demonstrations.

"If you're asking if I'm convinced it was that house reaching out to us here in New York, no, Kelly, I'm not convinced at all. Now, I will allow you this: I have no doubt that our environment can be altered. Ms. Tilden herself has obvious powers. Combine that with Mr. Lonetree, Mr. Cordero, and the expectations we all feel—well, I'm sure you can see my point." Peterson looked from Kelly to Feuerstein. "It's just a house, for crying out loud."

Abe Feuerstein nodded and stood from his seat. "I understand your consternation, Lionel. Before this morning I suppose that even I had certain . . . doubts about what we were trying to attempt here. But after what just happened— whatever just happened—I feel that no matter what, we at least have the makings of a very special show here." He held up his hand, silencing Peterson. "Whether it was Summer Place or just the power emanating from some of the people in this room, that's neither here nor there. If the event I just witnessed can be reproduced on Halloween, this will be the most spectacular special in this network's short history. Of that I have no doubt whatsoever."

"So, what are you saying, sir?" Kelly asked and bit her lower lip.

"I came in here this morning to see Professor Kennedy and his team, to judge what we had sitting in our laps, if you will. If I hadn't been impressed, I was going to pull the plug on this thing. But now? You are a *go*." He turned and hesitated, running his fingers slowly over the crack in the thick wood. He turned to look at Kennedy. "Anything you need, Professor, anything at all, it's yours." He turned toward Peterson. "Lionel, make this happen. God, I love this business." He opened the door, admiring the crack as he did, and then left.

Kelly Delaphoy nodded as everyone filed past her. She made as if she were gathering her notes and materials as she watched the others leave. It was Julie Reilly who stopped and gave Kelly a curious look, and neither of them saw Kennedy pause at the door with a glance back. As he turned to leave he saw Leonard Sickles looking at the left side of the double doors, running his hand up and down the crack in the wood. He looked up at Gabriel and they locked eyes, and then with one more glance back at the producer of *Hunters of the Paranormal* and her ace field reporter, Kennedy nodded at Leonard and they both left.

"Well, how do you think that went?" Kelly asked as she slid her notes into her case.

Julie didn't respond at first. Then she smiled.

"Impressive demonstrations—all," Julie answered.

"That Professor Tilden is something, isn't she? She's going to be great for the show."

Julie nodded slowly. She shifted her bag to her other shoulder and started for the door.

Kelly watched her leave, suspecting that the newswoman wasn't as easily impressed as the CEO. The demonstration here had made him feel his age, and started him questioning the hereafter. He had played his part very well. She grinned to herself and then turned for the door. She was startled to see a middle-age man, in a blue jumpsuit, looking over the crack in the wood. He turned his head and then closed the door, stepping inside.

"Maintenance, ma'am."

"Goddamn it, you could have waited for a few moments." Kelly glared at the heavyset man as he placed his large toolbox on the tabletop.

"Take it easy. Peterson called me to get down here and fix the door."

"You still could have waited," Delaphoy said as she placed the strap to her large bag over her shoulder. "Can you get that . . . that thing out of the door frame without being noticed?"

"I got it in there without anyone seein' me; I imagine I can get the hydraulic ram out without everyone knowin' you fleeced them." The man eyed Kelly in his arrogant way.

"What about the thermostat control?"

"Look, that first time wasn't my fault. I was monitoring the thermostat settings when it went haywire and went down all on its own. I figured it was something with the internal thermometer and the temperature release valve in the wall."

"The first time?" Kelly asked.

"Yeah. When that crazy professor broad was doing her ghost thing? I had nothing to do with that one. And that breeze that sprang up was pretty good. You'll have to tell me how you did that." The man finally eyed the smaller woman before him. "But the second time, when the door trick happened, the thermostat dropped without a hitch. That was mine, and that's what you owe me for."

The man climbed his small ladder and lifted out the wall panel above the double doors. Inside the small space rested the small hydraulic ram he had built the night before. The ram had placed just enough downward pressure on the left-side door to make it bow and then crack.

The night before he had also replaced that door with a cheap stand-in that matched the opposite door in color and texture, to make the small ram's pressure work more efficiently. He smiled to himself as Kelly started toward the door and deftly held out his right hand.

Delaphoy, without missing a beat, placed a folded check for five thousand dollars in the man's outstretched hand.

"Remember, if anyone finds out about this, I can always put a stop on that check."

The man didn't say anything; he just smiled and reached up, yanking the small system out of the door's upper panel.

As Kelly left the conference room, she saw Kennedy and his people waiting by the elevator. She nodded her head, and then turned without a good-bye and made her way to her own office.

PART III

BATTLEFIELD

12 The Waldorf-Astoria, New York, New York

The meeting room had been sectioned off for Gabriel Kennedy, John Lonetree, Leonard Sickles, and George Cordero.

"Before we start, may I ask Professor Tilden's condition?" Lonetree asked. He removed his suit jacket and draped it over the back of his chair.

Kennedy set his small black bag on the tabletop and then smiled at the large Indian. He had known even before John and Jennifer had ever met that there would be an immediate connection between them. As distant and quiet as John was, Gabriel had known he would feel a need to protect Jenny from any harm that might befall her—and that had been his number one reason for bringing Lonetree here. The number two reason was about to be revealed.

"Dr. Tilden is sleeping soundly upstairs. She is in deep REM sleep." He looked at John and then away as quickly as he could. "I just checked on her. Thus far, Bobby Lee is keeping his word. Now, Professor Tilden is someone we need to discuss at length. Before I allow our last guest to come in with the items he has brought for John, I want to ask your opinions on something that has been festering ever since the meeting this afternoon. I'll start with Jennifer. George, your opinion on the episode in the meeting, regarding her"—again Kennedy looked around at the three men sitting at the table—"possession?"

"Damn, you know my opinion on it. It goddamn near

chased me out of the fucking room. I have never in my life seen anything like that. If she's not the greatest ventriloquist in the world, that girl has one big-ass problem."

"Then you believe what you witnessed?"

Cordero tilted his head to the right, widened his eyes, and took a deep breath. "My talent is getting into people's heads. Number one, Doc, I couldn't get into Professor Tilden's head because it was too damn crowded. It was like I was being kept out by something stronger than me. Number two, while I didn't feel this McKinnon guy inside her, I did feel her thoughts. And let me tell you"—he looked at John—"she is close to insane." He looked down at the polished table. "Sorry, but she is."

John nodded his head. He told himself it was just sympathy for a fellow human being that made him care so deeply, but he knew he liked the small professor and had known it from the moment he saw her helped into the conference room at UBC.

"Good. Now, Leonard, your impressions?"

Sickles raised his eyes to the ceiling.

"I agree with this guy, Doc, that b—lady is off her fuckin' rocker." He quickly looked at Lonetree. "No offense, Red Cloud."

Lonetree said nothing, but from his look the small gangbanger knew he had better tread the Indian line far more carefully in the future.

"John, there's no reason to ask you. I could see that you felt McKinnon's presence when Jennifer came into the room."

Lonetree continued to look at Leonard, who had started studying the ornate wallpaper. He nodded.

"Okay, I think I know where Leonard stands on my next question, so I'll ask you, John. What about the second presence, the incident of invasion?" Kennedy asked, turning his back on the small group.

"Clever trick, but I felt no presence from your Summer Place," John said.

"George?"

"Didn't have the same feeling as with Professor Tilden. In other words, I wasn't scared at all."

"Leonard?"

"Fake. The wood on the left-side door was different from the wood on the right. It would take me a minute of study, but I would venture to guess someone tried to bullshit the intrusion—hydraulics, maybe. Good, but anyone capable of installing hydraulics on a car could do the same thing."

"I agree. Someone faked the door bending in and out—Ms. Delaphoy more than likely, or all of them, for the CEO's benefit. So that leads to my point: We trust only those of us in this room and Professor Tilden upstairs.

"Leonard, I don't want to keep our guest waiting. Would you let him in, please?"

Sickles stood and opened the meeting room door. An angry Wallace Lindemann stood there, his face scrunched into a ball of twisted flesh at having been kept waiting.

"Mr. Lindemann, would you join us, please?" Kennedy walked to the front of the room and held out his hand.

Instead of taking Gabriel's hand, Lindemann turned and waved two men inside. They were pushing two bellman's carts loaded with items that had been covered by a red tarp.

"I do not like being summoned like a deliveryman. I do not like removing items from my house, and I most assuredly will not be taking orders from you."

Gabriel lowered his hand and smiled as he turned back to the rear of the room.

"The delivery and use of these items will be the last favor I ask from you, Mr. Lindemann."

"You're goddamned right it will. And I hold you personally responsible for the items now in your possession. They are to be returned to Summer Place the day before Halloween."

"You have my word."

"A lot of good that is. The last time I signed something over to you the house was damaged and my reputation suffered the indignity of having to explain your mess. As a matter of fact, I ought to—"

"You ought to leave now and lay off talking to the doc like that, you silver-spoon-up-the-ass mother—"

"That's good, Leonard," Gabriel said. He tried hard to fight back laughter. "Your items will be returned in pristine condition, Mr. Lindemann, I assure you."

Wallace Lindemann, with one last look at the small black man standing in front of him, stormed out of the meeting room with the two bellmen.

John Lonetree was smiling at Leonard also. It seemed that Sickles disrespected everyone, and some of them deserved it. Lonetree was good with that—you always knew where you stood with the kid. Earn his respect and you'd be in.

Gabriel watched the double doors close and relaxed when they were finally alone again.

"Leonard, I am fully capable of handling Wallace Lindemann. You'll find out the little bastard is mostly hot air."

"Ah, Doc, the guy's a—"

Leonard stopped short of his name-calling when he saw Kennedy staring at him.

"Okay," Gabriel said, pointing at Sickles, "dim the lights a little and we'll start with John and George." Kennedy paced to the bellmen's carts and pulled the red sheet from the items.

Several items were immediately recognizable from the pictures they had seen of the interior of the house. The largest was the family portrait of the Lindemanns. Gabriel lifted the four-foot-by-five-foot frame and hefted the portrait to the easel he had brought in earlier. When Lonetree saw the professor was having a hard time lifting it, he jumped from his chair and assisted. As soon as his large hands touched the gilded edges of the frame, an electric current seemed to course through John's hands, arms, and then his entire body. As much as the large man tried not to react, he couldn't help it. He let go and stumbled backward from the massive painting, almost making Kennedy lose the portrait to the carpeted floor.

As John grabbed for the back of a chair, George and

Kennedy went to him. Leonard stood next to the long table, laughing at the look on Lonetree's face.

"Man," he said as he approached the painting, "you would think this thing was wired or something," he said, reaching toward the frame.

"Don't!" John said.

Sickles jumped at the loudness of Lonetree's voice. He turned and looked at the Indian as if he had lost it.

"Cool it, Geronimo, I just—"

"You'll interfere and block my feelings."

"Leonard, take a seat," Kennedy said as he helped John straighten up.

"Look, I'm getting bad vibes from this thing." George took to a chair next to Lonetree. "Something is coming off of that painting in waves. I didn't start picking it up until John touched the damn thing."

Kennedy looked from Cordero to Lonetree, who was looking at the portrait as if he were taking in every nuance of the artist's brushstrokes. The sepia tones of the background, the bright colors of the skin tones, and last of all, the smiling faces of the family.

"What did you feel?" Gabriel asked. He was tempted to go to his own chair to write it down in his notebook, but was unwilling to move in case he broke John's concentration.

"Something came through the portrait . . . but it wasn't the painting itself. It was like—"

"The house is here with us."

Everyone looked at Cordero, who was now leaning his head on his crossed arms on the tabletop.

"He's right." John stood, stepping closer to the portrait. "It may not be the portrait itself, but its attachment to the house. It has eyes on us."

Kennedy patiently listened.

Lonetree touched the old oil paint. He ran a finger over the faces of the small children, and then up to the older features of F. E. Lindemann. slowly went down in a zigzag

motion toward the beautiful face of Elena. There had been
nothing when he touched the other members of the family,
but now John sighed as a feeling of safeness came over him.
At the same moment Cordero raised his head and started to
shake.

"John . . . get away from there, I feel . . . like, hell, just get
away until I can sort this out."

George stood up, knocking his chair over. He was rubbing
his hands together, almost as if he wanted nothing more than
to tear the skin from the bone. Leonard backed away from
the table uneasily.

Lonetree didn't move. He felt like he was a child again—
no, even younger. He felt as though his mother's hand were
caressing his face while she smiled down at him in his crib.

"Gabe, pull him away from that damn thing. It's not what
it seems. The fucking thing is . . . is tricking him. He feels
safe around it, but it's taking something from him." George
stepped around the table and approached John, still wringing
his hands together. "It's like the picture is learning from him."

"You mean like a Vulcan mind meld or somethin'?"

Cordero started to reach out to touch Lonetree's arm but
he hesitated, and then went back to wringing his hands.

"John?" Kennedy said, stepping closer to Lonetree and the
portrait.

John tilted his head and then nodded like he was answering a question only he could hear. "Mama—"

John blinked several times and then removed his hand. He
continued to stare at the portrait for a long time; then, as if
coming from a faraway place, he blinked and looked at Cordero.

"She said that we are all welcome into the Lindemann
home. Summer Place has been waiting for all of us."

"Elena said that to you?" Gabriel asked. He took John by
the arm and led him back to the table.

"I think, uh, yes, it had to have been," Lonetree said as he
slowly sat down.

Kennedy looked up at George, who was watching Lonetree with a worried look on his face. Then his eyes went to Gabriel and he slowly shook his head. Gabriel tilted his head, not understanding what Cordero was trying to convey.

"That thing," he said, pointing at the portrait, "does not want us in that house. If it does, it's because . . . because—"

"What a bunch of bullshit. You buying this crap, Doc?" Leonard asked. He still stood his ground, far away from the rest of the group.

"Do you feel it?" John asked, sounding more like his old self. Far deeper, far stronger than when he was touching the face of Elena Lindemann.

"What?" Sickles asked, looking around the dimly lit room.

"I do," Kennedy said.

"What?" Leonard asked again, losing the bravado he had been feeling a moment before.

"Get your thermal laser, Leonard," Gabriel said. He ran his hand back and forth through the air, still looking at the portrait. "Now!"

Sickles jumped as if he had been goosed. He rummaged through his small black bag and came up with a pistol-shaped instrument. He turned on its red laser light and started pointing it in all directions.

"Seventy-four degrees, seventy-four . . . seventy-four . . . seventy-five," he said as he pointed it toward the double doors. He swung it toward George and John. "Seventy-three, seventy-three . . . seventy-four." Then he pointed it at the portrait. "Jesus Christ! Thirty-eight degrees, thirty-seven, thirty-six." He pointed it back at the interior of the meeting room. "Temperature dropping. Thirty-five, thirty-five, thirty-one, shit," he said. His breath had started to particulate into a fog.

"It's here, Gabriel. Goddamn it, it came into the room with everything Lindemann brought over," George said. Sickles returned to his black bag and started throwing things out of it, searching for something.

"What is it?" Gabriel asked. Leonard had found the object he was looking for, and now held a black box up and outward toward the center of the room.

"The electromagnetic field is off the freaking chart, Doc. This room should only have a point oh two, or maybe point oh three. We're at point oh nine and the damn thing's climbing. There's enough electricity in this room to start cooking our brains."

"Does that account for the temp drop?" Kennedy asked, his own breath coming out in a fog.

"I don't know. It's as if—"

Suddenly the portrait flew from the easel, barely missing George Cordero. It landed on the conference table and slid to the end, stopping just before it tumbled to the floor. Then the bellmen's carts with the remaining items on them tipped and were literally thrown, sailing only inches from Gabriel's head. They smashed into the wall.

"Fuck me!" Leonard shouted. He hit the floor, the magnetic resonance counter flying from his hand.

Kennedy looked around as calmly as he could. Then he smiled and looked at Lonetree and Cordero.

"It's gone," John said. He stood and helped Leonard to his feet.

"Yes, he's right, the house has withdrawn. It got what it came for," George said, wiping his brow. The temperature had already started rising.

"Doc, I don't know if I'm built for this," Leonard said. He looked around wildly as if expecting something to charge at him.

Gabriel smiled.

"Would it help you to know that whatever was here was afraid of you and your toys, Leonard?"

Sickles pulled his arm free of Gabriel's grasp and looked around at the disheveled room.

"Yeah?" he said as he finally looked back at Kennedy. "It sure doesn't seem like it's afraid of anything."

"Well," Kennedy said, patting Leonard on the back, "of anyone we're taking into Summer Place, you're the one it will fear, because of what you can bring inside to help defeat it."

Sickles blinked, and then his bravado returned. He stepped away from the professor and strutted back toward the table.

"John, why don't you take a few of the smaller items to your room tonight and see what you can come up with. The same for you, George."

Both men nodded. It was back to business, and they appreciated it.

"I'll keep the portrait and everything else in my room tonight. We wouldn't want anything disappearing on us."

A knock sounded at the door. When Leonard, who was nearest, pulled it open, a man in a red blazer and shifting uncomfortably stood in the doorway.

"Yes?" Gabriel said as he stepped forward.

"Uh, sir, I'm security. I was sent from the front desk. Are you related to the woman in five twenty-three?"

Kennedy frowned with concern. "Ms. Tilden, Jennifer Tilden?"

"Yes, sir. Small woman, red hair?"

"Yes," Kennedy answered.

"She's in the Astor Salon and is making quite a scene. She hasn't become a problem yet, just a little confusing, and rude perhaps to the group of gentlemen she's sitting with, perhaps—"

Gabriel and the others shot out of the room with the shocked security man turning and following.

It seemed Bobby Lee McKinnon was awake and had forgotten all about the deal.

As the four men hurried from the meeting room, Julie Reilly, Kelly Delaphoy, and Jason Sanborn walked through the ornate front doors. They caught sight of Gabriel and the others cutting across the ostentatious lobby at a quick pace and knew immediately that trouble was brewing. Julie exchanged a quick look of concern with Kelly and Jason and then started after the men as they made their way to the lounge.

Gabriel and the others entered the Astor Lounge and came to a sudden stop. Jenny was dressed in what looked like a very expensive evening gown. It was emerald green and glittered brightly in the small spotlights that lined the ceiling. She was sitting and looked to be conversing in soft tones at a table with four older men, all dressed in two-thousand-dollar suits. The men looked amused by everything Jennifer was telling them. They watched the woman before them with smiles and rapt fascination. Kennedy nudged John Lonetree in the ribs. Standing not three feet behind Jenny were three large men in black blazers; both Gabriel and John both smelled body-guards. They didn't look as amused as their employers at what Dr. Tilden was relaying to them.

"What's going on?" Julie asked. She nudged George Cordero's arm.

George only shook his head, but Leonard volunteered what he knew.

"Our crazy lady has something to say to these crackers at the table," he said. Julie looked at him, confused. "I mean the gentlemen she's speaking to, with the stuffed Armanis."

The table was only ten feet away, but Gabriel couldn't hear what was being said. He watched the reaction of the four men and saw that the smiles were fading.

"The rest of you, stay here. John, let's see what our lady friend has in common with these astute-looking business-men."

Lonetree followed Gabriel to the table. Jennifer stopped talking and with a dazzling smile looked up at the two men. She tilted her head and John could see that her eyes had been enhanced by makeup and she even had a dusting of glitter on her skin. Her appearance was nothing short of angelic as Lonetree smiled down at her.

"Jenny?" Gabe reached down and, with all of his acting skills, took her hand and kissed it, as though he were just stopping by to say hi. "How are you?"

"Gabriel! Funny running into you here, of all places."

The five-piece band on the stage wound down a slow rendition of an elevator Muzak classic and then prepared for another.

"And Mr. Lonetree . . . the first face you look for and the very last you see," she said. She pulled her fingers lightly from Gabriel's so that John could take her hand and kiss it awkwardly.

"Ms. Tilden," Lonetree stumbled.

"Who are your friends, Jenny?" Kennedy asked, taking a step back and looking at the four heavyset men with expensive suits.

Gabriel knew immediately that he was looking at men who usually would not tolerate having their evening interrupted by anyone. The man Jenny had been talking to had designer glasses and his black dyed hair curled under both ears in one of those European haircuts that old men got to make themselves look younger. The man's three companions were of the same ilk, and Gabriel took an immediate dislike to all of them.

"I can answer that for you, Dr. Kennedy," Julie Reilly said, stepping up to join them and shrugging out of her leather jacket. She had broken away from the group at the lounge entrance when she recognized the man at the center of Jenny's attention. "This is Stephan Martin, the CEO of Griffin Records. Of course, when he first started out in the music business in the early sixties as a twenty-one-year-old producer, his name was Steven Markovich, from the Bronx."

"I'm afraid you have the advantage of me. As well as this lovely young lady," the fat man said. He nodded toward Jennifer, who smiled demurely and tilted her head to the left. A very worrisome move—Gabriel saw that her eyes remained fixed on Martin, and they weren't showing the kindness of her smile.

"My name is Julie Reilly. This is Dr. Gabriel Kennedy, police chief John Lonetree of Montana, and this young lady is Professor Jennifer Tilden."

"Julie Reilly of the UBC *Nightly News*," Martin said as flatly as the words could be spoken. He nodded toward one of the bodyguards as an indication that the conversation was drying up.

"Jenny, if you're finished with these gentlemen, maybe you can join us for a drink," Gabriel said.

"Mr. Martin and I haven't finished our conversation yet, Gabe," Jenny said. She smiled even broader than before. "Now, if you and your friends here would fuck off, I'll say what I have to say to this fat pig bastard."

That was it; Martin waved the bodyguard over to the table.

Gabriel reacted first by taking Jennifer by the arm and standing her up. She easily shook off Kennedy's grip and then placed her hands—clad in elbow-length white gloves—on the table.

"November twenty-first, 1963. Remember that night, Mr. Martin?"

The man's face drained of color. He looked up at the small woman, and a questioning look crossed his acne-pitted face.

"A night long before you were squirted out of your mother. What of it?" he hissed.

Gabriel eased his hand over and stopped Lonetree from slamming the man's fat jeweled face into the white-linen tablecloth. He looked at John and slightly shook his head.

"It was rainy and cold on the Lower East Side. My apartment at the time had a hot water heating system and three radiators more musical than my piano. They clanked and vibrated and put out very little warmth. They were singing loudly that night in November. Remember, Stephan?"

"Who the hell are you?" he asked, tossing his napkin onto the tabletop.

"Remember the song?"

"All right, I don't care to listen to this any longer. This woman is obviously mad."

"That word isn't exactly descriptive, nor adequate for the way I am, man," Jenny said, hissing the words. Her voice became deep and man-like. "Maybe if I sing it for you?"

Gabriel tried to stop her, but she turned and made her way to the front of the lounge, bumping into several men and women who were dancing slowly to the nondescript music being played by the house band. She went directly to the stage and hopped up on it, tearing the expensive dress as she did. She wobbled at first, and then straightened as the lead singer of the band steadied her. The music stopped one instrument at a time. She exchanged a few words with the singer and then placed a gloved hand on his chest and pushed him away.

"That's it. Call security," Martin said to the bodyguard next to him.

On the stage, a confident and gorgeous Jennifer Tilden adjusted the microphone stand. At the table the four men, Martin included, turned to see what was happening. Two of the three bodyguards walked past the group still at the salon's door.

The small lights lining the stage went from gold to light green. Jennifer looked up. Her features had become harsher, but at the same time even more feminine. Gabriel had the feeling that for the first time since he had known Jenny and her traumatic state, Bobby Lee McKinnon was actually sharing the stage with her. This show belonged to both of them. For some reason he couldn't fathom, Kennedy smiled.

"I would like to dedicate this song to a longtime producer friend of mine who gave me a start in the business. He's in the back of the room, where he can sit in judgment of people and make deals behind their backs." She lowered her gaze. "I cowrote this with a longtime friend of mine you all know as Sonny Bono and Jack Nietzsche in 1962. I played it for this young man in the audience, and he told me it wasn't good enough."

Stephan Martin slowly started to rise, but John stepped up and placed a hand on his ample shoulder, making the remaining bodyguard take a step forward.

"Why don't we hear what the lady has to say?" John said into the ear of the record executive.

Jenny raised her face to the lighting above her. Closing her eyes, she started to sing a song that was immediately recognizable. "I saw her today, I saw her face . . ."

The band caught on and the drums rolled and joined in with the slow way Jenny and Bobby Lee sang the old song, "Needles and Pins."

On the floor in front of the stage, every person watching her onstage was enraptured by the slow way the old ballad was sung.

John Lonetree slowly removed his hand from Martin's shoulder and took an involuntary step toward the stage as Jenny started winding down.

The blood had drained from Stephan Martin's face. He seemed to shrink in his chair and as the bodyguard reached out he angrily shoved his large hand away.

The song finally came to an end and the audience was silent in rapt fascination. Jennifer had closed her eyes, and as the lights came up and the crowd started applauding and cheering, she slowly looked up. That was when Kennedy knew this wasn't going to be good.

Jennifer demurely stepped from the stage, this time assisted by the band members. Jennifer ignored the praise from the audience as she easily stepped between tables on her way toward Martin. She stopped just short of the table as every set of eyes in the room watched.

"Are you related to Bobby?" Martin stuttered his question.

"You could say that," Jennifer said as she pulled out a chair. Lonetree stood like a hulking guardian angel over her shoulder.

"Look, I don't know what you've heard, but Bobby sold me that song. It was all aboveboard."

"He was deeply in debt to some unsavory characters in 1963," Jenny said, staring at Martin. Kennedy slowly waved Leonard and Cordero into the lounge from their position at the door. Jason and Kelly followed, still stunned. "He had a chance at getting out from under that debt by selling a surefire hit to a foreign publisher. But that publisher found that I and my friends had a bit more music smarts than he thought."

"This is outlandish, and you better choose your next words

very, very carefully, young lady." Martin's greasy forehead
had started to break out in a sweat.

"So he sent those unsavory men to my apartment one
night, and when I refused to sign, they broke all of my fingers." Jenny leaned forward as far as the table would allow,
making Martin's company lean backward, away from the
woman's venomous looks.

"This is outrageous!" Martin stood, knocking the table
forward and spilling several of the drinks. "She's talking like
she was there!"

"Then I signed the papers, selling my song to Martin, just
wanting the pain to stop." Jenny's voice lowered as if she were
ashamed of caving in to torture. "They took me into my bathroom and then shot me in the head."

Jenny slowly turned and looked at Gabriel, then turned
back and looked at Lonetree. Her eyes were watery and she
looked lost.

The people who were closest to the table looked from the
small woman to the shocked, burly man. He slowly sat down
in his seat and couldn't look at his company. It was as if everyone in the room believed what Jenny was saying. Gabriel
leaned over and whispered something into Jenny's ear. She
looked at him and shook her head.

"All I ever wanted to do was write music. The money, although necessary, was never important to me. I didn't deserve
what happened."

With that, Jennifer slowly slumped down in her chair.
Gabriel and Lonetree went to her and helped her to her feet.
Gabe knew that Bobby Lee had gone. Jennifer had one last
thing to say before she let go. The strange thing was, Kennedy suspected that Bobby Lee McKinnon had left Jenny
long before the last words were spoken. It was if he trusted
Jennifer to say what he was feeling, and left her to say it her
own way. They lifted Jenny and started out of the room.

"I'm going to sue you. This is slander and it's . . . it's—"

"I think it's best that you leave well enough alone," Julie
said, leaning over Martin's table. "You know who I am.

Would you like me and my staff of twenty tenacious researchers digging into what was said here tonight?" She dug into
her purse and threw a hundred-dollar bill onto the table. "The
next round is on Bobby Lee McKinnon."

The four men watched the strange entourage leave the
lounge. Martin swallowed, trying desperately to get the lump
out of his throat, and then looked at the three businessmen
around him. They had accusatory, or at the very least specu-
lative, looks on their faces. For the first time in his long
career, Stephan Martin was afraid to look into a suddenly
changed and damaged future.

As the rest of the group made their way back into the meeting room, Kennedy and Julie Reilly had to smooth things
over with the Waldorf management staff. It seemed Mr.
Stephan Martin was a major spender and the Waldorf wasn't
very pleased about embarrassing the man. It was touch and
go until Julie Reilly started pushing UBC's weight around.
Needless to say, the Waldorf saw fit to allow a onetime in-
discretion by the group who was being fronted by the UBC
television network.

Jennifer and Lonetree were huddled into a corner, as far
away as they could get from the items that had been taken
from Summer Place. Gabe had to smile when he saw that
Jenny was actually looking at John with her own soft expression, Kennedy stepped up as the other team members settled
into their chairs around the table. Julie placed her tape recorder on the table but did not turn it on. She just watched
Kennedy, Lonetree, and Jennifer talk in low tones.

"How are you feeling?" Gabriel asked. "How's Bobby Lee
doing?"

"He's not here. Or at least he's not making himself felt."

"Was it enough for him to confront that jerk?" Lonetree
asked.

Jennifer looked from Kennedy to John's concerned face.
She shook her head in the negative. "I feel like he's confused
after what happened. When I was asleep upstairs, I suddenly

awoke as if someone had walked into a dream I was having. It was Martin, only he was far younger than the fat pig he is today. . . . It was like he was sitting right on the edge of my bed."

"Did you know who he was?"

"No, but Bobby did. It was like he felt it when Martin walked into the hotel. The next thing I knew I was out of bed, into my clothes, and out the door. Only . . ."

"Only what?" Gabriel asked. Jennifer had that faraway look in her eyes again.

"I was *wanting* to go with him," she said. "It was no longer Bobby Lee making me *do* something against my will, it was if I felt his hatred, his utter despair for the first time, at what happened to him." She looked at the green evening dress she was wearing. "You have to admit, Bobby Lee had very good taste in clothes." Jennifer had a pinched look on her face as she glanced over at the two women sitting at the table. Julie and Kelly were watching with mild curiosity. "I think I owe them a lot of money for this thing. Bobby Lee charged the dress to the room."

"Oh, I think they can cover the cost," Kennedy said, smiling and looking back at the two women. "Now, the question is, where's Bobby Lee?"

"He's not here, Gabe."

Kennedy was torn between being happy for Jennifer and feeling he may have lost an advantage in facing Summer Place. He smiled at Jenny and patted her hand. "I'm happy he's gone," he said. He straightened and moved to the front of the conference table, then turned and faced Lonetree and Jennifer once again. "You're going to assist John from here on out. That is, if you still want to be a part of this thing. I wouldn't blame you if you told me to go straight to hell and not collect two hundred dollars on my way."

Jenny looked from Kennedy to Lonetree, and nodded. "If he needs help, I'll stay."

"Okay. Come take a seat around the table and I'll tell everyone the starting lineup.

"I think everyone had a wakeup call, as far as things that go bump in the night. Jenny handled things as well as she could, and she will be assisting John in his dreamwalking. May I suggest you sleep tonight, and begin when Jenny has had some rest?"

John Lonetree nodded.

"The rest of us won't be here for the next two days. It's the final research push before we strike out for the mountains. We have to divide into teams to accomplish everything we need to cover, and still we won't have enough time. This process will continue through the live broadcast from Summer Place, when we correlate our findings. We may need what we come up with now, during the night."

"How many teams will we have in the field?" Kelly asked, writing on her ever-present notepad.

"Four teams. Mr. Sanborn and Leonard, you'll work on everything we need as far as electronics go. Leonard is going to be requesting some rather bizarre materials, and I expect you to ram through corporate to get them."

Jason Sanborn placed his pipe in his mouth and nodded. Leonard just sat at the table staring at Jennifer as if she were going to jump across and bite his head off.

"You with us, Leonard?"

"Huh? Oh, yeah, Doc, you got it."

"George, you and Ms. Delaphoy will be going to five different cemeteries and their corresponding halls of records, in New York, Pennsylvania, and Maine. You'll be digging for autopsy reports, certificates of death, and anything else you can dig up—pun intended—on the children of the Lindemanns."

"You think this has something to do with the haunting?" Kelly asked. She was frowning, apparently displeased to be teamed with George Cordero.

"I don't believe in coincidence, Ms. Delaphoy," Gabriel said. "You'll dig. George here will analyze in his own special way. I want impressions; I want you to feel what happened to these kids and young adults. This has a bearing on what's going on at Summer Place. Does that answer your question?"

Kelly didn't answer; she just wrote down her instructions.

"Good. I have the names and places. You can start tonight with the farthest burial site, in Maine."

George looked at Kelly and grimaced.

"Now, Ms. Reilly"—he said the name as if he had bitten into a bad piece of fruit—"will be visiting a few museums in New York and Philadelphia."

"Museums?" Julie asked as she adjusted her tape recorder.

"Yes. The Lindemann building in the garment district has been turned into a museum of turn-of-the-century clothing manufacture."

"And you expect to find something there that will help?" Julie asked, looking straight at Kennedy.

"The main office of Lindemann Sewing Machine is there and is not a part of the tour. They also have employee records—that is what we are interested in."

"And Philadelphia?" she asked.

"The Lindemann Historical Society," Gabriel answered as he made his way around the table. "Family history, artifacts, and the diaries of F. E. Lindemann and his wife, Elena, are there."

"Thrilling," Julie said as she reached out and snapped off the tape recorder.

"Watch out what you ask for, Ms. Reilly. The Lindemann Historical Society has been closed for the past twenty years, due to, let's say, disturbances in the building."

"Disturbances?" Jason Sanborn asked as he pulled his pipe from his mouth.

"It seems they can't keep a staff there because they scare off too fast."

"Wonderful. Not one, but two haunted locations." Julie stood and started putting on her coat.

"Yes, it seems Summer Place has a long reach, as we discovered this afternoon in your offices."

Julie looked at Gabriel and then, without preamble, walked

from the meeting room. Kelly scrambled to gather her things and also left the room, in a hurry to catch her ride.

"Good luck working with her. Talk about wrapped too tight," Leonard said.

"I think we all may be wrapped too tightly, young man," Jason said, "because I have the distinct feeling that is exactly what our good professor here is banking on."

13 Bright Waters, Pennsylvania

Bright Waters had rolled up its sidewalks at eight o'clock that night, so it was no wonder that there were so few witnesses to the strange events that took place as the hour hand struck twelve. It was a lone man in room number seventeen of the Bright Waters "Come As You Are" motel that heard the arrival of Summer Place into the town.

As Detective Damian Jackson lay in bed, he studied the case file he had opened on Gabriel Kennedy seven years ago.

Jackson closed the file folder and placed his large hands behind his head, staring up at the ceiling. It had been six hours since he had requested background checks on the people Kennedy had assembled for his foray into that damnable house. Thus far his superiors hadn't asked the dreaded questions about why he wanted these people checked out. Jackson had been specifically warned about not pursuing anything having to do with Professor Gabriel Kennedy on his personal time. The State of Pennsylvania wanted to keep distance from the goings-on in Bright River. They were trying to live it down, while Jackson was busy tearing away at the old wound in his effort to reopen it.

As he lowered his eyes away from the bland ceiling of the room that had been his for the past two weeks, Jackson leaned over to turn off the bedside lamp. As he reached the old pull chain, he felt his bed vibrate. He stopped and wondered how many of the motel's old pipes ran right under his bed, and if one of those pipes were about to give way. He shook his head and again reached for the light. Another tremor shook his bed. This time it was powerful enough to make him throw back his covers and stand up. The bed was indeed moving. As he placed a hand on the mattress, the movement stopped as suddenly as it had started.

He watched the bed closely and was about to place his hand on the mattress again when the loud blaring of a car horn made him jump almost out of his pajamas. Jackson cursed himself for being so skittish. He looked out into the dark night. The road and sidewalks were empty and for some reason Jackson felt exposed as he stood in the window.

"Goddamn ghost town," he mumbled. He was just getting ready to let the curtain fall back when a flash of lightning streaked across the sky, followed closely by a loud clap of thunder. Looking back at the bed, he shook his head. That was the vibration he had felt—the far-off sound of thunder. A storm had not been forecast for the area. He had heard the weather reports all night long on the cable access channel on TV. "Goddamn good detective." Out of curiosity, he turned back to the darkened street outside.

Rain had started to fall. With its coming, something settled into the small burg that happened to be the nearest settled town to Summer Place. It was like knowing you're about to have company for no other reason than you just know. Jackson shook his head. He had been reading the report on Kennedy too long, and it was starting to creep him out. That was all. As he let the curtain go, he saw movement across the street just in front of the old diner. He grabbed the curtain and pulled it back once again. A man was standing right in front of the twin glass doors. He was haggard—that Jackson could see—but the rest of the man was darkened by shadow and distance. Damian narrowed his eyes. When the traffic light flashed yellow, he saw something at the man's feet. His heart froze in his sizable chest for a moment; the man was standing over a downed body. His heart pounded loudly. He knew the man was looking right in his direction.

Jackson let the curtain go and started dressing. He found

his holstered gun on the nightstand. Pulling his door open, he was met with a cold blast of wind-driven rain. He hesitated. The man was still there, still looking right at him. Jackson pushed off from the door and leaped into the arms of the gathering storm. He splashed his way to the parking area directly in front of his room. In the flashing of the lone traffic light he saw that the man had raised his arm and was beckoning Damian forward. With gun in hand, Jackson crossed the street.

Damian raised the gun but was careful not to aim it. He stopped fifteen feet from the man's back-lit form and shielded his eyes as the rain blasted past his fedora.

"Who are you?!" Jackson shouted. He glanced momentarily from the standing man to the body at his feet.

The man said nothing. Jackson could see scraggly long hair silhouetted against the light, but not the man's face. He raised the gun a little more.

"What are you—?" Jackson started to shout, but the man stepped forward, moving easily over the person lying under the diner's awning.

"An offering," the man said.

"Your name! Give me your name!" Damian shouted against another roll of thunder.

"We are an offering, that's all I know. I'm hungry, we're both hungry."

"Yeah, well, we'll take care of that, but I have to know who you are first!" Jackson shouted, becoming nervous as the man kept walking toward him.

"It was dark, and we didn't know. It won't allow what is to happen, to happen. Its home . . . don't defile its home. It won't allow that. We are meant as a warning."

"All right, you have to stop right there." Damian cocked the nine-millimeter and aimed. "Who are you?"

The dark, bedraggled figure slowly turned and went back underneath the awning, where he stood like a sentinel over the prone figure at his feet.

"I have to go now, but you are left this as a reminder not to return to my soil."

Damian Jackson saw the figure stoop low to the ground and then swipe at the figure lying on the sidewalk. The gesture was quick and the detective had very little time to react. As the dark figure raised his hand once again, Jackson saw the gleam of a knife in the flashing yellow from the traffic signal. At the same moment, lightning streaked across the sky and thunder ripped apart the rain-laden darkness. Jackson fired his weapon. The bullet caught the man in the right shoulder and spun him around. He flopped against the front doors of the closed diner.

Damian cursed as he hurried forward, still training his gun on the slumped man. As he stepped onto the sidewalk, lights in the surrounding buildings started to come on. He held the nine-millimeter close by the head of the fallen man, who was writhing in pain. With his free hand, he pried the large kitchen knife from the man's tight grasp. He then allowed his eyes to shift quickly to the body that had never once moved. He saw the pool of blood running from around the neck area and knew that the rate of that flow was too great for the person to survive. The man he had shot was trying to rise to his elbows. Damian slapped the barrel of the gun onto the top of the man's head, and the long-haired man grunted and fell onto his face.

"Goddamn it," Jackson hissed. He looked around him for some sort of assistance. Then he saw that a light had come on inside the diner. A man appeared at the doorway, tying a rope around the waist of his old robe. Jackson waved the man out. Then he looked down and rolled the prone man at his feet over onto his back. In a flash of lightning, the man's face became visible. Paul Lowell stared back at Damian with dead eyes. His throat had been cut so deeply that Jackson could see the whiteness of bone in the wound. Damian gasped and removed his hand, standing slowly. The heaving rain was starting to wash most of the standing blood into the gutter, but the flow was heavy and would soon cover the protected part of the sidewalk.

Jackson leaned over the man he had shot, grasped him by his filthy hair, and raised his head. As the world flashed with lightning and the traffic signal flashed yellow once more, the face of Kyle Pritchard remained slack and unconscious.

"Good God almighty, what in the world did you do?"

Jackson let Pritchard's head fall back to the wet sidewalk and then looked up into the shocked face of the diner's owner.

"Call the local police," Damian said and held out his state police identification. He knew everyone in the small town already knew exactly who he was and why he was there.

The old man didn't move. He stood in the half-open doorway, almost as if he were preparing to run back inside.

"Move, old-timer," Jackson said. He placed his gun in his raincoat pocket and slapped handcuffs on Kyle Pritchard. "And you better put on some coffee."

When Damian looked up, he saw the man had left to comply with his orders. Jackson placed his hands on his hips and looked from the murdered cohost of *Hunters of the Paranormal* to the just-awakening sound technician. He stepped back out into the rain and looked up, letting the cold wetness strike his face. When he looked back, he raised his brows.

"Now that, I didn't expect," he said, as lightning flashed across the sky once again.

The Waldorf-Astoria, New York, New York

Gabriel Kennedy stood just inside the doorway to room 1809, looking at John and Jennifer. John sat on the end of the large bed, and Jennifer was at the desk, writing. Her energy level was almost off the charts now that Bobby Lee McKinnon had disappeared. She moved a small vase, and then counted something and wrote it on her pad. She was following John Lonetree's instructions to the letter about the way in which his part of the program would be conducted, numbering each item that she would place in John's hands after he had gone to sleep. She would then record his reactions as his dreamwalk went through its paces.

"Be sure that you write everything down, and record the whole session, too," Kennedy said.

"I think she'll keep everything in line," John said, kicking off his cowboy boots.

Jenny smiled but didn't look up from the notes she was writing. "What if Bobby Lee's not really gone?" she asked, as matter-of-factly as she could.

"Tell him he's had his moment in the sun, and then put him to work helping John." Kennedy smiled, but saw that Jennifer wasn't very appreciative of his sense of humor. "Sorry. I don't know, Jenny. I don't have any answers for you. All I can say is that if he does, end the experiment and call me. I don't want him mixing it up with John while he's under."

The slight woman nodded. She walked to the door and kissed Kennedy on the cheek, then placed her thin fingers on his chest and pushed him out of the door. She closed it without another word and then turned to John, who was stretched out on the bed with his large hands behind his head, watching her.

"I thought he would never leave," he said with a smile.

"Now, am I supposed to sing you a lullaby?" she asked, not appreciating his sense of humor either.

"Maybe just a bedtime story," John said, his smile growing wider.

"You wouldn't care for my bedtime stories at all, Mr. Lonetree, I assure you." He flipped off the light switch at the wall, and then the desk lamp. She slid into her chair and looked toward the bed in the total darkness of the room. She hoped and prayed that Bobby Lee McKinnon would leave her be and stay away. She truly wanted to help the team—and most importantly, she wanted to help John Lonetree.

Before long, she felt that John had slid off to sleep. She would give him twenty minutes, as his instructions had stated, and then she would slide the first item he had requested into the bed beside his sleeping body.

Looking at her notes, she could barely make out the first item's name: portrait number one—F. E. and Elena Lindemann, wedding portrait.

Kennedy went over each team assignment one last time and then tiredly adjourned the meeting. He and Julie Reilly would be leaving at six in the morning, and the others soon after. He wondered how John and Jennifer were doing. He was tempted to enter the room and eavesdrop, but he knew that John's dreamwalking was like a tightrope walker attempting a wire act in a high wind: any disturbance at the wrong time could send Lonetree falling out of whatever realm he was in. To Gabriel that could be dangerous; it would be like startling a sleepwalker out of his slumber while in motion.

As he returned his paperwork to his briefcase, he saw Julie Reilly waiting for him by the door. She had a curious look on her face and in a split second he saw the reason why. She pushed the door open, and standing in the hallway was a rumpled-looking Lionel Peterson. He was wearing a white shirt and black sport jacket, but that was where the neatness ended and the haggardness began. He was unshaven and his eyes were bloodshot. Kennedy could see the aftereffects of a long night of drinking. He pushed past Julie, making her step aside.

"I think you better slow down on your alcohol intake," Kennedy said as he snapped his briefcase shut. "I know the look—I've been there."

"I don't give a good goddamn where you've been, Kennedy."

"Can you tell us why you're here and what you want?" Julie asked. "We're tired, and we have an early day tomorrow."

At that moment Kelly Delaphoy stepped into the room, followed by the CEO himself. Abe Feuerstein still had on his customary bow tie and his brown suit. He slid easily into a chair at the table. He was looking directly at Kennedy as he pushed a chair out for Kelly to sit. When she did, the CEO placed a hand her shoulder and squeezed.

"I sure as hell will tell you, Ms. Reilly," Peterson answered smugly. "Although, you being the ace reporter here, I believe you should have had an inkling of what was happening right under your nose."

The CEO of UBC watched, letting it all play out without comment, but still he kept his aged hand on Kelly's shoulder.

"I was awakened an hour ago by the Pennsylvania State Police. I immediately called the CEO and he suggested we get here and sort this mess out."

"And that mess is?"

"Your intrepid detective shot and wounded Kyle Pritchard tonight in that small town out by Summer Place. He shot him after the man cut the throat of Kelly's other con man, Paul Lowell."

Shock settled on Julie's face as the news sank in. She sat hard in the chair she was standing near and placed a hand over her face. It was when she looked over at Kelly Delaphoy that her anger seethed to the surface.

"You stupid fool, what have you and your people done?"

"I don't know what the hell anyone is talking about. I had nothing to do with this. Those two have been missing since the night of the test. I had no idea they were still near the house!" Kelly looked to Gabriel for some sort of help, but immediately saw that there would be none there.

"Can you explain in detail what happened, Mr. Peterson?" Feuerstein asked, patting Kelly on the shoulder in a calming gesture.

"All I know is what the detective told me over the phone. He wants to talk to Kelly. He suspects, and rightly so, about her connection to Pritchard. I think she has something to do with this."

"Are you kidding me? Murder?" Kelly stood so suddenly that the CEO's hand flew from her shoulder. "In case you didn't realize, Lionel, you just told me one of my best friends in all the world just had his throat sliced!"

"I didn't think sharks had any friends," Peterson spat back.

"Most sharks are loners, Peterson. That's why you travel as a singular entity yourself," Gabriel said. "I doubt very much that Ms. Delaphoy's imagination would go to that extreme. I mean, to kill another human being for high ratings—"

"Now, you listen to me, you crack—"

"Professor Kennedy is right. Where would the gain be for Kelly?"

Peterson stopped in midsentence and looked at the CEO. He was attempting to get Kelly to sit once more.

"Obviously Kyle Pritchard was insane. He more than likely abducted the poor man, and did God knows what to him. And then, in the end, he snapped and killed him. Sad, but I think all we can accuse our little producer of is extremely poor judgment."

"Did Jackson say anything more?" Julie asked. She changed targets, shifting her glare from Kelly to Peterson. "Did Pritchard say anything at the scene?"

"Detective Jackson didn't go into any detail. He just wants to speak with Kelly."

"Well, he can do so, but in the presence of our team of criminal defense attorneys," Feuerstein said, rising from his chair.

"Sir, it's obvious we have to cut this program from our lineup. I mean, we have to use a little bit of taste and common sense."

"Common sense, yes, yes we do, Lionel. We have already spent a tremendous amount of money in advertising. Common sense is indeed needed. Good taste, however, is something that reality television left out of the equation many years ago. No, the show goes on. We will turn this Pritchard thing into a beneficial part of the show." He placed his hand back on Kelly's shoulder and squeezed hard enough to elicit a wince from the blond woman. "You'll see to that, won't you, young lady?"

"Yes, sir," she said, shrugging away from him.

"Good," the CEO said as he moved to the door. "Professor Kennedy, I would appreciate it very much if you would be present at any questioning. It seems Detective Jackson may have some preconceived notions regarding Ms. Delaphoy here."

"He won't be the only one there. I want a crack at Detective Jackson, also. How convenient that all of this happened right in front of him," Julie said. Kennedy stood and, without a word, bypassed the CEO at the door and left the room.

"It seems we are fast becoming a disappointment to our good professor," Feuerstein said, surveying the people still inside the room. "Lionel, please attempt to follow up and get as many details about this incident as you can," he said. Then he turned and followed Kennedy out the door.

"Goddamn you two, you're going to go down and you're going to take everyone with you."

Julie grabbed her bag and took a menacing step toward Peterson.

"That just may be worth it, you little prick."

Kennedy walked down the hallway in silence. Julie glanced back and saw that Kelly was waiting on the CEO and Peterson. She would like to have stayed and listened to Kelly try to explain the sudden reappearance and then death of her co-host, but she knew Kennedy wasn't going to allow this incident in Bright Waters to pass by without doing something.

"I'm coming along," she said as she caught up to Gabriel. He looked tired.

"No, you have the assignment; you don't need me to go to the Lindemann Historical Society. I've got business."

"I know, and that's why you need me along." She stopped suddenly and took Kennedy by the jacket sleeve. "Jackson's not going to allow you to talk with a murder suspect, not when he thinks you're one also. He not only believes you killed your student, he thinks you're possibly in on this, too. Professor, you need me."

Kennedy shook free of her grasp and looked around. His eyes traveled to the ceiling as he thought about leaving John and Jennifer alone upstairs.

"I'll get Jason Sanborn to sit outside Lonetree's door for the night. If anything happens we can be back here in a few hours. Look, Kennedy, if this is a part of Kelly's little plan that got away from her, we need to know that. If she was, she'll never admit to it and you know that. You need to know what you're dealing with here. The only way you can do that is by speaking to Kyle Pritchard, and I'm sorry, but you need me for that."

"Goddamn it," Gabriel hissed, finally sparing Julie a look. "What are you after? Tell me the truth. Do you believe what happened to us seven years ago, or are you just playing along until you can pull your *60 Minutes* spring trap on us?"

"I'll tell you the truth: I don't know. I think that maybe you have good reason to fear that damn place and that maybe you have justifiable reasons in your own head for what happened that night. But there is one thing I will tell you, Professor. Even after all the hocus-pocus I've seen today, there are no ghosts in that house. There are just people. People are capable of creating the true horror stories of our day, I've seen it time and time again. Kyle Pritchard is one of those—a part of the mystique of a wooden and concrete house that makes up a whole puzzle. If this is a fake, I will report it as so."

Gabriel nodded. "Okay. Report things as you experience them, tell people the truth after Halloween. I'll be satisfied with that."

"And Pritchard?" she asked.

"I've told you before; I'm not a big believer in coincidence. Why would Pritchard do what he did?"

"Maybe he's just crazy. Did you ever think of that?"

"That's a very clinical analysis, Ms. Ace Reporter, and I'll even grant you that and counter with my own clinical report—

yes, his cheese has slipped his cracker. Now that that's taken care of, why did Pritchard wait until now to kill Mr. Lowell? Why did he travel that distance to do it at that particular place and in front of the one policeman linked to that damn house? And here's one you'd better burn into that notebook of yours, Ms. Reilly: Just where the hell have Pritchard and Lowell been for the past eight days?"

Julie had posed the same question to herself in the meeting room, but it hadn't made her stop and think like it did now, spoken in the light of the hallway.

"But you're right. I will need you to get through to Detective Damian Jackson." Kennedy turned and started for the immense lobby of the Waldorf.

"Damn right you do," she said as she caught up with Kennedy once more.

"And it's just not for the reasons I just mentioned." He reached the front doors and stopped. "For some reason, that house knows Jackson is involved with what's happening on the thirty-first. It tracked him down to deliver UBC's missing people to him."

"Yeah?" She switched her large bag to the other shoulder.

"They were sent to deliver a message."

The light finally dawned in Julie's eyes. "We need to know what Summer Place communicated to him."

"Now you're starting to get just what may be crazy here, Ms. Reilly."

Julie smiled as Kennedy turned and went through the doorway. The doorman took Kennedy's valet ticket.

Julie shook her head. "My bet is still on the human factor."

"Yeah?" he said with a larger than normal smile.

"Yes, it is."

"Mine's on Summer Place."

Jason Sanborn yawned, leaning forward and pressing his head lightly against the door. He heard nothing but the hiss of air by his ear, so he pulled away and leaned against the wall. He pulled his pipe from his jacket pocket, looked from it to the NO SMOKING sign, and frowned. He placed the pipe back into his jacket and then leaned his ear to the door once more. He was rewarded with a mumbled shout and then sudden silence.

"No horrific sounds, no bloodcurdling screams yet?"

Jason's heart almost jumped from his chest. The voice caught him totally unawares. He turned and saw the smiling face of George Cordero. "Oh, God. You scared the living hell out of me." Jason grabbed his chest.

"Calm down, old boy. This is the Waldorf, not the House on Haunted Hill."

"What are you doing up here? It's nearly two in the morning."

"Ah, the lounge died down to nothing after Jennifer's magic trick, so I thought I would cruise the hallways looking for adventure and hijinks."

Jason rummaged in his pocket, fumbling for his pipe once more. He placed it in his mouth and tried to look as if he wasn't on edge. "Well, you're not missing anything up here, so I guess you'll have to find your hijinks and adventure somewhere else."

"Boy, everyone's just as friendly as hell tonight." Cordero leaned against the wall and folded his arms over his chest. "Still, I think I'll wait and see if our resident medicine man gets a line on anything."

Jason removed the pipe from his mouth and looked at George. He studied him for a moment and then looked at his empty pipe.

"You don't care for Mr. Lonetree, do you?"

George smiled as he looked to his left down the long and empty hallway.

"I don't care for most people, Mr. Sanborn. If you had the talent"—he looked at Jason with serious eyes—"or curse, you would find that the basic human being is a piece of shit. Always out to screw someone over."

"Then why are you here?" Sanborn asked.

"Kennedy. That man is tenacious. I was a patient of his many years ago; he hadn't been out of school very long. He found me in an alley in Pasadena. When he pulled me out of there and started talking to me, I would have never known he was a shrink. Then he took me to his house and I saw his diploma on the wall. At first I thought he was a freak or something—you know, out to diddle a kid off the street. But instead of being a perv, the man actually tossed me his house keys and told me where the food was, and then he left. I didn't see him for two days. You see, Kennedy had a feeling, too. He knew I wouldn't rip him off. After that, we spoke for weeks. He taught me that it was okay to be bitter about my talent."

"Did you ever use your talent on Kennedy?" Jason asked.

"No. If I did that, it would open a two-way street and exchange of information, and I don't need Gabriel Kennedy that far into my head. He did test my clairvoyance, though, and he did verify what I had wasn't natural. He believed me right off the bat, and didn't try to give me the full battery of medical testing that most doctors would do. You know, looking for the grapefruit-size tumor in my head, or the dark past that had me killing my immediate family. He knew it was a gift and never doubted that or tried to cloud it with medical terminology. That, Mr. Sanborn, is why I'm here." He stared down at Jason for a few uncomfortable seconds. "Gabriel Kennedy is my only friend in the world, and I suspect if he doesn't get answers this time around, it will kill him. Maybe physically, maybe mentally, but it will certainly damage him beyond repair. I won't let that happen."

"Well, that proves you have some humanity in you. So why don't you respect Mr. Lonetree's talent?"

Cordero chuckled and then examined the hallway. The elevator chimed, a hundred feet away. He heard the doors slide open and then close. He watched, but no one came from the elevator landing.

"I don't go looking for the feeling. My curse is the mere

touching of someone, or something. Our Indian friend goes in search of trouble. He wants to connect with his gift, and that can be very dangerous. It's like inviting a vampire into your house. Once done, it can't be undone. Mr. Lonetree is fucking with something that, once in his head, may not want to leave."

"That sounds ominous," Jason said as he once more bit down on his pipe.

"I guess that's why we're both standing in this freaking hallway in the wee hours of the morning. Yes, Mr. Sanborn, very ominous."

Jennifer checked the last item off her list, frowning in frustration when John groaned and pushed the latest and last item away in his sleep. The small silver-framed photo of the Lindemann children, taken around the pool at Summer Place sometime in the early summer of 1932, hadn't sparked anything in Lonetree's sleep-colored world. She laid the silver frame on the bellman's cart and then examined the sleeping man. His sleep wasn't what she would have called restful. He turned his head to the left and then to the right, and then became still again. He had released his long black hair and it was splayed out on the pillow. He shook, and then his body calmed once more.

"Well, that's it for the house items," she said softly. She leaned over, listening as John mumbled in his sleep. The words were in his native language; Jennifer couldn't understand them, but she found it all to be fascinating. She reached out and touched John's hair and he immediately calmed. She smiled and straightened. She would keep her little secret to herself. She didn't want John to know how she was starting to feel about him so early. She knew most men would shy away from her, but she felt the goodness in Lonetree and she clung to it like a drowning swimmer hugging a buoy.

She returned to the bellman's cart and the items Wallace Lindemann had brought from Summer Place. She felt frustrated that John had shown no reaction to any of the items on the cart, from the large framed painting of the family Lindemann, which she thought for sure would elicit some response, to the small household items such as the doilies from the sedans and armchairs. Even the bottles of very aged whiskey, which she thought may have been left there by accident by Wallace Lindemann, had no effect on John's sleep patterns. While some of them caused a stir, nothing seemed to make him dreamwalk.

Jennifer shook her head. She took the cart by its large frame and started pushing it toward the corner of the room. Something on the floor became entangled in the small wheels of the cart, stopping her. She knelt down, thinking that maybe her sweater had fallen from the desk chair. In the darkness, she felt the material. It wasn't her sweater. She pulled, and felt the fabric tear. Pulling the cart backward, she tried again. The material came free into her hand and she held it close to her face. It was a dress. She felt the straps and the length as she stood and walked toward the desk. With one look at John, who was still sleeping peacefully, she turned the desk lamp toward the wall so as not to wake him, and switched it on, holding the dress close to the light. It was a black sequined gown. Jenny froze. She scrambled to find her list of items that Lindemann had brought, scanning it one line at a time. She turned and looked at the bellman's cart, then at the old and dusty dress again. She knew she had not seen the dress at any time, when she had been inventorying, removing, or replacing the items on the cart.

"How did this get here?" she asked herself. She turned toward the bed, watching John's chest rise and lower in peaceful sleep. A few of the black sequins had fallen off, onto the desk. She closed her eyes and made a decision. Easing up to the large bed, she sat on its edge. The recorder on the desk still showed its red light; the small device was recording. She slowly brought the evening dress up and placed it over John's exposed hands, as if she were covering a baby with a blanket.

John's reaction was immediate. He sat straight up in bed

and his eyes flew open, staring straight ahead. Jennifer eased
herself from the bed and backed away, her heart racing at a
thousand miles per hour. John took the dress into both hands
and then twirled it into a knot; it was as if he were wadding
up a set of papers. Jennifer swallowed. His haunted eyes still
remained fixed on something straight ahead as if he were
seeing something that scared the hell out of him.

The temperature in the room suddenly fell by thirty degrees. She could see the vapor of her breath as she breathed
in and out. She absentmindedly reached for her sweater on
the back of the desk chair, but fumbled it as she watched
John's eyes. Summer Place was in this room.

The house was here, and John Lonetree was seeing it.

John looked around frantically. He knew, without ever having
seen the house, exactly where he was. He was standing in the
corner of a room. The bedside table lamp was on but it was
like seeing the room through a wet coating of gauze, or a
double-thick layer of mosquito netting. The light was diffused
and gave the large room a brownish, darker tint.

In his dream state, he felt another presence in the bedroom. *No,* he thought, *two others.* One was a young girl
standing at the foot of the bed, the other a tall and striking
dark-haired woman standing next to her. The smaller girl
nodded her head and left the room. The other turned and
looked down at the item the girl had left on the foot of the
bed. Lonetree looked from that blurry, hazy thing on the bed,
to the black sequined dress knotted in his hands. He saw the
woman lift the dress up and look it over. The black sequins
shined brightly in the lamplight from the table. John watched
as the tall woman held the dress up to her front and looked it
over in the full-length mirror by the dressing screen. He could
feel, not see, the woman snap the thin black strap. She played
with the dress a moment and then lowered it in thought.

In the haze of the diffuse light, John looked down at the
dress he held in his own hands and then shook it out. He saw
the broken strap on the left side and wondered if that was

what the woman was seeing. He looked up just as the tall woman opened the bedroom door. She stepped through and looked left and then right.

"Hallo, die junge Dame?" the woman said in thick German. John thought she was asking for the young lady. *"Mein Kleid scheint gerissen zu werden . . ."* The tall woman was frustrated. "Young lady, my dress seems to have been torn. . . . Young lady?"

John felt himself move from the shadows, and the woman seemed to have felt the movement. She half turned and looked around the room, but seeing nothing, she turned back to the hallway, then stepped out with the black dress in her hands. John followed with the ever-present veil confusing his vision. He saw the woman slowly make her way down the third-floor hallway. Lonetree knew he was in Summer Place, and he also knew he was in the presence of the German diva Gwyneth Gerhardt. She seemed to be examining doors as she went to the right down the hallway. She turned when John came out of the bedroom, almost as if she were feeling Lonetree close to a hundred years after the fact. She looked at the spot where he stood for the longest time, and then turned away and continued toward the end of the long hall.

John tried his best to get a bearing on exactly where he was, so that he could relay this information to Gabriel later. He started to get the uneasy feeling that he wasn't alone in his pursuit of the German opera star. There was another presence not far away from him. No, it was more than one, he thought. He didn't feel threatened by the multiple entities, but he knew that they were most curious as to what the diva was up to. John wondered if maybe he was only expressing his own thoughts outwardly to the point where he was flashing back on himself.

Suddenly the atmosphere changed dramatically, just as the diva approached a large set of double doors at the end of the hallway. John stopped in his tracks. He felt a warning shudder from his own body. He could sense concern from the other presences. Try as he might, John couldn't connect with whatever was there with him, but he knew that whoever it was feared for the diva. Suddenly the warm and inviting temperature changed in the hallway. From the end of the corridor to where he stood, the glass fronts of picture frames frosted over, and he even saw the diva's breath mist from her mouth. She placed an ear up to the large double doors. He wanted to warn her that something had changed, but found—as usual—that he was merely an observer with no voice or ability to affect his surroundings. He did, however, see the multiple presences in the hallway move forward, stop, and then move again, as if hesitant but wanting to warn the diva.

The loud slam made John jump. It was if a cannonball had struck the wall next to him. The diva didn't seem to hear anything. She reached for the handle on the left-side door. John held his hand out, wanting to warn her away. He saw the dress in his outstretched hand, and his attention was drawn to it momentarily. The German woman disappeared into the sewing room. John felt the other entities in the hallway all gather around the double doors, and he sensed wailing, crying—a horrible crucible of anguish from all around him. He tried to single out the voices but could only make out five or six. The rest were lost, as if coming from a farther distance. Gwyneth Gerhardt started screaming inside the room. John took three quick steps toward the sewing room but stopped as a door to his left opened. A man stepped out in a long-tailed tuxedo. He adjusted his tie and looked around the hallway. John wanted to grab the mustachioed man and shake him, awakening him to the fact that a woman needed his help in the sewing room. The man looked around as if sensing something, and then he shrugged his shoulders and stamped his feet. He was feeling the cold also. Gwyneth screamed, pounding on the giant double doors of the sewing room. The feminine voices cried out with her, sharing her anguish.

John watched the man in the tuxedo leave for the stairs. He tried to grab the man but his hand passed right through him. John yelled, "Stop!" But the man continued on his way.

The entities ceased their wailing and crying. John sensed

panic, terror, pure animal fear. Something was coming down the hallway from behind him. He slowly turned as all of the entities vanished in a sudden rush of warm air. Then the hallway grew even colder than it had been a moment before. The footsteps sounded like a hollow ball striking the carpet runner. They shook the house as they came toward John. He closed his eyes, forcing his body to turn. As he did, the giant footsteps came to a stop. He felt its breath as it leaned in close to him. When he opened his eyes, all he could see was a misty blur. But he knew that hiding underneath the trick of light was a living, breathing human being. The evil rolled off of it in waves that almost made John sick to his stomach. All the while, Gwyneth Gerhardt kept pounding on the doors and screaming for help. Her voice was breaking, losing all of its womanly humanity and becoming animalistic and desperate. Lonetree was reminded of a deer caught in a trap.

The thing came mere inches from his face. He heard the sniffing sound as it smelled him—first up, and then down. He felt the severe cold as it leaned in close. The thing turned toward the sewing room door, then it leaned down and came close to him once more. He felt triumph from the cold, evil-smelling entity as it studied him. He knew the thing was smiling, satisfied about something.

"They are mine, shaman, mine forever," it said in a husky, deep voice. "You are so easy to disperse, so easy to kill. You will never make it to your gathering. Stay out!"

With the last words John felt the thing push him into the wall. It suddenly moved away, the blur of its camouflage acting as a bubble of disguise as it approached the sewing room. The screaming stopped as the thing pressed against the double doors. John's eyes widened when he saw the oak press inward. He even heard the cracking of the thick wood. Then the doors snapped back and all of the air was sucked out of the hallway. He heard one last scream.

"You should not have followed!" came the thick, horrible voice from the sewing room. Then it was over.

* * *

John opened his eyes and saw the dress in his hands. He tried desperately to throw it off, but he had twisted it so thoroughly that it wouldn't free itself.

Jennifer, wide-eyed and in a state of terror at what John had been shouting aloud, reached out and tried to unwind the dress from Lonetree's hands. She finally managed to remove it and tossed it across the room just as the door opened. Jason and George had been trying to get in since the moment John's screams and shouts of warning had reached them in the hallway.

"What the hell?"

Jennifer held up a hand. She splayed her fingers as she watched John. Finally, he reached up and ran his fingers through his long hair. He looked up and saw Jennifer.

"Where're Gabriel and the others?"

Jennifer turned to Jason for the answer.

"He and Julie Reilly left for the Poconos. It seems Kyle Pritchard and Paul Lowell have turned up. Paul's very dead."

Jennifer sat on the bed and took John's hand. "Did you learn anything?" she asked him. As the two men stepped farther into the room, John turned and planted his feet firmly on the carpet. He was careful not to move his hand out of Jenny's.

"I think so," he said, looking into her concerned face. "I don't think we can beat whatever's in that house. It's been killing for a very long time."

"It seems the house has allowed at least Kyle Pritchard to live," Sanborn said as he fumbled for his pipe.

"That was its plan all along," John said. He rubbed his eyes with his free hand.

"I'm not following."

"It's attacking us even now. It doesn't want us to go to Summer Place, so it's reaching out for us."

"And?" Cordero asked, though he suspected he already knew the answer.

Lonetree looked up past Jenny and found Cordero's eyes.

"You know the reason. I can see it in your face."

Sanborn removed the pipe from his mouth and looked at the man next to him as if he had suddenly grown two heads.

"Tell them what you think," John said, holding his eyes on Cordero.

"Gabe and Julie have left. Kelly has been dragged off by Peterson and their boss, and we're heading out in the morning to pursue information about the house."

"Vulnerable," John said. "It will hit us when we're weakest, before we gather to fight it."

"Come on, you're speaking like a bad horror book. What are you saying?"

Cordero looked at the open door and the bright light in the hallway, grateful for the brief respite from darkness. Then he turned to the others.

"Summer Place wants us separated."

14

Julie tried to answer her cell phone once again, but for the tenth time in as many minutes she failed to get a clear signal. She looked at the screen in frustration and tossed the phone into her bag.

"Goddamn dead zone out here," she said. She watched the windshield wipers and their hypnotic rhythm as they swept the heavy rain away.

"Could you tell who was calling?" Kennedy asked. He leaned forward, trying to see through the water that covered the glass between wiper pulses.

"Jason Sanborn." She glanced at her watch, using the dashboard lights for illumination. "It's about four hours past his bedtime, which is worrisome in itself."

Kennedy was worrying more about John Lonetree. If something had gone wrong during the dreamwalk and he wasn't there, he would never be able to forgive himself. It was his experiment, and things seemed to be pulling away from him. In this line of research, that could be deadly.

"Are you thinking about Lonetree?" Julie asked, turning to look at Kennedy through the green and blue reflection of the dashboard lights.

"Yes. I should have been there. This Kyle Pritchard act could have waited."

"Act?" Julie asked, raising her left brow. "So, you do think the test broadcast was some kind of a put-up job?"

Gabriel spared the reporter a look, and quickly turned back to watch the twisting road. "No, not the ending of Kelly's little game."

"Just the beginning—the disappearance?" Julie asked.

"I think it may have started out as a prank, but the house one-upped Kelly and her friends, took it to the next level."

"The house?" Julie said with a skeptical look.

"Look, if you open a doorway and allow the house into your head, it will take the advantage—it will attack."

"You're going off on a tangent. Either you're advancing a theory that has yet to be discussed with UBC, or you're holding back historical information from us. Which is it?"

Kennedy shifted in the seat. Through the heavy downpour, he saw the road sign for Bright Waters. "Jesus," he said as they entered the town.

"Damn Jackson. Little does he know, he's playing right into the network's hands with this circus." Julie leaned over the seat and brought out a camera case and a digital recorder. She started filming the ten state police cars, flashing their blue lights outside of the small constable's office. There was still an ambulance out front, along with several news vans from Philadelphia with lights blaring. Julie saw that one of them was an affiliate station of UBC, so she stopped filming and put the camera back in its bag.

"Lieutenant Jackson is ever diligent, isn't he?" Kennedy asked. Julie tried her cell phone again as Kennedy pulled to the curb behind a news van.

"Finally, a signal," she said, punching numbers on the phone.

Kennedy turned off the car and watched the comings and

goings of the police as they made their way from the diner across the street to the constable's office.

"No wonder you have a signal. You have enough micro-waves emanating from this little town to light up Cape Canaveral." Kennedy opened his door and stood, letting the rain pummel his head as he watched the scene before him. He would let Jackson come to him. He needed coffee.

"Jason, what's up?" Julie said as she opened her door to follow Kennedy.

Gabriel didn't wait on her; he made his way through the rising water toward the brightly lit diner. A group of state policemen were standing over something on the concrete. He swallowed when he saw it was the taped outline of a man's body. Several of the policemen looked up and eyed him with suspicion. Kennedy averted his eyes and walked into the diner.

Julie came in close behind Kennedy and turned as the door closed. She watched the policemen as they noted details. One of those details was the brownish stain that had soaked into the concrete of the sidewalk.

"Okay, I'll pass along the message. Now inform the news division that I'll be filing a live report from Bright Waters on the murder, using the affiliate that's already here. Tell whoever you need to pull some strings and threaten whoever needs to be bullied, and get me that affiliate crew's cooperation."

Kennedy removed his coat and shook out the rain as he sat at the counter. He eyed the three policemen sitting farther down the counter and the four others in a booth eating breakfast. An old man in cook's whites placed a cup of steaming coffee in front of Gabriel and then started to move away.

"Quite a bit of excitement," Kennedy said. The man stopped and turned.

"Don't know how folks can eat after seein' things like that," he said. He placed a cup and saucer in front of Julie when she sat, and poured her coffee without asking if she wanted any.

"Did you see what happened?" Gabriel asked as he poured sugar into his cup. Julie placed her bag on the stool next to her and watched the exchange.

"You bet I did. I never want to see anything like it again." The old man turned and disappeared behind the swinging doors.

Julie sipped the hot coffee and then turned to look at the policemen, who were in turn eyeing her. She turned back and removed her own coat, laying it over her large bag.

"Jason said that John Lonetree had quite the experience; Sanborn's about to have kittens. He wants you to call him as soon as you can."

Kennedy held out his hand, indicating that he needed the phone. Julie started to place the cell phone into his hand, but when the door opened she pulled it back and raised her cup to her lips instead.

"Mr. Wonderful is here. That didn't take long," she said, hiding her moving lips behind the cup.

"It seems your cast of characters is fast coming together. Well, minus one of the players. Paul Lowell won't be making the cast party," Damian Jackson said as he removed his soaking raincoat. "Why don't we grab a booth so we can talk."

Kennedy sat motionless and Julie sipped her coffee. Then they slowly rose and walked over to the nearest booth. They sat, both on one side to face the grand inquisitor. Jackson watched them sit. He eyed the state policemen sitting at the counter, and then the four in the booth at the back of the diner.

"I think we have a prisoner almost ready for transport," he said to them. "Or do you want the local constable to handle it?"

As Kennedy and Julie watched, the three policemen at the counter and the four in the booth all rose.

"And leave the man a sizable tip. I have to eat here today and tonight."

The policemen started tossing dollar bills on the counter

and booth table. They didn't meet the large detective's eyes as they placed their Smokey Bear hats on and left the diner. As they did, the old man stepped out of the kitchen with his coffeepot, but Jackson waved him off. He sat down across from Julie and Gabriel. This was the first time that either of them had seen Jackson without a tie and not looking as if he had just stepped out of a *GQ* magazine ad.

He smiled at the two people across from him as he laced his fingers together.

Silence hung among the three like an invisible wall. Gabriel knew he was the focus here, even though he had nothing to do with Kyle Pritchard or Paul Lowell.

"I would liked to have seen Kelly Delaphoy sitting there. I have a few pointed questions to ask her about tonight's events."

"She's conferring with the network legal department at the moment," Julie said. Kennedy remained silent and kept his eyes on Jackson.

"I imagine she is."

"Detective Jackson, why would two missing men show up after eight days, and then one kill the other with a state police detective as a witness?" Julie asked. She pulled out her small digital recorder, which Jackson immediately covered with a bear paw–size hand.

"This is not your interview, Ms. Reilly. It's mine."

Julie pulled her hand and recorder out from under Jackson's palm and clicked on the device. "Then I'll forward you a copy. It will save us all a lot of time. Otherwise, you know what you can do with your questions."

Damian smiled, the expression falling short of his brown eyes. He pulled a sugar dispenser toward him and started rolling it. Kennedy recognized the sleight-of-hand gesture as a way policemen had of distracting the person they were questioning—a trick that only worked on people who were scared to begin with.

"Now, what condition is Kyle Pritchard in?" Julie asked, pen poised over her notepad.

"Okay, Ms. Reilly, quid pro quo. I'll play along and then I would like something answered."

"Fair enough," Julie said.

"I wasn't asking you," Jackson said. He was eyeing Kennedy.

"What questions could I answer that would cast light onto something only you witnessed?"

"In answer to your question, Pritchard is in shock. He looks emaciated and he's dehydrated."

Julie wrote down Jackson's answer.

"His last words to me, after he slit the throat of your network personality," he said, looking from Kennedy to Julie, and then back, "were, *they're mine*. Does that sound familiar, Professor?"

"In the spoken word, no. Not familiar at all; however, I've seen those words written on paper."

"Don't play games with me, Kennedy. You did that once before and you paid dearly for it."

"Yes, I did. Both of you saw to that. Let me add that a closed mind, coming from either you or Ms. Reilly here, is a very dangerous thing to have when you're facing something like Summer Place. I suspect, however, neither of you will realize it until that house jumps up and bites you both on the ass. Now if you'll excuse me, I have a phone call to make."

Jackson started to reach out and take Kennedy's arm, but stopped short. Gabriel looked at him with an intensity the detective didn't remember Gabriel having before. The professor leaned over and looked the detective in the eyes once more.

"And I would expect my antagonist to allow me an even playing field. Let me speak to Pritchard before you cart him off to Philadelphia for your own inquisition."

"Of course. That's why I'm happy to see you here, Professor. I want your take on his state of health and well-being."

Kennedy held Julie's cell phone up and waved it. "Excuse me."

Julie watched Kennedy leave. She jotted her observation

down in her notebook and then looked up, smiling at the detective. "He seems to have grown a set of balls since the last time you confronted him."

"No comment," Jackson said. "I take it you are seeing things quite differently nowadays too, Ms. Reilly?"

"Let's just say I have a little bit more of an open mind than I used to have." Julie turned off the recorder and gathered her things. "I'm going to give you some time to think about my question, Detective. Just where the hell were Pritchard and Lowell all this time? I mean, you searched high and low for them, and then all of a sudden they come strolling into Bright Waters to demonstrate to you personally their culpability in a hoax, and then one kills the other. And please don't stick with a pat policeman's answer. This is damn strange and you know it. So think hard, Detective, because in just two days Kennedy may have a point to ram home to you."

"And that is?" Jackson asked as Julie rose.

"The point is, that house is beginning to look like it just may be capable of reaching out and biting us both in the ass, just like it may have done to Pritchard and Lowell. And you know what else I'm beginning to believe?"

"What?"

"I think that house may have enjoyed scaring the hell out of you personally, and I can see by your eyes you don't like being scared. So now I guess you know how Kennedy felt all those years ago." Julie raised her brow as she said the words. "After all, the house may have just sought you out . . . on a more intimate basis."

Julie moved off to join Gabriel outside. Jackson watched her go, then turned and slid the sugar dispenser away so hard that it broke against the wall fronting the booth. He closed his eyes. The tables had been turned on him by both Reilly and Kennedy, and he knew exactly why. The reporter's theory had been spot on.

He was indeed scared, for the first time in his career.

* * *

Jackson stood to the side in the one-cell constable's station. Kennedy stood in front of the bars, and as Julie tried to join him, Gabriel gently pushed her back. She held up the recorder, and Gabriel reluctantly nodded his head in agreement. Julie placed the recorder on the locking mechanism on the cell door and then backed away to stand beside Jackson in the dark. Outside, the last of the storm was passing by and all that could be heard was the gentle falling of the rain. The lightning was now far off to the east.

"Kyle, can I speak to you a moment?" Kennedy asked.

Pritchard was sitting on the lone uncushioned cot that occupied the cell. His long hair was a tangled, wet mess. His head hung low, buried between his raised knees. Kennedy could see the shaking of his shoulders.

"Mr. Prichard, Mr. Kyle Prichard, my name is Kennedy. I would like—"

Pritchard's head shot up and he scrambled into the corner, as if he wanted to crawl up, around, or through the wall.

"I had no message for you!"

Gabriel didn't miss a beat. "That's why I'm here, Kyle, to understand the message you brought to—"

"Jackson, big, strong buck nigger!"

To Damian's credit, he didn't react to the racial slur in the slightest. He raised his right brow at Gabriel, wanting him to continue. These were the only words that Damian had heard the man utter since he was taken into custody.

"Yes, that's the man," Gabriel said. Kyle Pritchard lowered his head and started weeping again.

"Who gave you the message to give to the detective?"

"I . . . don't . . . know."

The answer was almost an extended whine.

"Why was it necessary to kill Paul Lowell?"

Pritchard looked up just as if he had been given a reprieve from his execution. His eyes were wild and he actually smiled.

"It . . . it . . . said that I would free myself if I allowed Lowell to escape. I did, didn't I? I kept my part of the bargain.

Now I don't have to go back there, do I?" Prichard jumped from the cot and slammed himself into the bars, striking his head hard enough to get a good flow of blood running down his forehead. Jackson took a step forward but Gabriel held out a hand, staying him before he reached the bars. "I . . . don't . . . have . . . to . . . go . . . back . . . there—right?!" he yelled into Kennedy's face. "You know it, Kennedy. You know it better than anyone. It keeps its word, right? I don't have to go back?"

Julie saw a man who had gone totally insane. She knew that Gabriel would receive no useful information from Pritchard.

"No, Kyle, you never have to go back. Not ever."

"I knew it. I knew as soon as you said your name. It's satisfied." Pritchard slid down the set of bars until he was on the cold concrete of the cell.

Kennedy was about to turn away when Pritchard spoke again.

"They tried to protect us, but that . . . that . . . thing would have none of it. It found us and . . . and"—he turned, twisting his neck until he could see Kennedy—"and . . . and . . . Paul was the lucky one. I wanted to be the message, but it chose Paul. It wasn't fair. Now Paul will never be afraid again. It's just . . . not . . . fucking fair."

Pritchard lowered his head and sobbed.

"He's not making any sense at all. He'll be away a long time before he goes to trial for murder."

Gabriel shook his head. "You didn't understand a single thing this man said, did you? All you heard was the rambling of a terrified man, just as you didn't hear me all those years ago. You stupid bastard, he told us everything."

"For instance?" Damian asked.

"Show up on October thirty-first. Summer Place can explain it to you better than I ever could."

Kennedy walked out of the cell area. Julie started to follow, but then remembered her recorder. She reached back to pick it up and stopped in front of Jackson.

"I guess Summer Place is the place to be, huh?"

"I'll be there, all right. You bet your ass I'll be there. I guarantee all of this bullshit will be laid to rest."

Julie turned at the door.

"Let's just pray that's all that's laid to rest on Halloween."

Julie laughed as Damian glared at the empty doorway.

"You don't believe all of this shit, do you?!" he yelled after her.

"No," she called back, "but it sure is going to be good television, one way or the other!"

When Jackson turned back around, his heart fell through to his stomach. Kyle Pritchard had stood up and was staring right into the detective's face, smiling a maniacal grin that made Damian step back another foot.

"Don't worry, Detective. If it has its way, they won't be showing up for any TV special. It's hungry now." A blank look crossed Pritchard's features. It was as if something had reached out and switched him off.

"These fucking people," Jackson hissed as he turned away from the cell. "I'm going to nail them all!"

Outside, the last of the lightning and thunder faded from the small valley as the storm worked its way toward the place that was calling the shots: Summer Place.

Gabriel listened to the call from New York and the dire warning from John Lonetree. The rental car was pulled off to the side of the road while Julie Reilly made her field report with the assistance of a very disgruntled affiliate team from Philadelphia. Their own field reporter glared from underneath an umbrella. Kennedy could understand the affiliate's distaste for Reilly; it seemed the UBC woman was used to stealing the spotlight from people. As he watched, he realized that Julie didn't even know she was doing it. Gabriel didn't know if that was a factor of her arrogance or if it was from a natural ability to lead. He watched her wrap up the report outside the diner. Maybe she had been climbing the ranks of reporting for so long that she had become insensitive to others trying desperately to do the same thing.

"Well, maybe we should get Leonard to break a few laws and get the information through the historical society database. We can do the same with the New York and Pennsylvania state records on the deaths of the children. Then we can do the research from Summer Place, if need be. I'm inclined to take John's warning seriously, if he thinks we're being separated for an attack. Listen, Jason, keep everyone together at the Waldorf; Leonard is the only one allowed out of the hotel to work with the UBC engineers. He needs access to their equipment, but see what you can do about getting a guard on him."

Gabriel listened and then closed the cell phone. He watched through the misting rain as Julie thanked the UBC affiliate crew. Then he saw Reilly take the frustrated young woman reporter by the arm and walk with her, steering her toward the covered entrance of the diner. It looked as though they were in serious discussion. Julie smiled, and when the Philadelphia reporter lowered the umbrella, she was also smiling. Julie handed her a business card and the younger reporter looked not only grateful, but also outright giddy. Julie shook her hand and then made her way back toward the car. Kennedy shook his head as he started the vehicle. Reilly opened the door, tossed her bag inside, and then followed, snapping her seat belt and looking straight ahead. Kennedy watched her a moment before placing the car into gear. The reporter was tired. He could see that much through the dim dashboard lighting.

"Oh, look, Detective Jackson looks downright sad that we're leaving him," Julie said, nodding her head toward the small motel across the street.

Kennedy saw Damian Jackson standing in the shadows near the ice machine, watching their car turn for the road out of Bright Waters.

"You know the look of a lion when he's surrounded by a pack of hyenas?" Julie asked.

"If I recall, you and he were business acquaintances."

Julie looked over at Kennedy with a curious slant to her features. "Professor, just because we were nonbelievers never made us allies. I particularly don't like that man. As for you"—she raised her voice just a little, making him glance toward her—"you seem to be just as unforgiving. Have you ever tried to consider my point of view, or Jackson's? No, it's always your point of view, because the rest of us don't have a Harvard-educated slant on the paranormal, so our perspectives don't count. To let you in on a little secret, Professor Kennedy, I have done my research and more than seventy-five percent of all Americans believe in some form of activity, paranormal or scientific. I went into your investigation seven years ago with my eyes wide open. I never do anything half-assed. Give both of us—Jackson included—a break. He sees the fucked-up side of things in his line of work. He's a skeptic, but all he's saying is that he knows it doesn't take a ghost to be evil. Maybe he knows that over ten percent of all people in the world are insane. As for me"—she looked away—"nothing fucking surprises me anymore. But I do know when to admit that I need to reexamine something, and maybe Summer Place, for one reason or another, needs to have its doors opened again."

Kennedy was silent as he steered the car out of town. Then he smiled.

"What did you say to that reporter from Philadelphia?"

The question caught Julie by surprise. She shook her head.

"You thought I would steal her crew and make a report using her field team and not apologize for it? If you must know, I told her I liked the way she and her news crew made it to Bright Waters so fast after the fact, and that I will see what I can do about getting her some light work out of New York, you know, weekend stuff. That should help her."

"But you've never seen her work, is that right?"

"That's right."

"Isn't that a leap of faith on your part?"

"Oh, so it boils down to you analyzing me about my conclusions seven years ago?" she asked angrily.

Gabriel spared her a look and laughed. "No, it just shows me that you're capable of not being a bitch all the time."

Julie raised her eyebrows and then she laughed.

As the car moved down the small road leading down the mountain, Kennedy didn't see the black shroud as it moved along behind them. It vanished into the tree line to the left, heading for the large bend in the road three miles away.

Summer Place was reaching out.

The limousine was quiet as Kelly Delaphoy worked on her laptop. She had thus far ignored the hateful looks from Lionel Peterson, who was sitting across from her. Abe Feuerstein sat sipping a drink, watching Kelly work. It was as if the old CEO were studying her.

"What do you think about placing your team onsite a day early?"

Kelly looked up from her computer, the light from the monitor casting her face in a wash of colors and shadow. Feuerstein took another swallow of his drink.

"I mean, if we're on the property, the state police would find it that much harder to have us removed if they were so inclined, wouldn't you agree, Lionel?"

Peterson looked from Kelly to his boss, sitting next to him. "That raises more concerns on expenses for the show. Having the entire production crew onsite is an expense not budgeted for. Lodging, tent rental, commissary, and the overtime, all of that would run us over an already extended budget." Peterson looked at Kelly. "Plus, with the police now so interested, it may not be wise to rock the boat at this juncture."

Feuerstein smiled and placed his crystal glass in a small holder on the wet bar in front of him.

"I see your concern on the budget. I have spoken to marketing and sales and they say we can push the envelope just a little farther."

"The contract with Lindemann only covers one night in the house; I would anticipate him throwing a fit about the added—"

"That's enough about Lindemann and quite enough about budget concerns, Lionel." The CEO looked out of the darkened widows as the limo pulled into the underground parking garage at UBC. "You are not just the president of programming for this show, you are also its producer. And let me put it another way and make this absolutely clear, Lionel: Your job is on the line, so you better damn well get on board. Kelly here deserves the benefit of the doubt, at least to this point."

"So you're a believer in this crap, too?" Peterson asked.

"Believer? No, I'm not. The scariest thing in the world to me is our stockholders, Lionel; they should be the scariest things in the world to you, also. They believe in their quarterly reports, and that's all they believe in. Now, inform the legal department that since Kelly was not present at the murder scene, I don't want her disturbed as long as she's in New York. They can have at her on the thirtieth, when she arrives in Pennsylvania."

As the limo came to a stop, Feuerstein looked at Peterson and waited for a confirmation of his orders, which the president of entertainment finally gave by a quick nod of his head.

"Good." The CEO reached for the door handle when the driver failed to open it for him. Another employee he would have to straighten out.

Kelly closed her laptop and started gathering her bags. She watched the CEO pull on the handle twice, then a third time. He reached for the lock on the door and pulled up on it, but it slipped through his fingers. Feuerstein angrily slammed his hand down on the intercom to the driver's compartment.

"Unlock the goddamn door!"

The slim locks popped up, down, up, and then down again in rapid movements that made them all flinch.

Peterson reached over and used the electric lock mechanism to pop the door locks, but the same rapid movements repeated. "What the hell is going on?" Lionel leaned over near Kelly and slammed his palm against the glass partition. "Open the fucking door, you moron!"

Kelly flinched at the loudness of Peterson's voice. She half turned in her seat. Through the glass, she saw the driver's shadow sitting motionlessly. Then without preamble the car's interior temperature dropped by about thirty degrees, frosting all the glass.

"What kind of fucking idiots do you employ here?" He slammed his hand on the glass, then repeated the move again. This time it was answered by the large black limousine rocking hard to the right and then the left. Kelly grabbed for the seat belt that she hadn't bothered to use. Feuerstein lowered his hands to the seat, bracing himself against the violent rocking.

"Jesus Christ!" Peterson screamed. He was thrown against his door just as the glass partition cracked. The break zigzagged downward and disappeared into the seat frame.

The glass broke free, showering them with tinted shards, and the radio came on. The electronic numbers scaled up and then down, far faster than the radio was capable of. Soon they started catching words from different stations. Although they had to be random, they came through as a full sentence.

"They are mine . . . they are mine . . . they are mine . . . they are mine. . . ."

"What the fuck?" Peterson said. The rocking of the car increased.

Kelly closed her eyes, praying for the assault on the car to stop. The radio volume increased, lowered, and then increased again, enough so all three put their hands over their ears.

"Mine . . . mine . . . mine . . . mine . . . THEY   ARE MINE!!!"

Suddenly everything stopped. Then the door next to Feuerstein opened and he was helped from the car. Peterson slid over and followed the CEO. Then Kelly slapped the laptop from her lap and got out as fast as she could. All three stood shaking and looking at the now normal limousine.

"Why the hell didn't you unlock the fucking doors?" Peterson advanced on the driver, who was looking around as if he were lost.

"What? I just did."

All three of them looked at the driver as if he had lost his mind.

"Was there a problem?" the driver asked, noticing the terror in their faces.

It was Kelly who started laughing first. The CEO turned and started for the elevator. Peterson watched them both as if they had truly lost their minds.

"What the fuck are you laughing about?" he asked as Kelly reached into the car to gather her things.

"I'm laughing at the fucking look on your face." Kelly stepped up to Peterson, looking at him closely. "Suddenly just about anything is possible, isn't it?"

"Why, because we have a bad driver and a malfunctioning car? That just falls in line with every other aspect of this fucked-up special." Peterson reached into the limo for the crystal cut decanter of whiskey and uncorked it.

"Keep thinking that way, Lionel, but you know and I know that house is building power. It's starting to reach out to everyone involved."

Peterson watched Kelly hurry to catch up with the old man. He took a quick swallow of the whiskey, and then he looked over at the driver, who still looked totally lost and confused. Peterson offered him the bottle. The driver looked taken aback, but then he accepted the offer.

"Yeah, what the fuck's the difference? You may be working here long after my ass is fired."

Peterson accepted the bottle back from the driver and took another long pull from the crystal decanter. Then he kicked the limousine, startling the man next to him.

"Yeah, they may be yours, you motherfucker, but this"—he

splashed whiskey onto the limo and then showed off the decanter—"is mine . . . *MINE!*"

The Waldorf-Astoria, New York, New York

Jason Sanborn, George Cordero, and John Lonetree stood at the door and watched Leonard Sickles pace back and forth in his long white boxer shorts and T-shirt. His baseball cap was turned sideways on his head.

"You woke me up to tell me Professor Gabe wants me to break into state death records and the Lindemann Historical Society? I thought you dudes was going out into the world to get this information tomorrow. What do you need me for?"

"John thinks the house is trying to separate us and attack us piecemeal," Jason said. He placed his pipe in his mouth and then rolled his eyes at Lonetree.

Leonard stopped in his tracks and turned to the three men at the door.

"What do you mean, attack? Are you serious?"

"Look, kid, Gabriel wants you to do this; so can you do it and still complete your other electronic work, or not?" Lonetree said.

The look on Leonard's face changed. He turned and grabbed a robe. They had been joined by Jenny Tilden, who stood next to George Cordero.

"Sorry, I didn't feel like being alone in my room," she said. She looked much better than she had earlier in the evening.

"I'm sure we all quite understand, my dear," Sanborn offered. He wished he could light his pipe.

"Damn, man, doesn't anyone sleep around here?" Leonard asked as he came back to the door, tying off the hotel bathrobe. "Yeah, I can do both jobs," he said. "I can farm out the computer theft through a friend of mine in LA. But if he gets caught, it's going to cost someone a lot of money."

"Ten thousand dollars for the information we need," Sanborn said, sucking on his empty pipe.

"Excuse me, but can we discuss this inside the room? It's getting cold out here," Jennifer said, crossing her thin arms over her chest. At the moment, the hallway lights and the room lights started flickering.

"She's right. Did someone leave open a window or something?" Sanborn looked around the empty hallway.

Lonetree and Leonard saw it first—a large transparent shadow that closed in behind Jenny and Sanborn. It seemed to rise up through the expensive carpet. John tried to react as the hallway lights dimmed, but he and the other men were pushed forward into the room and the door slammed, closing them inside. Whatever it was had completely sealed them off from Jennifer, who was still outside in the hallway. John tried desperately to disentangle himself from the three other men. Leonard was on the bottom of the fallen pile, screaming for everyone to get off.

Outside, Jennifer screamed and a loud thump smashed into the closed door. Then the door rattled as Jenny tried to turn the handle. She started pounding and slapping at the wood.

"Get off. It's out there with her!" Lonetree screamed. He literally lifted Cordero and Sanborn off of him and dashed for the door on his hands and knees. The room was warm, but when John touched the wooden door he felt the extreme cold emanating from the hallway. Jenny was crying and still slapping her hand against the door. Then she screamed again and the pounding and slapping stopped.

"What the fuck is happening?!" Leonard shouted. He finally gained his feet and ran for the door to help Lonetree.

John managed to pull the door partway open, but whatever was on the far side pulled it closed again. Leonard threw his own minimal weight into the battle and this time the door opened a foot. A large black hand made of mist reached inside and pulled the door closed with a hard slam. Both men screamed and fell back, wide-eyed.

"Goddamn it, help us!" Lonetree shouted to Cordero and Sanborn.

Outside they heard Jennifer scream and then heard a choking sound. The men grabbed for the door again.

"No, no, no . . ." John was saying over and over as they cracked the door once more. This time, with all of their strength, they had it almost all the way open. None dared to remove their hands while they had the advantage. A flood of freezing air rushed through the opening.

"Jenny, can you get inside?!" John yelled.

Jennifer Tilden's arm snaked in through the doorway. Leonard freed one of his hands and grabbed for it. He was slapped back by an invisible force that knocked him against the bed, and the small black man somersaulted against the wall. George watched, stunned, but he quickly recovered and took Leonard's place. He reached out and pulled as hard as he could. He was hit by an electrical discharge that made his eyes widen and his body shake, but his strength had proved the difference. Jennifer tumbled through the opening and a moment later the men lost control of the door. It slammed shut and bodies went flying. As Jennifer rolled over, holding her throat, she saw the door frost over. It started bending inward, cracking the material as the thing on the other side pushed.

"Jesus!" John stood and slammed his large body against the bulging door. Once his weight seemed to be doing the job, the room started to warm up. Just as they thought their visitor was done, ten loud blows sounded against the wood of the door. The blows were struck so hard that John Lonetree's head was thrust forward with every strike. Then the room fell silent and the lights stopped flickering.

"It's gone," George said from his knees. "Fuck me, it's gone." He reached out for Jenny. "You okay?" When she reached out to take George's hand, he flinched away as if afraid to touch her. Jennifer didn't notice the strange look on Cordero's face. She shook her head while holding her throat, and tried to sit up.

Leonard sat heavily on the edge of the bed. "This is one bad motherfucker. Look at that," he said, pointing at the door.

It was cracked from top to bottom, straight down the middle.

"I thought ghosts couldn't form that kind of power," Sanborn said. His pipe was hanging upside down in his mouth.

John turned away from the door and went to Jenny's side. He looked back at the large crack.

"We're dealing with more than your ordinary ghost. We have something here that can reach out and crush the life right out of you."

Sanborn reached out and touched the crack in the door.

"Just as Professor Kennedy has said all along."

"I don't know about the rest of you, but I can't do this," George Cordero said. He watched the door warily, as if he expected the entity to start up again.

"You promised Gabriel you would see it through," Lonetree said.

"I didn't promise to stay here and die, and that's exactly what will happen if we stay." He looked pointedly at Jenny.

"What do you know that you're not telling us? What did you perceive when that thing was at the door?" Lonetree persisted.

Cordero went to the desk chair and sat down hard. He placed his hands over his face and then slowly looked up.

"I had the distinct feeling, when we were holding that door open, that this thing was just playing with us. It was enjoying it, because deep down it likes scaring people, because it's not afraid of us. It's showing off. And we propose to walk right into its lair and try to kill it?"

"Yes, that's exactly what we are going to do," Lonetree said as he looked from face to face. "And I think you're wrong. At the end of that encounter, it was angry. We beat it by sticking together and fighting it together."

"It's waiting for us in that house, John, do you understand?" Cordero said. He lowered his head. He couldn't look at the others any longer, especially Jenny.

"Yeah, well, if that motherfucker wants me, it better bring a lunch for the long night ahead, because Too Smart Sickles don't run from nothin'," Leonard said with as much bravado as he could muster.

"That's what I mean, you stupid little bastard. We're the lunch."

That quieted Leonard's bravado. George stood and looked at the others.

"I'm sorry. Tell Gabe I just couldn't do it." He reached into his jacket pocket and tossed the envelope that held UBC's check onto the nightstand. He held Jenny's gaze as he left the room, not even hesitating at the cracked and broken door.

Summer Place had just eliminated one of its antagonists. Now it was going after two who were a little closer to home, just a ways up the road from Bright River, Pennsylvania.

Professor Gabriel Kennedy and Julie Reilly were about to meet the entity that lived in Summer Place face-to-face.

Ten Miles South of Bright River, Pennsylvania

The car clung to the depressions in the road like some fairy tale gone horribly wrong. Kennedy could barely see the road in certain spots, and that made him slow to a crawl. It wasn't until they moved past the bends and drops that he was able to speed up. The rain had vanished and was replaced by a heavy mist that allowed the wipers to go intermittently, but the covering of water on the windshield was still significant. Every time the car vanished into a dip in the road, the fog seemed to climb back out with them, and John Lonetree's warning kept echoing in their heads.

"Are we still on Route Six?" Julie asked when Kennedy slowed the car to ten miles an hour at the bottom of a small hill.

"Well, I don't remember turning anywhere, so I imagine we're still on course."

Julie's cell phone was equipped with a global positioning system. She moved it around, but the signal that she had received back in Bright Waters was gone.

"I can't get a damn thing on this," she said as Gabriel stopped the car. Outside the windshield was a wall of swirling, solid white fog. "Please tell me we're still a long way from Summer Place?" she said with a nervous smile.

"You, the nonbeliever, are asking me that?" Kennedy moved his foot off the brake and started forward again.

"The conditions are conducive to my question."

"Summer Place is thirty-five miles back in the other direction." Kennedy turned on the emergency flashers. "I'm more concerned about some farm boy coming along and plowing into us in this soup."

"Look," Julie said, squinting into the fog, "I'm going to take things as they come, through Halloween. A clean slate. Can we stop the jousting until we get through this?"

"I think right about now is a good time to lay down the weapons and at least get through this." Gabriel chanced a look over at Julie. He wanted to say something about the fear on her face but decided to let it slide.

They reached the bottom of a large dip in the road, and both were relieved when the car started to climb out of the depression. But the relief was short-lived. Without warning, the car jerked and then sped up, then jerked again. The lights dimmed and then the car stalled.

"No, no, not here. . . ." Kennedy brought the coasting car to a stop. He shut off the dim headlights and then tried to start the car again. They both heard the clicking of the solenoid, and then even that sound vanished, swallowed by the thickening fog.

"Oh, this is good," Julie said. "What did you do?"

Kennedy stopped trying the ignition and turned toward Julie. "What the hell do you think I did?"

"Well, we're not out of gas, are we?"

Kennedy looked away and shook his head, but still turned on the light switch to check. "Yes, there's gas."

Julie watched as the fog outside the car swirled and eddied. It was growing thicker by the minute and she wasn't liking it at all.

"Maybe that farm boy you were talking about will come along."

Kennedy looked at his wristwatch. "Not likely, at four in the morning."

"I know . . . the news van from Philadelphia will be coming by," she said, with the hope of a drowning woman reaching for a life buoy.

"They would have turned off on Highway Seventeen, six miles back."

"Why didn't we turn off at the same place?" she asked accusingly.

"Because we're going to New York and they're going to Philadelphia."

"Oh, sorry, it's just that—"

Something slammed into the car from behind, sending them four feet along the road with the locked tires screeching. Julie's head slammed against the backrest and Kennedy lost his glasses.

"What the fuck?" Gabriel quickly opened his door and stepped out. Julie, rubbing the back of her neck, reached out to try to stop him, but she was too late.

Gabriel looked around the car to see who had come up behind them blindly and struck them. The road, as far as the fog would allow him to see, was empty. The damage to the back of the car looked light. The trunk was sprung, so he reached out and slammed it down. It didn't catch, and he slammed it again. As it closed and locked, he saw that the lights inside the car had gone dark once more.

Julie opened the car door and stepped out. A breeze picked up, moving the fog in strange eddies and swirls. It rustled the large trees that lined the two-lane highway, and at the same time the air grew colder. Julie looked over at Kennedy, who held up a hand to stop her question before she could voice it. The wind slowly died, but the current of cold air stayed with them.

They both jumped when the car's headlights came on and then went off. The horn blared for a few seconds and then just as suddenly stopped. The radio snapped to life and then went silent.

"Tell me you've had an electrical system go haywire like this before?" Julie asked nervously, trying her best to see through the heavy veil of white.

Kennedy didn't answer. He moved slowly to the right side of the car, nearer to Julie.

"Something is out there, isn't it?" she asked. Kennedy kept his eyes on the side of the road, where they could barely see the soft outline of the large pine trees.

Gabe tried his best to keep his voice even and reassuring. As much as he would have liked to scare the hell out of this woman a few days ago, he now found he wanted to reassure her that things were fine.

"Ms. Reilly, we're in the mountains. There's always something out there."

A darker shade of fog seemed to break free of one of the larger trees. It passed by both of them and vanished into the whiteness in front of the car.

"Did you see that?" Julie took an involuntary step toward Gabriel.

"It went over there," he said, pointing.

As they watched the swirling fog, the black mist appeared again. This time it formed in front of the car and stayed. The veil was about thirteen or fourteen feet in height and just about eight in width, and Gabriel could swear he could hear deep, harsh breathing. The mist didn't move, as if it were studying the two people staring at it.

"Okay, this is the mountains, but this *something* doesn't look like it belongs here."

"Get your camera and recorder—go," he said, so low she thought she hadn't heard him right.

Julie stepped toward the car without taking her eyes from the hanging mist that stood its ground ten feet in front of them. "You think now is the time for taking its picture?"

"You seem so sure that it's cognizant of what it's doing."

Julie scrambled around the front seat and found the small camera and recorder. "Well," she hissed through closed teeth as she brought the camera up, "I say that because I've never seen two distinct shades of fog before . . . and add to that, the goddamn thing is breathing."

"Point taken." Gabriel took the small digital recorder from Julie's hand.

A stream of darkness broke away from the main body of the mist and shot forward, collecting into the shape of a large hand. It seemed as though it were about to slap the camera out of Julie's hand. She flinched, but the hand pulled back. It came forward again and then stopped, moving around the camera's lens as if it didn't know what it was facing, or whether the camera was a danger to it. Julie let out a small cry as the smell hit her nostrils.

"Hold your ground," Gabriel said. He stepped forward two paces and placed himself between the camera and the mist.

"Professor, I'm about to pee my pants. Believe me, I'm not moving."

"You're a long way from Summer Place, and I know you're not that strong," he said loudly to the mist in front of him.

The misty hand pulled away from the camera, as if Gabriel had shocked it somehow. Then they heard the deep rumble of a laugh. The hand shot forward and slapped the camera out of Julie's shaking hands. It flew twenty feet into the tree line and smashed against one of the pines.

"Did you take my student? Did you make that young man kill tonight? Who are you?"

The mist backed away as the laugh rumbled again. It was like something clearing its throat from deep inside of hell. The sound seemed to come from all around them.

"I am that I am."

The words were clear and made Julie shiver in the increasingly cold night.

"Is quoting God supposed to impress us?"

Just as the words cleared Gabriel's lips, the mist came forward. This time they both saw the outline of a humanoid form. The hand came up again and struck out at Kennedy, hitting him across the face. The laugh sounded again as the hand retreated. Gabriel jerked and then looked back with equal determination.

"Not very impressive. I still say you're too far from the house to be effective."

The laugh sounded again. Then the mist formed into a ball and moved. It came straight at Julie and then stopped, reformed, and then she heard the sound of sniffing. The thing was smelling her, she realized. She cowered away and closed her eyes. The hand came up and felt her hair. The smell of the mist was penetrating her senses. She managed to open her eyes and look at Kennedy, silently pleading for him to do something.

The mist expanded and the giant hand swept out, brushing the fog aside.

"Oh, God," Julie said.

Summer Place sat in its small, peaceful valley two miles away, brightly lit and inviting. Somehow they had driven in the wrong direction.

"Home," said the gruff, deep voice. "Come home, Gabriel."

"Am I yours? Like the others?"

The laughter was deep and loud and this time it didn't end.

"Stop it, stop it!" Julie shouted and ran to the open car door. Just as she reached it, it slammed closed. Then the driver's side door slammed shut. The darkened mist shot around Julie and slammed her against the car. Gabriel stepped forward, but the mist shoved him out of the way, as if he were made of paper.

Suddenly the night air warmed and the sound of birds came through the fog. The mist seemed to hesitate, its laughter fading. It drifted toward the front of the car.

"There's something else here," Gabriel said.

"Oh, God," Julie whimpered. She slid down the side of the car until she was seated on the ground with her hands over her face.

"No, don't you feel it? This thing doesn't like it, whatever it is. Listen." Turning away from the mist, he thought he could hear talking—many voices, soft and close by. The black mist seemed to hiss. Then it turned and dispersed into the thinning fog.

Gabriel pulled Julie to her feet just as the car started on its own, making them both yell in fright. Julie smashed her face and body into Gabriel's, and the unexpected force almost made his already unstable knees buckle. He strained to hear the voices, but they were slowly fading away.

"It's over." Kennedy stroked Julie's hair. "Look," he said, giving her a gentle nudge.

Julie looked up. "What?" she asked.

"Summer Place. It was never there. It tried to scare us. I was right—it doesn't have the strength to do its magic this far from the house. It can conjure and frighten, but that's all." He stepped back around the car and opened Julie's door, assisting her in. He then quickly went around to the driver's side door, looking to his left once again to make sure Summer Place truly was gone. He drove off as the last of the strange fog lifted.

"What happened?" Julie asked.

"Something stopped the house from having its fun. Several somethings, it sounded like. Are you all right?"

"Fuck no, I'm not all right. What the hell's wrong with you?"

Kennedy smiled for the first time in forty minutes.

"Can I ask what is so funny?"

Kennedy held up the small digital tape recorder.

"I just recorded the opening for your television special."

"I really don't give a shit about that right now." She turned away to watch the trees slip by out the window.

"Oh, I think you should open with that, followed closely by your official apology for the seven years of hell you and Jackson put me through."

"You'll need more than that to convince Damian Jackson," she said, carefully not mentioning the fact that she had been convinced.

Kennedy smiled and stepped on the gas. "I think that can be arranged."

"Yeah?"

"Yes. I think Summer Place wants everyone to know it's alive and in charge."

"It may be in charge, but it sure as hell is not alive."

In silence, they turned onto the highway heading for New York.

Thirty-five miles away, every door in Summer Place, from the front entrance hall to the attic pull-down, creaked, was thrown, or fell open, and the laughter reached every shadowed corner throughout the house. The only door that remained closed was the double doorway at the end of the third-floor hallway.

The sewing room was still and silent.

Lionel Peterson perched on the edge of his desk at the New York office, nearly sliding off the corner but catching his balance just in time. His drink spilled onto his pants but he paid no attention; he was basically covered in alcohol already. In the parking lot a few hours before, Lionel discovered something about himself that he had hoped never to learn: he was, at heart, a coward. Lionel had failed the one and only test of physical bravery that had ever arisen in his forty-two years, and he hated it. His grip tightened on the glass in his left hand and the phone in his right hand, with the memory of how trapped he had felt inside that car with Feuerstein and Kelly. The two of them had handled the situation far better than he had, especially that damned Delaphoy. Oh, he knew the woman was as scared as he, but she had recovered where he failed to do so. His hand shook as he raised the glass to his lips.

"This better be good," the voice said on the other end of the phone.

"Yeah?" Peterson slurred the word. "Well, it is."

"Mr. Peterson, you sound drunk. If this is a social call,

let me tell you, I don't appreciate it," Wallace Lindemann said from his bedroom across town.

"Social call?" Peterson laughed. "For some reason I don't think you or I get that many social calls at four in the morning these days. I mean, with you being in financial straits and me being tossed about like a man clinging to a fucking life raft."

"What is this about? I don't need commentary on my personal life."

Peterson drained the whiskey and allowed the empty glass to fall from his fingers to the carpeted floor.

"The matter we discussed this evening, I want you to proceed with it. How soon can you get them out there?"

There was silence on the other end of the line. Peterson swayed and placed his left hand on the desk to steady himself. He closed his eyes until the dizzy spell passed. When he opened them again, he looked around the office. He no longer trusted his senses after the events in the parking garage.

"My guess is that they won't come until the day after tomorrow."

"Not good enough. They have to be there in the morning. Pay them what they want—my money—but get them there first thing in the morning."

"Are you nuts, Peterson? These people are professors at Columbia University; they're only considering this job because they think Kennedy is a nutcase who makes them all look bad. As much as they despise him, they'll never come at such short notice. I can get them the morning of the show, and that's it."

"Get them there in the morning. The crew is going to be there a day early to set up."

"That's not in the contract; I won't—"

"When are you going to understand, Lindemann, that you don't have a fucking thing to say about it? Corporate will do what they want, and you can sit and suck on it. If you want that house to sell, you better do as I say, because if this special airs and Kennedy proves that Summer Place is what he says it is, we're both fucked."

"What's happened to change your mind about that ridiculous claim of his?"

Peterson fell silent. He knew he had to stand up before he fell over. As he did, he heard a buzzing. His heart pounded until he realized it was the overnight cleaning man, sweeping by his open door with the floor buffer. He closed his eyes and wanted to cry at his failure to keep his composure.

"Just get the cleaners out to the house. Neither of us needs Summer Place to demonstrate what it's capable of. I want that television special to be a mundane, boring tour promoting the sale of your house, and that's it."

"Okay, but it will cost you. These guys, as much as they hate Kennedy, want to be paid."

"I'll write you a check as soon as I can sign my name without shaking. Now get that house straightened out. Kennedy and the others will be there tomorrow afternoon."

Peterson placed the phone on his desk without hanging it up. He walked to the front of the office and stared out of the large window that looked out onto the street far below. He swiped at a tear that coursed down his cheek, slapping it away far harder than he intended to. He was ashamed, and knew he could be possibly ending his career, but after tonight that was a backseat consideration. He wanted to strike back at Summer Place and take Kelly Delaphoy down with it.

Far below, he watched the quiet streets of Manhattan, and knew he could never look at anything so innocent the same way again.

Summer Place had ruined his life.

The Waldorf-Astoria, New York, New York

George sat in the lobby lounge drinking a glass of milk—an order that had drawn questioning looks from several of the businessmen around him, and a not-so-friendly glance from the large bartender. With his tie down and jacket off, George sipped at the chilled milk and stared at the polished bar top.

The speakers, hidden in the corners of the ostentatious lobby bar, played a Muzak version of "Dirty Deeds Done Dirt Cheap" by AC/DC. That irritated George even further. Good society could screw up the simplest of pleasures. Cordero shook his head. It was a good way to assist his departure out of the city.

As he took a drink of his milk, he felt the eyes on him from the back of the room. He knew who it was without turning around, only because he and the man watching him were as close as two men could get in ability. He also sensed the woman with him, so he just waited.

As John Lonetree started into the lobby lounge, Jennifer Tilden stopped him. She gently tugged on his coat and then shook her head when he glanced down. She pointed to her own chest, indicating that she would be the one to talk to George. She pointed John to an empty table and went to ease herself onto the bar stool next to George's.

"Yes, ma'am?" the bartender asked. He looked as though he were expecting another strange request from the tired and worn-looking little woman who had chosen to sit next to the milk drinker.

"Double Wild Turkey, please." She placed both hands on the bar and laced her fingers together. She looked at the mirror above the bar. George continued to stare into his glass of milk.

"I thought you didn't drink," he said, giving her a sideways glance.

"No. Bobby Lee McKinnon didn't drink. I do."

"A musician who didn't drink? That's a little hard to believe," George said, turning to face her.

She smiled at the bartender when he placed the crystal glass of Wild Turkey in front of her. Jennifer impressed both George and the server, downing the drink. She placed it on the bar and slid it toward the large man. "Another—with ice this time."

When the bartender left, Jenny turned and smiled at Cordero. "We want you to stay, George."

Cordero smiled and then turned away. He raised the glass of milk and paused with it in front of his face. Its pure white seemed to mesmerize him for a moment. Then he suddenly set the glass down.

"Do you know what it's like to just simply touch someone and know—I mean, really know—what is going to happen to them? To see what was in their past, to know who they are in an instant, far better than anyone's ever known them before?"

"Only with Bobby Lee. Only, I think that I cheated a little. Your ability is what's called, at least in theory, electrical symbiosis exchange—the exchange of thought and memory through touch." She accepted the second drink from the bartender, and this time she sipped the cold whiskey. She then looked at George and smiled. "I wasn't under the whole time Bobby Lee was in possession of me. I was able to continue some of my work. Electrical memory and thought exchange was a pet theory I developed between assaults."

George glanced at Jenny and shook his head.

"So," she said as she raised her glass again, "you touched one of us in the room during the attack and got a bad vibe? Or maybe a sordid vision of one of our futures?"

George watched as Jenny slowly took a drink from her glass. She looked at him with the gentle eyes of someone who knew what true torment was. He also felt he could tell her the truth—the truth about a lot of things.

"When I was twelve years old, after my mother passed away after a long battle with cancer, my father put me on tour. You know, the daytime television circuit, Art Linkletter, Mike Douglas, shows like that. They would bring people out of the audience and I would take their hand and tell them the light side of where they had been, and sometimes where they were going. My father would insist, drill it into me, that under no circumstances was I to delve into the darker side of people and their nature. You know, marital affairs, things like that. He insisted it was all for fun." He looked at Jenny and then just as quickly looked away. "Fun when we were on-

stage. Offstage, he was a driven man. Money was everything to him. Onstage, loving and the pillar of fatherhood;
off, he was cold as ice."

"Is your father still alive?" Jenny asked, pushing her drink
away.

"No, he died . . . alone and unloved."

Jenny lowered her eyes. George wanted to tell the story,
so she just let him venture forth without pushing him.

"I never really questioned my father," he continued, "as
to why there was never any physical contact between us. Oh,
he would ruffle my hair onstage and act the part of the proud
parent, but every time I tried to get close off the stage, he
would be, like I said, cold. He would pat me on my head, at
the most. That was as loving as the man ever got."

Jennifer looked up and into the mirror over the bar. John
Lonetree watched them as he sipped a glass of beer. He was
watching with curious eyes. It was if he knew Jenny was there
to witness George become completed, as if there were a
cleansing going on. Jenny thought that maybe a little bit of
John—and maybe even a bit of George—had rubbed off on
her in the short time she had known them.

"One time, I had flubbed up pretty bad on a morning show
in Minneapolis. Afterward, he drank most of the day. When
he came back to the hotel, I really saw who my father was
for the first time. He slapped me around pretty good and told
me that after my failure on the morning show, three other
shows down the line had canceled." George drained the glass
of milk and then shoved the glass away from him as if it were
the bad memory. He rubbed a hand across his face.

"What happened, George?" she asked, draining her own
glass.

"After he passed out, I went into his room and watched
him sleep for the longest time. I saw his eyes moving underneath his lids, and that fascinated me like no other sight ever
has—even to this day. He was dreaming and I knew it, even
before I ever heard the theory of rapid eye movement. I knew
that son of a bitch was having a nightmare. I couldn't fathom

what could scare this man who so terrified me. I was so curious that, for the first time I could ever remember, I placed my hands on him; one on top of his head, one on his face. I could feel his eyelids moving underneath my touch. The feeling continued to fascinate me beyond reason, even when I was shown what he was dreaming. I closed my eyes and I became him. I was inside of him when he went to visit my mother in the hospital. I was inside when she spoke her last words to him. I heard them with his ears, I saw myself with his memory of me. I heard her say to my father, 'Love George, he needs you so.' I wanted to cry, which at the time was at cross-purposes to invading my father."

George closed his eyes, reliving the memory. Jenny saw the sadness, the terror, and the love for his mother in his eyes as they welled with tears.

"I watched my father. He slowly took a white pillow from underneath my mother's head and raised it up. I felt his hands as he placed the pillow over my mother's face and pushed. It was like while I was inside of him, I was adding my weight to his bulk. We both pushed that pillow as hard as we could. I remember fighting inwardly against the despicable way my father felt as he murdered my mother. There was no peaceful decision to allow her to leave this life with what little dignity she had left. It was a selfish, cold-blooded act to rid himself of a drain on time and resources. I screamed for him to stop. Then I could feel him, beneath my hands, becoming aware that I was invading his memories. I remember when his eyes popped open, but I still kept my hands where they were. I pressed as hard as the memory of my father pushing on that pillow—harder and harder. I saw the panic in my father's eyes as he realized that I knew. It was a trapped, animal look."

Jennifer swallowed. She could not imagine what George had gone through, witnessing his mother's murder at the hands of his very own father. She looked up with tears in her own eyes and saw the concern on Lonetree's face in the bar's mirror.

"My father gathered the strength to throw me off. He jumped from his bed and vomited. It was like pure evil was spewing forth from the man. It wasn't guilt, it was that someone else knew what a coward he truly was."

"What happened?" Jenny asked. George wiped his eyes with the palm of his right hand, as if he wanted to gouge out the vision from his memory.

"My father killed himself the next day without ever saying a word to me. He stepped off the street in Minneapolis into the path of a car. He died hating me for what I knew."

"It wasn't you who killed your mother, George, it was him. You need not feel guilty about anything."

George laughed, and then slapped the bar with his open hand. He swiped the last of his tears away.

"My mother? No, I didn't kill my mother. But I wished my father dead, and when I took his hand on that street that day, he didn't even realize what I was doing. I thought about that small little step off the sidewalk, and that small push of thought ended up being just as physical as actually pushing him in front of that car. No, I didn't kill my mother, but I killed that man who was my father. And you know what?"

Jenny sat silently, waiting.

"I wanted to do it. I had thought all night and all morning on just how it could be done, but I couldn't find the answer, or the bravery. Not until the opportunity presented itself. Then I pushed my father with my thoughts as I reached out and took his hand that final time."

They sat at the bar without speaking, George with his eyes heavy and Jenny with hers locked on the mirror, as if drawing strength from John, who still watched them from his table.

"I am sick and tired of death." George looked at Jenny. "Do you understand?"

"George, I apologize for bothering you. I know what it's like to have an ability you hate absolutely having. Whether you stay or go, we will respect any decision you make."

Jenny slid off the bar stool and squeezed George's

shoulder. She turned to leave him to think things through, but he quickly reached out and grabbed Jenny's hand. John Lonetree stood and started forward, but she shook her head no. John, observant as ever, stopped and watched from the distance. George squeezed Jenny's hand without looking at her.

"Don't go into Summer Place. Leave the East Coast and go anywhere but Pennsylvania. Hell, come away with me. Just don't go into that fucking house."

Jennifer reached up with her free hand and placed it over his.

"I have to go. I have to help my friend, just like he would help me. I know you're scared. You go, George, and no one will think the worse of you for it, please believe me. I think you need to—"

"It's you, goddamn it." He turned and faced her, his bloodshot eyes bearing down on her. A fire had grown in him and he was allowing it air to breathe. "I had a vision that would be you killed. You'll walk into Summer Place and you will never walk out. It wasn't clear, but I saw a part of you staying in that house and never leaving. Don't go!"

John Lonetree started forward and pried George's hand from Jenny. As he moved her behind him, Cordero deflated. He tossed a large bill on the bar and then got up and left without looking back. John started to go after him but Jenny stopped him.

"Let him go. He needs to go, John."

"What did he say to you?" Lonetree watched George Cordero disappear out the front doors of the Waldorf.

"Nothing." Jenny looked away. "Can we go? I need to sleep some more." She looped her thin hand through John's thick arm. "And I need you to watch over me, so I hope you like the floor."

"No place I would rather be," John answered. He knew Jenny was holding back the truth, but he didn't press about it.

As for Jenny, she suddenly wished that more than just John was with her. She also wished in a small way for Bobby Lee

McKinnon—he would have understood what they were facing far better than any of the rest of them could.

Maybe Bobby would know what was stalking Summer Place.

At seven o'clock, not long after the city of New York came alive, seven large tractor-trailers pulled out of the old Brooklyn Navy Yard, where UBC had leased space for its production facility maintenance and technical field support. The trucks carried all the elements that would make the live broadcast from Summer Place possible. Cameras, sound systems, production vans, backup generators, and even a portable commissary for the production crew. This was to be the largest live production in the history of UBC and it would only fall short of the Super Bowl for total coverage.

Several of the early risers who worked inside the Brooklyn Navy Yard watched with mild curiosity as the seven large trucks pulled out. Never had they seen such activity from the UBC buildings before. It was almost as if the network were mobilizing for war. As the string of trucks pulled out and onto the Brooklyn-Queens Expressway, they were followed closely by twenty UBC field vehicles, all starting their journey to a single place.

Tomorrow was Halloween, and their destination was Summer Place.

15 Bright Waters, Pennsylvania

Detective Damian Jackson walked out of his room at the "Come As You Are" Motel. The day was bright and the weather mild after the heavy thunderstorm the night before, as if the small town had been cleansed of the sordid events of the late night. Jackson was freshly shaven and wore his newest suit. He was in an exceptional mood because of the phone call he had just received from his contact at the NYPD. A convoy of UBC vehicles had just left

Brooklyn on their way to Pennsylvania, and that meant
Kennedy would be coming with them. It seemed that UBC
was attempting to take possession of the summer retreat before the contracted date. He was curious to see how Wallace
Lindemann took the news.

   He stopped just outside of his door, slowly placed his hat
on his head, and whistled an enthusiastic tune. His quest to
nail Professor Gabriel Kennedy to the proverbial wall was
close to an end; one that he had foreseen many years before.
He decided he would pay a visit to his guest at the constable's office—Kyle Pritchard might have thought things over
during the night and decided to throw his fellow conspirators under the bus. Jackson would take Kennedy, the Delaphoy woman, and everyone involved in the hoax the night of
the test broadcast, tie it all into the disappearance seven years
ago, and package things up with a nice little bow. Then he
could finally move on with his life—a life that had been on
hold since the cold case labeled "Summer Place" had stalled
out his career.

   Hands in his pockets, he stepped off the sidewalk and
crossed the street, careful to avoid the large puddles of water
from the rain the night before. He hopped the puddles with a
lightness to his step, as if he could just as easily have floated
over them—yes, things were starting to come together since
the reappearance of Kyle Pritchard. Jackson couldn't imagine what the Delaphoy woman was thinking and feeling
since her little scheme had taken the unexpected turn. He
knew his arrival and the murder of her cohost had not been
part of the plan, she had just chosen to bring in the wrong
schizoid to be a part of it. Still, it was a good day to be in
Bright Waters.

   The small town and its people were just starting their day.
At the diner, he could see the curious faces as he strolled by
the very spot where the murder had occurred. He could still
see the outline of the bloodstain and made no effort to skip
out of the way of it. He knew the townspeople were frightened

of him, and that was all well and good to him. He turned to the large window, catching those watching him off guard. He winked and smiled.

Half a block down the street, he stopped in front of the small office of the township's constable. He paused, straightened his coat and hat, and then opened the door.

"Good morning," he said to the heavyset man at the desk. It was obvious that the old man had not gotten as much as a wink of sleep. These kinds of things didn't happen all that much in small towns, and most people were not used to the reality of murder.

"I don't know what's so good about it," the constable said, removing his feet from his desk.

"No sleep?" Jackson asked. He sat on the edge of the constable's desk, a move the heavy set man didn't seem to appreciate.

"If you had to hear that maniac back there—crying one minute, screaming the next—I'd like to see how much sleep *you'd* get."

"Our young houseguest was in distress all night, then?"

"Distress, yeah. Being terrorized by any sound he heard, or screaming every time thunder clapped in the distance . . . I guess you could call it distress." The constable stood with a ring of keys in his hand. "I suppose you want to say good morning to your boy?"

"You bet," Jackson said. "Now may be a good time to get some truth out of him."

"Well, good luck. He's been quiet for the past half hour. And I hope he stays that way until your state boys come to collect him an hour from now."

Jackson frowned, concerned.

"Have you checked on him since he calmed down?" He took the key ring from the slow-moving constable and inserted the key in the lock.

"Why, so he could start up again?"

"Goddamn it." Jackson turned the large key and pushed

the door open. He took the three steps toward the double-cell setup and then he saw it. The key ring slipped from his fingers as he turned away, fixing the constable with a glare.

"Oh, my God," the constable said.

Inside cell number two, Kyle Pritchard had slammed his head so hard through the six-inch gap between the bars that it had pushed through to the other side, ripping off both of his ears and scraping the hair on the sides of his head clean away. The body hung limp inside the cell, with his head on the outside. It was like he had been shoved through with superhuman strength. Jackson flipped on the overhead fluorescents. Examining Pritchard, he came to the quick conclusion that the man had done it to himself. There were bloody footprints on the cell floor, showing the running starts he had made to slam his head through the bars. Jackson could visualize maybe three or four attempts, running from the far wall to the bars, until finally he hit it with enough force to push his entire head through. Damian felt for a pulse. The bones of Pritchard's neck crunched under his fingers. Then he looked down to the man's wrists. It looked as though he had tried to chew through the skin and into his veins. Putting his head through the bars hadn't been the first suicide method he'd attempted.

"What is that?"

Jackson removed his hat and looked up. Written on the far wall, in what had to have been his own blood, were Kyle Pritchard's last words.

"I await," Jackson read aloud.

"What the hell does that mean?" the constable asked. Jackson turned and left the cell area.

Jackson put his hat back on and stepped outside into the clean morning air, distancing himself from the foul smell inside. Pritchard's body had voided itself of unneeded material, and the smell hung in his nostrils. The constable followed behind him.

"Jesus Christ," Jackson mumbled to himself.

"Why did he write something like that?" the constable

asked. Damian squinted up into the bright sunshine. He knew it could not restore the good mood he had been in before.

"It's just the ramblings of an insane man," the detective answered. He turned back to the constable. "Take pictures, and then get that doctor you use as a coroner over here. Tell him you have more work for him. I want him pronounced dead so we can get the two bodies to Philadelphia for a proper autopsy as soon as possible."

As the constable turned away, he saw several townspeople emerge from the diner. They watched him with suspicion as he tried to keep down the bile that threatened his throat. He swallowed and crossed the street. When he thought he was far enough away, he turned back, the townies still watching him. An old man in worn overalls stepped forward into the middle of the dead street.

"Why don't you get yourself to that house and get it over with?"

Jackson straightened and looked the man in the eye.

"What do you mean?" he asked.

"You outsiders have stirred something up that was meant to be left alone. Now you go and stop what it is those TV folks are up to. No good can come from it."

The old man turned and joined his mates on the sidewalk. They all turned back into the diner without a backward glance at Jackson.

"Whole goddamn town is nuts," he said as he moved off toward the motel's office.

All the same, Damian Jackson of the Pennsylvania State Police was about to do just what the old man had suggested.

His next stop was Summer Place, where he and Gabriel Kennedy would settle things once and for all.

One way or another, this thing was going to end.

Delaware Water Gap, Pennsylvania

Almost halfway back to New York, Gabriel and Julie had gotten the call telling them that the schedule for taking possession of Summer Place had been moved up two days. Instead of heading all the way back, they had found the nearest motel. Leonard was still at the network working on his equipment and would be the last to arrive later that night; everyone else was in the caravan of network cars following the production vans into Pennsylvania. John had passed along news of George Cordero's change of heart, and Gabriel had no qualms about letting George go. He had been more high-strung than Gabriel had remembered from seven years before.

Gabriel had tossed and turned for hours, finally dozing off at about seven in the morning. It was now close to ten, and although he was bone weary, he forced himself to shower, shave, and try to greet the day with as much enthusiasm as he could muster, even though the network was sorely testing his ability to greet anything in a good way. Summer Place wouldn't react well to a hundred people hanging out on its property for two solid days.

Gabriel opened the door and shielded his eyes from the glaring sun. In the doorway, he removed his corduroy jacket and threw it over his shoulder. Slipping his sunglasses on, he stepped out into the beautiful Pennsylvania day.

"Good morning."

Julie Reilly was sitting on one of those ancient lawn chairs that were painted green and white, the kind with a back in the shape of a fan. She was sitting with her ever-present notebook open in her lap and pen poised over a clean page.

"Why don't you use a laptop like everyone else in the world?"

"I carry enough crap in this thing"—she patted her abnormally large bag—"without being weighted down by six more pounds of cyberspace."

Gabriel adjusted his glasses and nodded. "Uh-huh."

"Breakfast?" she asked, placing her notes back in the giant bag.

Kennedy looked around at the motel's small parking lot. "Yeah, coffee at least."

Julie gestured toward the motel's coffee shop next door.

"I'm afraid I've got a bit of a shocker for you this morning," she said as they started walking.

"And what could be shocking on this lovely day?" he asked.

"Lionel Peterson called. Kyle Pritchard killed himself this morning in the Bright Waters jail."

Kennedy stopped walking and closed his eyes behind the dark glasses. "Why didn't you wake me?"

"Could you have done something about it?"

Gabriel took a deep breath and started walking once more. "I suppose not. Did your boss say how he killed himself?"

"No. He received a call from a very pissed off Damian Jackson. That's all I know."

"So I take it he's not accusing me of murdering the poor bastard?"

Julie smiled but didn't comment. She walked beside Gabriel in silence.

"Let's get the coffee to go; I want to get to Summer Place before the marines do." He opened the café door for Julie. "I'll start the car."

Julie ordered two cups of coffee to go. By the time she made it back to the door, Gabriel had the car waiting. Julie climbed in and before she could fasten her seat belt or place the coffee in the cup holders between the seats, the car was in motion.

"Hey, take it easy. I was here last night, too, you know. I had nothing to do with it."

Kennedy glanced over at her. He had been taking Pritchard's death out on the only person available, and he knew he was wrong for doing it.

"Thanks." He slowed the car while Julie fastened her belt. Then he relaxed and accepted the Styrofoam cup of coffee.

"I didn't know how you took it, but considering how clinical you are, I thought dark and bland would suit you."

For the first time since they had met seven years before, Kennedy actually smiled in her presence.

"Clinical, huh?" He sipped his black coffee.

"Or something like that," she said, returning the smile.

"Well, I guess I have been kind of dark and bland for a while now. But hanging out with you could only make that worse."

"So I guess we won't be getting engaged anytime soon?"

This time they both laughed. For the time being, the day was as beautiful to Gabriel as it would have been for anyone else. The rainstorm of the night before had cleansed everything away, and even Summer Place didn't seem to matter for now.

It was the calm before the storm.

Gabriel had pulled over an hour into their trip back into the Poconos, giving Julie the wheel. He dozed fitfully in the passenger seat, and every once in a while he would mumble in his sleep. Julie would slow the car down to try to catch what the professor was saying. She heard the name Warren over and over, but could make nothing else out. Warren, she knew, was the name of Kennedy's student who had disappeared seven years ago. Unlike Kyle Pritchard and Paul Lowell, he had never turned up in Bright Waters, or anywhere else, for that matter.

They were just outside of Bright River, near enough to Summer Place that Julie was starting to feel an apprehension she hadn't felt before. It was what she imagined traveling through Indian country used to feel like for the settlers crossing the Plains—a warning of hidden dangers ahead of you. Kennedy mumbled once more, this time mentioning the summer retreat by name, and Julie turned her head. Her eyes left the road for only a moment, but when she turned back she nearly ran over a large carcass in the road. She hit the brakes and swerved. The tires caught and she avoided the dead animal by mere inches, but that was just the start of the gauntlet. There were three more dead deer strewn across the roadway, along with several other smaller animals. She struck one of the smaller deer and then swerved off the side of the road, finally bringing the car to a stop.

As she sat staring wide-eyed out the windshield, she felt Gabriel move beside her.

"Now, that was exciting. Did you manage *not* to hit something?" he asked sarcastically as he rubbed his eyes. Julie was breathing heavily, still gripping the steering wheel tightly. Kennedy turned in his seat and saw the dead animals lying in the road. There were even more carcasses off to the sides of the road. He counted seventeen. "I take that back; no one has aim that good." He opened his door and stepped out into the bright early afternoon.

"Fuck," Julie said under her breath. Her heart was finally starting to slow back to its normal pace. When she thought she could manage, she peeled her hand away from the steering wheel and opened the door. She swallowed and then stepped out. Gabriel kneeled beside one of the many deer.

Thinking quickly, Julie reached into the car and grabbed her small camera. She started videotaping what had to have been the most bizarre scene she had ever seen.

"Were they hit by other cars?" she asked, slowly walking to join Kennedy on the right side of the road.

"Not a mark on it." He turned and moved a foot away, to a small squirrel. "This one either. No blood, no damage to the outer skin. It's like they just dropped dead. They've been dead eight to twelve hours, would be my guess."

"But why wouldn't they die in the woods? Why cross into the road like that?" Julie taped Kennedy as he checked the animals. She focused on the dark eyes of one of the dead deer and felt cold chills along her spine.

Kennedy raised his head and looked around. A soft autumn breeze had come to life and was rustling the pine trees lining the road. He looked back the way they had come and saw the steep incline they had just traveled.

"Have you noticed where we are, Ms. Reilly?"

Julie panned the camera around. She could only focus on the animals. The corpses extended far back into the shadows of the trees. She shook her head.

"Look at this, over here." Kennedy crossed over to the

opposite side of the road. Julie followed and looked around but didn't see whatever it was that he was trying to show her. "Look down at the grass," he finally said.

There were tire marks in the grass. She looked from them to the tires on the car, and then it hit her: This was the exact spot where their car had stalled the night before, when the dense fog bank had closed in on them.

"Are you saying these animals may have been dying around us when we were stuck here?" she asked, lowering her camera.

"The time of death is about right. Hell, maybe they continued dying after we left. When we get to Summer Place, I'll have the police check this out. They may want to bring the fish and game people in on it. This is just too much death for one spot in the road, wouldn't you say?" He looked at her with a creepy little grin.

Julie gave him a *go to hell* look and then moved away from the spot where their car had sat the night before.

"You know, for an award-winning investigative reporter, you seem to be close-minded about the obvious. Do you think all of these animals walked out of the woods and then had heart attacks?"

"I admit that it's creepy, but a few dead animals are all we have here, Professor. I'm not going to go running off like a frightened schoolgirl when the boy in her class hands her a frog."

"Even if the frog is dead, and the boy has twenty to thirty more just lying around? I think whatever is in that house was angry that it didn't get us last night, so it took it out on the local wildlife."

"I get your point. Do you feel up to driving? I don't think I'm ready yet. Besides, I want to get this footage off to the network through my cell phone."

"For some reason, I don't think we'll be running into any more dead animals past this spot." He moved toward the car. "Also, if you notice, we have cell phone service now when we didn't last night in the exact same spot."

She looked at the dead animals one last time and then followed Kennedy.

New York, New York

The morning show cohosts for UBC's highly rated wake-up show were only minutes from their 11:00 A.M. sign-off when the CEO of the network and its parent company showed up in the wings. Everyone on the set became nervous when they saw the old man in his legendary bow tie, sipping a cup of coffee complete with china cup and saucer. He was speaking with the morning show's producer and talent coordinator, and the two cohosts looked on nervously during an extended commercial break. Then they watched as a videotape was handed over to the producer, and a gaffer ran a new script over with only thirty seconds to spare.

"Bob says to run the script and then hand it over to the morning news desk."

"But what about our last guest?" the male host asked.

"He's been cut. Do it. The CEO brought down this segment himself."

Both hosts looked over at Abe Feuerstein, who raised his china cup toward them and smiled. They nervously returned the smile. Offstage, they could see the bad news being delivered to the *New York Times* bestselling author, who wasn't happy about being bumped from the show.

"Okay, people, we're back in three, two . . ." The producer held his fingers up and stopped counting at two. On one, he pointed to the male host.

"We're back, and we've had a change in the program. We're delighted to bring you a tag-along segment coordinated through our prime-time ratings juggernaut *Hunters of the Paranormal*. As you know, tomorrow night here at UBC, a historical event is taking place at eight P.M. Eastern Time. The Halloween special, scheduled for a record-breaking eight hours of coverage, is one of our network's proudest achievements in programming. For more details on an ever-changing situation, we go to our news desk and Connie Towers. Connie?"

The producer cut off to camera four and the news desk. The desk was in the foreground, but viewers could still see the two cohosts in the background. Then the camera switched over to number five—a head-on view of the dark-haired newslady.

"Thank you, Richard. As you know, the special holiday presentation of *Hunters of the Paranormal* has been the topic of conversation, from this famous building to other programming rooms across the city. The special, which airs tomorrow night at eight, is the talk of the town and is expected to capture not only the top Wednesday night ratings crowd, but bring in record rates for its lucky advertisers. And now we actually have our first video coming in, not only of the house where the special will be taking place, but of the roads leading up to the famous summer retreat. The video was taken this morning by UBC reporter Julie Reilly, who is on assignment all this week at Summer Place. She will be hosting the live broadcast tomorrow night, and on her way to the assignment she came across a rather bizarre incident not far from the retreat, which many suspect to be haunted."

On the television monitors around the studio, the view of the news desk vanished and the pictures Julie had recorded not more than an hour before unfolded for the viewers of the nation's most watched morning program. In the wings the CEO smiled and sipped his coffee. As Julie's small camera panned the roadway, it caught the first dead animal, then she expertly pulled back and took in the entire roadway. Everyone was shocked. The strewn animal carcasses made for a view that would upset a lot of viewers. UBC had brazenly placed this segment on the air without warning, because that was exactly what the CEO wanted: gossip, talk, outrage, and interest about the show. He smiled. The segment concluded and faded to black.

"The video you saw was filmed by correspondent Julie Reilly, who was gracious enough to phone in her report. We have her live on her cell phone, reporting from the Pocono Mountains. Julie, this is Connie Towers in the studio. We understand you've had an exciting start to your day already, and Halloween isn't until tomorrow night."

"That's right, Connie. The unexplained deaths of over two hundred animals occurred not less than a mere few hours after myself and the former professor of paranormal studies from the University of Southern California, Gabriel Kennedy, passed through the area late last night. To see this much death surrounding the road is unlikely to be a natural occurrence. It has led this reporter to speculate that it indeed has something to do with reports about the house known as Summer Place. Thanks to our producers, we were able to research the area and have found that the land surrounding this stretch of road is part of the Summer Place property. It is possible that water contamination or a rare outbreak of animal disease has struck these forest animals."

"Julie, were these animals possibly struck and killed by automobiles after you and Professor Kennedy left the area late last night?"

"The possibility is there, Connie, but only if they ran the Indianapolis 500 here at four in the morning. Professor Kennedy has confirmed that there is no visible bodily damage to these creatures, and therefore the cause of death remains a mystery. Until I report live from Summer Place for the *Evening News*, this is Julie Reilly, sending it back to the news desk."

Connie Towers looked over at her producer. He was running his hand in a circle, telling her to continue. He held up ten fingers: she had ten seconds to comment on the report.

"Thank you Julie, that is sure some creepy stuff. I can't wait to watch the special. Now, back to Robert and Lynn. Guys?"

"I agree with you, Connie, that is something I wouldn't be happy to be covering," said the female host. "Julie Reilly will be reporting live on tomorrow's show from Summer Place, as we all prepare for this monumental special."

Abraham Feuerstein smiled and handed his cup and saucer to an assistant. He nodded at the cast of the morning show and then moved away, happy he had decided to make Julie file her audio report by phone. He didn't think about the events themselves; even after what had happened last night in his own limo, all the CEO saw were dollar signs scrolling across the teleprompter in his mind. He felt wise and beyond reproach for pushing the special.

As he waited outside of studio 1-B, Abe smiled wider than before.

"Brilliant," he said as he waited for the elevator. He then turned to his assistant. "I want twenty spots added to the show's promo package."

"That will squeeze out most of the prime-time ad time for our own shows," she said, taking notes as they both stepped into the elevator.

"I don't care. Every ten minutes, I want the Summer Place on that television screen. Add some more history script if you have to, but get the story out there. I want everyone in the country talking about Summer Place before the day's over."

"Yes, sir."

"I never thought Halloween could be so lucrative. I should have dug up Professor Gabriel Kennedy many years ago. We're going to piggyback that man right into ratings history."

Bright River, Pennsylvania

At least a hundred people were gathered before the closed gate to Summer Place. Some were fans of the show, while some were most definitely not. The fans carried signs that read *HUNTERS OF THE PARANORMAL* RULES, and others that told the two hosts of the show that they were loved. But they were being pushed and shoved by local folks from the small town of Bright Waters. Kennedy recognized a few of them—some of them had stood in front of the diner that very morning, aiming accusing looks at him and Julie.

In the absence of Eunice and her large husband, the network had brought in five uniformed security men. Gabriel knew immediately that the special was going to call for far more than that if this mess continued.

"This is a fucking circus already." He honked the car's horn when they were forced to stop thirty feet from the front gate by the two converging sides of the crowd. 'This is never conducive to a controlled experiment. The cameras and stuff are bad enough, but this?"

"Professor, when did you ever believe this would be controlled—by you, or by anyone else involved in the production? You were never that damn naïve, were you?"

One of the admirers of the show slammed into the car's hood. When the man saw that it was Julie Reilly in the passenger's seat, he turned and called out to the others. Soon the car was surrounded by those trying to get autographs. Some of them even tried to open the car's doors.

"Don't say it. You want me to sacrifice myself and get out of the car so you can drive right on through the gate, right?" She leaned away from the glass as a large man pounded on the window.

"Now that you mention it, that wouldn't be a bad—"

Before Gabriel could finish his small joke, someone hit Julie's window so hard that the glass broke. When he looked over, he saw hands reaching through the shattered window. Julie was actually being pulled at by more than one of the men. Gabriel opened his door without hesitation and pushed his way through the crowd, shoving several people out of the way. When he made it to the two men who were reaching inside the car, he pulled one away and pushed him down. The other turned and hit Gabriel in the face. Julie sprang from the car. Kennedy was on the ground with a rather large men sitting on his chest. She swung her ample bag toward the man's head and connected solidly. Then she was pushed from behind by an angry woman, and she knew immediately that this one wasn't an admirer of the show or her credentials as a reporter.

"Jesus Christ!" Kennedy shouted. He gained his feet and pushed Julie into the car once more. As he got back in and threw the vehicle into gear, he saw two of the security men throwing the gate open. Another three kept the crowd back.

Gabriel pushed the accelerator all the way to the floor, spun the wheels just to let the people around the car know that he was coming through, then let off the gas and slowly crept through the gate.

"What the fuck was that about?" Julie asked, trying to slow her heart and regain her breath. She looked over at Gabriel and saw blood running from the corner of his mouth. His jacket had been torn at the shoulder and his glasses were hanging down from one ear. The way he looked made her chuckle as she reached over and used a Kleenex to wipe the blood away. "That was one hell of a rescue, Professor," she said as she finally got the nervous laughter under some sort of control.

Gabriel looked at Julie. He slowly made his way up the long gravel drive.

"So glad you approve. I was about to get my ass kicked back there, until you waylaid that guy with the horse purse you carry."

"Believe me, that was many years of reporting from places like Iraq and Afghanistan kicking in. It's a self-defense mechanism. You have Summer Place, I have assholes the world over that wanted my ass."

"Well, thanks anyway," he said.

"No, thank *you*. I thought those assholes were going to pull me right out the damn window." She tossed the bloody Kleenex on the floor. "If it weren't for you I would—"

"What the hell is happening here?" Kennedy said, cutting Julie off as they drove under the large portico.

Stumbling and backing down the steps were several men and women, also being confronted by men who looked even angrier than the ones out front. Among the defensive-looking group was a man they both recognized: Wallace Lindemann. He was pointing and gesturing toward the large double front doors as he backed down the stairs.

"Is that Kelly and Harris Dalton, the director?" Julie asked as she opened her door and stepped out. Gabriel quickly followed, thinking that the world had gone completely mad.

As they both approached the scene of the argument, Gabriel saw all of the vans and trucks on the side of the house where they had been directed to park. The truck drivers, the production and technical staffs, camera and soundmen all watched in fascination as the argument progressed from the front of the house to the large stairs that led to the drive.

"I don't care! You broke our agreement, and if nothing happens tomorrow night, we're going to sue you, Lindemann!" Kelly was shouting. Gabriel removed his sunglasses and watched as the director, Harris Dalton, reached out and pulled Kelly Delaphoy back from the men Lindemann stood in front of, as if he were guarding them. Then Kennedy saw a man in a black coat and recognized him immediately. He stepped up until he was only a foot behind the men as they backed down the steps.

"Yeah, well, sue me for what? Because my house isn't haunted after all?!" Lindemann shouted.

"If you did anything to ruin this for the network, you little prick, you know they're going to hang you!" Kelly came back.

"What's going on?" Kennedy asked as Julie stepped up beside him.

Lindemann, the two women, and the man in the priest's coat turned and saw Gabriel and Julie as they stood there.

"Hello, Father," Gabriel said with a small smile creasing his lips.

"Gabriel." The older man held out his hand and actually smiled back when Kennedy took it.

"Who is this?" Julie asked.

"The father and I go way back. He's a professor of Seminary Studies at Columbia, and the only man who ever believed me about Summer Place." He smiled wider. "Well, maybe a little. His name is Father Lynn Dolan." Julie nodded at the gray-haired man.

"Yeah, and he'll be named in the lawsuit, too!" Kelly shouted. She was trying desperately to shake off Harris Dalton's restraining hands.

Gabriel looked curiously from Kelly to Father Dolan. "Lynn, what did you go and do?" He climbed the step to get eye level with his old acquaintance.

"The owner of this magnificent property asked us to bless it before the arrival of this travesty."

"Professor, he didn't bless the house. He went room to room, cleansing it. He may have chased off everything we're looking for!" Kelly shouted. She was wild-eyed and Julie thought she looked insane.

Kennedy shook his head. He removed a handkerchief from his jacket pocket and patted his lip where it had been cut. "You didn't?" Gabriel gasped mockingly, in a rather good impression of being stunned and shocked, Julie thought.

"I did. And do you know what, Gabriel?"

"Do tell," Kennedy said as he looked at the blood on his white handkerchief.

"Don't even speak to this man—this fake—he and Lindemann just fucked us all," Kelly called, finally shrugging off Dalton's hands.

"Ms. Delaphoy, would you shut up for a moment? You're making an ass out of yourself," Kennedy said as he tucked the handkerchief back into his pocket.

"See? I told you. Now let it go," Dalton said from behind Kelly.

"As I've been saying all along, my house is not haunted. If you decide to continue with this character assassination tomorrow night, the whole world will see it," Lindemann said, and turned on Kennedy. "And you'll finally get what's coming to you for starting this whole messed-up story."

"Pompous little ass," Julie said, holding her ground behind Kennedy.

"Tell me, Lynn . . ." Gabriel took the priest by the arm and took two steps up toward the house. "You didn't feel anything when you were inside?"

"Gabe, I felt absolutely nothing but envy that this house is owned by someone other than me."

Kennedy smiled and then looked up at Kelly and Harris.

"This man did nothing that will interfere with my experiment. If he did get rid of something that walks in this house, then it wasn't as strong as I believed it to be, and thus couldn't be responsible for all the tragedy that's happened here." He turned back to Father Dolan. "By the way, who are your two friends?"

"This is Kathy Lee Arnold and her assistant from the Pennsylvania Paranormal Research Society."

Kennedy laughed out loud, ignoring the heavyset woman's hand as she reached for his. She lowered it with a distasteful look on her plump face.

"Paranormal Research Society—ghost hunters, right?"

"That's right, and for the past three hours we have been conducting our own inquiry into Summer Place. It's our conclusion that this house was never haunted; or if it was at one time, is not now."

Gabriel nodded and then turned to Kelly Delaphoy.

"I think you have bigger problems out in the front, Ms. Delaphoy. I suggest you take care of that and let these people be on their way."

"Father, would you mind stating what you did, on camera for the show? I promise no cheap shots will be taken," Julie said.

"Excellent idea. You'll get good face time, Lynn—something Columbia University loves for its professors."

"I suppose I can stay a few minutes longer," the father said. Julie led him away, and they were followed by the two ladies from the PPRS.

Kelly Delaphoy bounded down the steps and rounded on Kennedy. "What are you doing? Do you know what he did?"

"Well, I'm guessing Lindemann hired him to cleanse Summer Place before the investigation tomorrow night."

Lindemann said nothing. He looked like he hadn't shaved in days. The smell of alcohol wafted around him like a hovering rain cloud.

"And you're okay with that?" Dalton asked Kennedy.

Kennedy looked up at Summer Place, even though he

couldn't see the bulk of the massive house from underneath the portico.

"Sure. As a matter of fact, if I were producing this show, I would try to get the father to be available on Halloween—for his expert opinion."

They were both dumbfounded.

"Plus, I would try my best to find out who was behind this idea of cleansing the house by purging the spirits out of it before the show," he said, turning to face Wallace Lindemann.

"I came up with the idea myself."

"Somehow I doubt that, Wallace. You just don't have the imagination," Gabriel countered.

Lindemann, instead of answering, pushed past Kelly and Harris and made his way up the stairs.

"You better watch it, moving that equipment into the house. Nothing gets in before seven in the morning!"

"We can tour Summer Place?" Harris called after him. Lindemann stalked off into the house, probably heading for the well-stocked bar.

"Professor Kennedy, what if they . . . they . . ."

He stepped out from under the portico and watched Julie Reilly interview the father, with the two ladies smiling in the background. "Forget it. That thing in there isn't going to be frightened away by a few Roman Catholic rituals and words." He looked up at the warm and inviting house. "Whatever is in there is waiting for its own show to begin. Whatever my old friend did, I'm sure it found it all very amusing."

"I'm glad you're so goddamn confident, Kennedy," Kelly hissed. "It's my ass on the line here."

Kennedy laughed sharply. "Summer Place may just avail you of that ass if you don't respect it, Ms. Delaphoy." He started toward the interviewers, to say good-bye to Father Dolan.

"I can handle that if anything really happens inside that house."

Kennedy turned back to face her and Dalton but continued to walk backward.

"I hope you can handle it. If you can't, you may just end up like your friends Kyle Pritchard and Paul Lowell. They didn't take this house seriously, and see what that disrespect did for them?"

Kelly and Dalton watched Kennedy go and then looked up at the looming house.

"He better be right," Kelly said, looking up at the blank windows.

"For your sake I hope he is," Harris said. "And then again, I really don't want to see anything like what happened during the test again."

"Why? That's just the kind of show we want. Well, short of getting people eaten, of course."

"You really don't believe Kennedy, do you, even after all we've seen?"

"Oh, I believe him, it's just that I'm not as afraid of the house as he is."

Harris Dalton watched Kelly stride up the steps toward the double front doors.

Summer Place looked down on him like a giant looking at its next meal. To him, the house didn't look cleansed at all—like Professor Kennedy said, Summer Place looked hungry. For the first time since the 1930s, the house would have a large menu to choose from.

As the large trucks started off-loading the heavy equipment, the clouds started gathering over the westernmost range of the Poconos. Summer Place was preparing for All Hallows Eve.

PART IV

THE GATEWAY

Halloween

I know that brother's blood they've spilt,
And sons of Cain must pay their guilt; I know the deviltries that stem
From dark abyss we must condemn; I know that but for heaven's grace
We might be rotting in their place: —God pity them!

—ROBERT WILLIAM SERVICE,
"The Damned"

16 Summer Place

As more security poured into Summer Place, the crowds seemed to sense that their presence was causing the desired effect—UBC was paying them the attention they desired. They became louder and the clash between townies and fans became more boisterous and at times violent—the townsfolk of Bright Waters wanted the UBC network and its fans out of Summer Place, and the fans of *Hunters of the Paranormal* wanted the townies to butt out of everything. The additional security was helping to keep the two sides separated, and most thought it would calm down as soon as the district judge in Bright Waters issued his orders for the protesters and the fans to vacate private property under the threat of arrest.

Kennedy and his team, still minus Leonard Sickles and George Cordero, set up their meeting space in a large yellow and blue tent the network had set up just in front of the large pool. The commissary tent, a sixty-five-foot-long monstrosity, was arranged not far away by the giant red barn and stables. All of the production equipment was off-loaded and sat under tarps for the move into the house. Dalton and Kelly were inside the massive ballroom trying to convince Wallace Lindemann to grant them early access so that the cameras and sound systems could be placed a day early. The expected setup time for Leonard and his experimental equipment was a looming threat to their timetable. He and his technicians still had not left New York.

At four o'clock, Gabriel, Julie, John Lonetree, Jenny Tilden, and Jason Sanborn—who had abstained from joining the argument with Wallace Lindemann—left their tent and started walking toward the wooded area behind the pool, following the riding trail that had eventually cost the life of gossip columnist Henrietta Batiste back in 1928. The rain clouds stayed far to the north for now, flooding the small valley with sunshine, something that Jason Sanborn frowned upon. They needed a dark and stormy night, and thus far their own meteorologists at the network were promising nothing but clear, cold skies.

"Now, according to the stable boys on duty that day, including the caretaker's father, John Johannson, Miss Batiste left the stables early that morning. By all accounts she was an accomplished rider, backed in tournaments by the likes of John Barrymore and Mary Pickford."

"How many horses did Summer Place accommodate at any one time?" Jennifer asked. She walked slowly beside John Lonetree.

"During the spring and summer, the Lindemanns emptied their Kentucky stables and brought over fifty horses here—pure Thoroughbreds," Gabriel added.

"Even if she were an accomplished rider, an accident can befall anyone on one of those horses. They can be very finicky," John said. "Without trying to cast too much aspersion, she just very well could have been lying, trying to cover up the fact that she was thrown from a horse. I mean, no one wants to admit that."

"I see the point you're trying to make here, John. The police reports on the attacks and the disappearances are the only facts we have. This story, like all of the rest, are all hand-me-down stories."

"Is this where it happened?" Jenny asked as Gabriel stopped in front of a copse of large pine trees.

"Right in here someplace. I believe she was indeed thrown,

and then she claimed the attack came on so suddenly that she was caught totally by surprise."

"I'm not feeling anything. There's no residual energy here at all." Lonetree placed a hand against the trunk of one of the large pines. "I think we will miss having George the most on things like this. He could be better at picking up residuals without having to sleep on it."

"Well, I thought it worth a try, John," Gabriel said. He turned back toward the barn and stables.

As the small group walked, they saw Kelly Delaphoy and Harris Dalton coming their way. Kelly didn't look all that happy, and neither did Harris, but that could have been because he couldn't stand being around Kelly.

"Julie," Kelly said, "I thought I gave instructions that Professor Kennedy and his team were not to go anywhere on this property without at least one camera crew accompanying."

Julie raised the small digital camera from her large bag and held it so Kelly could see it.

"Oh. Well, did you come across anything?"

"Nothing but a bunch of trees," Julie said.

"Well, at least I have some good news. Wallace Lindemann said he owes us one for allowing in the priest and ghost hunters, so he's letting us start setting up the equipment."

"That's good," Jason said as he pulled his pipe from his mouth.

"But?" Gabriel asked as he half turned toward Kelly.

"But we can't have anyone in the house past midnight; he said he doesn't want any accidents without independent witnesses."

"A cautionary but sane request," Sanborn said.

"Bullshit. It's a con man trying to keep his play hidden for as long as he can," Julie quipped.

Kennedy had to smile. Julie was far more observant than he gave her credit for.

"You do realize the person that let Father Dolan loose in

Summer Place was your boss, Lionel Peterson, don't you?"
Gabriel asked Kelly.

The question brought her to a stop.

"I would need proof of that," she said. "I mean, why would
he sabotage himself?"

"After becoming acquainted with you, Kelly," Julie said,
"I think the professor has a valid point. He would do anything
to see you fail. Men like Peterson always squeeze their way
out of trouble, but he figures no matter what, if the show fails,
you're gone for sure."

Again, Julie's assessment was right on. Gabriel decided
that she might not be so bad a partner.

As they strolled through the late afternoon, Lonetree was
surprised to see that Gabriel's attitude and demeanor had
changed from night to day. It was as if he had come home to a
welcoming reunion with a long-lost family member. It wasn't
only in the way he looked, but the way he carried himself, as
if the horror of seven years ago never happened. It was like
he hadn't recounted to him and the others the nightmare of
Kyle Pritchard's death in a town not an hour and a half away,
or the dead animals he and Julie saw on the road in a spot
that coincided with an area where they had broken down the
night before.

John waited for Gabe to catch up with him and Jenny, and
then intentionally slowed his pace until they were shoulder-
to-shoulder. He would not only see how Gabe reacted, but he
also wanted to gauge the others as well.

"Since we've been on the property, Gabe, have you felt it?"

Gabriel looked up at his old friend with a curious look on
his face. The others heard the question and listened in, which
was exactly what John wanted. He would judge each, especially Kelly Delaphoy, by their reactions to his upcoming
statement.

Gabriel didn't answer right off. He stopped and tilted his
head, as if trying to detect something he might have missed.

"You know what I mean," John said. "Without actually
going inside the house. It's changed, hasn't it?"

Gabriel turned and looked up at the massive summer home, watching as a light breeze blew the curtains in the third-floor windows. Eunice must have been by and opened the windows to air the house out for the big night, he thought.

"It's not oppressive to you, is it?" John persisted.

"What do you mean?" Kelly asked.

"I mean, for at least the moment, Summer Place is just a bunch of wood and stone," John answered as he turned to face Kelly. "Does that worry you at all, Ms. Delaphoy?"

"Why do you say that?" Julie Reilly asked, eyeing the concerned look on Kelly's face.

"Whatever was in there"—he faced Gabriel once more—"and I do believe your story, is gone."

"Goddamn it!" Kelly said loudly. "I knew that son of a bitch was here to fuck this show up!"

Gabriel wanted to laugh at Kelly's terror. The others saw his reaction to John's statement and probably wondered why he would take John's feeling so lightly.

"You're right, whatever is in the house, or walking these grounds, isn't active right now." He faced Kelly. "And if it doesn't choose to display its abilities tomorrow night, that's just what your show is going to report. Is that clear, Ms. Delaphoy? If you try to fake something and we catch it, we'll humiliate you. If there is one person in the world who can smoke out a rat, it's my friend Leonard. Don't try it."

Kelly closed her eyes and mentally made herself not react to Kennedy's statement. Instead she turned on her heel and went up the small incline to the large production tent.

"Jesus, I think you just scared her more than Summer Place ever could," Jennifer said as she watched Kelly leave.

Gabriel smiled. "I don't know about you guys, but I could use a drink. Miss Ace Reporter, may I assume your people brought the makings of a martini?"

"Oh, I think we can dig something up. If not we'll break into the ballroom and steal some of Lindemann's private stock."

On the way up the hill, Gabriel looked over at the tree line and wondered if anyone had seen what he had. When he locked eyes with Julie Reilly, who was trying hard not to show Gabriel's hole card, he knew she had seen them also.

Fifteen feet inside the tree line, beneath one of the large and ancient pine trees, Gabriel had counted more than twenty dead birds and three dead squirrels.

Summer Place was very much alive, he thought. Alive and waiting for its time.

George Cordero sat in the backseat of the cab as it slowly made its way along the Van Wyck Expressway in bumper-to-bumper traffic. The turnoff for JFK International Airport was nowhere in sight. The cabdriver looked in his rearview mirror and saw that the dark-eyed man hadn't moved since he had been picked up in front of the Waldorf-Astoria an hour before.

The driver reached over and switched on his radio.

"*This is the top-of-the-hour news from KWBW, John Stannic reporting. All is going well for one of the strangest television events to be launched in many years over at the UBC television network, as their highly anticipated* Hunters of the Paranormal *Halloween special is set to go off with widespread fanfare tomorrow night from the Pocono Mountains. While the outlook is bright for record-setting numbers of viewers to tune into the extended programming, many stockholders are furious over the cost of the program itself. They say that Abraham Feuerstein, CEO of the parent company, has overstepped his bounds in the expensive endeavor. Meanwhile, here in New York, many residents are anticipating a glorious night for all trick-or-treaters and partygoers. Expect some of the nicest evening weather of the year, mild and almost balmy all the way from Washington, D.C., to the Maine border.*"

George listened to the news report, thinking about the friend he had left high and dry. He knew he had let Gabriel down. Now he only had John Lonetree as a visionist, and he would only be good if he was asleep. That could be very dangerous, potentially leaving Lonetree vulnerable at the worst possible moment.

"Running away, George?"

Cordero's eyes widened. His father was sitting next to him, eating a Nathan's hot dog and looking straight out through the screen separating the driver from his backseat passengers. His father looked over at him and took a bite of the hot dog, and George watched as the food went through his mouth and into a throat that wasn't really there. In the time since his father had been buried in New Jersey, his features had more than just deteriorated; they had rotted away to the point where the only thing holding him together was the suit he was wearing. George fixated on the piece of hot dog and bun that rolled from his throat to rest on the seat between them.

"You wouldn't know a thing about it, outside of the coward part of the equation, you bastard."

The cabdriver looked up and into his rearview mirror.

"You're so fucking high and mighty, you're leaving your friends and running away when they need you the most," his father said. He looked over the hot dog and tossed it on the floor. That was the move George had been waiting for—it confirmed that it wasn't his father he was seeing, but a manifestation of himself. When he was a kid his father took him to Coney Island on several occasions and they always stopped for hot dogs at Nathan's. George always refused to eat his, no matter how many times his father thrust the dog into his face. He just never could stomach hot dogs. Now he knew the ghost wasn't his father at all, but his conscience coming out in the shape and rotting features of his murderous dad.

"All that time your mother was dying of cancer, you never once saw the pain. Oh, you heard it, you saw the tears, but you never in your life would have thought about ending it for her. You waited until I did it." His father turned and faced him, his cheekbones sticking through blackened and moldy skin. One eye was completely gone and the other had the lid hanging over it. The black hair was how he remembered it, but everything else was a rotten meat sack. "Ah, you knew what I was planning. You can't be that close to another person and not feel the hate, the desire to kill. She was holding us back from making a fortune with your ability." His father laughed. "You knew, and did nothing, because deep down inside you were a coward, George. You always were. You wanted to be free of her as much as I—oh, for different reasons, to be sure, but free nonetheless. So you allowed me to do the dirty work and then acted shocked when you touched me that day. You scum, you hypocrite."

George tried to look away from his father out the window, but the reflection told him his father was still there. He closed his eyes hard and then opened them. His rotting dad was still watching him.

"Maybe it's better that you stay out of that house, George. You know why?"

George didn't move or utter a word. He squeezed his eyes shut.

"Because that house is just like me—it despises people like you, George. Everyone who enters that house tomorrow night is on the list to have their ticket punched, just like you punched mine. You could never know what's waiting for you, and you can never imagine the power of what walks there. You see death for one, but you blocked out far more than you told your friends, didn't you? That thing is going to protect itself and its secrets, and now you're running away so it won't eat you, too. How typical."

"Would you shut the fuck up?!" George screamed. The driver slammed on his brakes, startled, and nearly swerved into the back of another car.

"What the hell is wrong with you, man?" the driver asked, looking in the mirror at the wild-eyed man in the back.

"How fast can you get off this speedway?" George asked, staring at the empty seat beside him.

"What? We're here for an hour more, at least," the driver said, shaking his head.

George pulled a wad of cash out of his wallet. He shoved three one-hundred-dollar bills through the glass opening.

"That's for getting us out of here now." He added three more hundreds. "And that's for getting me to Pennsylvania, and there's another three when you get me to the Poconos. Deal?"

The driver collected the six hundred dollars and met George's eyes in the mirror. "Double. Six hundred when we get there."

George decided what the hell. He pulled out some more money out and pushed it through.

"In advance. Now go!" His eyes seemed to go back to normal, as did his spirit.

"Can I ask why you have to get there in such an expensive hurry, my friend?"

"Yeah, you can ask. But first, get moving. There's a storm coming."

The driver pulled his cab into the breakdown lane and started for the exit more than a half mile ahead. He looked up and saw that there wasn't a cloud in the late evening sky.

"I'll get you there, my friend, but I believe you to be wrong about a storm."

George laughed to himself, then lay back against the seat and closed his eyes.

"I've never been more right about anything in my life, fella. A storm is coming and it's going to be a killer."

Three trucks wound their way through the small valley pass, forty miles from Summer Place. The vehicles were transporting the small trailers that would be used as dressing rooms for the one overnight stay for the participants in the Halloween special. Six trailers were on each truck, strapped down tightly for the rough ride. The sun was setting in the west, and the lead driver had to drive slowly to negotiate sharp turn after sharp turn.

At a steeply angled downhill grade, the lead driver

downshifted to slow even further. As he turned his head suddenly to avert his eyes from the blindingly bright orange ball of the sun at the horizon, he saw that he was no longer alone in the truck. A dark form was sitting next to him in the cab. Reflexively, he slammed on his brakes. As the truck screeched to a stop, the dark form seemed to take a more clarified shape. The head turned toward the bearded driver and the maw of the dark mist opened and then attacked, engulfing him from head to chest.

The second driver in line slammed on his brakes when the first truck's taillights flared brightly, but it was too late. The second truck, with its load of trailers, slammed into the first, starting a chain reaction that caused the third and final transport to ram the middle truck. The trailers that had been strapped to all three vehicles broke loose. The first truck was pushed over and through the railing, plummeting down the side of the treacherous mountain road. The second driver saw the cab of the first as it left the road, and just before his truck followed the first, he thought he saw the driver screaming and trying his best to fend off something dark and massive. As the first two trucks rolled down the side of the mountain, the third managed to hit an intact section of the guardrail at a slower speed and careen back into the middle of the roadway.

The third truck spun, throwing off its six trailers like a dog shaking off water. The driver started shaking, so shocked at having seen the two trucks slide off the side of the mountain that he didn't notice the car coming down the road as he stepped out of his truck. Just as his feet touched the roadway, the driver of the car saw the stalled vehicle, but it was too late. The car slammed into the driver and then the fuel tank on the side. Both vehicles immediately burst into flames. The trapped driver of the truck screamed, his body on fire. Just before the pain of his shattered legs and the flames sent him into shock, he saw a dark mist ebb and then swirl around his body. As he screamed, he saw a mouth form in the mist, becoming a gaping and foul-smelling pit that seemed to smile just before it closed over his head.

The game had started in earnest. Though Kennedy and his team didn't know it yet, Summer Place had started the murderous rampage that would end on Halloween night.

Summer Place

Inside the commissary tent, Gabriel sat and sipped coffee, watching as Kelly Delaphoy held court with her production team across the large tent. Gabriel could only imagine what the woman was instructing them to do. He suspected she was still upset because Father Dolan had tried to cleanse the house, and wondered if she was inventing new and better tricks to defraud her viewers with. Kennedy knew the type of woman Delaphoy was—driven, the pressures of her job could push her over the edge. Yes, he thought, even now she was showing signs of cracking under the strain. He would have to watch her. Summer Place would sniff out her weakness and use it not only against Kelly, but also against all of them.

"I haven't been a big eater for the past seven years, but that ham and cheese casserole left a lot to be desired," Jennifer Tilden said as she pushed away her paper plate. It was still half filled with the conglomeration the network cooks had come up with.

"I told you the chicken Kiev looked better," John said. He drank his coffee.

"Yeah, well, I see you didn't touch much of yours, either," Jenny shot back, looking at John's full plate.

"I don't think this atmosphere is conducive to big appetites," Gabriel said.

The tent was crowded and the voices mostly carried excitement. But Gabriel thought the party atmosphere went a little deeper. He thought it stemmed from the rumor that Summer Place had somehow been cleansed of the entity and that all they would run into tomorrow night was a dead and silent house, their frights solely dependent on any gags Kelly could come up with. Kennedy made eye contact with Harris Dalton, who sat alone. The two men looked at each other for the briefest of moments, then Harris averted his eyes and lowered his head to the notes he was studying. Gabriel pushed his coffee away and stood.

"By the way, Jenny, any sign of Bobby Lee?"

"I felt him on the car ride up, but as soon as we entered the front gate, he left. It was like turning off a water tap," she said, looking from Gabriel to John Lonetree. "I never felt anything frighten my little ghost before, but Summer Place—it's like he's afraid it'll keep him if he shows himself." She sipped her coffee, her small hands wrapping around the cup as if it were a talisman against what she was thinking. "No, Bobby Lee will be a no-show tomorrow night."

Gabriel nodded. "Will you excuse me? I have something I want to say to the director."

John turned to Jenny and smiled.

"To hell with Bobby Lee, huh?" he said, looking into her green eyes.

"I think he's afraid of that, too—hell, I mean," Jenny said with a smile, then lost it almost as soon as it had appeared. "But I think he's far more afraid of this place." Her eyes went from John to the house, through the mesh screen opening of the commissary tent.

"I'm a little busy at the moment, Professor," Harris Dalton said as Gabriel approached. He scribbled a note about a camera placement for the subbasement.

"Kelly—do you trust her?" Kennedy asked.

"I don't trust anyone, Professor Kennedy. That's why I'm a director, and that's why I'm good at what I do." Dalton looked up from his notes and gestured for Kennedy to have a seat. He looked around the large tent and saw only one set of eyes on them: Kelly Delaphoy's.

Gabriel sat down and leaned toward him.

"I'll tell you something up front, Mr. Dalton: If my team catches Kelly laying her special-effects gags in the house, we'll expose her and the network for fraud."

Harris Dalton spun his pencil between his fingers, looking Kennedy over.

"Professor, this is my last assignment. I don't give a flying fuck if you catch her, don't catch her, or chuck her out of a third-floor window. There's something wrong with this place, and as much as I hate that woman and her silly show, I really don't care to find out what it is. I want to get through these eight hours and then take my grandkids fishing for the rest of my life. So you have at it, Mr. Kennedy. This is your show, not mine."

Gabriel nodded and stood to return to his own table. The conversation had been enough to tell him that Harris Dalton would not try to whitewash any of the experiments' findings to suit what the network wanted.

Lionel Peterson and Wallace Lindemann came through the commissary tent's wide opening, in the middle of an argument. Lindemann was gesturing wildly in the air with an empty glass; it was obvious the alcohol had long since disappeared. Gabriel looked from the scene to his companions. They watched Kelly Delaphoy advance on the two men. When Peterson spoke to her it was with a short hiss. He moved off to a table, where he sat alone.

"Ignore me if you want, you can't stay in the house overnight," Lindemann said, glaring at Peterson.

Kelly smiled. She followed Peterson to his table, where she leaned over and said something as he took a bite of his salad. He grimaced, using a napkin to cover his distaste for the commissary meal. He looked up at Kelly and then nodded his head. The producer of *Hunters of the Paranormal* straightened and returned to her production table, issuing orders that sent many of her team members scrambling out of the tent. Then she turned toward Gabriel's team.

As he stepped up to the table, she was writing on her clipboard and tried to act nonchalant.

"It seems there's been a large accident with a few of our trucks. The trailers we were going to use as dressing rooms and bedrooms—well, they're nothing but splinters on the roadway. Mr. Peterson said he wants everyone to bed down in the house tonight."

Gabriel looked at Kelly in silence.

"I don't think that's a good idea at all," John Lonetree said.

Kelly lowered her clipboard and looked at the group, including her own producer. He was sitting next to Jennifer, shaking his head.

"Oh, we're not using the bedrooms. I just sent all of my assistants out to Bright Waters to get the hardware store owner to open up. They're going to get all the cots and air mattresses they can find. The rest of us will sleep with blankets on the floor, inside the ballroom—one central location for all."

"My team will sleep out here or in the barn. We'll not be stepping into Summer Place until tomorrow afternoon."

"Look, Professor, this gives us a chance to get our equipment in place and maybe even enough time to have a dry run of the show."

"We have nothing to do with that. Your cameras will either follow our lead, or you can run around Summer Place all night long on your own, something I would not recommend."

Harris Dalton was watching from his corner table. Kelly grimaced at him, and that told Gabriel that she was also leery of Dalton watching her every move. Yes, he thought, Dalton would be an asset to the experiment. He wouldn't let Kelly get away with anything.

"You do what you want, Professor," she said with a strained smile, "but I, for one, am not sleeping in a barn."

Gabriel stood, then moved off without saying anything more. John, Jenny, and finally even Jason Sanborn stood. John and Jenny followed Gabriel from the tent, and Sanborn gave Kelly a pointed look.

"Look, I know we need a hit, and I'm all for being enthusiastic, but please don't take this extra time inside the house to lay any tricks," Jason said as he pulled his pipe from his jacket pocket. He placed the cold pipe in his mouth and rubbed the two-day growth of beard on his cheek. "If you do, Kelly, I'll expose you myself."

"What's gotten into you?" she asked, her smile widening. "Have you become a disciple of Professor Kennedy?"

Jason Sanborn turned away and then stopped. He slowly turned and faced his fellow producer. "Maybe not a disciple, but I've learned that, while Kennedy may be a lot of things, he is not a liar. What he says happened that night, I believe happened. I'll be sleeping in the barn with them. And if I were you, Kelly, my dear, I would also."

"Oh, come on—"

"And one last thing. This is my last show." He placed the pipe into his mouth once more. "After this, I think I've had enough of ghosts and ghouls, on both sides of the camera."

Kelly looked stunned and couldn't hide it from the men and women watching her. She attempted to smile and then pretended to write something on her clipboard. She tried to figure out where she had lost one of her best friends.

Summer Place was starting to cost far more than she ever thought it would. When she looked up as Jason disappeared through the tent's opening, she actually did smile, and this time it was genuine. She would go through with her dream and all would be well. They would all sip champagne and declare that they had produced the most-watched television event in history. When that happened, she would forgive everyone who had doubted her.

She turned and saw Lionel Peterson looking at her.

"With the exception of a well-chosen few," she mumbled.

Gabriel pulled open the large barn door and found the power box. He turned on the bright overhead lights and looked around the immaculate barn. It was far nicer inside than most of the homes in the rural countryside.

"You feel safe here?" Lonetree asked. He walked over to one of the large stalls and looked inside at the freshly tossed hay.

"No, but there's no history of anything bad happening here." He looked up past the loft toward the towering roof of the barn. "So this is as good a place as any to sleep."

Julie Reilly approached them, carrying her large bag. She had a blanket wrapped around her right arm.

"Common sense tells me I should be crawling in the barn with all of the Ph.D.s, but my inner voice is also telling me not to leave Kelly alone in that house. Harris Dalton will have to fall asleep at some point. He can't watch her all night long."

Gabriel nodded. He had also worried about the reporter sleeping inside the house. And the thought that she might tamper with the house had also crossed his mind.

"Stay on the ground floor and around people. If Kelly sneaks out of the ballroom, let her go. Do not try to follow her. If she tricks out one of the floors, we'll find out tomorrow night—there's no need to take chances in there."

"You got it, Doc, no chances," Julie said. She half smiled in a nervous way and then looked at Jenny, as if envious of the fact that she now had a real man to watch over her, not just her inner ghost. She finally turned and went toward the house.

Jennifer had never been inside an actual barn before, and she had decided on the spot that she wasn't made to be a country girl—even though her profession had kept her in the country wilds most of her career. She had an inkling inside her mind that she was no longer cut out for fieldwork and that after Summer Place she would officially call it quits. Instead of trying to uncover the mysteries of the collective minds of tribes and peoples, she would learn about Jennifer instead. For the first time in her life she just wanted to be Jenny and nothing more. She looked from the roof above to the men and they were both watching her.

"I think Dr. Tilden has made a decision on something," John said, smiling at her.

"You think you can figure anyone out, don't you, Mr. Lonetree?" Jennifer asked.

"Yes, eventually," he answered.

It was obvious to Gabriel that they were forming some sort of attraction, and Gabe didn't know if it was a good thing or bad. He did, however, decide that it wasn't up to him to approve or disapprove.

"Jenny," he said, "since your friend Bobby Lee has vacated the premises, why don't you take the money the network gave you and get the hell out of here? We can manage fine without you."

John Lonetree swallowed. Gabriel had voiced just what he had been thinking, but he hadn't wanted to say the words. Part of him wanted Jenny to stay—not with them, nor even the experiment, but because he just wanted her near.

"Trying to spare the little woman the horrors of Summer Place, Gabe?" she said, and turned to John. "And you? Is that your opinion?"

"No," he said, quietly enough that Jenny took a step toward him.

"What was that?" she asked.

"No. I want you to stay. You know, to at least observe. We don't have very many people around here that we can trust."

"I see." She turned to Gabriel. "There you have it. I'm needed, so I'll stay. Afterward, I'll go learn to bake cookies and pick flowers, but for now you're stuck with me."

John looked from Jennifer to Kennedy and nodded. He removed his cowboy hat and placed it on the gate to the first stall.

"Well, it ain't the Waldorf, but it'll do, I guess," John said. He opened the polished wooden gate. "I'm claiming this stall; it's closest to the door."

Two hours later, the sun had completely vanished from the sky and half of the technical crew sat underneath the portico of Summer Place and along its magnificent steps. They were waiting for the argument to settle down so they could move in and get some sleep for the trying day ahead. As it looked right now, it would be quite a while before that could happen. Wallace Lindemann stood his ground like an eagle defending its kill.

"Look, it's academic until tomorrow morning. I misplaced

the keys to the house—I think I left them inside, on the bar—
and every call I've made to the Johanssons has gone straight
to voice mail. You'll have to throw your sleeping bags into
the tents and trucks, and that's it."

"You bastard," Kelly said, "you're intentionally keeping
us out of the house. All my people want is sleep. Look, Lionel Peterson took thirty of them into Bright Waters—he practically bought the two local hotels out—so it's only us," she
said, gesturing to those men and women sitting or standing
on the steps below them. "We'll stay put in the ballroom and
only use the downstairs facilities."

"As much as I hate to agree with Kelly on anything at this
point, I have to say she has a valid point. This group will
cause the house no harm. Why would we?" Harris Dalton
said. He ran a hand through his hair.

Kelly looked around. Jason Sanborn had abandoned all
pretense of being her ally and had vanished with some of the
more experienced crew into the large barn and stables with
Kennedy and his people. Jason would pay for his disloyalty
later; she would make sure of that. Right now she missed his
ability to calm people and force them into making sensible
decisions. That was exactly what he had done with a quarter
of her tech crew, but that decision had been to trust only Kennedy and sleep in the barn. She frowned.

"Look," Lindemann said, "there's nothing I can do about
it. Everything is locked up, and when Summer Place is secured like this there isn't so much as an open window to crawl
through. If you'll excuse me, I have a room waiting for me in
Bright Waters, which is where I suggest you go also."

Kelly shook her head. She knew Peterson had been behind
this little maneuver, as well as the house cleansing earlier. She
was about to attack again when something caught her eye.
She tilted her head.

"I think you may have misjudged the security of Summer
Place, Wallace." She nodded toward the front of the house.

The doors were wide open, and the glowing golden lights

of the massive entrance hall shone through them like an invitation to warmth and comfort.

"What the hell?" Lindemann took two steps down the stairs, bumping into Kelly. She watched him like a cat watching a mouse.

"This time, I'm afraid it was not Summer Place pulling a fast one," Harris Dalton said. He took the remaining steps up toward the house two at a time.

Just as he reached the entrance, a man stepped into the doorway and tossed Harris a set of keys. Kelly smiled. He was an ex-marine by the name of Howie Johnson—one of the best cameramen in the business and a close associate of Dalton's.

"Nothing to it, boss. These old window locks are far from burglarproof." The big man slapped Harris on the shoulder.

Dalton turned and then underhanded the keys to Wallace Lindemann, who stood fuming on the steps. He was angered not only by the break-in to his property, but also because for a moment he had thought the house had somehow opened up on its own. He swallowed and looked at Kelly.

"The downstairs bathrooms and showers, the ballroom, and that's it. I know how much liquor is in there, so keep your people in check."

Lindemann pushed past her. She wanted to laugh as she joined Harris at the doorway. The men and women left on the porch were starting to gather their things to join them inside Summer Place.

"That was pretty smooth," she said to Harris, admiring the large cameraman.

"I didn't do it to piss off Lindemann, Kelly, I did it because this crew needs sleep. I don't want anyone to leave the ballroom tonight, and I'm placing two of the security guards on the stairway to make sure no one gets lost or comes up with a sudden desire to explore. Work begins in the morning."

Kelly tried her best not to react to the thinly veiled insult.

She placed a hand in front of her mouth, pretending to cover a yawn.

"You'll have no argument out of me, Harris." She made her way past the two men and into Summer Place.

Harris watched her and then looked at Howie, who was grinning. "Don't snicker. Lindemann is right, this house is dangerous in more ways than one. Your job is to keep an eye on that woman. She's slick, and she will attempt to get a jump start on equipment placement. And one more thing: It's not that I don't want this goddamn place to eat her, I just don't want it to eat her until after this thing goes straight to hell tomorrow night. This damn place can swallow her up as long as she humiliates herself on national live TV first."

Howie laughed. "You got it, boss," he said. He wasn't thinking about Kelly's broadcast, but about her tight ass. "Wherever she goes, I'll be right behind her."

Gabriel watched from the barn as the crew slowly moved from the front lawn into the house. He also watched as Kelly Delaphoy came to the corner of the house and looked back at the barn. In the darkness of the barn's doorway, he knew she couldn't see him standing there, but he felt her gaze anyway. With one last look, Kelly turned and walked away. Gabriel took a deep breath and shook his head. All was quiet in the barn, and he knew that the others were already fast asleep. He wanted to stay near John in case he started a dream-walk. Being in such proximity to the house, he suspected, might greatly influence his sleep. He hadn't discussed it with John, but they both knew that it was highly probable.

Gabriel spotted Jenny's bag and heavy jacket on the partially open door to the same stall John had claimed for himself. He smiled. Instead of heading for the small cot that had been delivered earlier by Kelly's people, Kennedy stepped outside and looked up at the clear night sky. The clouds that had hovered just a short distance away earlier had vanished with the sun, and the clarity of the sky brought Gabriel a calmness he had never felt before on this property. He walked a distance away, avoiding the house and the windows on the second and third floors. He knew Summer Place watched, no matter how dormant it was at the moment. The house would keep a vigilant eye on him.

As he neared the pool, he wondered when the Johanssons would find the time to drain it in preparation for the winter months ahead. Their schedule had, no doubt, been thrown off by their son's illness—brought on by the very house that sat solidly watching him from above. As he approached the Olympic-size pool and its cluster of old-fashioned deck chairs and folded umbrellas, he saw the dark waters. In the daytime, the pool had sparkled. Now it looked foreboding, as if an inky blackness had replaced the chlorinated, clean-smelling waters of the day.

He stepped to the edge and looked into the pool's depths. He closed his eyes, thinking about everything in his life that had brought him to this point, this place, this predicament. The house had ruined his life, but he knew he had brought it on himself. It had been his arrogance, trying to prove that hauntings were nothing more than people's fierce imaginations. A haunting usually occurred around families that had financial troubles, or troubles of a far more personal nature. Money, or an uncle who liked to sneak into the rooms after a child's bedtime. A father who beat a mother, any stress inside a family. The mind, he knew, was the most powerful instrument in the world at producing effects that looked on the surface like a haunting.

He opened his eyes and smiled. All of his theories had come to a crashing halt that night in Summer Place seven years before. Now he knew that his hypothesis of stress-created hauntings had been full of what his students called Ph.D. bullshit. He half turned and looked at the lower floor of Summer Place. Something walked inside that house; either that something was evil and it was caught, or it chose to stay where it was. He also knew that the very house itself supported the entity and protected it. It was if the beams, the brick, the wood, and the plaster were all a shield for what stood guard inside the house. It all came together as a grand defense for the protection of evil.

Gabriel looked away from the house and placed his hands in his pockets as he remembered that night—the experiment meant to prove that stress brought on by surroundings could manifest a haunting. His students—grounded, academically sound students—were his choice of guinea pigs. They were volunteers from his classes, and the brightest knew what they were in for. The influence of the house would be brought into play by the stories they were told of its history. Stories were relayed slowly in the days leading up to the experiment, with time enough for them to be absorbed, dissected, and swallowed. Then when they arrived at Summer Place, it all came home to them. Each scenario had been documented in the stories he told them, from total nonbelief to factual, "I was there" eyewitness accounts. Gabriel had known the students would be affected by Summer Place. They would be convinced by the stories they had heard, the darkness that would surround them, and the influence of the actual house that would close around them as the night wore on. Only, he had never suspected that Summer Place was alive. It came at his kids with its full power and scared them all half to death, and had also murdered one as a gift to Gabriel for his doubt. What a fool he had been to mock what he knew nothing about.

Back then it had been about the theory, the book deal, and the power. It all seemed so trivial and mundane now that he knew there was a whole other world that most knew nothing about—a world that hated the world of the living, possibly to the point of open warfare.

Gabriel saw movement at the bottom of the pool—a shadow against a dark background, darker than the night. He went to one knee and watched as the darkness flitted and floated out of view. There was calmness to it that held him riveted in place; a ballet of movement that reached his soul. The shadow would dive and then rise, coming tantalizingly close the surface of the still waters, then hover for a brief moment before settling back into the depths. The form never took shape, but in his mind he felt it was female. It seemed to hum like a motherly figure moving about the house as she cleaned, never really stopping to attend to one thing, but gracefully moving to cover multiple tasks. It would sway left and then gently roll to the right, and then it would do a complete somersault and retreat back to deeper water.

Kennedy smiled. He reached out and touched the surface of the pool. It felt warm and inviting. He swirled his fingers through the water. He knew that if he went for a swim he would feel much better about the house and its surroundings—if only he could cover himself in the warmth of the black water. Soon his entire hand was in the water, not just his fingers, and he felt the warm, gentle grip of the dark form caressing his hand. He smiled again. He had been invited into the water so he could understand what this was all about. In an instant, he would have a clear and concise understanding of what made Summer Place so special.

The dark form brushed against his hand, and once more he felt the warmness of home. When the darkness within the water slowly withdrew to the deep end of the pool once more, Gabriel thought he heard his name being called. The voice was distant and seemed to come from another time, another place. It wasn't inviting, like the touch of the darkness was. It was harsh and full of concern and warning. Still, Gabriel placed his hand and arm even deeper into the pool.

As his name was called again, this time by more than one person, the blackness that had coiled in the deepest part of the pool seemed to grow agitated. It swirled as if a wind had churned it into a whirlwind of anger and jealousy. It wrapped itself around and around and then finally took the humanoid form of a beast, growing ever larger. As Kennedy smiled and placed his hand deeper, the blackness charged the shallower end of the pool. The voice grew louder and more insistent, and the entity charged toward him. It was coming on with such power that the surface of the pool parted in a wave as the entity plowed through the blackness. Still Gabriel smiled and waited, even as the front of that blackness opened up like a shark ready to swallow its prey whole.

Gabriel was suddenly grabbed from behind and pulled back hard. He fell against the concrete surrounding the pool, and a splash of water covered him. He heard a growl and a tremendous hiss as the water settled back into place.

"What the hell is wrong with you?" came the voice.

Gabriel snapped out of the dreamlike state.

"As much as you warned us about this fucking place, you start acting like you want to swim at eleven o'clock at night."

Gabriel shook the water from his face and then turned to see George Cordero. Coming up quickly from the barn were John, Jenny, and Jason Sanborn. They all had been calling after him, but it had been George, just dropped off by a taxi-cab, who had been closest.

"Jesus, did you see that?" Jason Sanborn ran past Gabriel and George and looked into the settling waters of the swim-ming pool.

"It damn near got you!" George struggled to his feet and removed his soaked suit jacket.

"It was in the water," John Lonetree said, staring at the pool.

"John dreamed Gabe was being pulled under the water. He woke up just a moment before we heard you, George, the first time you called out."

George tossed Jennifer his wet jacket.

"Good thing I came back, huh? Mr. Dream Man here was a little slow."

Jason Sanborn turned away from the pool. "If that thing can do this out in the pool, what kind of power does it have inside there?" he asked, pointing harshly to Summer Place.

Gabriel shook his head and cleared it as best he could. He then reached out and took Cordero's hand.

"Thanks, buddy. I was in a dream state, or hallucinating, I guess."

"My ass. I saw what was coming after you, and it sure as fuck was no hallucination. The goddamn thing had teeth!"

"Teeth?" Jason sat heavily into one of the deck chairs.

"It seems its power was enhanced this afternoon, not cleansed. I guess Father Dolan and the others only pissed it off."

They all looked at Gabriel Kennedy, then turned as one. The many windows of Summer Place stared down at them, as blank and foreboding as before, but now there was a kind of sheen to the glass that made the house look as if it were smiling.

"What about the others—the ones inside?" Jason asked, concern showing on his face.

"Let's hope they have their cameras ready. I think this monstrosity likes to fuck with people."

They looked away from the house. They all knew that Cordero was right.

Kelly watched as the section of her crew that volunteered to stay inside Summer Place made up their cots and used the five downstairs restrooms. Luckily for the fifteen men and women, there were also four showers on the ground floor. The commissary kept hot coffee on the long mahogany bar, and several trays of sandwiches were available for those who could not sleep. Kelly chose to stay awake. Although frightened of the house, she knew she had too much work to do.

A small man with glasses and long black hair tied in a ponytail strolled up to the bar and slapped his hand on top of it. Kelly looked up from her notes with her eyebrow raised.

"Bar's closed through the duration of the shoot," she said as she lowered her eyes to her clipboard.

"Then I'll just take one of these," the small man said as he took a sandwich from the tray before him. He took a bite, grimaced, and then leaned forward and spoke low so only Kelly could hear. "Harris assigned me to watch you. I see the way you keep looking at the doors. I hope you're not planning to take a little tour on your own tonight when most of us go to sleep?"

Kelly looked up from her notes. "Howie, isn't it?"

"That's what they call me."

"You're one of Dalton's boys from his sports and entertainment division, right?"

"The best field-camera jock the network has," Howie said.
He took another bite of the tuna sandwich.

"Then you know what it's like to get knocked on your ass,
right?"

"I've been ran over a few times."

"If I decide to leave this room and you follow me, I'll yell
'Rape!' at the top of my lungs. How's that for getting knocked
on your ass, you macho jerk?"

Howie stopped chewing and eyed the woman, who looked
at him as if he were a bug under scrutiny. He tossed the sandwich half in the wastebasket behind Kelly, sneered as best
he could under the circumstances, and turned from the bar.

The producer watched him leave, and then caught sight of
Julie Reilly in the double doorway, looking right at her. She
let her heavy bag and blanket slip from her arms. She nodded at some of the nervous greetings she received from those
making up their cots for the night, and then continued toward
the bar. She sat at one of the stools, facing Kelly.

"What was that about?" she asked, watching Howie stalking toward Harris Dalton.

"He's one of Harris Dalton's spies. He didn't like the way
I would handle a certain situation," Kelly said. She pretended
to make notes on her clipboard.

"I see." Julie, like the cameraman before her, reached over
and took a sandwich from the tray. Unlike him, she turned
her nose up at it and put it back. "Howie's a good jock. Nice
to have in a finesse situation if the chips are falling against
the house."

"And now I suppose this is the veteran field reporter warning the novice about treating her people with respect so
they'll respect you. That right?"

Julie didn't say anything.

"Let me tell you something. I've been through so much
with this show, I've seen things you would never believe, and

now because of one incident I'm labeled a fraud." Kelly placed the clipboard on the bar and leaned forward. "So when the day comes that I take advice from a person who climbed the ladder the same way, you'll excuse me if I tell you to go to hell. I'm the best at what I do. My show is the number one–rated program at the network—most likely, it contributes more than half of that inflated news salary of yours. I have the CEO backing me, and when this is over I'm going to use the popularity of this special to slam those ladder climbers back down to earth. And Ms. Reilly, you fall into that category."

Julie smiled and leaned as far forward as she could. "You want me, you take your best shot. I earned my stripes from Iraq to Afghanistan, from Iran to Saudi Arabia. If you think I'm frightened by your little spook show here or your power with the CEO, you're highly delusional. You can push me down the ladder, but you'll beat me to the bottom, because I know you're going to try something to boost your hypothesis of this place, and I'll catch you in the act."

"And on the way, you'll expose Kennedy for the fraud that he is?"

The sudden change in tactic almost stopped Julie from answering, but she gathered her composure.

"If Professor Kennedy is in any way involved with fraud, I'll bring him down just as readily as you, or the network."

"That won't do much for your personal life, will it?"

Julie was stunned at the comment, but Kelly kept her eyes locked on hers. She had never in her life met anyone with as much gall as the woman before her. Julie could now see that Kelly was indeed as formidable as everyone said she was. She could also see that Lionel Peterson was in way over his head.

"You bitch. I can't believe you would stand there and accuse me of not separating my job from my personal life."

"I've seen the way you look at Kennedy; any blind person could. I bet it took all of your willpower to come into the house tonight, didn't it? The desire to keep an eye on me pushed you into it, or you would be out in that horseshit barn right now, wouldn't you, Ms. Field Reporter?"

Julie slid off the stool under Kelly's glare. She turned and made her way back to the door, where she gathered her things, and then chose an empty cot in the far corner of the ballroom beyond the billiard table, out of sight of the producer.

Kelly watched until she couldn't see Julie any longer and then closed her eyes. Her attack on both the cameraman and Julie left her with a bad taste in her mouth. She knew she was gathering so many enemies into Peterson's corner that they would fall on her like a pack of hungry hyenas if she failed. If the special went down, her entire career would go down with it and she would never make it out alive. And that was exactly why she would not, could not, leave anything to chance.

Kelly looked around the ballroom and was tempted to reach for one of the bottles and break her own self-imposed rule about drinking; instead she looked over at one of her assistants—an intern who had witnessed the small confrontation at the bar. Her certificate said that she was a qualified makeup artist; she was also an associate of Kyle Pritchard's. Kelly gathered her clipboard, turned, and made her way from the bar. On the way by the young tech, she allowed her pen to fall from her hand.

"Three o'clock," she whispered as she stooped to retrieve it.

Kelly continued to the cocktail table, where Harris Dalton was working on his notes. She sat down, smiling, and greeted Harris with all the enthusiasm that had been missing from her act for the past two weeks.

All Dalton could do was wonder why the circling vulture had settled on him.

At 12:30 A.M., Kelly stood at the open double doorway of the ballroom and stared out into the expansive living room. The twenty-foot-wide fireplace was cold and empty. The sixteen couches, chairs, and love seats were arranged neatly and covered with fine white linen in preparation for the yearly rit-

ual of winterizing the interior. Kelly placed her arms over
her chest and watched the house as if she were studying a
potential ally, or an enemy.

Her eyes settled on the stairs, wide at the bottom and
narrowing as the staircase rose to the heights of the second
floor. At the base of the wooden banister two electric lamps
burned, but all they managed to do was cast eerie shadows
on the risers that made their way to the ominous floors above.
Kelly was trying to get a visual on how she could play the
darkness to the advantage of the show. She smiled, leaning
forward until she could see halfway up the broad staircase.
She knew the low-light cameras would pick up the way the
scene stretched away and then vanished after a certain point.
They could use that angle to good effect. Her eyes roamed to
the portraits lining the living room walls. Most were brightly
painted and colorful—too damn cheery. However, there were
several old black-and-white photos in old-fashioned bubble-
glass frames that she could get good angles on; possibly get
some warped reflections of Kennedy and Julie Reilly off of
those for a chill or two.

"Can't sleep?"

Kelly flinched. She wanted to scream out loud when the
voice came from behind her, but she knew she couldn't admit to any fear, even just fear caused by being caught off
guard. Harris Dalton's hair was a mess and his ever-present
vest was missing, leaving only the rumpled flannel shirt that
always seemed a part of him.

"Are you kidding? I won't sleep until I get the ratings in."

"No matter what happens, I think people are going to tune
in. If not to see a ghost, then to see a large network screw the
pooch and fall all the way from number one to laughing-
stock."

"That's real encouraging," she said sourly.

"I'm not here to blow smoke up your ass, Kelly, I'm here
to direct a show, that's all."

Kelly stared at the staircase that rose before them across
the room. "In case you don't, or choose not to realize it,

Harris, your reputation is also on the line. You're a major part of this, and if it fails you'll go down with the ship. All they'll know at corporate is that it was you who steered the ship into the iceberg."

"I think I can handle anything corporate has to throw at me. Besides, dear, they can only fire me, they can't eat me like they can you." Harris stepped by Kelly and into the expansive living room. Hands in the pockets of his khaki pants, he looked around and then up into the blackness of the ceiling three hundred feet above. He felt the producer step out with him and stand at his side.

"Still, you have to admit that this place has angles for some great shots, and you're the one who can pull it off," she said.

Harris smiled. He didn't favor Kelly with a glance, or even a typical roll of his eyes.

"I can make looking at rocks entertaining, Kelly, just as long as that's what the viewer tuned in to see."

Kelly Delaphoy smiled at the mischievous way Harris toyed with his words.

"Look, you were here and you know what this house is capable of, so why don't you give the magnanimous director thing a rest? At least when it's just us."

Harris nodded. "I need you to change the opening of the script. The house has to be the star, not Julie Reilly. I called in a favor to a friend of mine and he's going to record a voice-over in Los Angeles tomorrow morning. He'll recite the history of Summer Place as we show angles of the house, never the full frontal view. We'll record those instead of doing it live. I'll have the camera crew out before the sun comes up and get the shots for editing later. I don't want the audience to get a full view of Summer Place during the narration scenes, only snippets. That will solve concerns about the damn place not looking haunted."

Kelly was stunned. She almost panicked when she realized she didn't have her clipboard or notepad to write Dalton's ideas down.

"So you are on board, you want to make this work. That

is a marvelous opening. Who did you get for the voice-over?"
She loved the fact that the opening monologue had just been
taken away from Julie Reilly.

"Our retired anchor, John Wesley, is doing it as a favor—
but I had to give up my Super Bowl ticket allotment for it,"
he said, looking at Kelly sternly.

"I'll get you a damn suite for the game if we pull this off."

"You're damn right you will."

Both continued to examine the downstairs. Dalton was
wondering when Kelly was going to broach the subject of
heading upstairs, at least to the second-floor landing. He
didn't have to wait long.

"Why don't we see what kind of angles we can get on the
stairs? I think that's a creep factor we've yet to explore."

Harris laughed.

"Well, that didn't even take as long as I thought it would.
We're staying right here. You couldn't get me up there tonight
with a platoon of fucking marines backing me."

"This place has gotten to you, hasn't it?" Kelly asked,
amazed that this man who had been all over the world was
frightened by Summer Place.

Harris looked around, and his tired eyes settled on Kelly's. "Frightened, yes. Let me tell you something, in case your
exterior has grown so tough that you haven't noticed, or in
case you've faked so much ghost crap that you're immune
to your own senses: This place is wrong. It's like touring a
battlefield after the fact, and believe me, I've done that a
lot. There is death here, past, present, and future. I can feel
it. If you brought a combat veteran in this house, he would
feel it also. It's a sense that you're being watched and the
watcher wants nothing more than to do you harm."

"You're right. I don't get that sense. That's what worries
me about tomorrow night. Summer Place could fuck us all
and be as dormant as your grandma's house."

Dalton removed his hands from his pockets and strolled
over to the giant fireplace. He stared into it.

"This place is like an animal; a wild predator, I think. It

may go all night and just watch, or it could explode into a violent attack against what it may perceive as a threat, even though it's not hungry. Either way, this place is ruinous, Kelly, don't you understand that? If I hadn't heard all the stories, I still would have felt it." He turned away from the cold fireplace. "The one thing I'm not prepared for is for the full potential of this blackhearted house to reveal its secrets. I can see Kennedy feels the same, and if it weren't for his missing student seven years ago, I bet he wouldn't come within a state of this place—ever."

Kelly was about to respond when they heard a door creak open. She looked at Dalton with her brows raised.

Harris turned away from the fireplace and made his way across the living room to the entrance hall. The front doors were closed and secure. He grimaced, then moved through past the coat check stall and into the passageway that led to the huge kitchen. He pushed open the right side of the swinging doors and stepped inside. The smells of old meals still hung in the air. As his eyes adjusted to the semidarkness, the black-and-white checkerboard tile stood out as if it were painted in neon bright colors. Everything else was solely illuminated by the light that came through the open doorway. He felt Kelly behind him, trying to peek around his large frame.

"Look," Kelly said, squeezing past him.

The basement door, once locked, was standing wide open. The lock that had been used to secure it—the one that Kelly had witnessed Wallace Lindemann remove himself during the tour—was sitting on the large butcher block next to the door. "That door is always locked. Lindemann said so himself. He was afraid one of the Johanssons would take a tumble down the steep stairs."

"Well, obviously things have slipped while Eunice and her husband have been away." Harris allowed the swinging door to close as he stepped into the large kitchen. He felt around for the old-fashioned light switch and turned it on. The light fixture on the ceiling flared to life, casting a brilliant glow over the old appliances and counters. The kitchen was decorated with checkered tile floors, red countertops, and white paint on the walls with a belt of black tile halfway up. "I think I would have modernized the paint scheme in here," he said, stepping toward the basement door.

Kelly followed, watching as Dalton took the old crystal door handle and moved the thick wood door back and forth. It made the exact same squeak they had heard in the living room. Harris looked at Kelly and her brows rose questioningly. Dalton stepped to the open doorway and looked down into the blackness. He reached in and felt around but could find no light switch.

"It's a string above your head," Kelly said, remembering Wallace Lindemann clicking on the lights for the tour.

"There's no string here, or light switch, or fixture," Harris said.

"It's there. I saw it the other day," Kelly said in exasperation as she stepped into the landing.

"Yeah, well tell me where it—"

The loud bang from far below stopped the rest of the words cold in Dalton's mouth and made both of them jump. The sound reverberated through the kitchen.

"That was the root cellar door," Kelly said. She quickly stepped away from the steep staircase.

"How do you know?" Harris asked.

"I just do."

Harris grabbed her by the arm as he heard the first footfall far below on the staircase. Then suddenly the draft hit him and its force made the hair on his arms stand up. Goose pimples formed across his exposed skin. The landing, the doorway, and the entire kitchen felt like a door had been opened to the North Pole. Their breaths fogged in the air before them. Something had changed inside Summer Place, and this time it originated from far below.

"Listen!" he said with a cocking of his head to the right.

Kelly stopped and listened. There was a second step, and whatever was down there stopped. It was as if it were listening to see if it had been heard.

"Okay, that's it, back to the ballroom." Dalton pulled on Kelly's arm. She tried to shrug off his grip but it was like iron. Then she froze as the footfalls started again. This time it seemed they were coming on with a purpose.

"Jesus." Harris yanked Kelly off the landing and through the door. He slammed it shut and then bent over for the lock as the footsteps rose toward the landing. Kelly could tell that they had rounded the bend in the staircase and were just below in the blackness, just out of her sight. Harris retrieved the lock and fit it into the latch, slamming the mechanism home. A moment later, something that sounded like a bowling ball struck the door from the far side. Harris and Kelly jumped back and watched wide-eyed as the door rattled. The cut-glass knob turned rapidly.

"Shit," Kelly mumbled.

Suddenly the door, just like the one in the network meeting room a few days before, started to bend inward, cracking. Harris knew that if they stayed where they were, they would soon see what was creating such force. He knew that if they left, the power would die.

"Let's get out of here, now!" Dalton pulled Kelly back through the kitchen doorway. It swung as he backed out, and he could see that whatever was on the other side of the basement door gave one last powerful push inward. On the swinging door's rebound, Harris saw that the door had held. Then the door came to a rest, closing the view for good.

Harris didn't let go of Kelly until they were well away from the kitchen. They passed the coat check station and backed into the large living room. He finally stopped as he felt the heat return to his system. He let go of Kelly and placed his hands on his knees, trying to catch his breath.

"What the fuck was that?" he managed to get out.

Kelly, wide-eyed and staring at the small entranceway to the kitchen, kept her eyes on the door.

"Goddamn it, I should have known to have a camera on me."

Harris straightened up.

"You crazy bitch. When is enough enough?"

"When we have it on tape, Harris. That's when it's enough."

Harris walked toward the ballroom. "I have a feeling you just may find out tomorrow that this fucking house has the final say on that."

Kelly watched Harris leave the living room and decided that she no longer wanted to be alone inside Summer Place. She started moving in the same direction to force herself to sleep; she would need the rest.

"We'll see about that." She turned around and looked at the walls enclosing her. "You're going to talk to the world, so you better get ready."

Kelly tossed and turned on the small, uncomfortable cot. She kicked off the itchy blanket and stared up at the darkened ceiling far above her head. She eased her left arm behind her head and then closed her eyes, listening to the sounds of the old mansion as it creaked and settled. She wondered in her semidaze how long it took for a house to settle. She turned over and tried to keep her eyes shut, but the cameraman who had taken the cot nearest her own was snoring so loudly that she lost all thought of listening to the house.

Kelly tried to find a peaceful rhythm to the large man's snoring, but she couldn't. She shot the sleeping man an angry glance, then stood and ran a hand through her long hair. Julie Reilly was sitting on one of the stools at the bar, jotting something in her large notebook. Curious, Kelly eased past the sleeping men and women. Julie had the advance script that outlined the first four hours of the show, and it looked like she was furiously crossing things out and writing things in. Kelly cleared her throat.

"Jason and I worked on that thing all day. You're not even going to consult with us on your changes?"

Julie stopped writing for the briefest of moments and then started again without answering.

Kelly pulled out the bar stool next to Julie.

"Can we be civil for a moment, here?"

Julie added a line to the first page, then placed the pen down and looked at Kelly.

"Number one, I don't like you. We've been through this already, and just because we've entered your war zone doesn't mean we're going to become foxhole buddies. Second, I know what you have in mind and I—"

Julie stopped when she saw her breath condensate as she spoke the words. She looked around and saw those closest to the long bar were also breathing out a fine fog while they slept. Several people sat up and looked around; even more drew their blankets closer around them. In the corner, Harris Dalton sat up and put his jacket on. He stood up and nudged the man sleeping next to him.

"Get up; I want this recorded," he said. The ambience in the enormous ballroom had changed from one minute to the next. The room temperature had fallen by forty degrees, and it had awakened everyone. Julie slipped from her chair and wrapped her arms across her chest as she looked around. She saw the double doors and the living room beyond with its antique lighting, but saw nothing there. She looked at Kelly, who was actually smiling—Harris Dalton had three cameramen videotaping the event separately.

"I'll tell you something, Ms. Reilly, this stuff you can't fake," Kelly said as she stepped away from the bar.

The ballroom grew colder still. People were starting to huddle together for warmth, if not for safety. They all had heard the strange tales about the house, and now many were becoming concerned that this wasn't just a network stunt.

"Someone get a temperature gauge and hold it so we can get an image for broadcast tomorrow," Kelly said as she moved to her own cot and found her jacket.

Harris Dalton nodded. "You heard her, get moving. Get me a temp reading in the living room."

Just before the cameraman reached the opening, the heavy oaken doors slammed shut, making several of the women—and not just a few of the men—shout and jump.

"Jesus," Kelly said. Harris Dalton reached out and felt the wood, then pulled his hand back.

"Cold," he said.

The cameraman, a veteran of the Gulf War, stepped closer to get a better shot.

"Look!" a woman shouted. She stumbled over her cot, falling backward and hitting the floor hard.

A deep shadow had parted from the far wall, and it swept up and over the ceiling. It moved to the far side of the ballroom and then disappeared into the corner, joining the shadow there.

"We're down to twenty-two degrees in here," a man said. "Still dropping."

Julie assisted the woman who had fallen to her feet. She could feel the young girl, a script assistant if she remembered correctly, shaking beneath her sweater. Julie reached down to her cot for the blanket and wrapped it around the girl's shoulders.

"It's here," Kelly said.

"No, there isn't just one. I think there're more," Harris said, backing away from the door.

Julie looked back at where the shadow had been, just as it broke away from the corner. This time another came with it. As they watched the shadows sweep across the ceiling, the lights in the room started to dim.

"We're losing power here," one of the techs said. "It's like the batteries are draining."

As they listened and watched, several more shadows broke free and started floating throughout the room. Julie held the young girl, but for some reason she didn't feel the least bit threatened by what was happening.

"Harris is right. This isn't the power behind Summer Place, this is something else."

As Julie spoke, Kelly knew that she was right. The sweeping

shadows moved like someone swishing black sheets through the air—bulky at the head and trailing off to nothing, floating like spectral figures in a macabre dance.

"We're losing the camera lights," the man next to Dalton called out. "Losing batteries."

The shadows moved and danced high above them. The lights in the room dimmed to near nothing.

The shadows swooped and came closer to the amazed onlookers.

Kelly and Julie smelled the odor at the same time. It was a loamy smell, like freshly dug earth, full of dirt, leaves, and mildew. Julie flinched as one of the shadows swooped low. It seemed to hover around her and the young girl she was holding. Julie swallowed. The shadow seemed to reach out a tendril to the script girl. The girl flinched away, and that quick motion made the shadowy arm and hand withdraw, but only momentarily. It reached again, this time for Julie Reilly. The reporter stood her ground, although she flinched as the icy fingers, not more than tendrils of shadow, reached out and slid along her cheek. She could have sworn she could see a small opening where the mouth of a person would have been. It seemed to be smiling at her.

"God, are you seeing this? It's actually touching you." Kelly couldn't help but break out in a large smile. That changed in an instant when she saw the cameraman next to Dalton lower his camera. "What are you doing?" she asked with a hiss.

"We're dead here, no juice, no lights," the bearded man said. One by one the other cameramen lowered their cameras; they were just as useless as the first.

"Goddamn it," Kelly said.

"Shut up." Julie hissed again. The shadow kept in contact.

"What are you feeling?" Kelly asked, taking a step closer.

"It's not danger. I don't know. It's like my mother's checking on me."

"Remember everything you can so we can—"

The boom sounded from outside the ballroom. The

shadow before Julie pulled back like it had touched a hot stove, making the reporter and the girl flinch simultaneously. The other shadows became agitated, flying faster around the room. The boom sounded again, up higher than the beams of the ceiling, as if it had come from the very apex of the roof.

All in the ballroom felt the change in atmosphere; it became heavy, burdened. The shadows swept high and low, as if afraid of the sound they had heard.

The boom came again, and then again, and again. It was as if something were walking the third-floor hallway above and coming closer.

"Jesus Christ, Harris, what do you have up there, a fucking elephant?" a cameraman asked.

The booms started sounding louder and were coming with rapid frequency.

"God, where is Kennedy? Don't tell me they can't hear that!" Kelly said, watching the shadows above her head.

"Look!" another cameraman shouted.

The ballroom's double doors were icing over. The sounds upstairs grew even louder, and now there was a sound like crying; like a group of people whimpering in fear. No one in the room would claim it came from anything other than the panicking shadows above their heads.

The shadows flew to every dark corner of the ballroom and vanished. As they disappeared, the atmosphere changed dramatically. The room started to warm, and the sounds of the giant footsteps above them stopped. The double oak doors looked normal, as if they had never accumulated the slick coldness a moment before.

Power came back on, the lights glowing intensely before settling down to their original dimmed state. Several people jumped and gasped as the camera lights flared to life.

"What the hell did we just witness?" Harris reached for the camera and checked its power settings.

"Something upstairs chased off the . . . the . . ." Kelly stopped short.

"Yeah, I would say something upstairs was pissed at

something down here. And for the first time, I don't think we had anything to do with it." Dalton handed the camera back to its operator. "Audio, did we get anything?"

"Nothing. The damn recorders wouldn't even turn on." The audio tech let the recorder fall to his cot.

"The cameras didn't get dick," the man next to Harris said.

"Then we got nothing?" Kelly said as she looked around from face to face.

"Oh, I think we got something." Harris Dalton opened the double doors to reveal a quiet, warm living room. "I think we got the hell scared out of us."

More than thirty people slept just beyond the large wooden gate of Summer Place. The network had tried to get the state police to move the crowd off of the Lindemann property, but with Wallace Lindemann spending the night in Bright Waters they had no one to officially declare them trespassers. Twenty of the group that was laid low against the chill inside of sleeping bags were protesters against *Hunters of the Paranormal* from Bright River and Bright Waters, mostly made up of religious men and women who saw the show as an affront to their beliefs. The other ten, sleeping only forty feet away, were staunch supporters of the show, fans since its cable inception many years before. They had all calmed down as many had left for the more comforting confines of the local motels, hotels, and off-season ski resorts. The shouting and yelling stopped just as the moon rose into the night sky. At four thirty in the morning there wasn't so much as the glow of a flashlight to say that anyone was outside the gates at all.

Across the road, watching from the woods, was a large buck. Its antlers moved left and then right as it turned its large head, as if it studied the strange scene across the way: the tents, the people on the ground nestled in sleeping bags. The buck sniffed the air. Then its eyes moved over the two state police cruisers parked in the gravel drive, blocking the front gates. The men inside dozed with their hats pulled down over their eyes. Of the four men, only one was awake. He pulled open the cruiser's door and stepped outside for some needed air. The trooper adjusted his belt and stopped, seeing the pair of glowing eyes in the woods across the street. It was a deer—a large one, to be sure, but just a deer nonetheless.

The deer made no move to come forward from the tree line or recede into its protection. It watched the man as he stretched, yawning and shaking his head to clear it of sleep. As it watched, two more deer joined it inside the tree line. At first they playfully brushed the male, but when the play wasn't returned, they too looked across the way, first at the slumbering men and women, and then at the man who walked around the two police cruisers. Then the eyes of all three deer settled on the house. The large buck's eyes moved as a light came on in the large tent not far from the swimming pool. The chef and his two assistants the network had hired for the catering stepped from the large enclosure and looked around. As the two assistants fired up the stoves and ovens at the back of the large commissary tent, the chef made a beeline for the Porta Potti fifty feet away. Three more deer joined the group watching the house. Far off, an owl hooted and then settled back down to silence.

The male deer stepped free of the tree line and advanced four steps onto the shoulder of the road. The movement caught the attention of the man as he turned the corner of his police cruiser. He froze, but made no move to frighten the buck away. The male was soon joined by a female, cautiously stepping free of the trees. It sniffed the gravel lining the road, and then the male, before looking across the street at the man who stood next to the driver's door with his thumbs in his gun belt.

The trooper moved his left hand slowly away from his body and tapped on the glass of the driver's side door. Not enough of a tap to frighten away the beautiful creature across the way, but enough to get the driver's attention. He pushed his hat back up and out of his face.

"Sid, look at this," the man standing outside the car said. Two more deer moved forward to join the first two.

"What?" the driver asked, irritated at being awakened.

"The damndest thing I've ever seen. Look at these deer. They're just standing there staring at us."

"Jesus, Jessup, let me sleep. I don't need a nature lesson right now."

Three more smaller deer exited the woods and joined the others. Now he counted nine deer. A little unnerved, the trooper slowly removed the large-handled flashlight from his belt. He brought up the instrument and clicked it on as fast as he could, knowing the sudden flare of light would frighten the deer away. It didn't. The deer just stood there, watching him. The most frightening thing—and the trooper had decided that it was indeed frightening—was the way they made no move other than to keep chewing on whatever it was they were chewing.

"Shit," the trooper whispered. "Sid, wake up and look at this."

"Shit. I guess you're not going to let me sleep." The driver threw open his door and stepped from the cruiser. He adjusted his gun belt and then looked at his younger partner. "We're not out here to watch the animal population, we're here to—"

The driver stopped as a raccoon passed directly in front of the deer as it sniffed its way out of the trees. The trooper reached in and pulled on the headlight switch. The bright beams of light caught the deer and raccoon dead on, but the animals didn't so much as flinch in the bright lights.

"Damn. Have you ever seen anything like that before?" the first trooper asked.

"They must be, you know, like deer caught in the headlights or something. You know, too scared to move."

"Yeah, too scared. Is that why that larger male keeps coming, because it's scared?"

As the two troopers watched, the male advanced two slow steps forward. As it moved it lowered its antlers, and one actually scraped the roadway as it moved off the shoulder of the road. The two troopers took an involuntary step backward.

"You men have to get those people out of there."

Both policemen jumped at the sound of the deep voice behind them.

Standing at the gate were four men and a woman. They were watching the scene through the heavy slats of the wooden gate. The woman looked worried, rubbing her hands together.

Gabriel Kennedy had been awakened from an uneasy sleep by George Cordero five minutes before. George had gestured to the next stall where John Lonetree and Jennifer Tilden slept. As Kennedy came awake, George placed his right index finger to his lips, shushing Gabe before he could talk. A questioning look crossed Kennedy's features when George pointed to the stall across the way. As Gabriel listened, he could hear John moaning and stumbling, and then the stall door had shot open and Jennifer came through, supporting John, who staggered. It was obvious the large Indian had been dreamwalking.

"What is it?" Kennedy asked as he shook free of the blanket.

"John says something's going to happen outside," Jenny said.

"What is it, John?" Kennedy assisted Jenny with some of John's weight.

"Don't remember. Something was in the woods earlier, but it's no longer there. It's watching people and growing angrier by the minute."

Kennedy had led the way from the barn and had immediately seen the headlights of the police cruiser come on near the front gate.

As the two troopers had turned and saw the strange-looking group of people watching them, the second cruiser's doors opened. They were joined by the other two men.

"What's going on?" one of them asked.

"Don't know. The animals are acting strange." The buck had come forward another three feet, and was fully in the road. The other eight moseyed out with it, heads swinging from side to side.

"I'm going to get the key to this gate so you can get those sleeping people behind it," Kennedy said. He fumbled with the large chain that was wrapped around the main beams of the wooden gate.

"We don't have a key, and Lindemann isn't here," Jennifer said.

"Damn it!" Gabriel said with a hiss.

"Wake those people up and tell them to wait it out inside their cars until the sun comes up," Lonetree said. He had regained a little more of his strength.

"Hey, cut out those damn lights!" someone shouted from the darkness of the grass quad in front of the gate.

A man and a woman had popped free of their sleeping bags and were shading their eyes from the harsh glare of the cruiser's headlights.

"What's going to happen, John?" Jenny said.

George Cordero stepped closer to the gate and placed his hands through the wooden beams. He splayed his fingers apart and closed his eyes.

"Jesus, I'm not picking up the slow thoughts of animals over there. Whatever is approaching is something totally different." He opened his eyes and pulled his arms back through the gate as if he had touched a hot stove.

The first state trooper to have seen the deer turned to the men and women who had come awake.

"Uh, can you people wake those next to you and move to your vehicles, please? Please move away from the area."

"Oh, come on, Jessup, they're deer, for Christ's sake," the second policeman said.

That was when the nine deer charged. The buck moved so fast that the man standing next to his wife never saw him coming. The antlers struck the man just below the buttocks and lifted him high into the air, then struck him again before he came to rest on the man lying on the ground next to his sleeping bag. The other deer made for the astonished state troopers. The four men scattered as the rest of the protesters and fans came awake to a melee of sight and sound. Soon their screams and shouts were added to those of the state troopers as they ran to avoid the deer stampede.

John Lonetree climbed the fence and held his hand out toward the scrambling men and women on the ground below. As one of the state troopers reached up to take the offered help, one of the smaller deer plowed into his back, twirling the large trooper like he was a doll. He came to rest at the base of the fence, alive but badly bruised. Another, a woman, screamed as a male deer with large antlers charged from behind one of the parked state cars. She scrambled and dove for cover underneath the wheel base of the car, narrowly escaping the sharp antlers, which missed her leg and punctured one of the tires.

Suddenly several bright lights flared to life behind Kennedy and the others. Two film teams and Julie Reilly approached the fence. The camera lights froze the deer in place, some skidding and sliding to a halt as the camera lenses zoomed in on the animal attack outside the gates. Harris Dalton pushed through the two cameramen and past Gabriel. He raised a set of bolt cutters to the chain and snapped it into two pieces. Gabriel, shouting for everyone to get inside, pushed the right side of the gate open while the deer were frozen like statuary.

Men and women who had taken refuge farther away from the gate saw their opportunity to scramble to their cars, while the closest ran, stumbled, and tripped their way inside. Lonetree had hopped down from the gate and was helping the injured trooper to his feet. In that split second, the deer all came out of their startled trance. The large buck saw John and Jennifer and charged. Two others saw the slow-moving trio and also lowered their heads and came forward at a run.

Gabriel shouted a warning, but he knew he was too late. The buck was almost on them. Suddenly, a brighter than normal set of headlights swerved off the road and into the short driveway. While the truck didn't strike any of the deer, it made them veer away at the last, most horrifying second. The buck turned and actually hit the large wooden gate as John and the others dove through. Gabriel and Dalton slammed the gate closed before any of the deer could recover.

The deer seemed to settle down once the gate was closed and the people safe inside. The large buck looked around as if nothing were out of the ordinary. The other deer started to wander around, sniffing at this and that. Then, as if they realized for the first time that they were no longer in the covering blanket of trees, the deer looked startled and bounded away. Only the buck stood for a moment, chewing, and stared at the gate and the humans watching it. Then it shook its large head and slowly moved away, past the large truck with the headlights that had saved John and Jennifer.

"What the fuck was that about?"

Kennedy smiled when he saw Leonard Sickles looking out of the open passenger-side window.

"You piss off the Bambi family or what?"

An hour later, with the Bright Waters police on hand, the fans and protesters were treated for scrapes and bruises. The injured state trooper was the worst case, as he had his ass punctured with one of the buck's lethal antlers, and that seemed to be fine by his partner and the other two troopers. They laughed and teased the man to no end as the network first-aid man applied tape and gauze to the wound. After the strange attack by the local wildlife, the police had no trouble moving the protesters and fans off of Summer Place property, while Wallace Lindemann, who had been alerted in his motel room, warned everyone that they couldn't sue him because they had officially been trespassing on his property.

Gabriel stood next to the members of his team near the front gate. John Lonetree was responsible for saving a few lives, but if you saw him he looked more worried than relieved.

"What is it?" Kennedy asked as he made sure Julie Reilly and her camerapeople were far enough away as not to hear.

"The warning I received in my dream." John looked through the gate at the mayhem. There were sleeping bags and tents strewn all around the ground; people had not had time to care about their belongings. "It was a woman's voice, Gabe. She said that there was trouble in the woods. She said 'Get to the main gate,' and that was it."

"A woman's voice, you say?" Jennifer asked.

"With a German accent."

"Well, that may help us in the long run."

"How the hell is that helpful?" Leonard asked.

"The boy, Jim Johansson, he may have been helped by the same"—Gabe looked around again at the faces watching him—"entity."

"You mean we're dealing with more than one?" Leonard asked.

"Possibly, and that's where you and your computer friends at USC are going to come in handy, Leonard. We need to know what the connection between the German opera star and Summer Place really is. We need to know why her entity is helping us."

"You're kidding, right?" the small black man asked.

Kennedy smiled as he turned and looked at the house.

"You take allies where you can find them."

As they all turned and looked at the façade of Summer Place, the first rays of the Halloween morning sun peeked through the gap between two mountaintops from the east, casting the gorgeous house in a warm glow.

Upstairs on the third floor, as the first light of the new day entered the large window at the opposite end of the long hallway, the sewing room door stood open, and cold air swirled around the open space. The darkness at that end of the hallway hid the spectral shape that stood motionless, reaching out to feel the fear of those awake downstairs and those meandering after its brief display outside. A small chuckle sounded on the third floor. Satisfied, the darkness moved back into the confines of the sewing room. The door eased closed and a soft humming sounded throughout the third-floor hallway.

Summer Place was now resting.

The war was about to begin.

PART V

TRICK OR TREAT

ALL HALLOWS EVE

17

Lionel Peterson was putting off shaving and showering for as long as he possibly could. For the moment, he was content to sit in the small, smelly motel chair and stare at the water-stained carpet. He knew his actions against Kelly Delaphoy were taking a toll on his health. Not only had he endangered his career over his hate for the woman, he also had become obsessive in his drive to destroy her at all cost. He smiled. If the show flopped, millions upon millions of network dollars would be lost. He would be held responsible and fired unceremoniously. Still, he would have to root for the show to fail. He could always explain to the media that he had warned against such a risky venture as a live Halloween broadcast. On the positive side, if the show flopped, Kelly would never breathe the conditioned air of a network office again.

If the show came away with big ratings numbers for the entire eight hours, Kelly Delaphoy would end up sitting in his chair—as had been her design from the very beginning. That was a thought that almost made Lionel physically ill.

A knock sounded at his door, but Peterson kept his eyes on a particular stain that he found entertaining. The stain was in the shape of a man's head, and its wide mouth was open in a scream. The water stain (or was it something far fouler than water?) looked like a painting from a Salvador Dalí nightmare. The tongue was extended from the wide-open mouth and its eyes were closed so tightly that they were nothing but mere slits with wrinkles. Peterson tilted his head as the knock sounded again. He could hear one person speaking to another outside the flimsy door. He finally closed his eyes to block out the hypnotizing effect of the filthy carpet. He slowly stood from the chair and small table where one glass and one nearly empty bottle of Jack Daniels sat looking dejected after being ignored for most of the morning. Peterson made it to the door, removed the security chain, and cracked the door open a few inches.

The priest stopped talking and turned. He looked shocked at Lionel's unkempt appearance, but held back any rebuke he might have had.

"You do realize it's almost three o'clock in the afternoon?" Father Dolan said, wrinkling his nose.

"Of all the fools in the world, I believe I know how late in the day it is," Peterson said. He stepped back and pulled the door all the way open.

Dolan looked at the two women who had assisted him in cleansing Summer Place the day before, and then nodded that they could go.

"Good-bye, ladies. I'll hitch a ride to Summer Place with Mr. Peterson later."

Lionel raised his eyebrows and then moved as Father Dolan stepped in.

"The company you keep are rather suspect in their abilities as ghost hunters," Peterson said as he closed the door behind Dolan. "As a matter of fact, you're not that hot yourself, Father."

Peterson bypassed the chair and sat on the edge of the still-made bed.

"Has something happened at the house?" Dolan asked as he placed his black hat on the small table, making sure to miss the spilled whiskey. He sat down and watched Peterson rub the tiredness from his face.

"The phone has been ringing all morning, so in answer to your question, yes—several things." He looked up at Dolan with bloodshot eyes. "One, I guess your ghost cleansing isn't what it's advertised to be. Things happened last night that more than a dozen people witnessed, including Harris Dalton and Julie Reilly. Two, it seems thirty or more people were attacked outside the gate this morning by deer who thought they were commandos or something. Injuries were sustained, and some of it was actually caught on tape." He looked away at the closed curtains. "Not exactly a good start for a show that has to fail, would you say?"

"All I can tell you, Mr. Peterson, is that Summer Place was either cleansed yesterday, or it was fooling us and laying low."

"Now, that's a great explanation." Peterson stood and made his way to the bathroom. Before he went through the door he turned and looked at the father. "The house went dormant on you, is that what you're saying?"

"Didn't you hear those people yesterday? The house felt empty to them, so I wasn't the only one fooled. I would say that you have real trouble on your hands tonight, especially if I can't get back in there and try again."

"You'll get your chance." Peterson turned and slowly started to close the bathroom door. "They're almost done with the equipment placement, so they'll begin their final walk-through and dress rehearsal in about two hours. You'll be on that tour and in the rehearsal."

Father Dolan watched Peterson close the door and waited until the water was running before he reached for the bottle of Jack Daniels and the glass. He poured himself a glass and then made his way to the window. He pulled the curtain back and saw the heavy, dark clouds far off to the east. It looked as though they were in for rain. As he sipped the whiskey he couldn't help think that Summer Place was behind the weather buildup. Dolan had become convinced that the house had set him up, and worse than that, he felt that it knew it would be in the spotlight tonight.

As Father Dolan drained the glass, the first flash of distant lightning illuminated the window, and ten seconds later he felt the rumble of thunder through the soles of his black shoes. He turned and looked at the bottle of Jack Daniels, then quickly turned away. One drink was enough.

As he let the curtain fall back into place, the room once more became dim and dreary. He stood motionless for the longest time, listening to the shower run. For the very first time in his many years in the priesthood, he was frightened. Frightened because of the man he knew Gabriel Kennedy to be. Kennedy was a man who feared nothing in the normal, everyday world. So if Summer Place frightened him, he knew there was something in that house that he himself should be very afraid of.

Not since he had been a first-year priest in Vietnam had Father Dolan been so afraid to do what he knew was the right thing.

Summer Place

At nine o'clock in the morning, after forcing down a breakfast of cereal and coffee, Gabriel and his people entered Summer Place. Kennedy stood just inside the doorway with his eyes closed, taking in the smell of the large house. It was as if he were getting reacquainted once more with an old foe, or, Jennifer thought, an ex-wife—one whose marriage had ended horribly.

Gabriel took the others on a tour of the first floor, where it seemed he was most comfortable. He didn't seem frightened of the memories of that night seven years before, not until they started to climb the grand staircase to the second floor. His demeanor changed then—it was like listening to a recorded voice as he explained the second floor to the group. As they climbed higher, Jennifer left John's side to step up to Gabriel. Halfway up the stairs, he had stopped, unable to move another step toward the third floor. Jennifer took his hand. He swallowed and looked down at her face, filled with the early morning sunlight streaming in from the windows. Gabriel nodded his head and then took a step up. Then another and another, until he realized the house wasn't going to do anything about their presence for now. He showed the others the room where the diva had vanished, and the wall where his student had disappeared. He was shocked to see the sewing room door standing wide open, as he had never seen that particular door unlocked before. He only gestured to the sewing room before turning away, stating that they had a lot of work to do.

As the team moved away, John and George lingered, looking at the sewing room from about ten feet away. They were trying to get an impression of it, just as they had done the wall and the opera star's room. They looked at each other and shrugged, then turned and followed the others back down the stairs. As they moved, the third-floor hallway darkened, the window at the opposite end shut off from the sunlight outside. The clouds had started to move in.

The sewing room door slowly closed, and the lock turned on the inside with an audible click.

The technical crew along with Gabriel, Jennifer, John, and George assisted Leonard Sickles with the most bizarre electronics any of them had ever seen before. It took four hours to string what looked like nothing more than Christmas tree lights—small blue LEDs—along every hallway wall and staircase banister. Gabriel made his team reserve their questions for the end of Leonard's strange run-through. At every point where Harris Dalton, along with Kelly Delaphoy, placed a night-vision static camera, Leonard would be close behind to attach a small box with a lens to every stand. He explained that it was a spectral digital device that would not only pick up a color image of something that couldn't be seen by the human eye, but also an image that was etched in color by the variant air temperature, thus eliminating the need for an extra thermal cam placement next to the static night-vision cameras.

As Leonard looked over the final spectral placement, he saw Kelly Delaphoy standing nearby. She reached out to touch one of his black boxes, and the small black man jumped, startling her.

"That is one sensitive piece of equipment. You break it—you buy it."

"I already own it," she said with a smirk.

"The hell you do. Your network may have paid for the parts, but the patent is listed in my name. So hands off." Leonard's eyes blazed a hole through Kelly.

"I don't see any hookup for a feed to the production truck," she said, looking from Leonard to Gabriel. Everyone else, technicians and investigators alike, watched the small power play in silence.

"That's because there isn't one," Gabriel said. "The spectral cameras are for my team and their safety. If something shows up on one of these, it will be caught by Leonard down in the ballroom, and he'll warn us. We would rather not have any surprises coming down the hallways at us if we can help it, and we would rather not be seen running like frightened schoolchildren by a national audience."

"But—"

"But nothing. Leonard will be recording everything the spectrograph picks up. If and when I say so, you can put it on the air. Otherwise, it's a warning device only."

Harris Dalton walked up and handed a coil of electrical wire to one of the technicians. "May I ask, why the Christmas lights?"

Gabriel looked at Leonard and nodded.

Leonard looked smug. "This is a special air density meter." He removed one of the LEDs from the string of lights taped halfway up the wall and held it up. "This looks like a normal light-emitting diode, but it isn't. At the base is a small chip that measures air density, air temperature and humidity change, particulate matter disturbance, and air velocity."

"What?" Harris Dalton took the small blue diode from Leonard's fingers and looked at it.

"If something moves, it creates a disturbance in the air. I don't give a damn if it's a ghost or a freight train, if it's physically in this world, it creates a disturbance. Even if it's in-

initesimal. The laws of physics say it has to obey, and my
sensors will pick it up."

"You can track whatever it is when it moves?" Kelly looked
impressed.

"That's right. If it's moving down the hallway, or up or
down the stairs, we can see it just like tracking runway lights
at an airport. As it moves past one of my diodes, it will light
up."

Leonard hooked up the connection to the electrical line
that was snaked up and around all of the staircases and hallways. He then nodded at John Lonetree, who moved a few
feet down the hallway. As he stepped down the center of the
carpet runner, the small blue LEDs lit up as he passed.

"It tracks everything. And before you even ask, it's also
patented."

Everyone, including Kelly and Harris, laughed. Leonard
was enjoying showing everyone just how brilliant he was.

"Now, can you explain the four computers down in the
ballroom, besides the one you're using for recording?" Kelly
asked.

"Leonard has connections at UCLA and USC in California. The operators out there are going to break into the Lindemann family records in Philadelphia and New York for
photo archives and birth records. We have to do it as the show
goes out live, since we never had the opportunity to investigate for ourselves. And before you ask, no, Wallace Lindemann does not know about this, and we would appreciate it
not being mentioned, since computer theft is a crime."

"Why is all of that necessary?" Harris Dalton asked.

"The reason why we're all here tonight is because there is
something in this house that is inherently evil, and the reason it is here is in those family records—maybe in the plans
for the house, or in the property's history, or even in the family's past. Leonard will coordinate with the computer people
at the two universities and then feed up information as it be-
comes available."

"Will we have access to that information for broadcast?" Kelly asked. She looked worried that Kennedy would keep the juicy stuff all for himself.

Kennedy looked at his team and nodded his head. They agreed that since Julie and the network's cameramen and soundmen would be in the same danger as themselves, they deserved to hear anything that could be important.

"Yes, Ms. Delaphoy, we'll hook up a sound box so that Julie Reilly can hear everything we hear."

"Thank you," she said.

"Now, I need to know about power. Do you have a backup for the electricity coming in from Metropolitan Edison?" Leonard asked.

"Yes. We have three backup generators rated to cover everything on the property, plus the two production vans. They have a noninterruption contact start, meaning that there would be only a split second of light failure before the generators kicked in," Harris said, looking proud. "It's the same backup we use for sports events."

"Sounds like we'll have enough power in case that storm seriously hits us."

Kelly smiled at Gabriel. "As a matter of fact, our network meteorologist says we could be in for one of the largest storms of the year, hitting sometime after we go on the air."

"And this is good because?" Jennifer asked. She didn't like the look that came across Kelly's face at all.

"Ambience, Ms. Tilden, ambience. What's better than a haunted house investigation on a dark and stormy night?"

Kelly's smile deepened and she moved past them. Harris Dalton shook his head but followed along with the technicians, leaving Gabriel and his people alone on the third floor.

The group was quiet as they took in the gathering darkness in the third-floor hallway. John and George could feel the energy coming off of Gabriel in waves. They couldn't tell if it was growing fear of the night ahead or the hatred he felt toward Summer Place. The two men exchanged glances and a silent message—one of them would be at this man's side all through the broadcast.

"Jenny." Gabriel looked down the hallway toward the suite where the German opera star had once stayed, and then past it to the sewing room. He purposefully refused to look at the area of the wall where his student had vanished, but he felt the spot nonetheless. "You haven't felt the presence of Bobby Lee at all?"

Jennifer could tell that Gabriel had been banking heavily on Bobby Lee McKinnon's help. She could see it in his eyes as he finally turned to face her. She almost wished she could help Gabriel, even though it would have meant having Bobby Lee back inside her. Yet, she knew if that happened again, she would never survive the ordeal. He would make her go without sleep and practically sing herself to death. The past few days, she had regained strength and the perception of what a living hell she had endured at the hands of the mad ghost, and she didn't think she could willingly go back. It had been a fluke at the Waldorf when Bobby Lee had came across the man ultimately responsible for his death, and she knew how lucky she had been to get relief; lucky that Bobby Lee felt avenged when he confronted the man after all those years. It had been as simple as that, as if the old-time record producer had unwittingly performed a half-assed exorcism and sent Bobby on his way, content just to have had his say.

Jenny took Gabe's arm and shook her head. "Sorry, no."

"Gabriel, I don't mean to be an ass here, but you asking her that . . . it worries me," Lonetree said, studying his old friend. "You would be willing to risk Jenny over this house?"

Kennedy felt ashamed. He realized that was exactly what he would have been willing to do. He looked away.

"John, it's okay." Jenny smiled first toward Lonetree, and then Gabriel. "If I thought Bobby Lee could really be of some help here, and if it meant driving out into the open the thing that's inside this house, I would have done it. Don't blame Gabriel."

Lonetree nodded, unconvinced. They heard the creak of

a door opening. The sewing room door stood wide open; they could see the sheet-covered furniture inside, even through the gathering darkness. No one moved or said a word. It was if the five of them were standing in front of an old enemy and both sides were sizing each other up. If it weren't for Julie Reilly coming up the stairs with a script girl, the stare-down would have continued.

"What's wrong?" she asked as she gained the third-floor landing. Her eyes went from face to face and then settled on the portrait of the Lindemann clan on the wall facing the staircase.

"Oh, we were just discussing how to keep Kelly Delaphoy from making a mockery of our attempt to find out what's going on here," Jenny said, lying smoothly.

"Well, I think one of the answers to that just came in. He's down in the ballroom with Lindemann and Peterson. Detective Jackson made his grand entrance a few minutes ago. He's taken up station in a corner of the ballroom after threatening anyone that would listen about what will happen to them if they get his face on camera."

"Any other demands?" Gabriel asked, his eyes moving back to the sewing room door.

"As a matter of fact, yes," Julie said. She wrote something on her notepad and read it over, then tore the page out and handed it to the script girl. The girl didn't even see the instruction Julie had written out; she was staring at all of the camera equipment and Leonard's strange devices lining the hallway. Julie pushed the paper at her and the girl finally took it, then started for the stairs.

"Miss," Gabriel said, stopping the girl, "no one goes anywhere in this house alone. Leonard, will you see that she makes it back to the first floor?"

Leonard smiled at the young, pretty girl and nodded. "You bet, Doc." He took the girl by the arm and started down the staircase.

"You were saying?" Gabriel said, getting Julie back on track.

"He told Dalton and Peterson that he wants to travel the house tonight with your team. Specifically you."

"And this cop is camera shy?" Lonetree asked.

"Lionel, the big mouth that he is even when he's sober, said it would be no problem. They can get shots of the team without including Jackson. So I guess he'll be behind the cameramen and soundmen the whole night, but he'll be there, watching."

"It sounds like he would be better off watching Kelly, if you ask me. She's the real danger here."

They all looked at Jenny, who stood with her back to the sewing room, not wanting to give her cold chills any credence.

"Harris will have her in the production van right at his elbow. He'll be watching her. After all, his reputation is on the line here also."

Gabriel didn't say anything. Damian Jackson was one small problem in a chain of them. He finally looked away from the sewing room and at the four people with him.

"Remind me to tell Leonard to concentrate his investigation in the archives on that room and the person who used it the most—Mrs. Lindemann. I'm wondering if something may have happened to her inside there. It seems to be making sure it's noticed."

"I agree, there's more power coming out of there than any other room," George said. He took a step toward the sewing room. Gabriel took his arm and stayed him from going farther.

"Not now," Kennedy said. "We'll accept its invitation later."

Julie looked at her watch. It was well after four thirty. "I agree. Right now we have the final run-through of the opening sequences, and Harris wants a word with everyone. And, just so you know, since the promos for the show have been running, the anticipated viewership has risen to close to fifty million." Julie looked around the third floor and at the sewing room, then finally back at the others. "So if we fall flat on our faces, the whole country's going to witness it."

"I think we can bear up under the pressure," Gabriel said, staring directly into Julie's eyes.

"That's nice, Professor, but your career was already in the shitter. My fall will be from a much higher plateau than yours."

"That shouldn't bother you, Ms. Reilly. You should be more worried about what's going to cause your falling to your professional death—a flop, or a success?"

Julie looked at Jenny. Her tense smile said that she was only concerned about the flop portion of the equation.

As she watched the others start down the stairs, Julie looked up at the Lindemann family portrait and the smiling faces of the large clan. Then she heard a noise and turned. The sewing room door was once more closed. She shook her head as she turned and followed Gabriel and the others, wondering for the first time which death would be worse: the flop she fully anticipated, or something the Summer Place had in mind. The possibilities of the latter alternative might just be the worse of the two.

"Goddamn creepy place."

The commissary tent was packed with technicians, electricians, cameramen, soundmen, hair and makeup stylists, production assistants, and producers. And, of course, the people who were going to be seen live across the nation in less than three hours—the group that a lighting technician had dubbed the Supernaturals: Gabriel Kennedy and his team, along with Julie Reilly and Detective Damian Jackson.

While everyone sat around the ten long tables drinking sodas and coffee, Jackson stood in the far corner of the tent with one hand in his coat pocket and the other at his chin, listening but not hearing as Harris Dalton addressed the hundred or so crew. The lieutenant's eyes were squarely fixed on Gabriel Kennedy. And what was most irritating to the state policeman was the fact that Kennedy stared right back. Jackson realized for the first time that the psychologist actually believed this night would bring him the redemption he sought over the disappearance of his student seven years before. But Jackson knew he would never see that redemption. He knew Kennedy would throw up a smoke screen at some point during the night to mask his culpability in the incident years before—to make people believe, or guess at his innocence. Jackson would be right beside Kennedy the whole night and he would make sure that the smoke screen was not as thick as the professor would like it to be.

"The two generators are outside the production vans for quick and easy access," Dalton said as he looked at his notes. "The state police have moved the looky-loos three miles down the road, so we shouldn't have any interference from them."

"Just how many police will we have on hand?" a nervous production assistant asked. The pretty young woman was one of Dalton's own people, and he felt for the girl. This was a lot of pressure for her first live assignment.

"The state police will have six men stationed in and around the property," he answered.

"But not in the house, correct?"

All eyes turned to Kelly.

"Only Lieutenant Jackson, as per Professor Kennedy's request," Dalton answered. Kelly knew exactly who was to be allowed in the house, but was baiting both Wallace Lindemann and Lionel Peterson, who sat side by side in the farthest corner away from everyone, watching silently. Both men were impeccably dressed and cleanly shaved and showered.

"Can we discuss the roving teams?" Julie Reilly asked.

"Please do. It's time each team met their camera and sound people," Harris Dalton said as he gestured for Julie to take over.

As Julie stood, Jennifer nudged Gabriel's arm. She raised her right eyebrow as if to tell him to end the staring game with Jackson. Before she turned, however, she saw a small smile crease the state policeman's mouth. Then he relaxed, but not before placing his hands on his hips; in so doing, he uncovered the black pistol he kept holstered on his hip. Jenny lightly shook her head.

"Professor Kennedy's technical man, Leonard Sickles, will be with the four computer assistants inside the ballroom. They will be covered by a static and a remote-controlled camera. Lighting there will be minimal, so expect a lot of blurred close-ups," she said, smiling at Leonard.

"Blurred? Baby, this is the one face you want clear," Leonard said with a grin. He kept his smile on until his eyes went to Jackson, who was just looking at the former gang member. Then Leonard lost the smile fast.

"Just do your job in there, Mr. Sickles. Your research, which should already have started, will be going out live if you uncover anything."

"If there's something to dig up, we'll dig it up. But I will need clear access to the West Coast. Anything spotty may lose us valuable time and data," Leonard said. He glanced nervously at Damian Jackson, knowing the man could see right through his bravado.

"Your satellite link is secure and every computer has a battery backup," Julie reassured Leonard. "Team two, Professor Tilden, John Lonetree, and George Cordero. Team three, myself, Professor Kennedy, Father Dolan, and Detective Jackson." She looked at the lieutenant, who raised his brows. "Detective Jackson will be the only one not filmed, taped, or otherwise recorded."

Gabriel stood and looked at the others. "Only one team at a time will be on any floor of the house, with at least one floor separating teams for sound variance. When team two is in the basement, team three will be on the floors above. When three is in the barn, two will be on floor three, and so on. You will be told your assignments during the show and at commercial breaks. It's not perfect, but it will keep us from crowding each other."

"Shouldn't each team have a . . ." Lonetree looked around as if not being able to come up with the word. "Shouldn't each team have a seer?"

All eyes looked at John.

"No. With Professor Tilden's friend missing in action, I want her covered. I think she still may be a magnet for whatever is in there. She attracted Bobby Lee McKinnon; she just may do the same here. You two will watch her and try to feel if that happens before it happens."

John Lonetree looked satisfied at the answer, but not truly happy about it. It was like Gabriel was still using Jenny as bait. Jenny calmed John when she reached out and wrapped her thin fingers through his enormous ones. She smiled without looking at him.

"By Professor Kennedy's request, after the taped lead-in from New York, and after my intro from the front steps along with the introduction of the teams and their expertise, Summer Place will be secured—locked from the outside."

"That's just a little extreme, isn't it?" one of the soundmen asked from the back table.

"Integrity." Kelly stood, her clipboard held against her chest. "That's the modus operandi of *Hunters of the Paranormal*. No one in or out for the duration. At the very least, it compels the viewer to believe the teams are isolated, which is hard enough to do on television."

"Look, we all heard what happened the last time we had people in this fun house. What if we need to get out of there fast?" the same man asked. He didn't look the least bit ashamed at questioning the *Hunters of the Paranormal* routine.

"For all of those who have the same concerns, I present you with this magic talisman," Kelly said dramatically, holding something up like a cross to a vampire. "The key to the front and back doors!"

Everyone, including the nervous soundman, laughed aloud.

Lionel Peterson even grinned, to a point. He had to hand it to the queen bitch of the universe—she knew how to handle the production team.

"It makes me want to have the locks changed," Peterson mumbled.

"What was that?" Wallace Lindemann asked, leaning toward Peterson.

"Nothing."

An hour later, Harris Dalton stood on the upper tier of the production van while the three teams were in makeup. Without the roving team cameras and sound, he had to be satisfied with testing the static night vision and infrared cameras on each floor, bedroom, and basement. He would have liked to test Leonard Sickles's lighting system before the start, but he guessed that would have to wait—the ghosts wouldn't move on cue just because he needed a test.

"Go to one," he said. The view on static camera one showed the interior of the ballroom. There were three people inside sitting at the computers that had been installed. One of the state policemen was there as a precaution, as most were still outside the house. As the camera zoomed in, Harris could see the technicians tapping away at their keyboards. Every once in a while they would look up nervously. *Jesus*, he thought, *if they're going to do that all night long, they'll never uncover anything.*

"Okay, one, switch to infrared, please."

On the monitor, the scene switched and it showed three red-hot figures, two sitting at the table by their computers and one standing at the open door to the ballroom. Their body heat put out enough energy to turn their images red. The rest of the ballroom, with the exception of the computer monitors and their towers, was a soft blue, yellow, or green.

Harris continued the static camera check. Twenty minutes later the still camera and sound backup installed in the stable picked up movement, and just as Kelly Delaphoy walked into the production van Gabriel Kennedy came in view. Harris was annoyed at Kelly for coming into the camera check, since he usually allowed no one in or out during this critical time. He looked at her, annoyed, but went back to camera thirteen, inside the stables. Kennedy just stood there looking around, then moved over to the first stall and eased down on a bale of hay. He sat silently, rubbing the tiredness from his face.

"Tell makeup they have to hit Professor Kennedy again before airtime. He just rubbed his face off." Harris shook his head. Amateurs. He would have to watch everything these people did. A shadow fell on Kennedy and then a large man stepped into the view of the night-vision camera.

"Bring up the sound on the parabolic microphone on thirteen, please," Kelly said.

"You don't give orders in here, Kelly." Harris stared a hole through the smaller producer.

"Harris, turn up the goddamn mic, will you? Do you see who that is?"

Dalton looked again and saw that the man who had joined Kennedy was none other than Damian Jackson. The state policeman, with his hands casually at his sides, stood over the professor. Then Jackson moved over to a bale of hay feet away from Gabriel, sat down, and tipped his fedora back on his head.

"Do as she says, bring up the volume," Harris ordered.

At first there was nothing, only the camera picking up two men who seemed to be taking a quiet moment for themselves.

"I don't like eavesdropping on private conversations." Dalton leaned on the large console as he watched the scene before him.

"They know the stables are hot. That camera was placed where Kennedy himself wanted it. Leave it. I wouldn't miss this conversation for the world. In fact"—Kelly placed a set of headphones over her ears—"record this. It may come in handy."

Dalton shook his head but nodded to the playback technician anyway.

In the barn, the two men faced each other. Jackson leaned forward and entwined his fingers, resting his elbows on his knees.

"I guess you've been waiting for this night for quite some time," Jackson said.

Gabriel looked at the detective. Then he straightened and looked around the stables for a brief moment, his eyes momentarily settling on the camera and its stand in the far corner. He looked away and finally settled on Jackson.

"Even if I prove nothing, I know what happened that night seven years ago."

"You know, Doc, I truly believe that you think something supernatural happened at this house, but that doesn't make it right that you placed kids in your charge in danger." Damian held up a hand when Gabriel started to say something. "Whether it was you or one of your students responsible for the disappearance of that kid, it doesn't matter. He's dead and gone, and I'm going to bring the person responsible to justice. If that makes me the bad guy here in this sickening menagerie, then so be it."

"You'll never understand anything about this world, will you? All you see is black and white, and there's never anything in between. I used to believe that hauntings were simply self-induced illusions brought on by adrenaline and stress. Mass hallucinations by people expecting to see something, and the human mind producing the desired outcome."

"Now, that is a sound theory, Doc. You should have stuck to it." The camera couldn't see Jackson's expression as long as his back was to the camera, but it could pick up Kennedy's. His was tolerant, as if he were speaking to a child who didn't know any better.

"The theory is shit, and any clinical psychologist that subscribes to it is a moron. I was one of those, seven years ago. I assumed I knew the natural world, and this house is a part of that world. I didn't know a damn thing." Kennedy leaned forward until he was only a foot away from Jackson's face. Kelly and Harris did the same thing, unknowingly leaning toward the monitor for camera thirteen. "There is something in that house, Detective. As matter of fact, there are several somethings. If they show themselves tonight, you better be prepared to open up that pit you call a mind, or you'll find yourself in a purgatory, like I did—a place where nothing in the universe makes any damn sense at all. I know what it's like to have a closed mind forced open, and it hurts."

"Doc, your rhetoric is the best I ever heard. You talk a game that most can't follow, and those that can, well"—he gestured toward the stables' twin doors—"look at the ones who do believe; the people you assembled, they're all nuts. The true believers will get you every time. That's who I'm going to be watching tonight, Doc." Jackson stood and looked down at Kennedy. "And you, of course." Jackson turned and walked toward the doors but paused before opening them to the gathering darkness outside. "It ends tonight, Kennedy, one way or another; you're going to come clean."

Gabriel and those watching in the production van saw Jackson exit the stables, whistling a tune none of them knew.

"I'm using this. We'll find a place to plug it in later in the show," Kelly said. Kennedy turned his head and momentarily looked at the camera. She saw the small shake of his head before he stood and left the range of the camera and microphone.

"You really are a little cutthroat, aren't you?" Dalton asked, loud enough for everyone in the trailer to hear.

Kelly gathered her things and made her way to the plastic curtain that covered the door. Then she stopped and looked back at Harris Dalton.

"You better get this through your head, Harris: If this show fails, we'll both be wishing we had used everything we could get on the air. I, for one, am leaving nothing under, or on top of, the table. Cutthroat? Yes, I am. And you better be also, at least for tonight."

Harris watched her leave and then lowered his head. He heard one of his technicians punch a button.

"We have the opening angle, and it looks great."

Dalton looked up into the number one out-on-the-air monitor. Summer Place was glowing bright yellow and white in the setting sun. The house looked magnificent, but he knew it was a beast waiting for its prey to come into range. He had not seen a thing that night of the broadcast test, but he knew something was waiting for all of those who would enter.

Harris also knew that he wasn't going to be one of those people.

Summer Place wasn't going to eat him.

After Jackson departed, Gabriel sat and listened to the sounds around him. The stable, although empty of people, was alive with activity. He could hear birds in the upper rafters and wondered why they hadn't headed out of Pennsylvania with the turning of the weather. He could hear mice scurrying in the hay. He even thought he could hear the ghosts of summers past and the stable workers employed by the Lindemann family many years ago. The sound of horses anticipating a summer ride by privileged houseguests filled his ears, along with the laughter of men and women long dead.

Gabriel walked over to the old tack room and looked inside as the sun drained from the sky outside. He turned on the ancient light switch and saw the gleaming, oiled tack kept in immaculate condition by the Johansson family. The reins, saddles, and fancy horse blankets emblazoned with the Lindemann family crest—a shield, two horse heads facing each other with crossed swords. Gabriel knew that F. E. Lindemann had originally come from a family that would have had no crest. His ancestors were hardworking folk from the Alpine region of Germany, farmers for the most part, so he knew that the family crest had either been borrowed or outright manufactured for the benefit of Lindemann's American friends. Impressions were everything back then.

Gabriel reached out and shut off the light. He stood motionless, thinking. No, Lindemann and his ancestors were not people of historical significance, but Elena Lindemann was. With a last name such as Romanov, it wasn't hard to figure who carried the real family jewels. Gabriel turned away from the tack room. Elena, the matriarch of the Lindemann clan, had met F. E. in 1879 at a function regaling the Romanovs in New York. Old F. E. had already made his fortune by then and was continually adding to it. By all accounts, the romance was burning as soon as Elena found out about that fortune. Gabriel guessed it was enough to keep her good name in even better standing in New York circles. Gabriel had always thought he had a trail to follow with Elena's ambitions and the effect she had on the family and on Summer Place, but by every account, Elena had been nothing short of an angel on earth. Not only did she feed the hardworking women of Frederic's garment industry, she also fed the homeless of New York and Philadelphia. She actually recruited women from Europe, personally financing downtrodden women from all over the Continent to come to America and get a fresh start.

Gabriel shook his head. Nothing in Elena's past could be a key to the haunting of Summer Place.

Kennedy stood and looked into the darkness, toward the expansive wooden beams overhead. His historical research before that night seven years ago was a cause célèbre for his classes at USC. He had more than a hundred students volunteering for library research on the Lindemanns, their family legacies, and their philanthropic endeavors. They came up with nothing more than a five-hundred-page report on just how great an American family they truly were. Oh, Lindemann himself had his troubles, as every businessman in the nation did in those harsh times of early manufacturing. Fires were a big issue in the garment industry in those days. A hundred men and women lost their lives in one such incident in 1889. Even then, long before he met Elena Romanov, Lindemann had paid out to each family a thousand dollars for the loss of their mother, wife, or daughter. The payout was unheard of at the time, and he did all of this without admitting to having a sweatshop. He always came out smelling like a rose. Even more, his students' research report showed that his goodness was never a publicity ploy; newspapers only found out through back channels that Lindemann had made the contributions at all. There was no history of trouble at their

New York, Philadelphia, or German estates. They were as clean as his students found them to be.

He believed all of it, and that had been the basis for his beliefs seven years ago. The history of the disappearances, the assaults, and the strange happenings had to be brought on by hysteria, mass hallucination, or a group mentality that forced people into believing there could be such a thing as an actual haunting. The property that Summer Place was built upon also stood up to scrutiny. No Indian massacres, no settler disappearances, nothing. Only F. E.'s old hunting camp; the house was built over the small gorge once used as a hunting blind to catch deer and other animals off guard. No, the property was as clean as the family history. Since there was nothing in the past, there could be nothing haunting Summer Place. Easy: two plus two made four.

Kennedy smiled as he slowly made his way around the darkened stable. *Two plus two make four,* he thought. That night with his students, he had found out the hard way that Summer Place wasn't good at math. Two plus two equaled whatever the house wanted it to equal. All through the night he debunked his students' feelings, or sightings, or misadventures, one after the other. He was proving that he was in control, not only to them, but also to himself. He was proving beyond any reasonable doubt that his theory on haunted houses was the correct one. About the time that he was patting himself on the back for his brilliance was when Summer Place came alive and started showing its true power. The doors slamming, the power surges and outages, the screams, the cries, and finally the apparition that every student on staff claimed to have seen up on the third floor.

Gabriel felt his knees weaken at the memory of that night. He leaned heavily against one of the solid wood support posts in the stable and took a couple of deep breaths to calm himself. He thought back to that long climb up the stairs after Warren Atkinson, the brightest kid in the graduate program, had disappeared. At the top of the stairs, he saw the sewing room door close on its own and he heard the laughter—he had never told Damian Jackson, nor anyone in authority. He remembered finding Warren's glasses at the base of the wall. His class ring was also there; the bulging plaster, the wetness of the wall and paper that covered it. He had gone into shock at the discovery of those items on the carpet runner, and had torn into the wall with one of the table lamps that lined the hallway every thirty feet. He had seen the emptiness of the interior of that wall, and the slatwork behind it. Yes, Summer Place had done its own math that night—it subtracted very well indeed.

When the hand reached out and touched him, Gabriel jumped. Julie Reilly stood beside him with a makeup tissue still tucked into her collar. She looked at him curiously.

"I would say you looked like you saw a ghost, but that would be a little too cliché, considering."

"Past mistakes," Gabriel mumbled.

"Excuse me," Julie said, watching his face in the darkness. She reached out and turned on the light. The man did look like he was scared, and indeed looked as if he had seen a ghost.

"I will not underestimate this house again."

"I hope you don't. Even if I don't believe like you do, I always cover my bases."

"What do you want?" he asked when he got his heart and breathing settled.

"You're due in makeup; we only have forty-five minutes to air."

"I was already there," he said.

"Harris and Kelly said you messed up your makeup and that you have to go back in."

Gabriel smiled and looked back at the camera mounted on its tripod. As Julie watched, Gabriel raised his right hand and flipped the camera the bird.

"Any *particular* reason you don't like that camera?" Julie said as she turned to leave.

"Yeah, but none that I care to share at this *particular* moment."

* * *

Kelly Delaphoy stepped out of the production van to get a breath of air. The trailer was air-conditioned to accommodate all the electronic equipment, but she still found it hot and oppressive. Kelly was used to a small Chevrolet production van and a minimal staff, one reason for *Hunters of the Paranormal*'s minimal production costs. Being this close to an expensive special was starting to eat away at her confidence. She looked at her watch, and the bright lights of a camera caught her eye. When she looked up she saw a network crew setting up on the lawn just inside the half-moon drive in front of Summer Place. The news division had come onsite without having notified her.

Kelly saw Wallace Lindemann walking toward the network reporter, a woman not far beneath the stature of Julie Reilly. He was being tagged by one of the makeup people, who dabbed at his face as they moved toward the reporter and camera crew. She saw Lionel Peterson standing off to the side, impeccably dressed in a black three-piece suit, standing as if he were king of Summer Place. She made a beeline toward the head of the entertainment division.

"What is this?" she asked Peterson.

"Well, let me see. From this distance I'm not sure, but it looks like Wallace Lindemann is about to do a news interview." He looked at Kelly as she came to a defiant stop in front of him. Then he grimaced when he saw Julie Reilly come out of the stables, with Professor Kennedy not far behind her. She saw the bright lights of the news team, and then him and Kelly. She ripped the makeup guard from around her neck and sprinted toward them.

"What the hell is this?" Julie asked. Her question wasn't directed at Peterson, but Kelly.

"That's what I'm trying to find out."

"Look, both of you need to get a grip. This interview is going out live on the evening news. As much as I hate the news division piggybacking us the way they have"—he shot Julie an ugly look—"we need a solid lead-in to the show."

"We don't need a lead-in; all the projections are skyrocketing. And we surely don't need a loose cannon like Wallace Lindemann walking the news audience through his hoax speech."

"And if the network wanted this, why didn't they have me do it? I could have controlled Lindemann," Julie Reilly chimed in. As much as she hated Kelly Delaphoy, she knew the producer was right. Lindemann was dangerous with a live camera. She looked into Peterson's eyes. "You set this up, didn't you?"

Peterson looked from Kelly to Julie and shook his head. "Now, why would I try to sabotage a show that has control of the trapdoor underneath my feet?"

"Because, you sanctimonious son of a bitch, you actually think you can survive this thing," Julie said before Kelly could open her mouth. She looked beyond Peterson and saw two men who had been with the CEO inside the boardroom watching the test broadcast. They were standing side by side and seemed quite content with the happenings.

Julie's mouth fell open—she realized finally what Peterson's game was. He had played the dummy, acting his way through the indignity of the special as if he had no choice to do so, while all the while he had been playing a game, making fools out of everyone from the CEO to Julie and Kelly. Julie actually smiled as she turned from the two board members to face Peterson once more.

"You're not just out to solidify your position as the president of entertainment, you bastard, you're out for a full-blown coup against Feuerstein, aren't you?"

"That's one dangerous and foolish accusation, Ms. Reilly." Peterson straightened and removed his hands from his pockets. "As you've noticed, there are two board members right over there, and three more are on the way. Now, why they are here to observe the special is beyond me, but if you like working in this field"—he looked from Julie to Kelly—"I suggest you keep this coup idea to yourself." Peterson started to walk away, toward the two men who were waiting for him, but he stopped and turned with a smile on his face. "It seems the CEO's decision-making has come under scrutiny from the stockholders lately; he may have overstepped his bounds with this very expensive special, something that's a little out of his area of expertise."

"You bastard!" Kelly said loudly, drawing the attention of those around them. She started to go after Peterson, but Julie stopped her.

"Let it go."

"We have got to tell the chairman what's going on here. At least, the news division has to be notified that they're being used." Kelly glared at Peterson, who smiled even wider and turned away to join the board members.

"Do you think that son of a bitch would ever have chanced this without most of the board and division heads in his corner? He's not just making his play for control, he's trying to oust the chairman. The news division is in on it, and who knows who else. All we can do is what we're here to do."

"Yeah, and if Summer Place is dormant?" Kelly said, turning on Julie.

Julie smiled and shook her head.

"Then the joke really will be on us, won't it? I mean, I knew for a fact that Professor Kennedy was a nut and proved it once a long time ago. You, well, you were out to use him. Now we're both dependent on the nutcase for our professional lives." She started to turn away, but stopped. "Summer Place is either going to bail us all out, or make the real monster king of his world, wouldn't you say?"

Kelly watched Julie Reilly walk away. Then she turned to watch Wallace Lindemann as he extolled the virtue and beauty of his summer home, which just happened to be on the open market for a bargain price. Kelly looked up from the bright lights of the interview to the brightly lit façade of Summer Place. The house seemed to be looking on with only mild interest at what was happening below.

Kelly knew as well as Julie that they had been played. She also knew that Peterson had started setting her up the moment the CEO and chairman gave her the go-ahead for the special. She had been outmaneuvered, and she knew this would be her last night in broadcasting.

Summer Place had already beaten her, and the battle had yet to start.

18 UBC Network Headquarters, New York, New York

Abraham Feuerstein stood in the corner of the theater-style viewing room. The entire board of UBC and the top members of the General Television and Electronics Corporation board were on hand for the special. The buffet had been laid out and the drinks were flowing. Feuerstein watched certain members of the UBC board as they meandered from person to person, hardly sparing the CEO a glance. The old man with his bow tie sipped his club soda and watched, knowing the talk was about him. The game was afoot, and Abe knew for certain that Lionel Peterson and his allies were smelling blood. The plan was to oust him as head of his own network, and Feuerstein knew they could do it with the board's approval. He had stuck his neck out by approving Kelly Delaphoy's dangerous scheme, but he knew that Peterson and his young bunch could be shoved to the side with no problem if the ratings came in. If not, he would just go back to overseeing his electronics empire.

The fifty-by-twenty-foot screen was the main feature of the room, and at this moment it was blocked by lower members off the UBC board, here to see the fight between the young lion and the old. Everything in the world was in Kelly Delaphoy's lap. He knew young Kelly for what she was—a cheat, a liar—but she was also a showman.

"Mr. Feuerstein, we have ten minutes to showtime. Would you like to say a few words?"

The CEO placed his drink on a side credenza and shook his head. The man who asked the question was in Peterson's camp. Abe had watched him hang up the phone only a moment before; he knew he'd been talking to the shark on location in the Poconos.

Feuerstein moved to his seat in the center of the room. He nodded at trusted friends from the electronics board as they joined him. These were men and women who seemed genuinely excited for Abe, with the risky venture about to start. Test pattern from the Poconos came up on the screen, and Abe watched as everyone took their seats. The test pattern was soon replaced by the still shot of Summer Place that was to be used extensively in the special. The picture of the house was meant to portray evil, but Abe knew it could hold real horrors for him tonight—it held the power that was to be exchanged between him and his television empire. He couldn't help but wonder what Peterson was doing at that very moment.

Summer Place, Bright River, Pennsylvania

Lionel Peterson was standing just inside the large gate, looking up at Summer Place. The crowds, both for and against the show, had been banished three miles down the road, and the scene was quiet. Peterson was well aware that by now Abraham Feuerstein had to be aware of the board's consensus that he had overstepped his bounds on the television special. The outlay for expenses would never be recouped, and the old man would be the one to answer for that. Only ratings could save him. If the show was a hit, Feuerstein would survive and would be standing over Peterson's dead body this time tomorrow.

The sun had gone down, and the threat of the storm—one that the network weathermen had assured them would stay far from the Poconos—was building not only in intensity, but also in camera-attracting splendor. It could only add to the ambience of the show. Peterson cursed his luck, but what could one expect from the weathermen? They were, after all, part of the news division. When and if he became head of the network, he would make sure those incompetents were all off working for NBC, or at the very least, Fox.

He watched the house, knowing that the inert structure held his destiny in its hands. But with the Kyle Pritchard incident, he had an outstanding chance of making this look like a Kelly Delaphoy fiasco, designed and carried out by that power-seeking bitch. If only he could pull this off and destroy her, he would never crave anything so much ever again.

"Mr. Peterson, Harris says we're fifteen minutes from airtime. He asks that you come to the production van for the final meeting."

Lionel never looked down at the small woman. She had headphones on, with the cord dangling at her side. When he looked back up at the well-illuminated house without acknowledging her, she shrugged and moved away.

Peterson concentrated on the windows at the third floor. He felt that he was being watched, but knew it had nothing to do with Summer Place—the feeling came from all the remote cameras around the front of the house. He knew Kelly was in front of a monitor somewhere, watching him.

A small group of people moved out of the commissary tent. Peterson finally broke his gaze from the house and saw the professor's group of ghost hunters moving toward the front door. He watched as Kennedy shook hands with each member of the group. The professor actually looked sad as they moved into the house and into position for the start of the broadcast. Gabriel Kennedy stood just underneath the portico and waited for Julie Reilly to join him. Their first cue would be right after the narrative of Summer Place by John Wesley. After that would be the rolling of the opening credits and theme song.

"Are you coming? I mean, you are the executive producer of the show."

Peterson's spell was broken. Jason Sanborn stood beside him with his pipe in his hand. His other hand held a water bottle, which reminded Peterson that he would have to sneak off sometime in the first hour to get a drink. Maybe when the first segment was pushed upstairs.

"Yes, I'm coming."

"This should prove, at the very least, to be a most interesting evening," Jason said, placing the cold pipe into his mouth.

Peterson walked past Sanborn. With one last look up at the yellow-and-white mansion, he shook his head.

"I hope it's at least that."

The production van was silent, watching as the last commercial ran before the broadcast's eight o'clock start. At five o'clock on the West Coast, the show was going to be cutting a lot of the Pacific Time zone ratings, but New York had decided that the trade-off could not be helped. The Alka-Seltzer commercial started fading to black on Harris Dalton's orders.

"Cue up John Wesley," Harris called, and then, "Roll tape."

On monitor one, the view was what would be seen by all of North America on a seven-second tape delay. That was another decision made by New York, just in case something untoward happened, so that there would be a chance to censor untoward language from going out live over the airwaves. John Wesley, looking resplendent in a black coat, black turtleneck sweater, and black slacks, with his distinguished gray hair combed straight back, stood before Summer Place. He smiled the disarming smile he had shown the American public for more than twenty years while bringing them the world and national news. He placed his hands together and nodded as if lecturing in a schoolroom. He then released his left hand and gestured toward the house.

"This is Summer Place."

The monologue went on for a full ten minutes as John Wesley explained the history of the giant house behind him. As he moved through the morbid details, still shots of the interior of Summer Place popped on and off the screen. Kelly Delaphoy had won the fight about keeping the house under wraps for as long as they could. The first people seen in the house after the opening credits of the show would be Julie Reilly and Gabriel Kennedy, and even then they would only be standing on the steps leading to the house. Only after the introductions would they move into the foyer of Summer Place.

Harris Dalton knew these few moments were his last chance to relax. Monitor two was filled with the faces of Kennedy and Reilly as they waited for the cameraman, who would cue them on Harris's orders. Dalton glanced back at Kelly and Peterson. They sat quietly, both looking like ghosts themselves. In the darkened far corner of the trailer Harris saw the gleam of stainless steel flash in the glare of the monitors as Wallace Lindemann raised his flask of whiskey. Harris Dalton thought about reminding Lindemann that they were just as live in the van as out in front of the cameras. Instead he just eyed Kelly and Peterson until they saw Lindemann drinking. Kelly nodded to signal that she understood; if Lindemann acted like a jerk, Kelly would hustle him out of the van.

On monitor one, John Wesley gave a fatherly look toward the house, then slowly turned and faced the camera once more.

"So sit back, relax if you can, and join the greatest team of ghost hunters ever to work the field of parapsychology—welcome to the live Halloween broadcast of *Hunters of the Paranormal*." He gestured once more at the bright, glowing house, and the camera panned away from the retired anchor to bring Summer Place to full focus on the screen. "Let the hunt begin!"

"Cue intro, cue music," Harris called out calmly. The regular lead-in started and the opening strains of Blue Öyster Cult came through the speakers. "Don't Fear the Reaper" played, while famous still shots of the show's former hosts and scenes of their adventures flicked by.

"Camera two, close in. You've got a little too much space showing on the sides. Get Reilly and Kennedy framed up right!"

On monitor two, the shot of Julie and Gabriel tightened up.

"Okay, camera three, tight on Julie. You're up first. I repeat, just Julie for the initial shot."

Kelly smiled. After a full week of agony and planning, Dalton was now in his element.

"Cue three," he said as the music wound down. Kelly's opening started, and it sounded better than she had hoped. The song stopped like someone had placed a hand on the old recording and dragged it to a stop. At that exact moment, the live television broadcast kicked in with a still shot of the former hosts of *Hunters of the Paranormal*.

"Good evening and happy Halloween," Julie said. She looked into camera three for the close head shot. "Greg Larsen and Paul Lowell," she continued as the screen split in two—one side showing Julie, the other the still shots of the hosts—"will not be here with you tonight. While investigating the stories surrounding this house, this summer home of the world-famous Lindemann family, one host vanished and the other stepped down after the traumatic night of October seventeenth. One host returned only to commit suicide, the other never to return to investigative work again."

Inside the ballroom Detective Damian Jackson pushed his hat back on his head and frowned. He had asked that no information be given about Paul Lowell's demise. He angrily slapped the table, making one of the computer team jump, then pointed at the only other people in the room—John Lonetree, Jennifer Tilden, and George Cordero.

"That's one," he said with a hiss. "Any more and I'll shut this down for endangering an active murder investigation."

George waited until the large black detective looked away and then shot him the finger, making Jenny smile.

"And here with me tonight is the man responsible for bringing the troubles of Summer Place to the world's attention—or should we say infamy?"

Dalton rolled his eyes. Infamy? Julie was already going off script. He glanced back at Kelly, who had the script in her lap and was following along. When her eyes met the director's, she just shrugged.

"Professor Gabriel Kennedy. Professor, just why have you returned to a house that nearly destroyed you personally and professionally?"

"Goddamn it, what is this?" Harris yelled. "The goddamn Spanish Inquisition? I thought she was giving Kennedy the benefit of the doubt—hell, she opens challenging him and we're not one minute in!"

Kelly looked over at Peterson, who was sitting quietly. He frowned and shrugged his shoulders. Kelly wondered if he had gotten to the network reporter.

"Go to camera two—now!"

Gabriel Kennedy came into full focus. Gabriel was composed, not shocked, and he smiled and looked from Julie Reilly directly into camera number two. The wide-angle shot captured both of their faces.

"That's enough, camera three, focus on just Kennedy," Harris called out. He hit the mute button on his mic as he faced Kelly. "You put a bug in her ear that if she goes off on her own again, I'll have her fired by the next commercial. I don't care who the fuck she thinks she is or who the hell she knows. You got that, Kelly?"

Kelly went to the sound console and cued in Julie's earphone. She rapidly explained the situation and Dalton's threats. Off camera, Kelly saw Julie smile and nod her head as Kennedy explained why he had come back. He looked into the camera with all the confidence in the world. On the secondary feed, Julie Reilly looked quite annoyed by Gabriel's seemingly nonplussed reaction.

"Well, I guess he was expecting that, wasn't he?" Dalton said with a smirk. "Okay, New York, getting ready for the break in five, four, three, two—"

Oncamera, Julie took over from Kennedy and gestured to the house. "After a word from our sponsors, we'll take a look inside Summer Place for the first time, and then you can decide whether you agree with Professor Kennedy's statement: that this house is, by far, the *most* haunted house in America. We'll be right back."

"One, New York, you're a go for three minutes of ad time," Dalton said. On his monitor, Julie was looking at Gabriel, and the professor was smiling.

"So you expected me to corner you?"

"I never had a doubt you would revert to your old ways. How can a shark not be a shark?" Gabriel said. He gestured toward the steps that led up to the wide double doors of the house.

Julie shook her head, still disappointed that Kennedy hadn't stumbled at all in her surprise opening. She placed a hand to her earphone and spoke into her mic.

"Harris, or Kelly, any feedback from New York or the test family in Boston?"

Kelly flipped the switch that gave her direct communication to Julie.

"You mean any reaction about your little ambush, you little—"

"All right, that's enough," Harris said. "Kelly, settle down and do your job." Dalton looked over at the monitor that held the view of the family of four sitting on their couch in the suburb of Boston. The father was watching the commercial; the mother was admonishing the two kids, and a boy and a girl of about of thirteen or so, about holding still when they went live oncamera. "No test family reaction." Harris examined the construction worker and his dowdy wife. "And if I have my way, we'll not be showing much of Mr. and Mrs. American viewer tonight."

"Let me know if New York has any comment. Especially the news division," Julie said. She walked faster to catch up with Gabriel.

"Okay, everyone, places in the ballroom. Julie and the professor will be entering the house. They'll be in the ballroom exactly two minutes after we start rolling. For God's sake, look like you're busy doing something when the camera pans.

Mr. Sickles, I don't want to hear a smart-ass comment coming from your mouth, you hear me?"

Camera ten moved just far enough to show Leonard standing behind one of his computer researchers with his hands on his hips, looking angrily at the lens.

"Not a word, even when they introduce you," Dalton finished. "We're back from commercial in five, four—"

The view opened with Julie Reilly standing in front of the massive stone and wood fireplace. Gabriel had already gone inside the ballroom to head off any chance that Leonard might retaliate for the slight.

Julie started explaining how the television investigation would be conducted—how the three teams would explore certain sections of the house after the lights went out. As she spoke, she moved closer to the ballroom, which had been tagged "command central" earlier in the opening.

"Before we meet our teams . . . on a personal note, I want to state that while I reported on a massive breakdown by the Kennedy investigation seven years ago, I am only an interested observer here. I have no evidence or convincing argument to say that Summer Place is at all haunted. I believe that Professor Kennedy's original theory concerning this beautiful, mysterious house is nothing more than a conductor that allows the mind to roam freely, injecting anything it wants into the moment, and that includes things that go bump in the night and strange sounds coming from a very old house. Now, we'll meet tonight's team: the Supernaturals."

"Damn it, she's doing it again. Where the hell did that come from—the Supernaturals? She's making a joke out of the whole thing!" Kelly said loudly. Dalton turned and gestured for her to shut up, waving his hand angrily.

"Peterson, you're the executive producer. At commercial break, you're going to have to corner that woman and rein her in," Harris said, watching Julie Reilly enter the ballroom. She went directly to Gabriel, who started introducing the team. The only person off camera who looked pleased at all was Leonard Sickles. The grinning young man clearly thought that the new nickname was cool.

Peterson almost couldn't hide his smile. Instead of answering Dalton, he just nodded. He would indeed talk with Julie about naming the team and going off script. However, deep down inside, he wanted to thank the arrogant bitch for upstaging the maniac professor and his team of ghost hunters.

"And finally a man who is not a member of my team, but an independent observer, Father Dolan of Columbia University," Gabriel concluded.

"Well, there you have it, the three teams of men and women who will try to make America believers in the supernatural. Right after the break, the hunt is on. We'll be right back."

Julie nodded to the cameraman, who gestured that they were off live TV. Jennifer Tilden came forward.

"The Supernaturals? Are you joking?"

"I thought the team needed a name. It's far better than calling you the group, or something."

"Well, let me tell you what I think," Jenny continued. Lonetree took her arm, but she wasn't dissuaded. "It may not be a joke to you, but you're trying your best to turn *us* into one, on live TV, no less. Why now? Why make us think you were coming on board as a fair and impartial observer? You know, Gabriel said he expected this much from you."

The last statement caught Julie off guard. She felt hurt that Kennedy never had trusted her; that all of her acting had been for nothing. Had her insincerity been that obvious? Kennedy ignored her, and he didn't even seem upset. He walked up to Damian Jackson and looked at his watch. He had one minute to say what he wanted to express to the state policeman.

"You see, Detective, I'm more observant that you thought. I picked up on Julie's little game early on, and now I'll tell you what you're hoping for in this mess. You think that I'm here to publicly declare that I was responsible for what happened that night. That maybe this is some grand stage for my confession and I've been waiting all of these years for the big moment."

"Personally, I bet you *want* to confess that you had the disappearance of your student staged. That's what I'm hoping for. And then I'll arrest you all over again."

"I guess we'll see eight hours from now, won't we?" Gabriel smiled and started to turn away. "By the way, are you armed?"

Damian Jackson smiled and patted his coat. "Always. Professor. Always."

Gabriel allowed his smile to grow. The policeman's grin vanished as he wondered what the professor's question had been about. Why would he need a gun against ghosts? Now he had to wonder if Kennedy was running a game, just as Julie Reilly had been.

Dalton absentmindedly watched the commercial airing from the New York studio. The soap advertisement showed a small girl in a clean, unbroken field of wheat as the image of the bar of soap spread across the screen. Dalton blinked and then caught himself.

"Okay, we're back in ten, people, get to your places. Professor, Julie, you'll start off by taking Leonard up to the second and third floors to explain his tech. Then we'll switch to Lonetree in the stables and his walk-through of the pool area. Then after the next three-minute commercial break, we go dark. All power inside the house gets turned off, save for the ballroom. Okay, here we go in five, four, three, two—"

As the camera panned backward, bringing the base of the large staircase into focus and showing the expansive stairs leading upward—just the effect Harris Dalton had been hoping for—Leonard Sickles, Gabriel Kennedy, Father Dolan, and Julie Reilly began their slow climb to the second floor. Leonard started explaining the technology behind his motion detectors. He pointed out the small blue LED lights that had been strung along the thick wooden banisters of all the stairs. From the first floor to the third, the little lights were designed to detect the slightest variance in temperature and air movement; the minuscule swirling of dust particles to the minute drop in temperature. The system would track anything moving along the stairs or hallways. The blue illumination would be picked up in the dark by the naked eye, and would also show brightly for the infrared cameras.

After Leonard finished and Julie and her team started back down to the first floor of Summer Place, Dalton switched over to John Lonetree, Jennifer, and George in the stables. John repeated the story of the assault on the riding trail and then moved the show outside and along the colorful pool. The atmosphere was developing well. Inside the van, Kelly allowed herself to breathe. Everything was going smoothly for the moment. She chanced a glance over at Peterson, who brushed at a nonexistent piece of lint on his black slacks. While he looked outwardly bored, Wallace Lindemann, who sat next to him, was anything but. He continually shifted in his seat, as if his ass were on fire. He watched nervously for anything on the monitors that might spell disaster for his plans to sell Summer Place.

After the teams finished their tours, the commercial spot for their main advertiser came on. Everyone had three full minutes to gather themselves. Julie stood to the side and listened for any instructions that might come over her earpiece. She glanced at Gabriel, who stood silently, mostly ignoring those around him. He didn't even flinch when the makeup girl started tapping at his face and neck with a sponge.

"Okay, Julie, make sure the professor is ready to go lights out after the break. We'll start with your team on the third floor," Dalton said over her earpiece.

"What about the basement and the subbasement? We didn't cover them yet." She stepped farther away from her team, brushing off the makeup girl who attempted to get at her.

"If things bog down, we'll send Lonetree and his team to

the basement. If anything happens down there, we have remotes."

"Harris, I think it's important for the creep factor. If we—"

"Look, if you want to direct this thing, I'll go home right now."

"Okay, okay." Julie ducked away, knowing that Gabriel was hearing all of this in his own earpiece.

"Everyone, this is Leonard," came a voice cutting into the chatter.

"What is it, Sickles? Make it fast," Harris called out.

"We have something interesting on the computers here. We have some photos from the Lindemann Foundation showing the wedding of Lindemann and his wife, Elena."

"I think we have enough background on the Lindemanns, Mr. Sickles, maybe we—"

"That's not what I'm getting at."

"Leonard, what have you got?" Gabriel cut in, silencing everyone.

"We have plenty of pictures of Elena after her marriage, but not one photograph of her before. Even the Romanov family history and family tree don't show any Elena Deleninov—that's her maiden name."

"The official Lindemann family lineage declares publicly that Elena was a member of the Romanov family." Gabriel stepped toward the ballroom door so he could see Leonard inside.

"Look, Gabe, we know from the archives that Elena was the daughter of a lowly fifth cousin of Nicholas the Second, but these photos and records show that family as two parents and three boys. There is no Elena."

"Hold on to that for now, Leonard. See what else you can dig up," Gabriel said. He nodded into the ballroom, toward Leonard and his three computer hackers. Sickles gave him a thumbs-up and then leaned back over the shoulder of one of the operators.

"Sounds like old Lindemann may have been sold a bill of goods," Dalton said from the van.

"I don't think so. The history is clear on this: Elena and her family financed Lindemann's expansion into the United States. We're talking five million dollars. Quite substantial for that time. It's on record."

Julie looked over at Gabriel. He was concerned about Leonard's revelation, even with his secure knowledge of the financial history of the old family.

"Keep digging, Leonard. Mr. Dalton will check on you again in an hour."

"Okay, people, we're back in one minute. We're ready for team one to go to the third floor, and then we go lights out."

"Hey, be sure not to cut the power to my equipment up there. Only the spectrograph has battery backup."

"Mr. Sickles, do not break in on me again," Dalton said angrily with a hiss.

"Okay, okay. Chill, man."

"Thirty seconds. All other teams go to the ballroom as per the professor's instructions. Okay, where is Father Dolan? I don't see him."

"He's praying over by the coat check station. He's coming now," Julie said. She took her place by the broad stairs and Gabriel joined her in silence.

"Camera ten, we'll start with you. Take the opening shot at the stairs and just follow them all the way up to the third floor."

The camera operator, a man named Steve, moved his remote camera up and then down. He had worked with Harris before and knew when not to speak.

"Okay—three, two, one, back from commercial, cue Julie."

"Welcome back," Julie started. "We're now ready for the start of our ghost hunt, so if you, America, are ready, we'll begin with arguably the most haunted part of Summer Place, the third floor. Professor Kennedy has instructed our technical team that it is most effective to conduct the experiment with as little light as possible, so at this point we will go to the very expensive ambient night vision. Don't attempt to adjust your television's picture if everything seems to be green-tinted; this is normal. Your screen will be absent color only. I promise you that you will see everything we see. Shall we start, Professor?"

Gabriel stayed as professional as he could and smiled down at Julie. He took the first step up the staircase and raised a small handheld radio to his mouth.

"Gentlemen, let's go with lights out, please."

As the world watched, every visible light inside the giant summer mansion went out. The property was thrown into inky darkness. If it weren't for the faraway flash of lightning, the grounds would have looked nearly primeval.

Halloween had truly begun.

Damian Jackson watched from the coat check area just inside the massive entranceway. He saw Gabriel, Julie Reilly, and Father Dolan take their initial steps up the staircase, and that was when the lights went out. Jackson placed his heavy raincoat on the counter of the hat check station and then his fedora on top of that. He straightened his suit collar and moved to the stairway. The soundman was the only person to turn, but was careful to keep his microphone boom pointed forward toward Kennedy and Julie. Father Dolan would only answer questions or give an opinion when asked.

The trio climbed the staircase with the cameraman and soundman in tow. Once more the soundman turned and looked at Jackson in the darkness of the staircase. Damian raised a finger to his lips and then pointed ahead, indicating the soundman had better watch where he was going. As the team reached the second-floor landing, Julie stopped in front of the giant Lindemann family portrait.

"As we showed you earlier, this is the family that originally built Summer Place—the matriarch and patriarch, Elena and F. E. Lindemann," Julie whispered in a low, mysterious voice as she gestured up at the portrait. "An interesting bit of information has been learned by way of Professor Kennedy's computer research team, which we met earlier. It seems our motherly figure, Elena, had no pictures ever taken of her before her wedding day. How do you account for that, Professor Kennedy?"

Gabriel wasn't the least bit surprised that Julie would use the partial information that Leonard had given them earlier, and he really couldn't be mad since he hadn't told her not to use it. Still, Gabriel knew he had to fight fire with fire where Reilly was concerned.

"As a matter of fact, Ms. Reilly, I don't account for it at all. Our research has only indicated that there are no photos of Elena that we have yet found. You must remember, she was a part of a very tightly protected royal family. Sometimes daughters, beautiful though they were, were not photographed for security reasons. We should know more later in the evening."

Julie was silent for the briefest of moments. The cameraman zeroed in on the face of Elena Lindemann, casting her features in the ghostly green and grays of the ambient-light system. Behind them, even Jackson had to stifle a chuckle at the way Kennedy had turned the tables on the reporter.

"I'm sure our viewers will be waiting with anticipation," Julie said in the lowest tone of voice she could muster. "For right now, we will pause on the second-floor landing and view the extraordinary hallway from here. As you know from the tour, the Lindemanns placed the second-tier guests on this floor, where the rooms were much smaller. Royalty from Europe and guests from Hollywood stayed upstairs, on the third floor. If there were any incidents on this floor, they were kept quiet by the family. Let's listen."

Inside the production van, Harris Dalton shook his head. He knew that Kelly could see Julie setting herself up to be the firm and sound mind on this little experiment—she would leave Kelly and Kennedy holding the bag for its failure.

"You have to hand it to her, she's like a clairvoyant when it comes to sensing danger to her career," Harris mumbled.

"Harris, New York is on the line. Mr. Feuerstein would

like you to call him at the next commercial break," one of his assistants said, lightly placing a phone back in its cradle.

"Jesus, this better not happen all the way through the next eight hours. The damn woman was his choice, not mine."

In the corner, Lionel Peterson watched without comment. His eyes never left the low-light photography of the second floor, but he heard all.

The camera swiveled and caught Father Dolan as he tried his best to peer into the blackness of the second floor. Gabriel turned a low-power flashlight on, casting a pinpoint beam of soft light ahead of them down the hallway. They saw the still cameras and the digital audio equipment right where they had been placed. Kennedy slowly walked up to the equipment, and the camera followed with the soundman in tow. Julie squeezed past them to see what Kennedy was doing. Then she spoke softly into the mic clipped to her blouse.

"The professor is checking the activity of the digital sound recorders and the infrared still cameras. Professor, exactly what do you hope to find on this very expensive equipment?"

Gabriel was leaning over the sound devices, hiding his frown of annoyance at Julie. After checking both the cameras and the digital sound recorder, Kennedy straightened and looked into the camera. He would explain once more to the viewing audience and ignore Julie completely. Down in the ballroom, Lonetree, Cordero, and Jennifer smiled at the slight.

"As we explained earlier, with the infrared cameras we hope to pick up any variations in heat and cold emanating from this floor. That could be an indicator of paranormal activity. The digital sound recorders are something totally different. They can pick up sounds that the human ear cannot, or will not, hear."

"And have we caught anything on either the cameras or the sound equipment, Professor?" Julie asked, though she knew the answer.

"Not at this time. The cameras have not been activated by any sudden changes in temperature, and the digital recorders have detected only us coming up the stairs, and our own voices."

"I see. So that means there is no activity on this floor."

"Not as of yet, Ms. Reilly."

The cameraman zoomed in on Kennedy as he answered. Damian Jackson watched as his eyes grew more and more accustomed to the darkness around them. He had also guessed the answer to Julie's question. Any mysterious sounds or sights detected by this equipment would have been placed there by Kennedy, Kelly Delaphoy, or both. He saw Gabriel look up at him in the darkness, and though he couldn't see well, he knew the man was smiling at him. That made Jackson lose his own sense of humor.

Inside the production van, Lionel Peterson raised his eyebrow. Was Feuerstein's own girl going to throw a monkey wrench into this whole thing and save him the trouble? He looked over at Kelly, who was seething. She gripped her clipboard tightly.

"Okay, we go to commercial in ten. Julie, wrap up the second floor, and try not to lose any more viewers than you already have," Harris Dalton said. He, too, was seething at the way Julie Reilly was handling Professor Kennedy. "The second we go to black, I want the CEO on the line. If he sent Reilly here to sabotage his own special, we need to know right now."

Kelly looked over at Peterson, who returned her look with a shrug of his shoulders. Then he smiled and leaned toward her, ignoring the questioning look from Wallace Lindemann. The owner of the house tilted a stainless steel flask to his lips and drank deeply.

"She's your girl in there. I suspect that her agenda is entirely from yours and old Abe's."

"I swear to God, Lionel, if you had anything to do with this turncoat bullshit, I'll go straight to the board with it."

"Honey, I've been threatened by far better people than

you, and guess what? I'm still standing, and they're back at their old cable channels with handheld cameras."

New York, New York

Abe Feuerstein accepted the phone from his assistant. His eyes lingered on several of the board as they stepped away from their seats at the commercial break. Their eyes wandered over to the old man sitting stoically in his large chair, but quickly moved away when they saw him looking at them. It seemed Lionel had far more supporters than even the CEO had realized.

"Harris, what is that woman doing to my special?"

Feuerstein listened as Harris Dalton asked him the same question from the Poconos. The CEO kept his smile on his face so the others would see him in control.

"I was just handed the ratings for the first hour. We started at sixty-two five—that's over sixty million viewers—and in a single half an hour we lost ten million and counting. There is a cutoff point, Dalton, when I have to pull the plug on this thing. We cannot sit through seven more hours of nothing; I want you to pass Ms. Reilly a little note from me. You tell her that if she thinks she'll escape this thing unharmed, she's sorely mistaken. Tell her she better appear to be giving Kennedy the benefit of the doubt, because he's the star of the show, not her."

The old man adjusted his bow tie and listened to Harris Dalton on the other end of the phone. Several members of the board started returning to their seats with fresh drinks in their hands.

"I never said that. Nothing gets faked, Harris. She can make it far tenser with her delivery. Explain to her that as of right now, the loss of viewers is on her head." He smiled and handed the phone back to his assistant. "Get a message to the entertainment division, and for God's sake bypass Lionel Peterson. Talk to LA directly. Have them get alternate programming ready in case this thing goes bad on us."

"Yes, sir."

Feuerstein smiled again, nodding as though he had been given good news. He nodded his head at the men and women of the board as they waited for the disaster from the Poconos to start once again.

The CEO knew he was facing another kind of horror if this special fell flat on its face. He would not only lose the confidence of the shareholders, he could possibly lose the backing of many for control of the manufacturing divisions. As this thought crossed his mind, he absentmindedly accepted a drink from his assistant. She nodded her head, letting him know that his message had been passed to the entertainment division. Abe sipped his drink and regained his confident air. The commercial—a small green lizard pushing car insurance—ended, and the show started again from Summer Place.

Abraham Feuerstein knew that if this failed, he could very well end up joining those ghosts out at that damnable house.

19 Bright River, Pennsylvania

With the second hour into the special having passed with no discernible recording or image having been relayed to the remaining forty million viewers, the mood in the production van was sticky at best. At the beginning of the last four-minute commercial break of the hour, Harris Dalton tossed his headphones down and stepped out of the van. He stood looking up at the darkened Summer Place. After the test broadcast, he had been sure that they would at least have something in the first two hours to hang their hat on, but thus far the show was sliding steadily downhill. He felt his reputation sliding with it.

"It's playing with us."

Kelly Delaphoy had come out just behind him, her clipboard still pressed to her chest as if she were preparing to ward off his ill humor with the thin piece of plastic. Harris shook his head and turned back to the darkened house, just as the first real drops of rain started to fall from the cloud-laden sky. He turned his face upward and took a deep breath as the rain cooled his face.

"Professor Kennedy doesn't seem too worried about the nonhappenings in the house," Kelly said, flinching as a streak of lightning crashed over the property.

"What the hell does he have to lose?" Harris said. "His career was already in the shitter." He brushed past Kelly and returned to the van.

The small producer watched the door to the van close and then looked back at the house. With the darkened windows, it reminded her of a dangerous animal as it slept, its eyes closed and breathing lightly. Lightning illuminated the sky once more, reflecting off the glass on the second and third floors. She felt as if the house were mocking her and the entire effort to bring out what was hidden inside. The wind picked up and the rain started to come down in earnest, but instead of running for cover she stood her ground, looking up into the silent face of Summer Place.

"Show yourself, you bitch," she said as the thunder caught up with the last bolt of lightning. The house remained as still as before. Silent and sleeping.

The real threat to Summer Place was coming, in the form of a package carried by a messenger who had been dispatched from Philadelphia two hours before.

That package was a result of a theft from the Immigration and Naturalization Service center mainframe computer. It was so hot that the man Leonard Sickles had hired to break into that system had decided to deliver the package himself. For the moment, Summer Place sat unaware of the threat coming its way.

Gabriel, Julie, Father Dolan, and Damian Jackson—who still stood back from the camera's lens—stood on the third-floor landing and looked through the darkness toward the sewing room at the end of the long hallway. It was a corner room facing the back of the property, standing like a dark sentinel. They would have to pass it to turn the corner and get to the guest rooms on the far end of the floor. Jackson, the last person in line, took the opportunity to examine the device that Leonard Sickles, the little hood from LA, had engineered. It looked like a string of ordinary Christmas lights to him, and Jackson suspected that Sickles was running a game on Kennedy. Jackson had taken the opportunity to have all of Kennedy's team checked out, especially the little gang member, so he knew the kid had recruited some friends from Los Angeles to do God-knew-what for him. As long as the gang members didn't show up at Summer Place, Damian had more important fish to fry.

A flash of lightning produced a soft rumbling through the floorboards of the old house and brimmed brightly around the shuttered third-floor windows. Jackson heard Kennedy explain to the television audience that the intermittent light from the lightning outside could affect the ambient-light photography they had planned. Damian smiled in the darkness as the team started moving down the hallway toward the sewing room and the suite where the opera star had supposedly disappeared.

The team, with Julie in the lead, stopped just outside one of the rooms and directed the camera toward the spot where Kennedy's student had vanished into thin air—or thick wall, if you believed the professor's story. Lieutenant Jackson watched Kennedy's expression as Julie once more explained the incident of seven years before. Gabriel looked away as the camera zoomed in on the spot where the kid had supposedly vanished, and Jackson knew the professor was looking right at him. He couldn't say for sure, but he suspected Gabriel was mocking him. Jackson placed his hands in his suit jacket and waited for Kennedy to look somewhere else, but he kept looking Jackson's way. Jackson found it unnerving.

"Professor Kennedy will try to re-create the circumstances surrounding that night years ago. If he is successful, one of the greatest mysteries of Summer Place may be solved right here before the UBC cameras," Julie said. The team moved away from the wall, the last place Kennedy's student had ever been seen.

As the soundman slowly followed the others down the hallway, Damian intentionally rubbed his large hand across the spot on the wall. The velvety wallpaper was cool to the touch. Damian pressed hard onto the wall, making sure nothing creative was lined up for later discovery. It felt solid.

Julie and Kennedy stopped just beneath the ventilation grill where Damian had stood himself with the state police not two weeks before. The low-light camera adjusted and the world saw for the very first time the vent that had supposedly consumed the man Kelly Delaphoy had hired to trick out the house.

"And now, for the first time anywhere in the world, the UBC network will broadcast the actual incident that happened right here in Summer Place two weeks ago."

Damian wanted to jump right out of his skin. He realized suddenly that he had been lied to, not only by Harris Dalton, Julie Reilly, and Kelly Delaphoy, but also by UBC as a whole. The footage had supposedly been lost forever, and they had sworn they had nothing to turn over to the police. Jackson clenched his teeth as Julie raised a concerned brow at the camera.

"A warning, the footage you are about to see is graphic and frightening. As most of our viewers are aware, this man, Kyle Pritchard, turned up yesterday. Mr. Pritchard committed suicide before he could give a full accounting of his experience. Once again, this footage is graphic, and has been proven to be real."

They all heard the voice of Harris Dalton in their earpieces as the canned footage started playing. This allowed five minutes for the team to relax.

"You lying sons of bitches had that footage all along and didn't tell me. That's tampering with state evidence, and I told you I would hang you for it!" Jackson shouted, pushing past the soundmen and cameramen.

"Lieutenant, I have been authorized to explain to you that

our network technicians only a few hours ago came up with
a workable copy of the videotape. As we speak, a copy of this
tape has been forwarded to your office in Philadelphia—by
U.S. Mail."

"If it takes me a year, I'm going to get someone at your
network for withholding evidence." Jackson looked from
Julie to Kennedy's smiling face. "And if I find you had something to do with the decision-making here, Kennedy, that's
going to add to your problems."

Gabriel took a step toward Jackson. The men were of equal
height, and for the first time Jackson realized Kennedy wasn't
easily intimidated. Even in the dark he could see that the professor's eyes were filled with a challenge the detective had
never seen in them before.

"Hang around, Detective Lieutenant Jackson. You may get
all the answers you ever wanted."

Julie nodded toward the cameraman and he gave her a
quick thumbs-up. The scene had been filmed, and during the
next commercial break he would feed it quietly to the control van for broadcast at the appropriate time.

Both men were being set up by Julie Reilly.

George Cordero followed John Lonetree and Jennifer Tilden
down the steep basement stairs with the use of low-power
penlights. The cameramen and soundmen were taking up the
rear of the line and were still in the kitchen as the group
slowly made their way down the steps. George hadn't mentioned anything to either Julie or John, but since they had
opened the door to the basement, he'd had a feeling that
something was down there. He corrected himself—something
had been down there. Deep down, he felt as if they had
missed an opportunity by delaying their movement to the
cellar and the subbasement. He stopped on the third step
down, causing the cameraman to almost bump into him. They
were currently going out live, which was the only thing that
stopped the cameraman from complaining that Cordero had
almost killed them all with his sudden stop.

Julie and John continued down. It took a nudge from the large man behind George to get him moving again before the two lead team members hit the bend in the staircase. As George started downward, he smelled the dank cement floor below, and possibly beyond that the loamy smell of the sub-basement. He shook his head, wanting to catch up with Lonetree and tell him that something wasn't right. In his earpiece, Dalton extolled them to step up the pace.

As John and Jennifer hit the turn in the stairs, they heard a loud thump from the floor twenty-five feet below, as if something had hit the concrete floor. John picked up the pace as Jennifer communicated quietly into her microphone. The crewmen wanted to push George out of the way so they could catch up with the two lead investigators. Finally the camera-man, the same large ex-marine who had run that night two weeks before—a man wanting to regain some of the dignity he lost that night—finally hissed into his microphone that Cordero was slowing them up too much for them to get a visual on Lonetree and Tilden. Everyone heard the complaint and John and Jennifer slowed their pace, not wanting to get George into further trouble with Dalton. As they stopped only ten feet from the darkened floor, they heard a loud moan coming from the recesses of the basement.

"Okay, did everyone hear that?" John called out softly.

Cordero heard it. Instead of slowing, he started moving faster down the stairs. As the two technicians hurriedly followed, taking the steps one at a time, they heard Cordero mumbling "This isn't right, this isn't right" over and over.

"Our colleague George Cordero is voicing an opinion." Jennifer positioned herself to assist George as he came stumbling down the stairs. She held both hands out to the darkness, keeping George from continuing past when he caught up with them.

"Whoa there," John said. "What are you feeling, George? Is it something to do with the moan we just heard?" John spoke for the benefit of the microphone clipped to his collar.

"Something's not right down here," George said, catching his breath. "Something's going to happen."

In the darkness, the cameraman and soundmen focused the low-light lens on the team.

"I'm not following," John said as Jennifer looked nervously from one dark face to the other. "I'm not picking up anything. No cold spots, nothing."

"I don't know what it is. Something has been here and was waiting for us."

"Waiting for us?" Jennifer asked.

"Well, we won't know what it is until we move down the rest of the way."

As the tension became palpable, the three investigators moved down the stairs and finally onto the concrete floor of the cool basement. Around them, something grew in power, and everyone watching the show could almost feel it.

"Damn. Now, this may get good," Harris said. He remembered the lost little boy feelings he'd had during the broadcast test two weeks before. He could only hope that his visuals were relating those same feelings to the viewers watching from the safety of their warm homes.

Was it possible Summer Place was finally coming alive?

Inside the production van, Kelly Delaphoy smiled over at Lionel Peterson and Wallace Lindemann. She knew Summer Place wouldn't let her down. The two men kept their eyes on the many monitors and acted as though they didn't know she was looking at them.

"About goddamned time," Harris said. He leaned over and patted the sound tech on the shoulder. "I need more gain; I want to hear their steps. That'll add tension. And you tell visual to keep on Cordero; he seems to be the star of this thing."

The technician nodded her head and passed the instructions along.

Kelly watched the monitors as the basement team hit the floor and stood their ground momentarily. Another loud moan came through the speakers, clear as day. Chills ran through Kelly. This was far better than any sexual encounter she had ever had. She was about to be proved right to her network and forty million television viewers. Her eyes settled on the team that stood on the third-floor landing. Professor Kennedy and the others couldn't see what was happening in the basement, but they were following the audio progress of Lonetree's team far below them. In the low-light camera angle, Gabriel looked concerned about something. Kelly thought that he may have been wishing he were with the basement team as they proved to the world that Summer Place was haunted.

In New York, Abe Feuerstein nodded his head and took a drink from his glass of whiskey. Things were finally happening, and even the board members were riveted to the large television at the front of the room. The man whom he knew Peterson was closest to turned and looked at the CEO. His smile was faltering as he nodded. Feuerstein nodded back, enjoying the advance surrender of the board and the first of many humiliating congratulations from his detractors.

For the first time in three hours, Abe was feeling his oats. He was tasting his drink for the first time that night. He turned the glass up, draining it, and held it out for his assistant to refill. Yes, this was going to be sweet—from being on the verge of having to pull the plug on the rest of the special, to getting the greatest ratings coup in history. Yes, the whiskey tasted just fine.

The basement was dark. To the many viewers still watching, it was scary enough to make children hug their mothers. Fathers made silly, teasing noises to cover their own Halloween night chills.

John held the small penlight up and examined the basement. The old kitchen appliances, from the ancient wood-burning stove to the bathroom fixtures lined against the walls, helped to lend the room an eerie feeling. It was like the history of the house were a time capsule stored in the basement and the viewing audience was seeing it for the first time.

The team spread out with John in the lead, all heading toward the center of the basement. The camera adjusted the green-tinted picture to show the detritus from more than a hundred years—accumulated appliances and a family's boxed-up life. There were boxes and boxes of antique children's toys. Though worth a fortune on the open market, in the dark of the basement they seemed forlorn and lost. At the top of a pile in a box that had split open after years in the damp cellar, Jenny spotted just what the viewing public would want to focus on. She held the toy up so the camera could zoom in. The ancient jack-in-the-box was wooden and old-fashioned, its handle overly large and its lid thick with dust and rotted with age. Jenny turned the box over. On the side, a child's name was written in gold paint: Garrett. As Jenny turned the box back over, the clown suddenly sprang out. Everyone, with the exception of John Lonetree, let out an exclamation of surprise. Even the cameraman jolted the camera.

Inside the production van and at the New York headquarters of UBC, everyone, including Abe Feuerstein, jumped.

Jennifer almost dropped the antique toy. She examined the features of the clown. The paint on the face had chipped, leaving the mouth turning at a downward angle. Instead of a happy smile, the clown had a look of terror etched on its once-happy face.

"Oh, yeah, that'll keep a child occupied," George said, standing next to Jenny. John Lonetree took the toy from Jenny's hands and placed it back in the box. He straightened and moved off toward the trapdoor that led to the subbasement.

"George, are you still feeling something?" he asked.

"Only that there was recent activity down here."

Jennifer remained in place and the camera zoomed in on her. She felt a momentary flutter of her heart, as if she had just wakened from a dream and didn't know where she was.

John caught her attention with a look that asked if she was all right.

Jenny nodded, but her thoughts felt distant and not her own. She realized Bobby Lee McKinnon was making a return to her subconscious. She didn't feel threatened by his presence; she felt only his curiosity as to what she was doing. It was as if he were feeling her unease. Then the feeling was gone. Either Bobby Lee didn't like the basement, or his curiosity had been satisfied. For the first time since her own personal haunting had started seven years before, Bobby Lee's presence, brief as it was, had been comforting. She almost felt he was looking out for her.

As the camera moved away from Jenny and focused on the trapdoor in the concrete floor, a loud bang sounded, frightening everyone in the room. Even Lonetree felt his heart jump. Just as the team started to settle, another loud bang sounded, then another, and another. Three in a row, and they could all feel the power behind them. They felt the beats through the soles of their feet.

"This isn't right," George said once again. "Something isn't right. Do you feel it, John?"

Lonetree looked around, trying to pinpoint where the banging had come from, but he was having trouble. It had come from two different directions. He tilted his head.

"There's no change in room temperature," George said, and John knew that George was right. "If this was real I would feel something."

Another bang sounded and Lonetree started forward, away from the trapdoor. He stopped in front of the box of toys and without hesitation reached over and upended the torn box. Toys, music boxes, and children's art supplies spilled all over the floor. With the aid of the penlight he examined the toys and the box. His foot kicked at something big and round. The camera zoomed in on the object, but no one recognized it for what it was.

"What is it, John?" Jenny asked.

Lonetree turned on his heel, moving directly for the large

wood-burning stove in the far corner of the basement. He ripped open one of the large oven doors and rummaged inside. Then he slammed it shut. He went to the next door and pulled it open, rummaging through its interior. Then he yanked and pulled and finally emerged with a small black box with an antenna on it. It was attached to the same kind of big, round object that was in the toy box.

Inside the van, Harris Dalton's gut wrenched as he watched John. He closed his eyes and ordered the cameraman to get a better shot of what John was holding. In the green-tinted low-light filter, they saw Lonetree hit a small switch. Suddenly the basement was filled with the sound of the banging they had heard a moment before. First the round, black object that had spilled from the toy box boomed loudly, then the one John was holding.

George smiled, but Jennifer looked angry. Lonetree threw the speaker and transmitter, smashing them into the large stove.

Harris Dalton felt his heart sink. Abe Feuerstein, more than 150 miles away, also felt his stomach churn with the whiskey that was washing around inside. Back in Pennsylvania, Lionel Peterson's eyes widened. He laughed out loud, unable to stop himself. Kelly Delaphoy buried her face in her hands and bit hard into her left palm to keep from screaming. On the third floor, Kennedy watched Julie Reilly. There was no surprise on her face.

"Goddamn it, go to commercial—NOW!" Harris shouted.

Suddenly the phones started buzzing. Harris knew without being told that New York was on the line, screaming for his head. He looked back at Kelly Delaphoy with murder in his eyes.

"Go to the extended commercial package. We'll need ten minutes here!"

"Sir, New York wants to know exactly what they just saw," his assistant said, holding the phone to her chest.

"What do you think? We just saw all of our careers and

possibly the entire network go under. Someone placed those goddamn speakers inside the basement!"

Lionel Peterson stood and patted Kelly on the back, then opened the door and stepped out into the night. They didn't need him to tell them that they were as fucked as a turkey the night before Thanksgiving. Kelly had done it. Against every order from New York, she had tried to put one over on Professor Kennedy's team, and she had gotten caught. It was just too good to believe. Nothing had happened inside the house for more than three hours, and now this. It was over for the special, and he would swoop in to save the day with the alternate programming he had arranged.

Summer Place, it turned out, was nothing more than a house.

New York, New York

Abraham Feuerstein felt the wolves gathering at the bar at the end of the large screening room. The board members who had been backing Lionel Peterson were no longer hiding that alliance, but outwardly flaunting it. Just thirty seconds into the extended commercial break, not only had he been handed the last ratings report, but he had also been informed that three major sponsors were all demanding release of their sponsorship agreement. The compartments of Feuerstein's ship were filling with water fast, and there was nothing he could do to stop the flooding.

The CEO slid his empty glass over to the bartender and nodded that he wanted it filled. He calmly sipped his drink and waited for the network wolves to attack.

Bright River, Pennsylvania

Harris Dalton sat hard into his chair and tossed his headphones onto the console before him. Below his elevated platform his technical team was silent as the first of ten commercials played on the broadcast screen. The monitors were all full of the camera views coming from inside Summer Place. One of them showed Julie Reilly hurrying down the staircase from the third floor. The only other monitor showing movement inside the house was number fourteen, in the kitchen. John Lonetree stepped through the door, carrying the damning evidence of the hoax in his hand: two large subwoofers and the transmitting box that had produced the loud banging and the moaning. Harris thought it would be people's exhibit number one in their fraud trials.

"Harris?"

Dalton didn't turn at the sound of Kelly Delaphoy's voice. He ran his right hand through his graying hair and sat motionless, waiting for the ax to fall from New York. His eyes roamed over to monitor seventeen. The Boston family was sitting confused in front of their television. The father was snickering and the mother was motionless. The kids had wandered away to another room, which was merciful in and of itself. The hoax was called, and the world knew it.

"Harris, I had nothing to do with this, I swear to you," Kelly said through the tears welling in her eyes. "I really thought we didn't need any gags to get through the night. I really believed that Summer Place would be the proving ground Professor Kennedy needed."

Finally Harris turned, a thin smile on his lips. He placed a hand on Kelly's shoulder and then took a deep breath.

"If it's any consolation, after the broadcast test two weeks ago, I really thought this place was special, too. I thought we had a chance to really prove something. I don't blame anyone for this mess but myself." On monitor number three, Gabriel Kennedy had just reached the bottom floor behind Julie Reilly. The lights came on throughout the house. Lionel Peterson was standing in the center of the foyer with his hands on his hips. Wallace Lindemann was walking past him toward his favorite spot in the house: the ballroom. "What's going to happen to him?" Harris asked, pointing at the image of Professor Kennedy.

"Sir, the network is on the phone. They're pulling the plug and they want Julie Reilly to wrap things up with script describing the hoax attempt. She's to use her own wording and try to exonerate the network as much as she can." The assistant was unable to meet the director's eyes.

Harris nodded his head. "Pass that along to Julie. No, wait. Kelly, take the instructions in to her. You'll need to make an appearance anyway. Accusations are going to be flying and I don't want you to give one inch to that son of a bitch Peterson."

Kelly bit her lower lip but nodded anyway.

"Explain to the new head of the network that he's got eight minutes to do his firing. Then we're back on the air," Harris said. He shook his head and headed for the door for some much-needed air.

Kelly slowly moved past him toward the front portico of Summer Place, now brightly lit. Other technicians were outside the production van taking a break and talking among themselves. Many were not hiding their mirth at what had happened inside the house. They assumed Harris Dalton himself had been in on the hoax.

Dalton was about to turn and walk back into the van when he heard a honking coming from the front gate. He watched a black van pull up to the gates, but shook his head, figuring it was just another nut coming out of the woodwork. Harris started up the steps of the production van just as a security officer stopped him.

"Sir, there's a couple of gangster-looking men out here in a van that say they have information for Leonard Sickles. They say he's expecting them."

Harris looked toward the large front gate.

"No one gets in, I don't care who they work for. If they have a package for Mr. Sickles, tell them you'll take it in to him." Harris turned and entered the production van.

The security man returned to the gate and passed on his instructions. The two men cussed but knew they had to give over the yellow envelope. They admonished the security man and told him that Leonard owed them money for their work, and the security man said he would pass on that also.

The black man in the passenger seat reluctantly handed

over the large yellow envelope that contained the material they had stolen from the Lindemann Foundation in Philadelphia. The package also included information from a bribed source at the Immigration and Naturalization Service offices in Washington.

The envelope exchanged hands. Just as the security man locked the gates once more, deep inside Summer Place, in the basement where John Lonetree and his team had just uncovered the hoax of the century, the trapdoor leading to the subbasement lifted on its hinges. The push from below was so strong that the wood cracked and the hasp and lock bent. The dust of a hundred years plumed up from the old wood as the door strained against its restraints.

Upstairs, on the third floor, the sewing room door shook in its frame. The crystal doorknob turned once, twice, and then the door shook again.

Suddenly Summer Place was awaking from its sleep. Two kinds of hell wanted to be freed.

Gabriel Kennedy met his team in the large foyer. George caught Kennedy's eye and shook his head. He stepped up to Gabriel and pulled him aside.

"Gabe, the feelings I was getting down there—I knew there was something going on. I mean, I felt the lie before Lonetree found the speakers."

Gabriel's attention was focused past George, trying to hear what Lionel Peterson was saying. Gabriel was surprised to see Julie Reilly arguing with him. If he heard right, she was denying the fact that she had anything to do with planting the speakers. Father Dolan had moved to the bottom step of the stairs and had sat down. Gabriel saw the father look away, as if the conversation involved him in some way.

"Gabriel, listen to me, goddamn it!"

Lonetree and Jennifer heard George's loud exclamation and broke away from the group. John pushed the two speakers and transmitter into Peterson's chest, hard enough that the executive flinched.

Jennifer and Lonetree joined Gabriel and George. "Look," George was saying, "that wasn't all I was feeling down there. I was to the point where I couldn't breathe."

"What are you saying?" Kennedy overheard Peterson telling Julie that they were pulling the plug on the special. He saw that Kelly Delaphoy had joined them.

"It was like someone had thrown a ton of dirt over my face and I couldn't get any air." George took Kennedy by the arm. "Something is down there, Gabriel. And I don't mean the basement. It's deeper. Maybe in the root cellar."

Kennedy turned to Lonetree. "Did you get any feelings down there?"

Lonetree shook his head.

"I got something," Jenny said. "Bobby Lee popped in for a minute. I thought it was just my memory of him, but it was like he was curious about something. It went away as soon as it appeared, but it was there."

"And John's a dreamwalker; he wouldn't have picked up on what I did. I'm telling you, something is down there!"

"Professor, can you join us, please?"

Kennedy looked up and saw that Peterson was looking at them. His eyes went from the small group to his watch. Kelly was standing with her head low and Julie Reilly was fuming, ignoring the makeup girl who tried to get her face. Kennedy walked up to the group, followed by the rest of his team. He saw Leonard Sickles standing in the ballroom doorway, watching curiously. Not far behind him was Wallace Lindemann, draining a glass of whiskey, content that his house had been proven clean of anything that went bump in the night. One of the security men gave Leonard a large yellow envelope, but Peterson interrupted his thoughts before he could wonder about what was inside. Leonard held the envelope at his side and returned to the ballroom with it.

"Professor, since an embarrassing hoax has been perpetrated on my network, the board has decided to pull the special from the air. Ms. Reilly here will go live and explain that we are having technical problems and cannot continue, and we will switch to alternate programming."

"You bastard, you know I had nothing to do with this. If it was anyone, it was Kelly," Julie said. Kelly Delaphoy didn't make any attempt at denial at this point. Kennedy turned and looked at Father Dolan, who was still sitting on the stairs. He was wringing his hands and making a point of not seeing the argument taking place right in front of him.

Julie Reilly held her ground.

"Now, I don't believe this house is haunted, but I would not have sabotaged what may have been an even bigger story: Professor Kennedy being held responsible for his missing student's disappearance."

Kennedy saw Damian Jackson step away from the coat check room with his overcoat in hand, smiling from ear to ear. He stopped short of the group and just listened.

"Look, whoever was responsible, it's a moot point at this juncture," Peterson said. "I'm sure the board will want a full investigation—we've lost them forty million dollars in revenue alone. For now, let's get this wrapped up and get the hell back to New York. I want everyone in the office at nine in the morning. And I will not be accepting any resignations."

Julie and Kelly, along with Harris Dalton, knew then that they wouldn't be spared. They would be fired and their careers were done.

"Okay, all nonessential personnel clear the house. Ms. Reilly, you have five minutes. Father Dolan, you are excused. Please clear the area, everyone. I want our intrepid reporter to do her stand-up at the staircase."

Dolan stood without looking at Peterson and moved to the side of the staircase. Kennedy smiled, and the others of his group looked at him, clearly wondering what he found humorous about all that was happening.

"I think we have our culprit, boys and girls." Most of the eyes in the room went to Father Dolan, who couldn't bring himself to look any of them in the eye. "James, you and your friends were the only ones allowed into the house before the broadcast team arrived. Would you like to do a little confessing?" Gabriel asked.

"Look, we know who is responsible for this fiasco; there is no need to call Father Dolan's reputation into question," Lionel Peterson said.

"I thought you would come to the defense of the good father, Peterson," Kennedy said. He looked toward Julie Reilly. He knew she wasn't a part of what happened in the basement, but he also knew that like a shark, she was smelling blood in the water. He was going to take advantage of that.

Julie caught the unvoiced instruction. She half turned and whispered into her microphone.

"Get the audio out to New York. Hurry."

"The two women with you this afternoon, James, they weren't from any paranormal society at all, were they?" Gabriel asked, stepping even closer to Father Dolan. "Or if they were, they were also experts at rigging up houses. Am I right? Is it so they can say they produce evidence?"

Father Dolan finally looked up at Kennedy. His eyes roamed from the professor to Lionel Peterson, and then to Wallace Lindemann, who stood in front of the ballroom with an empty glass in his hand.

"I see where you're going with this, Kennedy, but you're on the wrong tack. Our culprit is right here," Lionel said, nodding toward Kelly.

Father Dolan shook his head. "The supernatural, these shows, people all over the world turning away from their faith. I thought that—"

At that moment, every door upstairs on the second and third floors opened and slammed against the walls. Then, all at once, they slammed closed again. The lights flickered and the house shook. Lionel Peterson, about to follow the technicians out of the house, stopped and turned. The smile on his lips was wide and mocking.

"Really, it's a little late for that, isn't it?"

Just as the words exited his mouth, the front doors

slammed shut, hitting the last of the makeup girls in the back of the head and sending her flying onto the front porch of the house.

"Good God!" Father Dolan stepped forward, his confession all but forgotten.

The lights flickered again. Then they went out, and a grunt accompanied the sound of someone falling. Then the lights started flashing on and off. In the strobing illumination, Father Dolan lay sprawled on his stomach. Gabriel and Lonetree started forward to assist the older man to his feet, but as they neared him, something took the father by the feet and started pulling him up the stairs. The cameraman who had been following Lonetree and his group in the cellar thought fast and sprang forward almost at the same moment as Kennedy and Lonetree. He immediately started filming.

"Harris, Harris, get us back on the air, Goddamn it!" the cameraman yelled into his microphone. This was no elaborate hoax.

Gabriel and John reached Father Dolan and grabbed his hands. In the flickering light they all saw the panic on the old man's face as he was pulled away. Finally George and the second cameraman joined the two men trying to pull Dolan back, actually throwing their bodies on top of the black-clad priest.

The tug-of-war continued. On the twentieth step leading to the second floor, the small red indicator on the ambient-light camera started to glow red.

"We're going live!" the cameraman shouted.

At the front door, Lionel Peterson stood motionless. Then he also sprang into action, taking Julie Reilly's headphones from her. In front of the ballroom, Wallace Lindemann let the tumbler of ice slip from his fingers as he watched what was happening on the stairs.

"Who gave you the go-ahead to go back on the air, Dalton?!" Peterson shouted.

As they all watched, John Lonetree was shoved down the stairs. Gabriel was hit hard enough that his head slammed into the wooden banister. The cameraman and George Cordero were tossed back down the stairs with enough force that the gathered men and women heard bones break as they hit the tiled floor.

Kelly Delaphoy screamed. In the flickering light, she watched Father Dolan being pulled up the stairs hard enough that his head bounced against every step. It was all silent as he disappeared over the second-floor landing. Then as suddenly as it had started, the house quit. Then they heard the laugh, deep and booming, coming from upstairs.

Yes, Summer Place had awakened.

20 New York, New York

The screening room was silent, save only for the sound of ice striking the bottom of a glass. Everyone started, turning away from the large screen for the briefest of moments to look for the source of the sound. Abraham Feuerstein looked up in mock apology and smiled, pouring his own drink for the first time in years—at least, in front of others. He nodded toward the screen.

"Inform Harris Dalton that we'll stick with the special for the time being. Also inform Lionel Peterson he is not to leave the house, he's to stay inside with Professor Kennedy. We do have the state policeman on hand?"

"Yes, sir," his assistant said as she helped the old man back to his chair.

"Good. That should preclude anyone calling the authorities."

"Sir, what if—"

The CEO stared at the man who fronted for Lionel Peterson until the skinny little man closed his mouth.

"I believe our good Professor Kennedy made everyone aware of Mr. Peterson's culpability in the basement hoax. He stays, and the special goes forward. Instruct Dalton that he has control of commercial interruption time."

The audio and the visuals that had come in from Summer Place had shocked everyone.

"It looks like Halloween may just turn out to be something special after all."

The men and women in the screening room had never seen the old man looking so smug.

Bright River, Pennsylvania

They all heard the moan coming from upstairs. It was Kennedy who acted first, swiping blood away as he gained his feet. John Lonetree acted second, standing and eyeing Jenny, his unvoiced command making her stand in place and not follow him. Both men bounded up the stairs just as the lighting inside the house came on strong. Everyone else remained in the foyer, motionless. Lionel Peterson heard the command coming from the production van that instructed everyone to keep their places. Not only was the special to continue, it also would do so without commercial interruption at Dalton's discretion. But by far the most shocking news was the order that Harris passed on directly to Peterson himself, and this order made everyone who heard it over their headphones smile: He was to stay inside the house with the investigating teams. Peterson tore the earpiece from his ear and threw it to the ground. A soundman collected it and placed it in his own ear as he and the first cameraman bolted after Kennedy and Lonetree.

Inside the production van, Harris Dalton was practically screaming for the first cameraman and soundman to catch up with the professor. On monitor number one, the picture was jumbled as the cameraman took the stairs in pursuit, jostling the camera about. They had switched from ambient light to regular exposure, and the lens finally caught sight of the two men kneeling before a prone figure on the second-floor landing. The picture jostled once again as someone pushed past the two technicians. It was Damian Jackson, who went to Lonetree and Kennedy.

"If this man is hurt because of anything you pulled,

Kennedy, I swear to God I'll place you in handcuffs in front of the entire fucking world!"

Gabriel didn't even look up when the state policeman bumped him. He was busy feeling for a pulse. When he found it, he finally spared the lieutenant a glance.

"Shut up and help us get him out of here. He needs a doctor. I think his neck's broken."

All three men lifted the father as carefully as they could. The movement made the old man moan, and then there was silence. They brushed by the cameraman and soundman on their way down the stairs. The others gathered around the staircase as the three men went through the foyer with Father Dolan in their arms, and on to the front doors. Lonetree let go of one of the father's legs and reached for the door handle. He turned the knob and pulled, but nothing happened. He looked to make sure it wasn't locked and then tried again. This time the left side opened about six inches and was pulled closed, yanking the handle from the big Indian's grasp. He tried again and this time had it almost all the way open with the assistance of three or four people on the front porch. The door was pulled from his grasp once more.

"To hell with this," Damian Jackson said. He helped lower Father Dolan to the expensive carpet. Then he went to the large plate glass window on the side of the double doors. He took a large wooden chair that had flanked a small table, and with all of his strength he raised it above his head and slammed it into the window. The glass spiderwebbed, but held it shape and form. The heavy wooden chair splintered in Jackson's hands. Nonplussed, the detective picked up the second chair from the small table set and repeated the process. This time the chair bounced backward, almost hitting the policeman on the rebound. The spiderweb cracks not only held, they also looked as if they were shrinking. As if the glass were healing itself.

"What the hell?" Jackson exclaimed. The curtains blew with an unfelt breeze and, before all of them, the glass became whole again.

"It's not going to let us out," Gabriel said. "John, you and George take Father Dolan into the ballroom and make him as comfortable as you can."

Damian Jackson heard the instructions, but his eyes were on the window. It looked as if he had never assaulted it with two heavy wooden chairs. Through the sheer curtain, Damian could see other people on the front porch as they tried communicating with him through the glass. Then, as everyone watched, a coldness came through the first floor of Summer Place. It went past Jackson and slammed into the front wall. They watched as the pane of glass frosted over.

"Kennedy!" Jackson called. "This has gone too far. Call off your people, wherever you have them hidden. We have an injured man here."

Gabriel shook his head as he joined Jackson at the window.

"You just won't understand, will you? This house is waking up. Get that through your head, damn it. For now, we have to figure out what awakened it." He turned and ran for the ballroom, followed by one of the two sets of cameramen and soundmen.

With the two film crews going on instinct and with no real direction, and Julie sequestered in a far corner of the ballroom to speak quietly with the production van, Gabriel checked on Father Dolan, who had been stretched out on one of the large billiard tables. Jennifer Tilden and George Cordero had the elderly priest awake, and it looked like he had suffered no more than a broken right leg and possibly a concussion. In the corner, Julie cut her conversation with Dalton short when she saw that Gabriel was approaching Father Dolan. She waved the closest of the cameramen and soundmen toward the billiard table. Lionel Peterson saw the gathering and moved off to join Damian Jackson as he entered the ballroom.

"How is he?" Gabriel asked Jenny.

"For someone who was dragged up a flight of stairs, he's doing remarkably well," she said. She was wrapping the

ather's leg in one of the sheer curtains from the ballroom's
vindow.

"Keep him warm. In case you haven't noticed, winter's set
n down here." Kennedy blew out a deep sigh to demonstrate
he frosting of his breath.

"Professor, I'm sorry for what I did," Father Dolan said,
truggling with his words.

Gabriel placed a hand on the man's chest and patted it.
'You just lay still, we'll try to get you some help."

"I have a feeling that may be more of a problem than you
know." Dolan raised a hand and pointed toward one of the
plate glass windows. Wallace Lindemann was using one of
he ornate bar stools to smash at the glass, but every time he
struck the frosted glass, the barstool would rebound as if he
were hitting a pane of pure rubber.

Julie Reilly stepped up with the camera crew right behind
her.

"Professor, can you absolutely rule out a setup? You and
your team members were actually in a tug-of-war with something on that staircase. What can you tell us?"

Gabriel smiled and shook his head. Then he looked around
the room. It seemed that everyone was watching him, waiting for the explanation that would make sense of the sudden
shift in Summer Place.

"Something changed in the few minutes leading up to the
attack. An element may have been introduced that brought
this slumbering beast to wakefulness."

"So what is the plan for the Supernaturals, Professor?"

"First, we have to try to get Father Dolan and the nonessential personnel out of the house. Failing that, we will have
to secure them in the ballroom."

The lights flickered once more and a whoosh of wind
traveled from upstairs. It hit the ballroom doors with such
force that it slammed both doors closed. Wallace Lindemann was so taken by surprise that he dropped his bar stool
and quickly made his way over to Damian Jackson and Lionel
Peterson.

"Jesus, it must be thirty degrees in here."

"This woman, ladies and gentlemen, is the producer of *Hunters of the Paranormal,* Ms. Kelly Delaphoy. She has decided to join the inside team," Julie said. The camera, with its regular light lens, zoomed in on Kelly's face. She looked frightened but exhilarated.

The second camera team moved closer to the detective and Lionel Peterson just as Wallace Lindemann joined them. Damian interrupted his conversation long enough to push the camera and its operator back.

"I told you, I am not to be on the air. Now get away," he said, hissing.

The cameramen and soundmen backed away just as the lights went out, and then just as suddenly came back on. Outside the house, the harsh rumble of thunder immediately followed a flash of lightning.

"As we make plans for how to handle the sudden awakening of Summer Place, it seems we have an enormous storm cell moving into the valley. I am informed by our production crew that the winds have picked up and the sudden heavy rainfall has caught several of our support technicians off guard," Julie explained, moving around the ballroom with her camera team in tow.

Inside the production van, Harris Dalton allowed Julie to run with it. He looked to the preview monitor and saw that they were cued up for an extended commercial run in case something happened that required them to do things they didn't want the viewing audience to see. Thus far, New York had confirmed that they were indeed going out live and that ratings were still falling. That meant that no matter what, the CEO was telling him in no uncertain terms that they would sink or swim on what Kennedy had to say.

Harris looked around and saw the empty spaces where a half hour before Lionel Peterson and Wallace Lindemann had been sitting. Kelly's chair was also empty and he smiled, breathing a sigh of relief. He was alone with complete control and no one looking over his shoulders. He would now go

n his gut instinct, which was telling him this was his moment
n the sun—the once-in-a-lifetime event that would send his
name into the stratosphere. He smiled again and spoke into
his microphone.

"Julie, this is now Professor Kennedy's show. You had
your chance to put your monkey wrench in the works, and
so did Peterson. Now we become believers. I think that damnable house has something to say."

Julie Reilly knew Harris was right; this was now Kennedy's
show. She made her way back to Kennedy and pointed at his
back, indicating to the cameramen and soundmen that they
should lock on to him and not leave.

"George, anything?" Gabriel asked, pulling Cordero away
from his work on Father Dolan.

"I am getting conflicting thoughts, Gabe. Although we
know something from up there"—he pointed toward the ceiling—"is active as hell and mean as a snake, I'm getting the
feel of massive activity from below, possibly the root cellar.
Not the basement, but deeper."

Kennedy bit his lower lip. He had been expecting activity
on a large scale, but not from two very different directions.

"John, how about you?" he asked Lonetree.

"You mean besides the fact that whatever is up there is
strong as hell?"

"Yeah, besides that," Gabriel said with a smile. He was
aware of the camera and sound boom hanging over their
heads but did his best to ignore them.

"I'm afraid you'll have to go with what George is feeling
for right now. I have nothing. If I could close my eyes for a
while, I may be able to get a grasp on what's happening."

Gabriel patted John on the arm and then looked at Jennifer. She just shook her head, telling him without voicing it
that Bobby Lee had not rejoined her.

"Professor Gabe, maybe you better see this."

"That is the voice of Leonard Sickles, whom our viewing
audience met earlier in the evening. Leonard, as you recall,

is in charge of the technical side of things for the Supernaturals," Julie explained as she followed the cameramen and
soundmen over to Leonard, who was standing next to the
large bar. He heard the name of Kennedy's group as dubbed
by Julie and smiled. He was the only team member who actually liked the comic-book-sounding moniker.

"What do you have?" Gabriel asked as the camera joined
them.

With the thump of thunder and the flash of lightning outside the windows, the camera zoomed in tight on the small
black man's face. He pulled out the contents of the yellow
envelope that had been delivered by his friends from Philadelphia. Gabriel could see they were photographs.

"What we have here is the photo history of the Vilnikov
family," Leonard said. He spread the stolen photos out on the
bar for Gabriel and the camera to examine.

"For the benefit of our viewers, Mr. Sickles, could you explain just who the Vilnikov family is?" Julie asked.

"Uh, yeah, sure." Leonard looked into the camera with his
eyebrows bunched up, trying his best for that Clark Gable
look. "The Vilnikovs are third cousins to the former Romanov dynasty from Russia. They were the family of Elena
Lindemann, or so we were led to believe."

"Explain the phrase 'led to believe'?" Julie asked. The
camera looked over Kennedy's shoulder as he examined the
pictures.

"Put simply, we can't find any evidence that Elena Lindemann, or Elena Vilnikov, ever existed."

"You mean to say that there is no evidence of Elena in any
of these family photos?" Julie asked. Kennedy raised one of
the pictures and examined it closer. It was a father and mother,
both of stern visage, and two daughters—each the wrong age
to be Elena—and a son. No older daughter was apparent in
any of the photos.

"The boy in the pictures is Vasily Vilnikov. There is no
Elena."

Gabriel laid the photo down and looked at Leonard, not

saying anything. As he turned, the camera stayed on him, but before he could say anything to Julie, the house lights went out completely and didn't come back on.

They were now cut off and in the dark.

Gabriel ordered the double oak doors to the ballroom closed and locked. Through his twenty years of research, he had learned that the worst thing that paranormal researchers could do was let an entity control the situation. When entities struck, they did so brazenly and with little tact. After a supernatural encounter, most people preferred to move on and not attract any scrutiny. Yet those encounters were exactly the ones that needed to be researched, analyzed, and documented. Gabriel excelled where others had failed because he made those shy individuals want to tell him their stories. And now this was what they were working with tonight—his and others' experiences.

"Okay, let's get some battery-powered lighting up and running," Kennedy said as he surveyed the large ballroom. The number one camera and sound crew that had been assigned to his team kept the camera on him and him alone. "We'll use the ballroom as our starting point, and with our battery-powered lights, we're declaring this room out of bounds to whatever is out there."

"What the hell are you talking about?" Jackson said, moving the camera's lens from his face.

"Again, you have heard the voice of a Pennsylvania state policeman as he questions the professor on his tactics," Julie Reilly said into her personal microphone.

"If what's out there is what you think it is, why the hell would it follow your rules of conduct?"

Kennedy smiled and tried his best to ignore the constant hum of the camera as it zoomed in on him. The first set of small klieg lights came on in the corner, adjusted to shine light on Father Dolan and his injuries.

"It won't follow the rules, but this is the best spot in the house in which to work, at least for the time being. This is where we have Father Dolan, and I don't think it's wise to try to move him. This is where we start."

Damian Jackson looked taken aback. He hadn't been expecting Kennedy to have such a clear and concise answer to his question—and one that made sense.

"Professor Kennedy, why the sudden shift in the power of Summer Place? I mean, why would it come alive so fast?" Julie stood next to Kennedy, watching as he placed a rolled-up jacket underneath Father Dolan's head.

"To start with, the attempt of Father Dolan and Lionel Peterson—"

"All right, you have nothing that shows I was involved with that," Peterson interrupted, forgetting that his denial was going out live to forty million viewers. He looked toward Wallace Lindemann, who was pouring himself a drink at the bar. The small man caught the accusing look and started to protest, but he saw the camera turn his way and decided to fight for his defense another day.

"We already have his confession, Peterson," George Cordero said. He stepped up beside Wallace and opened a bottle of water, not so gently moving the owner of Summer Place to the side with his elbow and a stern look.

"Regardless, all we've seen here is that the man who admitted to placing the speakers down in the basement was involved in another hoax that went wrong, and now that man is hurt." Peterson finally realized that the camera was following him. He dipped his head and decided he may as well start fighting for his job right then and there. "There are several people in this room and in New York who have far more to lose than I."

Kennedy shook his head. "These are all things that the network can take up tomorrow in the daylight. Right now we have something upstairs, and it became active as soon as Leonard here was brought the information on Elena. That's the starting point. Why would the house care whether there's history of Elena Lindemann as a child or not?"

"Working on that right now, boss. We're trying to get an independent phone line out. All cell phone service is down. It's like it's being jammed," Leonard Sickles said. He and three of the computer techs worked to reestablish contact with the satellites above.

"Dalton, are we attempting to enter the house from the outside?" Kennedy asked into his production microphone.

"Harris Dalton is the director in charge of tonight's special. He is in the network production van outside of Summer Place," Julie explained. She went to one of the frozen windows and pulled back the thick curtain.

"Uh . . . yes, Professor, we have three men trying to break through the front doors and the rear kitchen door as we speak. I am surprised you haven't heard them."

The voice coming from the production van was but a whisper that was picked up on the air. Harris Dalton didn't like the fact that the viewers could hear him, but they were all flying by the seat of their pants.

"Thus far, we are unable to break through. I can't explain it yet," Harris said.

Outside they saw another flash of lightning through the frozen glass, followed by the roar of thunder. Damian Jackson wondered why they could hear that and not the sound of men with axes trying to batter down the doors. He turned and left the ballroom and made his way out to the front doors through the darkness of the living room. Leaning toward the double doors, he thought he could hear thumping noises, but they seemed distant and far away. He pulled back and placed his hand on the frozen pane in the center of the front door. The glass was like ice. As he stepped back he could see some light passing through the glass from a lightning strike not far away. As he did, he saw the figure start to take shape, as if someone were dragging a finger through the frost on the window. As he watched, he saw a rough outline of a pole, and attached to that pole was the figure of a man. A hanging man—lynched. The dark figure was hanging by a rope and as another lightning strike hit, the body attached to that rope swayed. Jackson backed away from the glass. The large room had become colder.

"What is it?"

Jackson felt his heart go into his throat. He turned and saw John Lonetree standing behind him. When he looked back at the glass to point out the anomaly, the pane of glass was completely frosted over and there was no figure etched in the moisture.

"Nothing," he said.

"Can you hear anyone out there trying to get in?" John asked.

"They're out there, but that's about all I know."

Lonetree turned back to face Damian.

"Not like your typical police investigation, is it?"

"I'm still not buying it, Lonetree. Come on, you're a cop. You can't believe this shit, can you?"

Lonetree shook his head. "Detective, I learned a long time ago not to question the natural world. There are things out there that our science has never touched on. There are worlds we know nothing of, and one of those worlds is alive and well and in this house. Now, that may not be the answer you're looking for, but it's one you better start considering. Your closed mind just may be your undoing."

Jackson snorted.

"If your mind is closed off to those things, just how can it come up with a defense?" The big Indian moved away toward the ballroom. "And you may want to join us. Gabriel's getting ready to explain the plan of attack."

"Attack?"

Lonetree stopped and turned. "You didn't think we came here just to study, did you?"

"What else would you have come here for?"

"To go to war. Did you think Gabriel was going to allow this house to kill one of his students and get away with it?"

Jackson watched Lonetree disappear into the ballroom. He

turned and looked at the glass again, and then turned just as quickly away from it.

"Yeah, well, in case you hadn't noticed, he's already down a man."

Damian placed his hat on his head and started to follow John back into the ballroom. Upstairs he heard the sound of a door slamming shut. He wondered if it was something entering a room, or coming out. He glanced up the broad, darkened staircase, and quickened his step toward the ballroom.

Harris Dalton removed his headphones, careful to mute the microphone. He turned and looked at the lead mechanic, who was trying to explain what was happening.

"You mean to tell me you have all of this power flowing into the breaker boxes, but nothing is flowing into the house? How can that be possible?"

"It isn't possible. It's like the electricity is being siphoned off before it reaches the breakers."

"Siphoned? Do you know how that sounds?" A thought slowly crept into Dalton's mind. "Look, you stand by outside the van. You're going to go on live with Julie Reilly, and she'll interview you remotely from inside the house. Explain to those people inside Summer Place what's happening out here. Tell that fireman to also stand by. I want him to explain why they can't bust in through the windows or doors."

"Oh, I don't think our union will allow—"

Harris almost exploded. He took the man by his right shoulder and squeezed. It took all of his willpower to calm himself. Using his most menacing voice—the one that had carried him through five Super Bowl telecasts—he leaned in toward the man.

"I don't give a good goddamn if you worked directly for Jimmy Hoffa in the day. If you don't go on, I swear to God I will make sure you're bundling electrical cable in Oklahoma City this time next week. Clear?"

"Yes, sir," the mechanic said. He turned and left through the plastic strip curtain.

Harris Dalton placed the headphones back on and took a deep breath.

"Julie, you'll be conducting two interviews after I run a three-minute commercial break. One is with the lead mechanic and the other is with the fire chief."

After Julie had her questions answered, Harris watched the monitors in front of him. He examined the ambient-light cameras on the second and third floors and saw absolutely no movement on either. He changed headphones and then checked the directional microphones on those floors. All he heard was the distant sound of thunder outside. He switched to the basement microphones next, and then he froze. He pressed the headphones into his ears and waved everyone in the control room to silence. The sounds he was hearing didn't seem to be coming from the basement, but the subbasement. They were distant and hard to define. He turned a switch and brought the sounds out through the large speakers.

"Can anyone tell me what the hell that noise is?" He tilted his head and closed his eyes as his brain worked to identify what he was hearing.

"Sir, it sounds like crying," his assistant said.

"That's what I get. Women, a lot of women. At least more than three or four," said the sound engineer.

"Can you boost the gain on the basement microphone?" Harris asked..

"That's as high a gain as we have. We need to place the microphones in a different area, like as close to the trapdoor as we can."

"Okay. As soon as Julie finishes with her interview, we'll see what Kennedy wants to do."

"Maybe they can convince that asshole Peterson to go and do it," his assistant said.

The elicited laughs told Harris that his production team was at least thinking about what was happening. And if they believed something was afoot inside Summer Place, then most of America would be believers.

"I'll suggest just that, but don't hold your breath. I don't think Peterson will risk his neck for a job that won't be there tomorrow."

The van quieted as they all listened to the sounds. The crying was definitely female, and full of anguish.

Just as Harris was about to order the commercial break from General Motors, incoherent gibberish started to replace the crying, like a hundred voices speaking a hundred different foreign languages at once. It was joined by another noise: pounding on the trapdoor to the subbasement.

Each pounding on the wooden door made everyone in the production van flinch.

"Julie, get Professor Kennedy on the line. Tell him to connect his microphone, damn it. And while you're conducting the interviews, we need someone to check out the basement. We have something happening down there. We're picking up voices . . . and what sounds like crying."

The main monitor showed a man standing in front of a brand-new Chevrolet Silverado, explaining why all of America should own one. Harris started counting down the seconds to the fifth hour of the Halloween special. He had been informed by the CEO himself that the show was just now climbing back to the ratings values they had anticipated, but the polls were still showing an overwhelming degree of disbelief by the viewing public. They had lost the test family completely—they had given up on the show, and were now watching reruns of *Family Guy* on another network.

Inside Summer Place, Cordero, Lonetree, and Gabriel stood in the darkened kitchen. The cameraman and soundman waited anxiously for their cue as Julie started her brief interviews with the men trying to get power to the house, and the fire chief who couldn't seem to break a pane of window glass or batter down a door.

Julie Reilly was right outside the double swinging doors of the large kitchen, her remote setup complete. She started off directly with the lead mechanic first. He explained how the power was connected to the house, but that it was being lost somewhere between the breaker boxes and the distribution points. Julie asked the question everyone was thinking: was the power being used by something inside Summer Place? The mechanic laughed. It was an impossibility, to put it mildly.

Julie grimaced at the answer. She had hoped the man would be more of a team player. She then started questioning the fire chief from Bright Waters.

"Chief, what problems are you encountering trying to break into the house?"

The camera cut to the chief, who was standing outside on the veranda of Summer Place, looking up at the house.

"It seems the storm has built up the barometric pressure to a point that—"

"Chief, we need to stop you right there. We can see the shadows of your men from the inside through the ice that has formed on the glass; they don't seem to be doing much in the way of breaking in. Is it true you have had orders to stand down?"

The question took the chief by surprise. Even Harris Dalton and his production team looked at one another. Harris picked up the red phone and was connected directly to the CEO in New York.

"Sir, have any orders come from New York to stop attempting to get inside the house?"

Harris listened, and his knuckles turned white on the phone's handset.

"Damn it, sir, we have an injured man inside that house. We need to get him out." Dalton listened and closed his eyes. "Yes, sir, right now it's a possible broken leg and a concussion. Yes, sir, a dramatic break-in in the sixth hour, I understand. Now, I also understand that it's your orders to not get help inside the house at this time?" Harris listened and made a sour face. When he hung up the phone, he rubbed his eyes. Then he looked up at the greenish image of Julie Reilly as she ended her remote interview with the two men outside.

"I must admit, you're damn good, Reilly. I never saw that

one coming," Harris said on cue. The preview monitor switched to the live shot of Kennedy, Cordero, and Lonetree as they stood at the basement door inside the kitchen; only she could hear him.

"Yeah, well, what about Father Dolan? Are they going to get him help anytime soon?" she asked. She placed her hand on the kitchen door, wanting desperately to get inside before they started down into the basement. She listened to Harris. "The sixth hour? Has everyone here and in New York gone nuts? The fire chief will be crucified if this gets out."

"Yeah, and in the end you'll find out our small-town chief just earned five times more in retirement benefits than he would have normally received. I don't think he gives a flying fuck about getting fired, not after what the network must be paying him to stay out of the house."

"Harris, maybe we should ask Kennedy to get the father out of here. I think whatever is in this house may have a hard-on for the good father."

"Okay, okay. Ask Kennedy if we should get him out through one of the back windows or doors, so no one can see."

"You got it. I'm going with Kennedy to the basement now."

"Okay. Be careful what you say. They're live in there."

Julie pushed open the double swinging doors, leaving her own camera crew behind. Kennedy had opened the basement door and was getting ready to enter the stairwell leading down. Julie nodded her head at the soundmen and cameramen she had just joined. The camera stayed trained on Kennedy, following his green-tinted image down into the blackness of the cellar.

Immediately, Julie started hearing the sounds that had so scared the production team in the van. The cries were getting louder and far more insistent. They were indeed women—a lot of them.

From the van, Harris Dalton informed everyone that the noises and voices were coming through loud and clear. The world was hearing what they were.

"George, are you picking up anything?" Kennedy asked. He slowly moved down the stairs in the total darkness.

"Anguish . . . yes, anguish. Not physical pain. It's . . . it's like a mental torture."

Gabriel reached the turn in the wooden stairs and stopped. He could now hear spoken words mixed with the crying.

"I don't know about you fellas, but I'm hearing German, maybe Polish, some Italian . . . a few other languages."

Julie was also hearing what Cordero described.

The cameraman and the soundman, with his mic boom hanging out over Julie and Lonetree, were both nervous. The soundman was of Polish descent and knew the language from his grandmother. He leaned toward Julie and muted his microphone.

"One of them is calling out for Leana, no—begging for Leana," he said nervously.

"And Magda," Kennedy said. "German, although I haven't studied it since high school. The accent is right—Magda."

"Our soundman, David, off the air, says that one of the voices he understood was in Polish. It's calling the name Leana. And now Professor Kennedy has confirmed a name being spoken in German—Magda," Julie explained. She started down again, holding tightly to the handrail. Just as her feet touched the small landing where the stairs turned sharply to the right, the kitchen door above them slammed shut. The sound was like a cannon going off and made Julie almost lose her footing on the landing. She bounced off of one rail and nearly went off backward on the rebound. George Cordero and John Lonetree reached out in the darkness and grabbed her. John switched on his small penlight and made sure Julie got her bearings.

Julie mouthed, "Thank you."

The camera had been jostled as it tried to focus on Julie's face. She grimaced and nodded toward Kennedy as he was nearing the bottom steps. She felt embarrassed at her near misstep and feared she would now be perceived as a klutz by the viewing audience. She would have to redeem herself below.

Kennedy paused at the bottom of the stairs, allowing his eyes to adjust to the pitch-black basement. He heard the door open at the top of the stairs, and suspected that Damian Jackson was joining them. He ignored the heavy footsteps that descended the steps slowly and carefully.

Gabriel turned toward the root cellar door, moving forward so that Lonetree, George, and the camera crew could step onto the concrete flooring.

"The voices and the weeping have started to fade down to almost nothing," Kennedy said as he listened.

Damian Jackson joined them on the floor and looked around. He was only able to make out the camera crew in front of him. He pressed his earpiece into his right ear and listened to what the professor was saying to the live audience. He shook his head. Kennedy was having a field day with this fiasco.

Gabriel finally switched on his small light and shined it toward the far side of the basement, illuminating the trapdoor. He started forward.

"Gabe, I'm registering a massive temperature falloff on the digital thermometer," Lonetree said. He moved the small device around, taking readings. "It's colder around the center of the room." John stepped toward Kennedy. "Okay, it just dropped another ten degrees."

George joined them with the thermal imager. The camera zoomed in on the screen of the handheld boxlike device. The blue wave it caught seemed to be flowing freely from the cracks around the edges of the subbasement door. George held the imager out for Kennedy to see.

"Professor, could this image be caused by much colder air rising from below, as would be natural for a deep root cellar?" Julie asked in a whisper.

"A normal drop-off would be a three-to-five-degree difference. But as you can see on the thermal imager, we have a massive drop of more than thirty degrees. Unless the root cellar is refrigerated, no, this is not normal."

Julie heard a small snicker of laughter from behind her.

When she turned, Damian Jackson held up his hand in apology.

Julie knew that Kennedy was scoring points off her. She was starting to understand that he was out to get her now.

Gabriel squatted and examined the old lock.

"The owner of the property gave the professor the key to the lock earlier, with the dire warning that no one has been down in the root cellar since the Lindemanns last stayed at Summer Place back in 1940. Whatever we see down there hasn't been seen in more than seventy-five years," Julie informed the viewing world.

From somewhere above them a loud bang sounded. Then another, and then another.

The ballroom doors had been standing wide open, and then they both slammed shut. They opened and then slammed again, then yet again. Leonard Sickles looked up as everyone in the room fell silent. Even the injured Father Dolan came up on one elbow and looked toward the doors. Jennifer Tilden took Leonard's arm and nodded in the light of the computer monitors. Leonard nodded in return. The camera team joined them just as Leonard pushed the mic button on his belt.

"Professor Gabe?"

As Kennedy answered from below, the camera zoomed in on Leonard's face. Then it caught Jenny as she leaned in with a small device, the same one that was being used in the basement. She held it so Leonard could see.

"We have a temperature drop of nearly twenty-five degrees up here. The ballroom doors just slammed closed three times on their own. We also—"

The computers shut down without warning and they lost the light from their monitors. The cameraman immediately switched to his ambient-light camera.

"Stay with the ballroom," Harris Dalton said from the production van.

"Okay, we lost power in here," Leonard said as he started checking the connections.

As they waited for Gabriel to comment, a pounding started from upstairs somewhere. Everyone in the ballroom turned their heads to look at the ceiling.

"It sounds like it's coming from the third floor," Jenny whispered. The camera had her framed, and all the world could see that Jennifer was frightened as the pounding started to take on the sound of footsteps.

At that moment in the production van, Harris Dalton looked over at preview monitor five and his blood froze. Everyone around him stared at the ambient-light picture coming from the third-floor hallway.

"Okay, people, we have activity up on the third floor. Both the sewing room and the master suite doors are standing wide open. I suspect that's where the pounding originated."

Indeed, the heavy pounding sounded as if it were moving from the far end of the third floor toward the center of the hall—toward the landing.

In the cellar, the temperature was rising and the voices and crying had disappeared completely. Kennedy pressed his earpiece in tighter, as Jackson had done just a moment before. He shook his head, straightened, and then started moving for the stairs.

"Something is happening upstairs and team one is now moving to investigate," Julie said. She scrambled to keep up with Kennedy, who was taking the dangerous steps two at a time. Jackson, who had stepped out of the way to allow everyone to pass by him, shook his head at the dramatics.

"This is getting good," he said as he turned to follow.

"Go to two," Harris said as he watched the monitor that showed "Preview," and then he switched to the live shot of Kennedy running up the darkened stairs. "Okay, back to one." The shot moved from Kennedy's camera team to the ballroom just as the camera moved from face to face. The soundman was picking up the heavy pounding heading toward the third-floor landing. Harris thanked God they had left a team inside the ballroom.

"Camera one, great job. Now turn eighty degrees to your left and get that little shit Lindemann in the shot."

The cameraman zoomed in on the owner of Summer Place, who had stood from his seat at the bar and was watching the doors, the drink in his hand forgotten. He didn't know he was on the air live, but the man next to him did. Lionel Peterson shook his head and tried to move away from the live shot.

"Don't let Peterson slip away. Get him!" Harris said excitedly into his microphone.

The camera caught Peterson and he froze. He tried his best to look as if he were the man in charge, placing his hands on his hips. He stood stock-still, watching the ballroom doors. Even in the blackness around him, he could see the camera frozen on him.

"Okay, get a shot of the ballroom doors. Audio, you're doing real good, but move over into the shot and get your mic boom close to the door. Camera one, make sure you get him doing it."

In New York, most everyone was impressed with the way Harris Dalton moved from shot to shot with the same kind of quick thinking that had won him all of his Emmy awards. Abe Feuerstein smiled and took a deep swallow of his whiskey. On the large screen, the greenish image of the soundman placed the sound boom as close to the door as possible.

The footsteps moved to the third-floor landing and then they stopped. The silence was even more frightening than the noise had been. The cameraman caught the father crossing himself.

"Great job, one, that was a once-in-a-lifetime shot there," Harris said.

Kelly Delaphoy moved over toward Lionel Peterson. Although it was dark, she could feel the anger radiating off of him in waves.

"Convinced yet?" she whispered.

"Fuck off," he said with a hiss, not really caring if the sound equipment heard him.

"Go to camera two. Kennedy is at the top of the stairs," Harris said quickly.

The camera view switched with a fluidity that made Harris proud.

Gabriel slammed into the door that led back into the kitchen. The camera lost him for a moment as the technician pushed past George and Lonetree, but finally focused on him just as he turned the cut-glass doorknob. Nothing happened. Kennedy tried it again.

"It's locked from the other side." He pressed his shoulder against the door and pushed. This time the door opened a few inches and then was suddenly thrust back, shoving Gabriel away from the door.

Lonetree stepped past the cameramen and soundmen and placed his large bulk against the door. Then, as one, they pushed. This time the door opened about a foot, and the camera caught both men struggling to maintain the opening. They could see the resistance on the other side of the door. Then they all heard the sound at the same time, right along with the live television audience. The growl was deep, as if it had come from a tunnel, and it made Kennedy and Lonetree lose their battle with the door. The force on the far side pushed it closed once more.

"What the hell was that?" Harris said into his microphone.

"Jesus!" the experienced cameraman said. His lens focused on the door in front of Gabriel and John.

"Goddamn it, camera two, we can hear you!" Harris hissed into his mic.

His assistant patted his arm. "Take it easy. That was intense, and I doubt TV-land minded at all."

Dalton knew she was right. Like it or not, the cameramen and soundmen were now part of the show, no longer just technicians in the background; they were now living this right along with the team down there.

In the green darkness on the screen, they could see Kennedy place his hand on the door about midway up and then quickly withdraw it.

"Freezing," he said, moving back to allow Lonetree to feel it for himself. "George, what are you feeling?" Gabriel asked Cordero.

"Scared, damn it."

"Nothing else?" Kennedy asked.

Breathing heavily, Cordero stepped up to the door and held his hand out without touching the wood. His fingers closed into a fist as he gathered himself, and then they spread again as his hand moved closer. He came within an inch of the wood, then suddenly withdrew his hand and stepped back, making Gabriel and John do the same. The night-vision camera zoomed in on Cordero's features. The man looked around like a trapped animal.

"What?" This time it was the soundman who said the word. The technicians were scared and the whole world now knew professionalism was being overridden by that most basic, overwhelming sense.

"That's not a ghost out there. Whatever it was, it was never human." George took a step back off the landing and onto the first stair, nudging Julie Reilly out of the way.

The cut-glass knob turned and the door slowly opened a foot. Everyone stepped back, their eyes turned toward the darkness beyond.

New York, New York

Every person in the screening room stood as the basement door creaked open. Abe Feuerstein lowered his crystal glass. His assistant knelt by the CEO's large chair and shoved a printout in front of him.

"Ratings have shot through the roof. Word is spreading

fast. The general consensus is still that this is all a put-on, but they don't seem to care."

"Of course they don't. This is goddamn good television!"

Bright River, Pennsylvania

They watched the door open. Gabriel felt it first, but it was John who voiced it.

"The cold is gone."

"It's not there anymore," George agreed.

"Our team leader has indicated that the presence beyond the door has left us," Julie said as the camera turned in her direction.

Kennedy reached out and gently pushed the door open. He suddenly flinched when the loud boom sounded. They could all tell it came from the direction of the ballroom.

"Go to camera one, now!" Harris said.

Inside the ballroom all eyes were on the giant, thick ballroom doors. The pounding on the wood started almost at the moment the basement door opened and the cold vanished.

"Professor Gabe?" Leonard said into his battery-powered mic, "Temperature falloff of . . . His eyes widened. The pounding was growing louder, more insistent, "Jesus, forty degrees."

Then the pounding stopped. The doorknobs on both ballroom doors rattled and turned.

"Camera one, tighten up on that shot!" Harris said.

The cameraman zoomed in on the ornate door handles as they both turned, slowly at first, then with more persistence.

Sudden motion blurred past the camera. Jennifer shot forward and reached the doors before anyone knew what was happening. She turned the old skeleton-style key in the locks and then backed away. The pounding started again. Whatever was out there, it was angry that she had locked the doors. Jennifer and the others threw their hands up and covered their ears. Leonard was flinching every time the doors were struck. The pounding was so hard that plaster from the ceiling started to cascade. The boom mic picked up Father Dolan's prayers.

The pounding stopped and the doors started bending inward with a loud crack that froze everyone in place.

"Holy fuck," Lionel Peterson said. His words went out live over the air, making legal execs flinch in New York.

Part of the oaken left door cracked and splintered with a loud pop. It was bent inward so far that the wood could endure no more.

Wallace Lindemann's drink slipped through his fingers and hit the carpeted floor. No one, not even Lindeman himself, noticed.

The right-side door cracked as it bowed inward. They could all hear heavy grunting and breathing above the din of cracking wood. Jennifer was pulled back suddenly by Leonard, who was staring at the double doors. They were being pushed beyond what they could take. The grunting became louder still.

Suddenly the doors relaxed and sprang back to their original shape and position.

"Feel it?" Leonard asked.

Everyone did. It was over and they all knew it, even as Wallace Lindemann fainted dead away.

The cold was gone.

Suddenly the pounding started again, but this time it was minuscule compared to before. The doorknobs rattled and turned. Leonard ran to the doors and turned the ancient key in their locks.

"No!" Lionel Peterson shouted. Most could hear Kelly Delaphoy's snicker even over his loud exclamation.

Everyone in the van smiled. Lionel Peterson seemed to be quickly becoming a believer in the supernatural.

Leonard threw open the left door and leaned heavily against the door frame when he saw Kennedy and the others standing in the dark.

"Everyone okay?" Gabriel asked as he pushed into the ballroom, quickly followed by Lonetree, Cordero, and Julie Reilly. Damian Jackson came in after the cameramen and soundmen. "I think it's over for now," Gabriel said. He looked around at the terrified faces framed by the dim glow of their flashlights.

"Professor Gabe?" Leonard said as he quickly closed the ballroom doors.

Kennedy turned. The cameramen had each of the two framed, so that Harris could choose the shot he wanted.

"I think you have a real haunted house here."

"Fade to black, commercial in two, one, go," Harris said into his mic.

On the screen, a rabbit was smiling and rolling a roll of toilet paper down a grassy hill.

"Tell New York I need ten minutes here to sort things out. Tell them to line three four-minute spots," Dalton said as he sat heavily into his chair. "I want to be able to go back ASAP if something happens, so be ready to cut into the spots if need be."

On the screen labeled "Preview," Kelly Delaphoy stepped into the picture and looked into the camera lens.

"What news is coming out of New York, Harris?" she asked, pressing her earpiece to her ear.

"All quiet on the Eastern Front at the moment, but I think you'll have the rest of your special," Harris said. He paused and downed an entire bottle of water. When he finished, he looked at Kelly, who was smiling. "What's so funny?"

"I knew this would work." She lowered her voice, looked away, and then looked back at the camera. "Did you hear Lionel scream when Sickles went for the door?"

"Yeah, we saw, along with the rest of the world. But before you start getting too thrilled over Peterson's state, you better get a hold of yourself and start making a plan with Kennedy, because I think you've got a real problem."

"What in hell can be a problem now?" Kelly asked.

"In case you haven't noticed, you've all been herded into one place. On camera five, up on the third floor, something isn't right."

"What's that?" she asked, her smile fading.

"The doors to the sewing room and the master suite are now closed. That means whatever was down near the basement and the ballroom more than likely came from the third floor."

"I get you, Harris."

"No, I don't think you do."

"What do you mean?" she asked.

"We can see the lights on in both rooms, even though the power has been out for the past fifteen minutes."

New York, New York

The network ad executives were on the phone throughout the ten-minute break in live programming. The din in the screening room was music to Abe Feuerstein's ears—they were now actually turning down requests from the main sponsors of *Hunters of the Paranormal* to add additional time to their commitment.

The CEO watched as the men and women who had supported Lionel Peterson in his coup also scrambled to try to save their positions. As they attempted to approach Abe one and two at a time, he simply held up his hand and waved them away. Several left the screening room altogether. The night was his, and he only wished Lionel was here himself to see his complete and utter failure.

"Sir, all indications are that we are now nearing a fifty percent share on the night. The late-night audience is just now tuning in, and the sequence of events at Summer Place could not have come at a better time."

Feuerstein nodded and shook his glass, which contained nothing but melting ice. The young lady took the glass and the meaning but stayed, as she needed to say something else.

"What is it?" he asked.

"Our legal department is concerned about what's happening. I guess they are now believers themselves and—"

"Tell them to shove their concerns."

"They would like all nonessential personnel out of that house, Father Dolan especially."

Abe smiled and tapped the glass the young assistant held in her hand.

"The good father stays. I believe he and Lionel Peterson need to be in on the finale, don't you?"

The assistant turned and went to refill the CEO's glass.

On the main viewing screen, a brand-new Chevrolet Malibu shot down a Rocky Mountains highway. The scroll at the bottom of the screen warned the viewing audience that *Hunters of the Paranormal* would resume in five minutes. Abe smiled as he accepted his whiskey.

"Yes, sir, this is television."

Bright River, Pennsylvania

With the storm breaking in earnest outside the walls of Summer Place, the occupants inside the ballroom were becoming concerned. The men, including Lionel Peterson and the very frightened Wallace Lindemann, were crowded in front of the massive oaken doors. They had been trying to open them and the smaller side door for the past ten minutes, to no avail. It was as if the ballroom had been encased inside a concrete block. Kelly Delaphoy and Julie Reilly were standing next to the sofa where they had moved Father Dolan, while Jennifer Tilden and Damian Jackson tried in vain to smash the glass at the French doors in the front. Chair after chair met a similar fate to those in the living room an hour before.

"How about taking one of the doors off at the hinges?" one of the cameramen asked as he zoomed in on the greenish figures standing at the doors.

Gabriel looked at John and tilted his head, then smiled. "I guess they didn't cover everything at Harvard, did they?"

Lonetree looked at the cameraman and nodded, as if to say, "one for you."

One of the soundmen reached into his bag and tossed Gabriel a large screwdriver.

In the front of the ballroom, Jackson stopped swinging the bar stool at the ornate glass of the French doors, out of breath. Jennifer patted him on the back.

"Still think things around here are rigged, Lieutenant?"

"I'm not ready to admit to anything yet." He tossed the stool away and reached into his coat. He pulled out a two-way radio, winking as he brought it to his lips. "We'll see how this place stands up to a ten-ton battering ram on wheels."

Jennifer gave him the faintest of smiles, as if she knew what was going to happen.

A flashlight illuminated Jackson. He and Jenny were joined by Wallace Lindemann and Lionel Peterson.

"Thank God someone's thinking around here," Peterson said. He pulled over the same soundman who had produced the screwdriver for the men working at the large doors and yanked the headphones from the man's head. He placed them on and started to call Harris in the production van just as Jackson, after giving Peterson a distasteful look, initiated contact with the state police.

"State police barracks seventeen, do you copy? Over."

"Harris, this is Peterson. Get every technician and firemen you can and get those fucking front doors open. We're coming out now!"

At the same moment, a voice came over both the technician's headphones and the police radio—one that didn't originate at either the production van or the state police barracks. The voice was deep and booming and brought everyone in the darkened ballroom to a complete and utter standstill. The sound was not only coming from the radio and the headset, but also from the powerless stereo speakers and ornate jukebox in the far corner, which had illuminated to its full glory. Everyone in the ballroom smelled the odor at the same time, as if it had flooded into the large room and clung to everything and everyone. It was the smell of lilac.

"You cannot have them, they are mine!"

Jackson figured it was more interference and technical wizardry from Kelly Delaphoy, Kennedy, or even Peterson himself. Both camera teams were now on the small group by the French doors. Jackson tried again. "State police barracks, this is Lieutenant—"

"Get out!"

With that chilling, dark voice still echoing inside the ball-room, the lights came on and the tall doors clicked and then slowly opened. The smell of lilac immediately vanished, as if it had never been there. Then they heard the cracking of the glass: the French doors, which Damian Jackson had struck time and time again, and also the plate glass windows in the living room. A few of the small panes of glass were weakened enough that they gave way and fell outward onto the large front porch.

Peterson slowly removed the headphones and let them fall from his hand. Jackson lowered the radio and shook his head.

"Amazing what happens when we threaten to bring my colleagues in, isn't it, Professor?"

Gabriel looked at Jackson, and the small smile told him it was a nice try at goading him into a statement. Instead of saying something to the state policeman, Gabriel quickly walked over to the small couch and leaned down to Father Dolan.

"Let's get you out of here. I don't think our host cares very much for your profession."

"I would prefer to stay."

"Not a chance. We may have enough legal problems on our hands," Peterson said. His fearlessness was returning brighter than the lights now illuminating the ballroom. "It's time we shut this thing down."

"I don't think you have that authority anymore, Lionel," Julie Reilly said as she gathered up her microphone and headset. "As a matter of fact, I'm not sure you work at this network any longer."

Peterson looked over at the camera and saw that it was still trained on him. "Get that off of me!" He shoved the lens away from his face.

Gabriel and John assisted Father Dolan to his feet. Then Gabriel looked at the camera team that was free at the moment and gestured that they should take Dolan outside for help.

"Gabe"—John leaned toward him just as Jenny and

George walked up beside them—"have you noticed the cold is still here?"

Gabriel nodded. He turned to face the others in the ballroom.

"Regardless who works at the network or not, we need to clear the house of everyone except my team, Ms. Reilly, and one cameraman and soundman. Everyone else needs to leave—for your own protection."

"What?" Kelly stepped forward.

"You heard me, Kelly. There is still activity in this room," Kennedy said as he adjusted the small microphone to his mouth. "Harris, what have you got on the third floor?"

There was a burst of static, and then Dalton came through loud and clear from the production van.

"The hallway lights played hell with the infrared and low-light cameras; they're just now clearing up. Wait, okay, it looks like the master bedroom suite is—yes, it's closed, but the sewing room door is still wide open. Now it's the only light on that floor that's out."

Gabriel nodded and looked at Jackson.

"This is not a good place for a nonbeliever, Detective."

Jackson shook his head and placed the radio back in his coat. "I think I'll see it through, Professor."

"You can't say I didn't warn you." Kennedy looked around the room at the faces looking back at him. "Now, did everyone take note of the smell of perfume?"

"Why do you say 'perfume' and not 'flowers'?" Kelly Delaphoy asked.

"The odor was too powerful for flowers. No, that was perfume. When the voice finished what it had to say, the smell left, and the doors opened at the exact same moment. It went wherever the entity did when it left the ballroom."

"Whatever we're dealing with is slowly getting stronger," George said. He stepped to the bar and eyed the bottle of whiskey. He grimaced and then turned away, much to Kennedy's relief.

"Professor Gabe, you better look at this," Leonard said from the large worktable. He waved his three technicians up and out of their chairs and then told them to vacate the house. "Go on, do what the professor says. Get while the getting's good." The technicians did as they were ordered.

Kennedy looked at the nearest monitor. The woman's face was clearly made out, and then the picture changed to that of another, this one equally mysterious. Then another face appeared, this one a full-length picture. She was dressed in turn-of-the-century clothes, and the picture must have been more than a hundred years old. Then another, and another—all dressed in the same period clothing. Some had husbands or other family members in the shots, others were alone.

"Where are these coming from?" Gabriel asked Leonard.

"It's from the same program my people were running just before the power was sucked out of here." He typed more commands. "These are Ellis Island shots. We were running employee records for the Lindemann sewing machine company and the textile companies."

"Why is it doing that?" Julie Reilly asked as she and the others started crowding around the table holding the computer monitors.

"It's doing it on its own," Leonard answered.

Julie and Kelly simultaneously shoved the first-team cameraman in front of the table.

"Harris, are you picking this up?" Julie asked into her headset.

"We're getting it. I don't know what we're getting, but it's going out clean to the rest of the country."

On the monitors a picture flashed, then the revolving show stopped. The lights flickered but stayed on. All eyes were on the pretty young woman framed on the monitors. She was dressed in the same clothing style as the others and she looked to be about seventeen, eighteen at the most. She was sitting at a small table with an old-fashioned sewing machine and she was looking at the camera and smiling shyly.

"The happy workers of the Lindemann Textile Company,"
Leonard read the caption, "taken from the *New York Post,*
February 3rd, 1925."

"Gabriel, we've seen that face before," Jenny said.

Gabriel sorted through a stack of folders until he found
the one he was searching for. He opened it and studied something for a few moments. When he looked up, he wasn't fo-
cusing on anyone in the room.

"Professor, we are live," Julie reminded him.

Kennedy finally turned back to face the camera, and
brought out an old eight-by-ten glossy photograph—a repro-
duction of a promotional still. The heading was in German,
but everyone focused on the face alone. They all saw it at almost the same time.

"Gwyneth Gerhardt," John Lonetree said.

"The opera singer who disappeared," Julie said to the
camera.

"No, but a relative. Maybe a sister. The resemblance is too
close," Gabriel said. He nodded for Leonard to do his thing.

Sickles leaned over and started typing his commands.
While he did so, Kennedy waved George Cordero over to his
side. On the computer monitors, the picture of the pretty girl
was replaced by a very old-looking employment record.

"You hit it on the head. Magdalena Gerhardt, eighteen
years old. She worked for the Lindemanns for eight months.
Gerhardt was her maiden name. She married Paul Lester, a
foreman at the mill, three months after arriving from Germany."

"Her sister, I'll bet anything on it," Gabriel said. "Now,
did she leave the company after she married?"

"She left, all right," Leonard answered, "but it doesn't say
why. Her husband, too. Wait, here's a note from the personnel office. It seems they both quit without notice."

"George, I saw that look on your face. What are you feeling?" Gabriel asked.

Cordero cleared his throat and then looked away, as if he
were reluctant to answer.

"George?" Kennedy asked again, this time with force. "Whatever it was, made you want a drink."

Cordero shrugged the camera gently away with an annoyed look and raised his hand. But then his eyes met Kennedy's own.

"I'm not picking up much. It's like looking at a scene through a bowl of milk. It's the opera star's sister, you're right on with that. And I think, I *feel,* Leonard's computers are being manipulated from . . . from—"

"The sewing room," Kelly said, not being able to hold back, much to Julie Reilly's annoyance.

"The basement. Or more accurately, the subbasement," he finally said, moving his eyes from Gabriel's.

"George, is that all?" Gabriel asked.

"The presence earlier, the voice . . . it was male . . . I think."

"We all heard it, for Christ's sake, of course it was male. I have to hand it to you, Professor, your people don't miss a trick." Peterson walked toward the bar and retrieved his raincoat, pushing Wallace Lindemann to the side.

"I don't know if it was . . . male. It had, I don't know, an acting quality to it. Hell, Gabe, I don't know."

"Maybe it was old man Lindemann, my great granddaddy. That would be my bet," Wallace said. He sipped his drink.

"Okay, let me know if you pick up anything else. For right now, Wallace here may have something—it's a start, anyway."

George nodded, knowing that he didn't convey his true thoughts the way he would have liked.

"Look, Gabriel, we're kidding ourselves if we think we can get the answers here. The house hides its secrets well," John Lonetree said. He looked from Kennedy to Jenny. "I have to go under. You know it, and I know it."

"I don't think this is the environment for it, John. You've never dreamwalked in anything like Summer Place. I don't trust it—or, more to the point, I don't trust whatever lives here."

"What if Summer Place clams up? What if it goes dormant again?" John asked. Jenny took his arm and shook her head no.

"Then it goes dormant," Gabriel said, feeling the camera on him and knowing the CEO and others were cringing at his words. "I'm not losing anyone here tonight."

"I'm not a student, and I'm going into this with my eyes—well, while not open, they will be aware. I'm doing it."

The rumble of thunder ripped outside almost on cue. In the corner, Damian Jackson listened to the men. He didn't understand anything that was being said, but he did see one thing: for the first time, Professor Gabriel Kennedy looked scared. Of what, Jackson didn't know, but he saw the defiant professor vanish, replaced by a man with memories of a night long ago etched on his face.

"Jenny, do you still have the sleeping pills I gave you at the hotel?" Gabriel asked.

Jennifer was silent. While she thought about what was being proposed, Kennedy turned to Kelly Delaphoy.

"Call Dalton and tell him to get to that EMS truck. Get me thirty cc's of Adrenalin and two one-milligram doses of epinephrine or atropine, whichever he has. Bring in the defibrillator, also." He looked up at the others. "We may have to bring John out of his deep sleep fast, and I don't know if his heart will be able to take it," he explained. His eyes locked on Jenny's. She reached into her bag, angrily pulled the small bottle of pills out, and tossed them to Gabriel.

"We had better hurry; I don't think our host is too happy we're not leaving. Feel it?" George asked. He pulled his coat tighter around his chest.

"It is getting colder by the second," Julie said into her mic.

The lights flickered as a streak of lightning illuminated the outside world.

"Okay, we'll go with John's plan."

As Julie Reilly explained to the television world what was going to happen, Jennifer felt a small twinge that signaled the first assault of a massive headache. Deep down, she knew what it meant.

"Jenny, what's wrong?" Gabriel asked as John reached out to steady her.

Leaning heavily on Lonetree, Jennifer brought her right hand up to her temple.

"I think . . . I think we're about to have company." She stumbled, with John's support, to the couch.

"Who?" Leonard asked, afraid of the answer.

"Bobby Lee McKinnon."

Jennifer stood from the small love seat. She looked into the lens of the camera pointed right at her, and then looked at John Lonetree, who was holding her hand. She gave him an odd, curious look and then shook her smaller hand free from his.

"Whoa there, man. Comfort is one thing, but I'm getting a vibe that says you have a much darker intent, and at Jenny's expense."

John stood up so suddenly that everyone took a step back. The voice that had commented on John's affections was deeper than Jenny's; still feminine, but booming, as if it were coming from a male. She looked around the room.

"You people are playing with fire here. This ain't ol' Bobby Lee you're dealin' with, this is blackness," Jenny said in that strange voice. She paced to the French doors and looked out at the storm-tossed bushes and awnings. "I knew you would get Jennifer into some kind of trouble, so I bugged out for a while." She turned and looked into the camera that had followed her to the doors, and smiled a creepy and tired-looking grin. Jenny placed her hands into her hair and brushed it back, creating what momentarily looked like an old-fashioned pompadour with a large curl breaking free at the front.

"Oh, shit," Leonard said, watching from his keyboard.

"Jenny may hate my guts, man," she said, turning her blue eyes to Kennedy, "but I didn't come vistin' her just to see her eaten by that thing upstairs." She snapped her fingers to a beat only she could hear. "She's my Angel Baby. I guess you can call it an attachment of necessity. So if you don't mind, Doc, we're splitsville."

They all watched—including the number one camera—as Jennifer started for the double doors of the ballroom. Julie Reilly explained in hushed whispers what was happening to Jennifer. John made a move as if to stop her, but Gabriel held a hand up. Jenny stopped at the door and looked back at the amazed faces of the others. Then she looked at the camera and winked.

"If I was you folks, I would be on the next train to music city, because somethin's comin' for you.'"

With those words Jennifer turned and walked out of the ballroom, this time brushing Damian Jackson out of the way, just as he had done to Lindemann a moment before. Kennedy quickly followed and watched as Jenny slowly moved toward the front door, looking at the room's décor as if she had never seen any of it before. Then she stopped at the large stair-case.

"Roll over, Beethoven," she said, looking up the stairs.

"Guys, the sewing room door just opened up on three," Harris Dalton said from the van. The live picture switched to the third floor. "The thermal imager is picking up a bright blue form standing inside the room, motionless. Hell, I swear whatever it is, is looking right at the camera."

Gabriel slowly stepped from the ballroom, quickly fol-lowed by Julie, Kelly, and the others. Even Wallace Linde-mann and Lionel Peterson joined them in the brightly lit living room.

Jennifer placed a hand on the banister. She seemed to be transfixed on something near the second-floor landing.

"Powerful," she said. Her words barely picked up on the parabolic microphone.

"Sound, boost your gain," Harris called from the van. The soundman didn't move, concentrating on the scene before him. "The figure is still in the doorway. The camera is clearly picking it up. It's a human form, large and framed exactly in the middle of the open door."

"Angry." Jenny turned and looked at Gabriel. "He blames you. He wants you out."

"He? Who are you talking about, Bobby Lee?" Kennedy asked.

"Hell, man, I'm not sticking around to be introduced to this cat, he's like—like, not of this world." Jenny started to back away but stopped. She once more grabbed hold of the banister and then actually took a step up the red-carpeted stairs.

"I'm not letting her go up there alone." John Lonetree stepped past Kennedy and made his way to the staircase. He took Jenny's hand, and she stopped and turned.

"Man, you're startin' to freak me out a little here. I don't swing that way," she said in her husky voice.

"Yeah, but Jennifer does," John said, still not releasing her hand.

A look of relief came over Jenny's features and then she nodded her head.

"Yeah, man, I hear ya. If anyone needs someone, it's this chick, let me tell ya. But right now, if you don't mind, it's still creepy." Jenny pulled her hand free of John's and took another step up. "Man, this place feels like a prison, and up there's the warden."

"Stop," John said. "Not alone. Don't go up alone."

"Follow if you want," Bobby Lee said, and just as the words escaped Jenny's lips, she collapsed.

Small, firefly-like orbs appeared, dancing in the air where Jenny had just been standing. John took a step toward the stairs and the sparkling objects moved upward. Looking apprehensively at the strange phenomenon, Lonetree pulled Jenny off the step and onto the carpeted runner at the base of the stairs.

Gabriel joined him but kept his eyes on the strange sight, taking the stairs very slowly. The entity would stop and seem to hesitate, but then keep moving upward.

"What happened?" Jennifer said when she came to.

"We don't know. You collapsed, right after you said"—
John looked up at Gabriel, and then back at her—"or Bobby
Lee said, 'this place feels like a prison, and up there's the
warden.'"

Jenny suddenly stood and looked up the stairs. The strange
twinkling reached the second-floor landing and continued to
the right, toward the hallway.

"Bobby Lee, it's bad. Don't go up there," she called out.

The cameraman and soundman were slow to react to
Jenny, still trained on the entity that was Bobby Lee as it disappeared into the hallway above. Soon the camera had Jennifer framed and the soundman was recording and sending
out her scared voice to the nation. On live television the
screen was split in two, showing both Jenny and the orbs as
they moved to the opposite stairway.

The roar of thunder shook the house, and the lights
dimmed once more.

"Okay, everyone has to leave with the exception of the first
team. Kelly, take Peterson and Lindemann out of here. Detective, you and Jason Sanborn had better beat a retreat on
this one also," Gabriel said as he left John and Jenny's side.
"John, you'll do your dreamwalk in the ballroom with Jenny,
Leonard, and George, with the doors locked."

"And your plan is?" Damian Jackson asked, still looking
up the staircase at the spot where the strange gleaming orbs
had vanished.

"I'm going to do what I came here to do, Detective
Jackson—I'm going ghost hunting."

"I've been waiting for you to say that, Professor," Julie
Reilly said.

Detective Jackson watched as Gabriel went toward the
ballroom followed by John, Jenny, and the camera team. "Exactly my thoughts," echoed Jackson. He removed his nine-
millimeter automatic from his shoulder holster and made sure
the safety was on.

Gabriel stopped at the doorway and looked at Jackson and then the gun.

"I don't think that will do much good with what we're up against, Detective."

Jackson smiled, and then brushed past Kennedy and entered the ballroom.

"For what I'm hunting, it will."

21

John stretched out on the largest of the four sofas. Jenny tried one last time to talk him out of doing the dreamwalk, but he only smiled and placed his giant hand on her cheek.

"This is what I do," he said, and then lay back against the hand-stitched throw pillow.

Gabriel entered the room while looking back one last time at Kelly Delaphoy, Jason Sanborn, Lionel Peterson, and Wallace Lindemann, who were standing just outside the two large ballroom doors. Only Lindemann and Peterson looked anxious to be on their way. Kelly Delaphoy stepped forward.

"I think one of the producers should be on hand for whatever happens."

"Forget it, Kelly, get these people out of here," Kennedy said. He nodded at Leonard, who moved to close the double doors. An ominous streak of lightning flashed through the French doors and lit up the shadowed room brightly.

Kennedy reached into his coat pocket and brought out the small bottle of pills that Jenny had returned to him. Just four of them would be enough to send John into a coma; five would stop his heart. He took a deep breath and shook out two of the sleeping pills. George Cordero came over with a glass of water from the bar. Gabriel smiled as he looked down at his oldest friend. He held out his hand and dropped the two small pills into John's own.

"Is this enough?"

Kennedy nodded his head. "Jenny, do you feel anything from upstairs?" he asked to break the tension. Kennedy could feel the camera on him and knew the microphone picked up his question.

Jenny shook her head.

"I do," George said as he looked away from Lonetree. "Bobby Lee is terrified. I think he's moving closer to the third floor, but I can't be sure. For a ghost, he seems to have a fear of something worse than the death he faced when he was alive. I'm not sure, but I think Bobby Lee's backed off and is hiding . . . yes, he's stopped." George opened his eyes. "That's all I'm getting." The camera zoomed in on his dark countenance. A rumble of thunder accented his foreboding words.

John squeezed Jenny's hand and popped the two pills into his mouth.

"I haven't had this much anticipation about pills since an acid trip in college," he whispered so only Jennifer could hear. She didn't smile. John drank from the glass that George had given him, and then handed it to Kennedy.

"Good luck, buddy."

"Listen, maybe you should hold off on this third-floor trip until I find out what we're dealing with."

"Before my last visit, there had never been one documented case where an entity hurt a human being."

"Just my thought exactly," Jackson said. "I believe your earlier excursion into this house a few years ago was also a human-on-human encounter."

Just at that moment, the lights in the ballroom went dark. The cameraman switched back to his ambient-light settings and everyone in the ballroom moved silently toward the couch. Thunder rumbled the floorboards under their feet.

"I don't think whatever's up there is going to give you the time, John. But with us up on three, we may be able to occupy it long enough for you to get some answers."

"People, we have activity up on the third floor," Harris Dalton said from the production van. "The lights in the hallway are acting like strobes, playing hell with the camera view.

We also have what sounds like mumbling coming from the recorders, both on three and in the subbasement."

"Time to go," Gabriel said. He pressed his hand to his ear so he could hear Harris better. "Dalton, did Kelly get the people outside?"

"What?"

"Did Kelly get—"

"I heard what you said; our outside cameras have not shown anyone leaving the house."

"Damn it." Kennedy straightened from John's side and looked at Jenny, and then to Leonard. "Watch him closely." He looked at his watch. "He'll be out in about two minutes. Leonard, lock the big doors after we leave, and if something gets in here, don't be a hero. Get everyone out, any way you can."

"Don't worry about that. I'm thinking about splitting as soon as you're out that door, Doc. If that thing up there wants in, it'll get in."

"He's right," George said. "Its power is building. It's getting stronger."

Gabriel looked at the dark faces around him. He switched on his penlight and studied each member of his team in turn.

"Let's go."

Kennedy, Julie, Jackson, and Cordero left the ballroom preceded by the cameraman and the soundman. The large living area was dark, with only the brief flash of lightning illuminating their view of the staircase. Gabriel moved the small light around. Wallace Lindemann stepped through the swinging doors from the kitchen, his face slack and white as he hurried to the front doors. The cameraman sped to the front doors and zoomed the ambient-light lens onto Wallace as he tried the doorknobs.

Kennedy followed the camera team as Lindemann started pulling on the doors. As he did, Lionel Peterson came through the kitchen doors, far more calmly than Lindemann, but in a hurry nonetheless.

"Where are Kelly and Sanborn?" Gabriel asked.

Lionel shied away from the camera's lens and joined Wallace at the door.

"The damn things won't open!" Lindemann cried. He slammed his body into the thick doors.

"Calm down and turn the handles, you idiot," Peterson said as he leaned in and tried the handles himself. They turned in his hands and he even felt the clicks of the locking mechanisms as they gave way, but the doors remained tight to their frame. He pulled, as did Lindemann, but the doors were frozen shut.

"Where is Kelly?" Kennedy repeated more insistently.

"Her and Sanborn went down into the basement. She said she would call Harris and let him know what's going on. Now help us get these doors open."

"The basement?" Kennedy asked, turning from the two struggling men bent on escape.

"Gabe, feel it?" George asked as he looked around the room.

Kennedy turned toward the staircase. The room had once more gone ice cold, making everyone's breath fog, as if they were deep in a winter frost.

"Detective, tell that madman to get this door open. We've had enough of this," Peterson said. He gave up and turned around, pulling his coat closed around him and shoving his hands under his arms.

Jackson didn't respond. He was also looking toward the stairs. The coldness almost seemed to roll down them, like a slow-moving waterfall. The darkness mostly hid the staircase, but the image was one Jackson would take to his grave. For the first time, he was wondering if Kennedy might have been telling the truth; he could not figure out how Kennedy could have pulled off the sudden freeze without a refrigeration unit the size of Yankee Stadium upstairs.

"Okay, people, we have the sewing room door closing and the cold image we were seeing is now gone," Harris reported from the van. "The lights on three have gone completely out and the night-vision and thermal imaging cameras have stabilized. We have a good view of the hallway."

Kennedy ignored the noise that Wallace Lindemann was making at the double front doors. He pulled up his coat collar and took three steps toward the staircase.

"What about Kelly and Sanborn?" George asked in the dark.

"They're on their own for now. Harris can hear them in the production van, and when they reach the basement he can see them on camera."

Gabriel took two more cautious steps toward the staircase. He felt Julie step up to his side. The air was actually growing colder.

"Still think your gun's going to help?" Kennedy asked as he moved by the detective.

This time Jackson had no snappy comeback. He just watched Kennedy move by him as the house grew quiet. Even Wallace Lindemann gave up and turned away from the door.

"Damn you, Kennedy. Tell whoever is helping you to open this goddamn door!" Wallace said, almost in a child's cry. "I'm going to sue every one of you sons of bitches!"

Kennedy, without turning back around, intent on the steps ahead of him, smiled. He knew Julie was doing the same next to him, but it was George who said it out loud. This, the soundman did pick up, and Harris Dalton hissed a silent curse in the production van.

"God, what a dick."

Leonard was just starting to feel the coldness as it wafted through the bottom of the doorjamb. He looked back at Jenny, who was on her knees by John Lonetree, who closed his eyes. Leonard looked back at the large double doors and thought about how easily they had been bent inward by whatever walked upstairs. He had tried the French doors twice and failed to open them. The ice had re-formed on the glass and was thickening. If he had to, he thought, he could smash his way out—but that would have to be with the largest Indian he had ever seen in his life heaped over his shoulder and the smallest haunted woman by his side. The prospects of breaking out looked dim.

At the couch, Jenny flipped on her small light and brought the beam up until it just illuminated John's relaxed features. She watched his eyes, but they lay still underneath his eyelids. He had not entered the dream state yet.

Jennifer was hoping the pills would actually keep John from dreaming; she knew she hadn't dreamed when she used them. Just as she was about to turn off the flashlight, she saw the first movement of John's eyes. She felt Leonard come up from behind.

"Goddamn, it's cold in here," he said as he shook his head.

Suddenly John's body went rigid as a board and his hands clenched into fists. Then his long hair blew up and off the pillow, flowing off the arm of the couch as though he were standing in a strong wind.

"Do you smell that?" Leonard asked, taking a step back.

Jenny nodded. The smell was like dead winter, but there was also an odor of wet woods in the rainy season, and then the smell of a wood fire. On the couch, John moved his head left and then right. An unseen wind still blew his long hair.

Leonard turned away and paced to the static camera that had been set up on Harris Dalton's orders to catch John's dreamwalk. He knelt down and made sure his face was framed in the night-vision picture.

"Look, if you're hearing me, we may have to get out of here fast, so we may need help from you people. If you see us moving toward those glass doors, come runnin'."

Inside the van, Harris smiled. He had just switched to the ballroom camera, and had caught the concern of the small black man.

As Leonard stood and turned, he saw Jenny suddenly stand and back away from the prone John. In the weak light cast by Jenny's flashlight, Leonard could see that John had sat up and was staring at the ballroom doors. His hair was still being blown by an invisible wind.

"Shit, I sure hope you guys are getting this."

John was in a brightly illuminated hallway. The smell of a gas lamp wafted into his nostrils as he stood before a door. It was open about a foot and John saw movement inside the dimly illuminated room. He heard the laughter of young children, possibly two girls, and then the booming laugh of an adult. As John maneuvered his head he could see that indeed it was two small girls lying on an ornate, covered bed. A man, possibly their father, was sitting on the bed's edge and looked to have been reading to them. He had stopped and they laughed together, and John could feel the love of the father for his two daughters. The man spoke, but John didn't understand the language. It sounded Russian. The man was well dressed and had a large beard. He reached out and tickled the two girls, who laughed uncontrollably. They looked about six or seven.

John heard a squeak behind him in the hallway and saw the door had been opened farther. The father had turned and the girls fell silent. The man stood from the bed and walked straight at John, raising his hand. Lonetree flinched in his dream as the hand came down and the words exploded from his mouth. John was surprised when the hand passed right through him and struck something he hadn't seen. When he ducked, he saw the small boy in a long nightgown. The hand connected solidly with the boy's face and he slid to the wooden floor. The father screamed at him.

John felt badly for the boy. He wanted to reach down and help the dark-haired child to his feet. But as suddenly as the thought struck him to help, it seemed the boy's eyes moved from the man, who was obviously his father, to look right at John. The dark eyes stared at him and through him. They penetrated him. Then the father struck out again, yelling in Russian. The boy was lifted to his feet and then thrown out the door. John looked on, horrified. The girls in the bed were silent as they watched the boy's punishment, but they both had small smiles stretched across their otherwise innocent faces.

John turned and left the room. The hallway was now dark. He leaned back into the bedroom and saw the light there was also out. The girls were sleeping soundly in their bed. Just as he started to turn, John felt the presence behind him. It was the black-haired, dark-eyed boy. He was looking right at John, and even in the darkness John could see the boy's eyebrows were raised. The child tilted his head and Lonetree could see the bruises on the boy's face, and knew for a fact without seeing that there were even more, darker, uglier scars underneath the child's dressing gown. The boy's head turned but his eyes lingered on John a moment. The cold chills coursed down John's spine as he watched the boy reach out and pull the girls' bedroom door closed. He reached into his nightshirt and produced a key and locked the door. Then he moved down the hallway and inserted the key into another door. When the boy turned around he had a smile stretched across his feminine features. The boy slowly raised his hand to his face and brought his index finger up to his lips, shushing John.

John swallowed in his sleep. The boy went to the far wall of the hallway and bent over in the dark. John heard a splashing sound and the floor was doused with something wet and oily-smelling. The boy looked at Lonetree with that horrible grin on his face. Then brightness filled the hallway and John flinched. He could see the flare of the match. John tried his best to swipe at the match, but the boy giggled as Lonetree's hand passed through the flame. John knew he was helpless to stop what was happening. The boy raised his left eyebrow once more as he let the match fall though his fingers to the wooden floor. The whoosh of flame bit into the wood and held. It quickly crawled up the walls and engulfed the two doors the boy had locked moments before. The boy stared at John, who raised his arms to shield his face from the intense heat. The boy remained where he was, smiling, as if he wanted John to witness what he had done.

A feminine scream sounded in the hallway, from the far end of the house. Then suddenly John could see her. It was a woman of about thirty; her face bruised as badly as the boy's had been. It had to be the child's mother. She grabbed the boy and tried to reach for the door handle of her daughters' room, but the flames licked at her dressing gown. She screamed in frustration and then turned and ran, holding the boy, into the flames and the smoke.

John could hear the screams of the two girls and the father as they started to burn to death.

As the flames traveled up his own legs, John placed his hands over his ears. He could not drown out the horrible screaming.

There was blessed silence. As John lowered his hands, the smell of smoke faded. He opened his eyes and saw that he was now standing on a small rise, watching the snow being blown by a strong wind that carried not the smell of smoke and burning children, but the smell of forested hills. The sound was that of rain, which mixed with the snowflakes to produce a slush that penetrated the body with its cold. He felt that coldness sink deep into his soul, mingled with the relief of being out of the burning house. Looking around, he spotted the large, dark object in front of him, its skeletal ribs standing out against the blackness of early winter.

It was Summer Place, in the first stages of rising from the countryside. The house was not yet framed but the outer shell had been completed before the weather had turned. As he looked at the house, he felt it. It wasn't evil, it had no dark intent; for now, it was just wood and nails. The moon broke through the clouds for the briefest of moments, showing the frame of the massive barn and the hole for the swimming pool. He even saw the deepest pit that would become the root cellar and subbasement. As he looked at these, he felt the first presence of something that made him afraid, as if he were staring into the bowels of hell itself. He looked away, not wanting to know the true depths of the basement and its root cellar.

He felt better when he focused on the house. Then he heard the sound of an engine. At first he couldn't place the direction of the sound, but then he thought of his waking self and concentrated on what he knew. His gaze moved to where the front gate would eventually be built, and then beyond that to the road. It was hard to pick out because of the slushy snow that had accumulated, but he saw the carriage lights of two wagons as they came forward from the darkness beyond. They were large wagons, each drawn by six large horses.

For a reason John couldn't fathom, he stepped back and stood behind one of the large trees that lined the property. He knew in his current state he was invisible, but for a reason he knew not, he didn't want the occupants of the two wagons to see him. The first wagon looked to be fully loaded with wood that protruded from a large tarpaulin. The second looked to be covered, like an old wagon from the Westerns John used to watch as a child. The second wagon maneuvered around the first and advanced toward the incomplete Summer Place. It stopped about where the kitchen would eventually be built, and the driver, a person of large size, hopped down. He stepped into the framing of the house and then stopped. The area below flared to life with light. John could see that the man had lit a lantern and was moving it around. John froze as the large man seemed to stop and look up at the small rise where he was standing. Then after a moment he turned away. The moon above was once more covered with black clouds, and the snow had vanished with it. Rain started coming down in earnest as the man below moved farther into the house.

John took a cautious step out from behind the tree and watched for the man to return. Three men were unloading the first wagon, placing the wood under a makeshift shed at the front of the framed house. They seemed in a hurry to be on their way. Soon they had the wagon unloaded, and the three men climbed back in. Without speaking to the occupant of the second wagon, they turned and whipped the horses forward onto the dirt road fronting the property. The lantern attached to the wagon's front slowly disappeared beyond the bend, and the second wagon was left alone at Summer Place.

The large man came back into view, carrying something John couldn't make out. Before he could recognize the object, someone stepped down from the covered back of the wagon. This person was smaller and was bundled against the cold and rain. And John knew immediately that this person, like the one before him, was looking right up at him. The figure stayed still a moment and then turned away when a banging was heard. John quickly stepped back against the tree as the smaller person turned back in his direction. The figure stood and watched the trees, and then finally turned away.

John took a deep breath and then found the first man. He had brought the object to the pit that would become the root cellar and the basement. It was a ladder. He pushed it over until the weight was greater on the dangling end and then secured it as best he could to the dirt surrounding the hole. The second figure walked up to the hole and then nodded. Then both turned back, out of the skeletal house, and returned to the wagon. They pulled someone out of the back. The smaller person was struggling, but the two men were far stronger and quickly brought her under control. John swallowed as he watched the scene play out. He knew in real life he never would have been able to see anything from this distance, but that was the advantage to dreamwalking; he could sometimes do the impossible.

As the two men maneuvered the woman, John could see bright red hair spilling from a woolen cap on her head. The larger man struck the woman hard, and her struggling calmed somewhat. John wanted to call out to stop them, but he knew from past experience that either they wouldn't hear him, or his call would be ignored. He was meant to see this, not prevent it.

They placed the woman down on the ground in front of the hole. She was wobbly from the blow she had just received and held on tightly to the leg of the smaller of the two men. The man brushed at the woman's hand, but it held firm. Then the man punched at the woman's hand and she finally let go. He pulled something from his coat and John knew exactly what it was. Before he could shout out, the gunshot reverberated through the valley. The small woman fell forward into the large hole. John screamed, knowing that, as in other dreams, his voice wouldn't be heard. As his voice joined the echo of the gunshot, the small man turned and looked in his direction. John could see the blazing dark eyes underneath the hat as they searched the woods looking for the author of the scream. John closed his mouth, and fear seized him.

He knew those dark eyes had found him. For the first time in a dreamwalk, he knew it was far more than a dream; he was actually there, and as vulnerable as the woman who had just been murdered.

On the second-floor landing, Gabriel paused and examined the ambient-light camera that had been placed on a swivel base to roam the left and right of the hallway. The movement of the remote camera was stopped and it was facing to the right, which meant that it had detected movement in that direction in the past few minutes. He checked the motion sensor and found the small blue light blinking, meaning it was still working properly. Gabriel pressed his hand over his earpiece and called Harris Dalton.

"Has the production team picked up any movement on the second floor in the past five minutes?"

"Negative. If there had been movement, we missed it. Hell, everything was so active a few minutes ago we would have missed a train coming through. Sorry, we'll keep a sharper eye out."

Gabriel straightened and looked at the darkened faces around him. He nodded at George Cordero. "Go ahead and activate the laser systems here and on the third floor."

"Professor," Julie said in a low voice, "can you explain what this laser system is?"

Kennedy closed his eyes for a moment in frustration, but decided that shaking off the question wasn't an option. He really did want the country to take interest in what was happening. Gabriel reached down and plucked a small object off the floor. It was the size of a basketball and weighed more than six pounds.

"This is a laser grid generator. These small holes are laser emitters. Each device has two hundred small lasers, the power output of a small laser pointer. Once turned on, each laser light will create a grid in each of the two hallways. For us to see the light more clearly, each designator also has a built-in fogger that will spread a veil of mist."

"And what does this accomplish?" Julie asked.

"In theory, anything moving through the lasers will possibly become visible. With these lasers, coupled with our ambient-light cameras and the new motion sensors that detect the movement of air, heat, cold, even dust particles, we should be able to avoid being surprised by anything near us."

Kennedy didn't wait for another question from Julie. He turned and placed the laser designator back on the floor as George Cordero switched on the device with the remote control placed by the camera stand. Suddenly red, green, and blue lasers shot free of the round, battery-driven orb. The grid it laid down covered the hallway from floor to ceiling, left and right of the landing. Another emitter, at the far end, illuminated, as did another two on the opposite side of the house on the far hallway. George then made sure the motion sensors lining the hallways were activated. This was confirmed by a beep as he switched the sensors on and off, and then on again. He nodded at Gabriel.

"This way to the sewing room," he said. The team fell in line and continued up the stairs. Gabriel again pressed his hand to his ear and spoke into his small microphone. "Harris, what do you have on Kelly and Jason?"

"Nothing. They've hit the blind spot halfway down the

stairs. We should be picking them up visually in a moment. We have them on audio walking down the stairs."

"Any word from the electrical people outside?" Gabriel asked.

"The power company says it's not in their lines. Our own people have confirmed that power is being directed into the house, but that's where it ends. It's like something is sucking up the juice."

Damian Jackson frowned. It was more likely the storm had blown the breakers. He shook his head but continued to follow the professor.

"How are John and the others in the ballroom?"

"Mr. Lonetree is out like a light, but we do have activity. It was like a windstorm had erupted inside the ballroom, but things are a bit calmer now. Leonard Sickles just let Wallace Lindemann inside and he's at his usual spot at the bar."

"Keep an eye on Kelly. She and Sanborn should be your priority. If anything starts to happen, pull them out until we can all get down there. Order her if you have to."

"Yeah, all I have to do is threaten to kill her live feed. She'll comply," Harris said. There was a momentary pause as Harris asked something of Julie. Gabriel picked it up on his earpiece and thought about the answer to the question he knew the reporter was about to ask.

"Professor, for the sake of our viewers I want to reiterate: Before your experiences in Summer Place seven years ago, you were not a believer in the supernatural, is that correct?"

Kennedy paused. This was not the question Harris had just asked Julie to relay to him.

"No. At the time I believed most hauntings revolved around living people. The human mind is capable of many things, including creating things inside a person's head that would make it seem they are dealing with the paranormal."

"You've stated mass hysteria as one of those causes, is that correct?"

"Yes," Kennedy said. He wondered where Julie was going with the questions.

"Before we continue our journey to the sewing room and the third floor, Professor, I am sure the viewers would like to know your opinion on what's happening here tonight. Are we dealing with the theory of mass hysteria?"

Gabriel looked at the others. They waited silently, and in the darkness he could feel them anticipating his answer. He saw a brief reflection of the red, green, and blue laser lights off the ambient camera lens and knew that many others, the people Julie and Harris Dalton were playing for, were waiting also.

"This is no mass hysteria, Ms. Reilly. In my opinion, we are dealing with something that has never happened before in the annals of supernatural activity. A haunting such as this, the activity we have experienced tonight, has never been documented before. We may be dealing with an entity that is powerful beyond reason. No, Ms. Reilly, not mass hysteria. Something doesn't want us here because we are a danger to it. It knows that unlike other visitors to this house, we can cause it harm."

Julie Reilly swallowed. She heard the prompt from the production van and hoped her voice didn't crack when she spoke.

"On that note, we'll take a brief commercial break."

Inside the production van, the number one monitor faded quickly to black and was replaced by a small green lizard selling auto insurance.

"Jesus, give me a break. That's some scary shit, Gabe," George Cordero muttered, pulling his coat tighter around him.

"If I were you, I would have stuck with the mass hysteria theory, Kennedy. When my lawyers get done with you and the CEO of this company, you'll need a good story to keep your ass out of litigation," Lionel Peterson said, stepping up from the darkness below. He tilted his head back and took a drink from a silver flask. His earpiece was hanging free, so he didn't know they weren't going out live.

Gabriel had already turned down the second-floor hallway,

toward the stairs to the third floor. He stopped as he felt the breeze of cold air grow even colder. The presence was out of the sewing room and waiting for them—he knew it. He also knew the others could feel it as he stopped and turned. He nodded at each. Then his eyes lingered on the large state policeman.

"Don't accidentally shoot me with that thing," he said, nodding to the gun in Damian Jackson's holster.

Jackson looked at the cameraman. He saw that, for the moment, the camera was concentrating his view on the bend in the hallway a few steps away. He didn't know they were in a two-minute commercial break. He smiled at Kennedy.

"If you have someone in a bedsheet up there, Professor, I would warn him that I am just a tad jumpy at the moment. I never said you didn't have a gift of the narrative."

Kennedy returned the smile. For the first time, he felt relief that Jackson was along.

"If we come across someone in a bedsheet, Detective, give me the gun and I'll shoot him."

Kelly Delaphoy stopped no more than ten steps from the bottom. It had taken almost five minutes to get down the steps in the darkness. The small flashlight only served to cast dangerous-looking turns and drop-offs on the steep stairs. Jason had twisted his ankle, misjudging the turn halfway down. He had to sit and rub his ankle a while before he was sure he was okay to continue, but thus far he hadn't said a word in complaint.

She stood still, looking into the darkness, seeing the even blacker outline of the audio and visual equipment in the middle of the room pointing toward the trapdoor she knew was there. The hulking shapes of the old kitchen appliances ringed the basement, just as they had before, but they looked far more ominous now. She swallowed and reached behind her, taking Jason's hand in her own. His, as hers, was ice cold to the touch, but it still felt good to know she wasn't alone. She used her free hand to adjust the earpiece and then contacted Harris in the van.

"Okay, Harris, we're a few steps from the bottom of the stairs. We can see into the basement. Are you picking up the audio?"

"We have you, just a second and we'll adjust the camera to pick you up as you step into the basement. We'll lead with you after the break in fifteen seconds."

"Okay." Kelly squeezed Jason's cold hand even tighter, and he reciprocated. "Well, here we go." As she took another step down the steps, she heard the whine of the small motor on the camera tripod turn the lens their way. "I hope this was a good idea," she said. Jason didn't answer, just squeezed her hand tighter.

"Okay," Harris called out. "We're back in five, four, three, two . . . camera five, basement . . . go!"

On the green-tinted picture, everyone watching—from the production van to Mr. and Mrs. America—saw Kelly take the first step onto the basement floor. She stood motionless, allowing her eyes to adjust to the darkness. She moved her small penlight to the far wall, and then over to the trapdoor. The basement was silent as a morgue as she took another tentative step. As she moved, she felt Jason become hesitant about going forward, but just as she was about to say something, he squeezed her hand almost to the point of breaking it.

"Hey, Jason, take it easy." She took another step toward the center of the room. The whine of the tripod motor sounded lightly as it followed her. "Come on, Jason, you're breaking my hand!"

Inside the production van, everyone watching the monitor froze. Harris tried to speak but couldn't. He fumbled with the small switch on his mic but missed. Everyone watching the television special saw what they were seeing, but few really picked up on the horror of the moment as Kelly, with her arm behind her, came clear of the wall that had blocked the camera's view.

"What did you say?" came Jason's voice from the stairs.

Kelly froze. The pressure on her hand was becoming unbearable. A whimper escaped her lips.

Jason finally made the bottom step and froze. Kelly was standing in front of him with her arm trailing behind her, and holding her hand out.

The black entity was just behind Kelly, and part of that darkness was connected to Kelly's outstretched hand. The obsidian blackness was enormous, far darker than its surroundings. The illumination of his small penlight penetrated through the towering darkness. Jason saw Kelly slowly turn around and open her eyes wide.

The hand she was holding was not Jason's.

The small penlight and the power to the camera went out just as Jason and Kelly both screamed.

Gabriel stopped at the top of the third-floor staircase. He looked around and made sure the laser designators were working. George Cordero moved up the stairs and stood by Kennedy.

"Gabe, do you feel it?" George said just as Harris Dalton started his countdown for coverage to begin again. "It's warmer now. I'm not getting the black feeling like I was a few minutes ago."

Kennedy did feel it. As he looked at the others he saw that there were no more shivers due to the cold.

"Are you saying that the entity has left this floor, Mr. Cordero?" Julie asked for the benefit of the live audience.

"No, I'm just saying something's different."

Gabriel thought for the briefest moment. In his earpiece, he heard the order to go to camera five, the static camera in the basement. He stepped onto the third floor and looked down the laser-lined hallway. The sewing room door was standing wide open. He could see the blackness beyond, as if it were a gateway that soaked up the possible, leaving only the impossible behind. He continued down the hallway.

As the others followed, they each heard the static in their earpieces—soft at first, but growing louder and stronger as they moved toward the sewing room and the master suite next to it. Julie tapped her earpiece.

"As we move down the hallway, our electronic equipment is starting to malfunction," she explained to the audience, just hoping her words were going out to the van clearly.

"How surprising," Lionel Peterson mumbled at the back of the group.

Damian Jackson looked at Peterson with the laser grid spread out over his features. He could see in the multicolored light that the entertainment president was getting drunk.

Suddenly the static became unbearably loud. Each of them grabbed at their ears, pulling the cords and letting them dangle. As a result, they missed the few discernible words from the production van: Harris Dalton screaming Kelly's name.

"We have just lost communication with our production facilities outside," Julie said. She shook her head, trying to clear the ringing in her ears.

An alarm sounded from the staircase. Gabriel ran back to the landing and looked down onto the first floor. In the blackness, he saw the first of Leonard's motion sensors go off. The lights tracked something up the stairs a few steps and then stopped. Again the lights on the banister registered movement as whatever it was moved five more steps up. Whatever it was, it was stopping to peer upward at the group gathering at the landing. It would take a few steps upward, then stop, look, and then continue.

"What are you feeling?" Gabriel asked George as the cameraman moved forward and switched to infrared. The soundman pushed his boom microphone out over the banister.

"I'm picking up footsteps," he said quietly to the others. "Heavy freaking footsteps."

"This is the thing that lives here, and it's pissed, that's what I'm feeling. This thing wasn't human, it couldn't be. It has grown in strength. It isn't even close to what we were experiencing before," George answered. His breath was starting to fog once more.

As Damian Jackson watched the red lights illuminate, following the movement up to the second-floor landing, he swallowed. He had to give Kennedy and his team credit—if it was an intentional trick through electronic means, it was a good one. He could see the ply on the stair runners actually being depressed in the beam of the professor's flashlight.

Lionel Peterson watched the blinking lights as they progressed up the stairs. Then he capped the flask and tossed it away.

In the freezing ballroom, John Lonetree was sweating as his head tossed from side to side on the pillow. With shaking hands, Jennifer wiped the cold sweat from John's brow, wanting to say calming things to him but knowing that her voice could wake him from his walk—something he had warned her not to do. She wasn't even supposed to be touching him. Leonard reached out and pulled Jenny's hand away, shaking his head.

They both turned at a noise in the ballroom. Wallace Lindemann, using only his free hand because a sloshing drink was in the other, was tossing wood into the massively large fireplace. Leonard rushed to him and pulled a piece of wood out of his hand, shoving him away from the fireplace.

"Get your ass back over to the bar and stay there. In case you haven't noticed, asshole, we have a situation going on here."

Lindemann shot Leonard a dirty look. "Keep your hands off me, you nig—" he started, but saw the look on the small man's face.

"Go ahead. Say it, rich man, and see what happens."

Lindemann turned and weaved his way back to the bar.

"You better lay off that shit. You just may need your senses about you later," Leonard said. John took a deep breath and tensed up on the couch, scaring Jenny so badly she nearly fell backward.

It was hot, summer possibly. John tried to get his bearings. At first it seemed he was in a small room that had no windows. Then, very slowly, light started to filter into the world he had stepped into. There was noise, a lot of it, resolving into the sound of machines—possibly hundreds. He tilted his head as his vision cleared. There were windows, possibly a thousand of them. Some were open, some closed. The ones that were open were not producing enough of a draft to even begin to cool the large room.

John took a tentative step forward into the room and saw row upon row of small tables. On the tables were sewing machines, and above them were thousands of strung threads— threads of all colors and thicknesses. Working the machines were women dressed in very old clothing, and Lonetree knew immediately where he was. He saw the room's foreman moving around the women, who tensed when he walked past, allowing only their eyes to glance at the large man as he passed behind them. Lonetree felt the women's dread and knew the shop foreman was a scoundrel of the first order. They were all afraid of him. It was only during the summer months in the city that they were afraid, because the rest of the time the Lindemann family stayed close to the factory. The man always was a model citizen when the Lindemanns weren't away at their retreat: Summer Place.

John heard a commotion in the back of the large room. A woman screamed, and the noise from the sewing machines dwindled to almost nothing. A young woman had collapsed at her machine and was being picked up by two of the women closest to her. John could see the poor thing was dripping with sweat and was very much pregnant. The shop foreman was soon standing over the girl, who looked embarrassed and was white as a sheet. The kerchief she had on her head to cover her hair was soaked through with sweat. John took a few steps forward between the rows of machines, where the women watched the scene before them. He felt their tenseness.

"I was afraid of this. I warned Mr. Lindemann about keeping you on. Your work has slipped and now you're costing me time and money." The man with the thick mustache turned to the hundred women in the room. "Get back to work, you lazy swags!" he shouted in a deep Irish brogue.

"The Lindemanns kept her on because she's pregnant and without a man," said one of the women who was helping the young girl. Her Irish was as deep as the foreman's.

"Well, the Lindemanns ain't here, are they, swag?" the foreman said with his hands on his hips.

John felt anger rising up in him, but knew he was helpless to do anything.

"'Tis all right, Molly, I just got a little dizzy is all," the girl said.

"Yeah, well you'll not be causing a shutdown with your dramatics again, you lazy slug."

"You can't fire her. What will she do?" the older woman supporting the girl asked.

"Your only concern is how long I'm going to stand here and not fire you, Miss Big Mouth."

"The last I heard I was running this company, Mr. Coughlin."

The women and the foreman turned to see a smallish man in a very expensive suit standing at the door. He also had a mustache, and long sideburns. He removed a high-priced hat and looked on toward the back of the room. His German accent was there, but after years of trying the man had fought to limit the sound and tone of his German and English; he found here in America it was far better to speak as one of them.

"Why, Mr. Lindemann, I thought you were vacationing in Pennsylvania, sir," the foreman said.

"I can very much see your belief in your actions."

F. E. Lindemann tossed his expensive hat on one of the worktables and stepped forward. He reached the young woman in ten very quick steps. He took her arm and looked her over.

"She fainted and was causing the others to stop work. I was just—"

Another stern look shut the Irishman's mouth.

John wanted to laugh at the worried look on the foreman's face. He wanted to slap old F. E. Lindemann on the back—he obviously hated bullies.

"My dear, you are obviously too far along to be working in this heat," Lindemann said as he helped the girl forward. He paused for a moment, letting her to get her bearings.

"Yes, sir, but I need the money, at least for the next two weeks; I'll be traveling to Baltimore to stay with my aunt. That's where my baby will be born."

Lindemann reached into his pocket and pull out a roll of bills.

"Now you ladies, staring at me is not conducive to making me any money, so I suggest you return to your sewing."

Most of the women smiled at the polite little man. They didn't understand the word "conducive," but did as he asked.

"Take this. It's more than a month's salary for you, and more than enough to get you to Baltimore by train to have your child."

"Mr. Lindemann, I couldn't, I would—"

"You can and you will, young lady." Lindemann placed the rolled bills into the girl's hand. "Now, you listen. As I am more than likely to sever Mr. Coughlin's services, I suggest you take that train to Baltimore this very day." Lindemann looked back at the large Irishman, who was still standing arrogantly with his hands on his hips, watching the exchange. "I trust him not to pay you a visit for causing him to be exposed."

The young girl looked back at the foreman and nodded her head. She understood the threat.

"Good. I'll see you to your room, and then to the train." He pulled out a gold pocket watch and examined it. "If I don't return to Summer Place by tomorrow evening, Mrs. Lindemann will eat me for dinner."

John watched Lindemann pull the girl away. He saw the smirk on the shop foreman's face. John wondered when Lindemann was going to fire the man, but allowed his mind to ease when he felt the girl's tension fade. Lindemann helped her toward the door, and toward a new life in Baltimore.

John felt the dream starting to fade, but was startled by the look in the foreman's eyes. It was not one of embarrassment at being caught behaving as an overbearing and cruel man—it was one of a job satisfyingly done. John realized he had been watching an act of some sort on the foreman's part.

The light and the heat faded as the girl and Lindemann walked toward him. John tried to step out of the way, but the strangest thing happened. The girl acted as though she saw him. Her blue eyes looked right into John's. She smiled and maneuvered at least three steps over to her left, pulling the smaller Lindemann with her, and then she passed right through him. John felt a jolt of electricity, something he had never felt before in any dreamwalk. He felt the growing child inside her, he felt the sweat on her face and brow. Then she was through, and he wanted to collapse. As she reached the door, she turned her head and looked in John's direction once more, as if she were apologizing to someone she couldn't possibly see. John raised his hand and wanted to say something, but the dream faded and then he was gone into the dark void that was his dreamscape.

The pain made him sit straight up on the couch, but in his dream he was sitting on a large hardwood floor. He turned his head as the sharp pain came once more, his body shaking as though the pain were so bad he couldn't bear it any longer.

He heard the cry of a baby, then another ripping pain. Then a cloth was placed over his mouth and nose and pressed down firmly. He managed to raise his head slightly in the brightly illuminated room. He saw an old wood-burning stove and, most shockingly, he saw his own blood-covered legs and ripped-open belly. He knew for a fact that he wasn't looking at his own body. It was the body of a young woman, kicking out from the excruciating pain. He tried to focus on the faces above him, but the girl's body wouldn't cooperate. He knew somehow that they had tried to put the girl out with chloroform but it hadn't taken.

"This crap isn't working anymore," said a husky voice with a Russian accent. Then a fist slammed down into John's face, then again. Then the chloroform-soaked rag once more.

"Never mind, just take her below and dispose of her. Give me the child. No, no, watch its poor head. There, there," the Russian voice said. "It's all right now."

John felt his legs rise into the air and then he was being pulled across the tiled floor.

"You're dragging blood all across the kitchen!" the voice said angrily. Somewhere, the cry of a baby started.

There was silence from whoever was dragging him. His legs were tossed down and then he heard the sound of a door opening. He was once more pulled away and into the semi-darkness of another room. Then, with searing pain coursing through his body, he was dragged down a flight of stairs. His head hit every one of them. Then he was dragged onto a concrete floor. He tried to scream, and this time he did. It came out not as his voice, but the voice of a young woman.

"Stop it, please stop it. Please, I cannot stand the screaming!"

John recognized the voice that had spoken, even though his host body kept screaming. Through the pain-seared voice of the girl he heard the click. It was loud and he knew exactly what the noise was. The gunshot sounded and John felt the impact of the bullet as it sunk deep into his skull, and then there was blackness. When he screamed next, it was his voice. The sudden scream nearly took ten years off the life of everyone in the ballroom, and of those who were watching on national live television.

The dreamwalk continued as the battle upstairs began.

Lionel Peterson bumped the cameraman at the banister on the third-floor landing. According to the string of motion sensors and laser designators, the dark mass vanished as it made the turn into the second-floor hallway. That meant the next time they would have any indication of where it was would be when it came to the base of the third-floor staircase. Peterson, for one, didn't relish waiting until then to decide what to do. After all, the staircase was their only avenue of escape.

"Kennedy, I hope you have a back door to this floor." Peterson stared fixedly at the base of the staircase.

"I have a better idea, Professor. Why don't you just call off your dogs? Enough is enough," Detective Jackson said. He turned from the banister and saw that Gabriel wasn't even close enough to hear. He was a few feet away, using his small penlight to examine the wall. He was running his hand over the flowered print wallpaper. In frustration, Jackson moved toward the small light.

"See it?" Gabriel asked, tracing a bulging outline along the wall.

"Yes," George answered, and swallowed. His heart began to beat faster.

"This wasn't here when we first stepped onto the landing. I remember looking this way." Kennedy straightened. "Ms. Reilly, can you place your hand right here?" Kennedy ran his fingers along the wall about four and half feet up from the carpet runner. "Tell me what you feel. George, you do the same, then allow our intrepid detective to do so."

"Shit," the soundman muttered.

Julie made sure the cameraman had turned and zoomed in on her. She didn't know what the professor was angling toward, but for dramatics, she nodded. She slowly reached out and placed her small hand on the wall. "Higher," Gabriel said. He took a step back so the large cameraman could get closer with his night-vision lens.

Julie looked at Kennedy but did as he asked. She moved her hand up the wall about a foot, then suddenly froze. She felt the chills course down her spine as she pulled her hand away and took a step back, her eyes never leaving the bulging area of the wall.

"Professor Kennedy has just pointed out an anomaly in the plaster of the third-floor hallway, the very same spot where his student reportedly vanished more than seven years ago. When I placed my hand on the exact spot, I felt . . . I felt a . . . beating heart." Julie swallowed, her mouth suddenly dry. She wiped her hand on her slacks, trying to get the feeling of the beating heart off her skin.

George decided he didn't need to feel the wall. However, Damian Jackson roughly shoved his hand against the wall as if by mere bravado he would dispel the truth of what was there. After all, this was the part of the story that had made him Kennedy's enemy seven years before.

"This is foolishness. In case you forgot, you have two people down in a very dangerous and darkened basement, I suggest we—"

Damian Jackson froze just as his hand came into contact with the wall. At first he thought he was only feeling his own pulse, but he quickly realized that it was indeed coming from the wall. He wanted to pull his hand away just as Julie had, but it was because of the temperature difference that he kept his large hand in place—the wall was growing warmer.

As Damian felt the heartbeat in the wall, the soundman suddenly turned, pressing his right earphone into his head. He swung the boom mic around, searching for a sound that at first was flitting, and then constant. The others watched the soundman as the boom swung first one way and then the other. Finally he moved a few feet down the hallway and raised the mic toward the old iron grill. Gabriel swung his light up, and the small beam illuminated the ornate grillwork where the special-effects man had disappeared more than two weeks before. The soundman looked at his audio gain. The noise was growing stronger. He took a step back.

"Jesus, what could be in there?" he muttered.

"What are you hearing?" Julie asked. Her eyes locked on the grill. Now she could hear the sounds coming out of the vent. It sounded like someone crawling inside, their weight moving toward the grill. "Come on, what did you hear?"

"Listen," the soundman said with a hiss between his teeth. The camera zoomed in on the black-painted grill.

"Run."

"Oh, shit," the cameraman said, panicking. He wanted to do just what the voice ordered.

Damian Jackson turned around. He had stood in front of this grill just after the disappearance of the special-effects man during the broadcast test and had never felt a thing—at least nothing as strong as some of his troopers had felt that night. Now he was hearing something for himself. This voice, coupled with the beating heart in the wall, was adding up to him starting to believe Kennedy had every right to believe in ghosts. The evidence seemed to be piling up right before his eyes and ears.

"Run!"

This time the voice was more insistent and far closer. If Gabriel were tall enough, he would have aimed the light into the vent and tried to get a glimpse of the owner of the voice. He knew it was Kyle Pritchard warning them to get the hell out of there.

"Oh, damn, what in hell is that?"

Everyone, including the cameraman and soundman, turned toward the landing and the banister where Lionel Peterson was staring down.

"What in God's name—" Damian Jackson started to ask.

"God has nothing to do with that, Detective," George said. They looked down upon the large black shape standing in the light of the sensor at the base of the third-floor stairs. The laser cast a red glow to its inky darkness. "Gabe, it's grown in power, I feel its . . . hatred . . . no, *his* hatred."

Kennedy looked at the entity and knew it was looking directly up at them.

"Is it Lindemann, George?"

"I . . . I . . . think so . . . no. . . . Yes, it's a man, definitely man."

Damian raised his gun but Kennedy placed a hand on the detective's and lowered it.

"Come on, what the hell do you think you're going to hit with that?"

Jackson was breathing deeply, hearing Kennedy's words but also hanging onto the gun and its aim, simply because it was real, it was solid, and he could believe in it.

"Oh, man, listen to it," the soundman said. He swung the boom mic over the edge of the banister.

Below them, the black shape stood its ground. It rolled like a thundercloud, turning its midsection into a jumble of mass, and every time it moved its chest area, they heard the ragged breathing. It was a deep, foreboding sound. They could make out the neck and the head. They all knew it looked up at them with extreme hatred; they could feel it.

"Temperature reading is twenty-five degrees and falling," Gabriel said as he checked the thermometer on his digital watch.

"May I suggest that we move away from the landing?" Peterson said. He took a step backward, brushing by a frozen Damian Jackson. "I think Professor Kennedy has proven his point."

As Julie Reilly stepped back from the railing, she heard a crack and the wall gave way, hitting her hard and pushing her forward into George Cordero. The cameraman turned just as the skeletal remains of Warren Atkinson fell across Julie's backside. She screamed and George, who had turned, also froze just as Jackson had at the landing. Gabriel moved first and pulled Julie out from under the bones of his former student. He was shaking and almost screaming. As soon as Julie was free, he angrily turned back to the third-floor banister. He gripped the rail, moving slowly at first, then faster, to the stairs.

"You son of a bitch!" he shouted at the thing staring up at him. The movement sensors flashed upward as the entity took a step up. "Is that what you're good at, scaring and killin' kids?"

"For God's sake, you fool, what are you doing?!" Peterson yelled, trying to pull the professor back from the stairs.

"MINE!" came the roar from the second floor as the thing took another two steps upward. The sensors illuminated brightly as it moved.

Gabriel shook himself and then looked at the faces lined in the green, red, and blue laser grid. They were looking at him for an answer. For the first time, he knew he had a house full of believers. He turned back to the stairs.

"F. E. Lindemann, we know who you are!" he shouted.

The laughter came immediately—thick, full of spite, and accompanied by the smell of putrescence, as though a graveyard had opened and spilled forth its corpses.

"YOU'RE MINE!" the entity bellowed. The sound boomed, as if it had originated in hell and not twenty steps just below them.

Julie was trying to keep the bile down as she stared at the skeleton of Kennedy's lost student. The voice called from the grill again.

"RUN!"

Only Julie and George Cordero heard, and then saw, the door three rooms down slowly open.

"The room . . ." Julie actually spit some of the bile from her mouth as the cameraman swung to his right, from the entity to Julie, as she spoke. "The room where the German opera star vanished close to a century . . . ago, has opened." She quickly pushed George forward, and then the soundman. Then she screamed for Jackson and Peterson. Gabriel turned, and with one last look at the entity roiling and shifting three steps up from the bottom, turned and followed the others into the lost diva's room.

"NO!" the entity screamed. The sensors illuminated the mass as it shot toward the third-floor landing. The boom of footsteps sounded inside Summer Place, and the house was shaken on its foundation.

As Gabriel and Jackson slammed the thick door home and bolted it, the entity slammed into the opposite side. The door bent inward but held. Jackson didn't care any longer—he again pulled the gun and quickly fired two bullets through the door.

"Don't do that! That door's barely strong enough to—" Peterson started. The entity struck the door again, creating not only a dent in the wood, but also a boom, as if it had been struck by a cannonball. In the blackness of the room, they all gasped each time the mass struck the door. Damian was slowly backing away.

"Jesus, that thing wants to actually kill us!" the soundman screamed.

"Listen!" Gabriel said.

Out in the hallway, just as the entity struck the door a tremendous blow, they heard the deep and booming footsteps moving back down the hallway—in *both* directions.

"George?" Gabriel asked. He stared at the door as the beast outside hit it once more, shaking the thick wood in its frame.

"It's still there. . . . No; wait . . . part of it is going to the sewing room, and . . . and—"

"What, goddamn it?!" Peterson screamed.

George tilted his head and closed his eyes. "Part of it is going to the ballroom . . . and another part is going outside!"

"Good God, it's going for John and the others," Gabriel said.

"But why outside?" Julie asked.

"The production van," George said, his face draining of all color. "It wants to stop it all."

Julie once more put the static-filled earpiece into her ear and started calling a warning out to Harris Dalton and the production team outside.

"Use the camera to warn them," Gabriel shouted, "and pray it's still transmitting a live feed!"

Just as the words escaped Kennedy's mouth, the door cracked straight down the middle.

The entity laughed, and then began screaming a sing
word that was heard all the way into the ballroom and th
production van two hundred feet away.

"Mine, Mine, Mine!"

22

John's breathing would go shallow one moment and the
he would gasp for air the next. Jennifer and Leonard wer
both becoming worried that he was too far under. The wa
Lonetree and Gabriel had explained the dreamwalks, h
never went so deep that his own movements wouldn't wak
him. But now he was thrashing, screaming and whimpering

"Maybe we should try to wake him," Leonard said.

Jennifer swallowed and bit her lower lip. There was
chance they would have to do just that.

John stood in the middle of the brightly lit ballroom watch
ing men and women in formal attire roam the room with
drinks while a string quartet played. People coursed in and
around the rows of chairs that had been set up in front of th
small stage. There were close to a hundred people of vary
ing ages, and their dress was obviously from the twenties o
thirties. John quickly stepped back as a small woman in
maid's outfit walked right through him. He gasped as he fel
the woman's thoughts and feelings. When he turned around
she was offering a glass of champagne to a couple who ac
cepted without a thank-you. She was angry that she had to
perform two jobs during the night. As he watched, the small
woman headed toward the crowded bar and placed the tray
of filled glasses on the end. Then she wiped her hands and
made her way toward the large double doors.

"Leanne, what has become of Mrs. Lindemann? She needs
to be down here with her guests."

The man was the same one whom John had seen at the
factory in New York. It was F. E. Lindemann, and he looked

none too pleased. His tuxedo was of the finest cut and he grinned as he asked the girl the question, but John could see he was seething underneath. Now he knew who the girl was. She was one of the maids from the nearby village, and was also the spitting image of Eunice Johansson. He thought a moment—Leanne Cummings, if he remembered right. She was the last person to see the German opera star Gwyneth Gerhardt alive.

"Yes, sir, she had a last-minute alteration to her dress. She is in the sewing room; she shouldn't be but a moment."

"And Miss Gerhardt?" Lindemann asked.

"The staff reironed her dress and I am on my way to deliver it now, sir."

"Be off, then, and tell them both to hurry. Our guests are waiting."

The girl half bowed and made her way quickly from the ballroom. John followed.

As he stepped aside to avoid two guests who nearly passed through him, he saw the girl disappear through the kitchen's swinging doors. Looking from the moving doors to the staircase, he played a hunch and started to climb the stairs. In the wink of an eye, John found himself on the third-floor landing, and then across the hallway to the far side of the house, where he was looking straight at the master suite and the sewing room. Both doors were closed. He stopped and looked at the wall where almost a century later Gabriel's student would disappear. This wallpaper was different from the current wallpaper in the hallway. He felt the wall and found it just that: a wall, normal and cool to the touch.

Suddenly a door opened down the hallway. A woman stuck her head out and checked the hallway before stepping out so that John could see her. She looked right at him, and then through him. She was wearing a dressing gown and slippers, and her hair was coiffed to perfection. John could see her stocking as she stepped from the room. Her eyes seemed to meet his for the briefest of moments before she started across the hall. She moved like a cat, with her eyes firmly placed on the sewing room and the master suite next to it. She stepped into the room across from hers and then quickly closed the door behind her.

John didn't have to follow. One moment he watched the woman disappear into the bedroom, and the next moment he was standing next to the bed in that very same room. He watched the robed woman go to her knees and look under the neatly made bed. She straightened onto her knees and crawled to the closet, then stood, pulled open the door, and quickly rummaged inside. It looked as if the woman were looking for something. While John watched the woman's strange behavior, he kept feeling his stomach. He could still feel the pain from the previous walk. John found he was still shaking from the pain of the murder he had endured.

The woman stepped from the closet and then stopped cold, as if she had heard something. She went to the bedroom door and cracked it open. She then quickly hurried out into the hallway. John followed this time as she made her way to the next room and tried the knob, but at that moment the maid came around the corner. She was carrying a dress in her hands, held out as if she were carrying a baby. The black-sequined gown shimmered brightly in the lights lining the hallway.

"Oh, I was just looking for you," the woman in the dressing gown said. She released the handle of the door to the next bedroom she had been about to search. Her words were spoken in a heavy German accent. John knew then who he was looking at—the opera star Gwyneth Gerhardt. The diva was about to disappear from Summer Place, and John's dreamwalk had placed him right at the center of the action.

"Yes, ma'am, Mr. Lindemann has requested that you join the party as soon as possible," the young maid said as she went to Gerhardt's room and opened the door. The diva moved into her bedroom, followed by the maid carrying the dress. John stepped over but didn't enter the room; he just watched from the hallway.

"Just lay the dress on the bed, please, and tell Mr. Linde-mann I'll be down momentarily."

The maid did as she was ordered and then half bowed and left. Turning to the right, she walked toward the master suite. John watched her knock. She knocked again and then moved over ten feet to the door on the left—the sewing room—and knocked, looking uneasy to John's watching eyes.

"Yes," came a voice through the door, just as soft music was turned down.

"Ma'am, your husband is anxious for you to join him in the ballroom."

At first there was no answer, but then the sewing room door opened a few inches. Though John tried, he couldn't hear what was said. Then the door closed and the young girl hurried away down the hallway and past John. The soft music started again inside the sewing room. He started walking toward it, but movement from the opera star's room caught his eye. She stood at the open closet. John felt something, or maybe he felt what Gwyneth Gerhardt was feeling; he couldn't be sure. He moved easily into the room and watched as the woman removed a fur stole and tossed it onto the bed, then stepped farther into the closet. She was feeling around at the back of the closet. Occasionally she would stop and listen, and then feel around some more. Then John heard it—the same music he had just heard coming from the sewing room.

Now just as curious as the opera singer, John came up behind her. For a moment, John knew she could feel his presence. She stopped probing the back of the closet and turned to look right at him. Then, satisfied she was alone in the bedroom, she went back to feeling the back wall of the closet. John hesitantly reached out. He nearly touched the German star, but withdrew his hand. He wanted to feel exactly what she was feeling, but was afraid to complete a chain that linked the past with the present and that therefore might stop her from doing what she had done in that past. Waves of long-ing, of missing something, came off Gerhardt as she finally found the spot she had been seeking. As she pushed in on the back of the wooden closet, it popped open like a small door. Beyond was a darkened passageway that led off into a false wall. She hesitated.

John gathered his courage and reached out and touched Gerhardt on the shoulder. She froze for a second, looking into the dark passage.

Lonetree closed his eyes, feeling what Gerhardt was feeling. She was indeed looking for something. She was looking for . . . for . . . her sister. Lonetree moved his hand from her shoulder, and she seemed to relax. John watched as the opera star gathered her courage and stepped into the hidden passage. He wanted to shout for her to stop, but another wave hit him from the woman's mind. She was here to sing, but she had only accepted the invitation because she had wanted to search for her sister. She suspected that the Lindemanns were involved, and suspected her sister was here. John was starting to get a sick feeling in his stomach again.

As the woman felt her way along the passage, the music grew louder. Finally she stopped at another doorway. John knew they were right outside the sewing room. There were two doors almost side by side, mirroring the two in the hallway: the master suite and the sewing room. As the opera star reached out in the darkness, John came close to trying to stop her. He knew that her death, or at the very least the reason for her disappearance, was right behind that thin panel of a doorway.

A sliver of light filled the small tunnel that ran between the thickened wall of the third floor. Gerhardt stood motionless, peering inside the sewing room. John touched her again, so that he could gauge her feelings and thoughts. Suddenly he was thrown backward. Gerhardt's heart lurched in her chest. She panicked and, with a gasp, turned and ran back the way she had come, running right through John. He felt eyes on him, and turned. The small door had opened wider, and a face was staring through him. The naked body and fierce eyes penetrated his soul as if he were looking at Satan himself, and then everything about Summer Place became crystal clear. John panicked himself and fought to gain control as he backed away from the figure. He stumbled in his dream and fell to the wooden floor of the passage. He heard Gerhardt up ahead as she gained the closet in her own room. John finally managed to get to his feet. Before he realized what was happening, he was in Gerhardt herself as she squeezed out of her closet.

John could still hear the music, and now he could feel Gwyneth's pounding heartbeat and her terror as she stumbled to her door. John tried with all his ability to assist the woman, who was now in a blind panic to get out. She was crying, whimpering, and John was also. She went to her knees as she reached for the crystal glass doorknob. It turned and she used it to stand, then she choked back a scream. The figure from the sewing room was standing at the door when it flew open. Inside Gerhardt, John screamed in horror right along with her as the knife plunged down and into the opera star. The figure pulled the knife free and slammed it into the German star again.

Lonetree fell backward with Gwyneth Gerhardt. He felt the body strike the hardwood floor just in front of the large bed. She tried to roll over and crawl to safety under the bed, screaming in pain and terror. He felt the large knife plunge into her back. Then all was still as the diva was roughly rolled over. John could see the person standing over Gerhardt clearly. The naked body was sheathed in a fine sheen of sweat, and its horrible, hate-filled eyes stared down. John felt his stomach heave.

John felt her heart stop beating at the moment of her death. Gabriel and the team were facing something far more terrible than just ghosts at Summer Place, he knew. The secret of the house was now in his memory, and all he had to do was wake up from the dreamwalk to let Gabriel know what they were dealing with.

It wasn't Summer Place that was evil, it was what walked there that came from hell itself. Lonetree feared it might be too late to stop it.

New York, New York

CEO Feuerstein stood from his chair as the sounds inside of Summer Place went down. They could still see the live picture of Kennedy's team as they ran for the open doorway of the bedroom. The basement camera was dark and had shown nothing since the attack on Kelly Delaphoy. The ballroom camera was blank, but they were receiving sound.

"Sir, the ratings are skyrocketing and the advertisers want to extend their time. The phone lines are going down due to overload. Most of the callers want to know if this is on the level or a practical joke. The news division wants more reporters on site, and the Pennsylvania State Police want to know why they weren't informed about the live broadcast," Feuerstein's assistant said from his side, "and I have Harris Dalton on line one."

Feuerstein, without taking his eyes off the screen, reached for the phone and pushed the flashing light connecting him with Harris Dalton in the production van. He placed his hand over the receiver and leaned toward his assistant.

"Inform our sponsors that we are not going to break. They'll get a scroll at the bottom of the screen." Feuerstein thought a moment as his assistant scribbled furiously on her notepad. Everyone in the room could hear Harris Dalton at Summer Place screaming into the phone. "Tell the news division to dispatch their news team from Bright Waters, and also please inform the state police that we have a detective lieutenant from their Philadelphia barracks in attendance, and that he is thus far reporting that everything is under control!"

The assistant stopped writing, and her eyes flicked to the large screen. The door of the third-floor bedroom that had once been used by Gwyneth Gerhardt slammed and locked, with Kennedy and his investigative team inside. She looked back to the CEO, and his glare told her she had better get moving at once.

Once the assistant was gone, Feuerstein raised the phone to his ear. "Dalton, you are putting on one hell of a show. The phone lines are going down due to the volume of calls. I want to—"

"We need the state police out here in force, and don't hand me any crap about ratings! We have people in serious danger in that house!"

"Now, now, why don't we let the good professor continue the experiment? After all, we haven't really seen anyone get hurt, so why—"

"If you don't allow us to call for help, I'm shutting this goddamn thing down!"

"You will do as you are told. We have several police officers standing by in Bright Waters. Until ordered otherwise, you will keep this show going."

All eyes in the screening room were on the CEO, whose face had just turned murderously red. Deep down, they also wanted the show to continue; each and every person in the room, with the exception of Peterson's people, were feeling the drag of money in their pockets.

"Now you listen, Dalton, you know how many millions we have riding on this special. It's a smash success thus far. If you jeopardize what we have—"

The CEO froze as the phone line shut down. The light was still active on the phone console.

Suddenly, in the phone's receiver and the overhead speakers of the screening room, a deep and booming voice escaped from Summer Place loud and clear, chilling everyone who heard it.

"They are MINE!"

Bright River, Pennsylvania

Harris threw the phone down into the row of technicians operating the monitors. The voice was so loud it hurt. He quickly turned to one of the assistant producers.

"Call the goddamn police—now!"

The woman nodded and held up the phone. "I did five minutes ago, and I don't give a shit if they throw me in jail."

"Good girl," Dalton said as he placed his headphones back on. "Now, let's see if we can get the damn camera operating inside that basement to see if Kelly is still alive."

"Jesus, oh, man, look at camera seven," one of the technicians called out.

They saw the motion sensors on the bottom floor light up just as the black mass hit the last few steps of the staircase. "I didn't notice on the other static cameras before, it was coming down the stairs the whole time," the tech said, half rising from her chair.

"Sit down, and let's at least start doing our jobs!"

As they watched camera seven and its ambient-light picture, the entity once more split in two. One black mass headed straight for the ballroom and the other for the front doors. The camera couldn't follow both, so it kept its motion activation motor on the closest segment of the oozing and towering mass—the one that was heading for the large double doors of the ballroom.

"It's going for Lonetree and the others. Try to get some communication up and warn them," Harris said as calmly as he could. "Get camera five to get ready outside. Tell him they are on the clock again and to train all eyes on the front doors. We may have company."

The camera team that had been dispatched when Kennedy ordered Father Dalton evacuated didn't have to be told anything; they already had camera and sound trained on the front of Summer Place because of the banging and booming noises coming from the inside. The cacophony of noise rivaled the booms of thunder that were inundating the small valley, almost as if bombs were going off inside the house.

Harris's relief was short-lived. The front doors exploded outward and landed somewhere just in front of the production van. The cameraman and soundman were knocked from their feet, and the camera went in the opposite direction.

"Oh, God!" Harris cried, watching the mass exit the house. Even though the camera had fallen far from its operator, it was still trained on the front of the house. It was on its side, skewing the picture, but still functional.

"Go to five, go to five!" Harris shouted. The picture switched from inside the living room to the live view of the entity as it crashed through the open space where the thick front doors had been. All over the country, viewers got their first clear look at evil. The black, swirling mass stopped at the top of the stone steps, just under the portico. Suddenly a tendril of inky blackness shot out from the still form and went south into the storm-tossed night.

"Oh, shit," Harris said aloud.

"Is it—is it coming at us?" one of the technicians called out worriedly.

On the screen that showed a sideways view of the mass, it started down the stone steps, smashing the bottom of the giant wooden portico as it came on.

Harris couldn't open his mouth as the entity, or the part that was outside, came right at the production van, scattering emergency personnel in its path. He and the others turned toward the clear plastic curtain that sectioned them off from the heavy steel doors at the front of the trailer. Harris pulled the curtain back and ran to the double steel doors. He slammed home the large lock just as the entity struck the thick doors, bending them and warping them in their frame. The large van shook as it was knocked from its stabilizing blocks, knocking Harris backward.

In New York, the first inkling of panic began to set in inside the screening room.

Bright River, Pennsylvania

The six state police cruisers received their orders to move on Summer Place. They screamed out of the small town and took the curves of the wet road at breakneck speed, making the other cars fall behind. Suddenly, eight miles out of town and only three miles from Summer Place, the woods lining the roadway lit up as if an explosion had rent the forest. The bright green flash made the lead driver flinch, but he recovered quickly and kept going. As he accelerated back up to speed, a brief flash of movement caught his attention. A deer had shot from one side of the road to the other, barely missing the cruiser. The state trooper figured the hard storm with its lightning strikes was spooking the animals. Then as that thought struck him, another large buck sprang from the woods to the cruiser's right and stopped right in the middle of the road. The headlights picked out the large deer, just standing its ground against the police cruiser. Suddenly the animal started forward, first at a trot and then at a full gait. The state trooper turned his wheel, hitting his brakes and putting the heavy cruiser into a spin. The deer struck the car in the rear quarter panel and flew into the roadway, dead. Then another deer jumped in front of the spinning car, smashing the headlights. As its body was tossed underneath the car, the rear wheels struck it. Then the cruiser was airborne. It came down on its top, crushing the flashing lights, and skidded down the center of the road.

The second car in line took the corner dangerously fast. The driver saw the wreck and tried to turn, but he was too late. His vehicle slammed into the first at more than seventy miles an hour, bursting into flames. The third cruiser in line actually had a chance to avoid the disaster ahead, but just as the driver tried to apply his brakes and turn the steering wheel, a large owl slammed into the windshield, shattering it and momentarily throwing off the trooper's concentration. The bird was thrown clear just as the third car slammed into the first two. Flames were spreading fast in the downpour of rain, illuminating the woods, but the false light wasn't enough to prevent the pileup that followed, and the next three cars ended in a similar, disastrous fate.

As men and cars burned in the stormy night, the fires lit up the woods. Standing six and seven deep in those woods, thousands of scared animals regained their wits and turned and fled back into the forest.

The part of the entity moved over the burning, screaming men in the cruisers, absorbing their pain and anguish. Then, stronger than before its assault on the roadway, it rose and entered the woods.

The black and shimmering mass was returning to Summer Place, and the men and women trapped there were now on their own to face hell itself.

Summer Place

Gabriel pushed his weight against the door and was soon joined by Damian Jackson and even Lionel Peterson. The entity slammed into the door for a second time, and the wood actually splintered down its center. In the far corner of the room, George Cordero and Julie Reilly were trying frantically to open one of the bedroom windows. They struggled with the lock, but it wouldn't budge.

Damian Jackson tossed his nine-millimeter away and placed his hand over the crack that had formed in the door. Suddenly the state policeman screamed and then pulled his hand away. Even in the dark Jackson knew that at least two of his fingers were missing.

"The goddamn thing bit my fingers off!" He threw his weight against the door.

"Hell of a special effect, isn't it?!" Gabriel said as the door bulged inward once more.

"Yeah, just about as good as your theory that ghosts never really harmed anyone!" Jackson screamed back.

"You got me there," Kennedy said as he strained against the wood.

"Jesus, what the hell is that thing?" Peterson whined. He slid down the door and pushed his back to it, keeping pressure on it.

George and Julie turned from the window. The psychic grabbed a chair and slammed it against the glass. The wooden chair bounced back and struck Julie in the arm. She let out a small yelp.

"It's not a ghost," George said, out of breath. He examined

the glass, which hadn't broken into a thousand pieces, as he thought it would. He tried to catch his breath. "It may have been, once . . . and it may have also been human . . . but not now." He straightened, pulling Julie farther away from the window, and once more picked up the wooden chair. "No one has ever dealt with anything like this. Nowhere in the annals of the supernatural is anything like this mentioned. Its power is building from our fear of it, I can feel it. It wants out of Summer Place and it's going to go through us to do it!"

"He's right," Kennedy said. The entity laughed out loud in the hallway, bringing a spate of shivers to the people trapped inside the room. The laugh was booming and hardy, as if it were amused by what it was hearing. "The goddamn thing has evolved into something that's never been seen before."

"Well, may I suggest we get the hell out of here and allow it to go on its merry way?" Jackson said, cradling his mutilated hand.

"Where? We're trapped!" Peterson screamed as the mass struck the door again, this time breaking the crystal doorknob from its stem.

A tendril of mist entered the room through the crack in the door and slapped Kennedy away. With his weight off the door, the entity was able to push the thick wooden door inward by three inches, breaking away a portion of the frame.

As Gabriel crawled hurriedly back to the door, the roar of an enraged animal sounded from the hallway. They knew that the next time it struck the door it would give completely.

Whatever walked the halls and rooms inside Summer Place was mad and very hungry. It was tired of hiding among the wood and mortar of the old summer retreat and wanted to break away for good.

The entity smashed into the production van from the side, bulging the thin steel inward and shorting out several of the monitors. Harris Dalton threw himself over a production assistant just as the overhead fluorescents shattered, sending the van into darkness with the exception of the few still-functioning monitors left. With all thought of the Halloween special purged from his mind, Dalton went into a mind-set he thought he had forgotten. Just as when he'd been on assignment in Afghanistan, it was now time to try to stay alive.

The entity had smashed a large hole in the center of the ballroom doors in its attempt to get inside and stop the only being in the world that could cause it harm: John Lonetree. Leonard Sickles was throwing anything he could find at the large double doors; he was terrified, and that was the only action he could think of to take. Wallace Lindemann was sitting behind the bar with his hands over his ears, rocking back and forth, his mind slowly leaving him.

Jennifer was shaking John as hard as she could, but all Lonetree was doing was shaking his head and sweating cold moisture from his pores.

"John, wake up!" Jenny cried.

At the large double doors, Leonard froze with a bar stool raised as the top half of the left door smashed inward and flew into the ballroom. The stool slowly slipped from his grasp as the entity showed its face. It grabbed both sides of the opening with its black swirling hands and leaned its head through the opening. Leonard stumbled backward as the beast roared in animal triumph. Its obsidian eyes settled on John.

John felt Jenny shaking him, but he knew if he ended the dreamwalk now the beast would get them all. It would become powerful enough to leave Summer Place forever.

John watched the scene in the hallway. The entity was smashing into the large door over and over again. He heard his friends inside. Suddenly the beast turned its black eyes on John. He couldn't see it in the darkness, but he knew it was staring at him. It roared like an animal and John knew it was about to spring at his dream self. John closed his eyes and remembered what he needed to remember. When he opened them again, the entity was gone—not far away, but not after him any longer. He knew what he had to do. He had to help Gabriel and George, and then he needed to get help. There was only one place he knew of that could provide it. He reached out with his hand and pushed.

"Look!" Julie Reilly called out.

Gabriel, still helping to hold closed what was left of the door, looked up in time to see the large closet door slowly swing open. Warmer air permeated the cold room. He knew immediately it was John.

"George, put that chair down and get inside that closet. Feel around. I think Lonetree is trying to tell us something!"

Cordero slammed the chair against the window one more time. As it bounced off, he turned and ran for the closet. He also felt the large Indian's presence, and shoved aside the aging black-sequined gown on its lone hanger. As George struck the back wall of the wooden closet, he felt something give. He heard a squeak and then he felt a draft of even colder air. He reached out just as a loud boom sounded from the bedroom.

"George, we're running out of time here!" Kennedy shouted. "I think old F. E. Lindemann wants this bedroom!"

"In here! There's a passage of some sort."

"Julie, go!" Gabriel shouted. The door gave another two inches inward.

The reporter scrambled over the bed, hit the closet, and without hesitation she ducked inside.

"Peterson, get in there and follow," Gabriel said. He grimaced with the effort of keeping the entity out.

"You don't have to tell me twice. Good luck!" Peterson scrambled to his feet and vanished into the dark closet.

"Don't even say it, Kennedy. You get out of here!" Jackson screamed over the grunting and roaring of the beast outside of the bedroom.

"I wasn't going to say anything. Neither of us can leave without Mr. Wonderful coming inside and chasing down the others. I'm afraid we're pegged to be the heroes here."

"You could have at least argued for me to leave," Jackson said with a snarl.

The entity crashed into the door, and this time it gave way.

John moved back out into the hallway. He didn't know exactly how to get the mass of darkness to pay attention to him, but that became a moot point as he felt the black mass back away from the door. It had finally succeeded in cracking the wood to splinters. It turned toward John and roared. Forgetting all about the bedroom, it turned and came forward. John backed away. Then the beast roared in anger and came at him in earnest.

"Now, Gabe. Run, get to the sewing room, the answer is in there!" he shouted as he ran for the staircase.

Gabriel pushed broken shards of wood off his hurting body and turned his attention to Damian, who was covered in the remains of the door. When they both heard the call for them to run, they didn't hesitate. They covered the floor to the closet in moments and smashed inside the dark space that was their escape.

Once inside the passage, Gabriel searched his pockets for his penlight. "Damn it, the flashlight's back in the room!" he said with a hiss.

Jackson pushed by him in the tight passageway.

"Well, go back and get it, but don't mind if I don't go with you."

Kennedy had to smile as he turned on his heels and followed the detective.

They traveled along the passage until Damian, not being able to see clearly in the dark, bumped into Peterson, who let out a scream.

"This door or that one?" George asked in the darkness as Gabriel caught up.

"John said the sewing room. If I have my bearings straight, that's the one to your right."

George tried the panel in front of him. It didn't move.

"Try sliding it," Julie said at his shoulder.

George placed both hands on the panel and pushed to the left—nothing. Then he tried to the right, and the panel moved. He pushed it all the way open and then slowly and cautiously stepped into the sewing room.

As they all joined George, Gabriel brushed a small table and bumped against something. He picked it up to examine it and some liquid splashed in his hands: kerosene.

"Anyone got a light, a match, anything? I have a storm lamp."

Suddenly the room flashed brightly as Lionel Peterson lit his lighter. Gabriel raised the glass chimney on the storm lantern and Peterson lit the wick. Kennedy closed the chimney and adjusted the flame.

The sewing room was laid out neatly. There were three sewing machines, half-body mannequins, and old bolts of materials of all colors and make strewn across the room, all covered in a thick layer of dust. This was one room Eunice Johannson never touched in her daily cleaning of Summer Place. The dust and disarray made the room seem frozen in time. The many closets in the room were all locked with small padlocks. Damian Jackson noticed them just as Gabriel did.

"I guess Mrs. Lindemann took the security of her wardrobe seriously," Jackson said. He walked up to one and grasped the old brass lock with his uninjured left hand. The big state policeman pulled down as hard as he could. The lock held, but he heard a small cracking of the wood that the hasp was attached to. He pulled again and this time the old wood gave way and the lock and its hasp came off in his hand. "Oops."

Gabriel came forward with the lamp as Damian pulled open the closet door. Several items hung inside. Jackson took a step back in stunned silence. Julie mustered all of her courage to keep the sickness she felt from exiting her stomach.

"My God, what are those?" Peterson asked. Now they

knew who they were dealing with, and what was walking the hallways of Summer Place.

John had made it to the second-floor landing, but he felt the entity close behind. The flashing of the motion sensors and the beeping of the laser grid told him the beast had gained the second floor and was just across the house from where he was. He knew beyond a doubt that if the entity could catch him in his dream state, it could kill him just as surely as if it were confronting his real body.

John held his ground on the landing, waiting for the black mass to reach the corner of the hallway, baiting it away from Gabriel and George. The black force rounded the corner, and John knew he could lead it away successfully—his bait had worked.

Suddenly, as he turned to run down the stairs in his dream, a cold splash—or flash, really—struck his face. It was so cold that he gasped for breath. Then, to his horror, he opened his eyes. The entity roared in pure animalistic anger and turned back the way it had come. John knew it had figured out where Gabriel and the others were.

"No, it's going back to the third floor—it's going to the sewing room!"

He tried to scream at the retreating entity to regain its attention, but just as he opened his mouth in his dream state, another splash of freezing cold struck him. Like the witch in *The Wizard of Oz,* he began to dissolve.

John opened his eyes and tried to catch his breath. He was coughing and spitting as the cold water ran down his throat and windpipe. A pair of reaching arms helped him to sit up.

"John, are you okay?"

John tried to clear his head, shaking cold water from him and slinging his long wet hair around. He managed to draw in a deep breath. He finally opened his eyes and looked around. Shaking, he saw Jennifer standing over him. She was holding a large glass that still dripped water.

"You . . . you woke me," he said as he rubbed his swollen eyes. "I wasn't done."

"You were dying, John. You were breathing too hard and your pulse was racing. You were about to go into cardiac arrest, or have a stroke."

Before John could say anything, a crash at the door brought his head around. The entity, or the part that took occupancy near the ballroom, had smashed the left side of the door to splinters. Leonard Sickles was still throwing anything he could through the large opening at the roaring beast.

"We're out of time here!" Leonard shouted as he threw a computer monitor through the doorway.

"I have to get to the subbasement!" John stood. "Can we get out of one of the French doors?"

Jenny shook her head. "We've been trying ever since you went under."

"Damn it, we're going to lose them if I don't get to the basement!"

Jenny suddenly felt weak. She sat on the edge of the couch. At first, John thought the situation was just overwhelming her, but then he saw her eyes roll into the back of her head. Her entire body shook and then she moaned deep in her throat. She suddenly stood and looked down at John.

"I didn't think that bitch would ever let me squeeze though that hole," Jenny said, her voice decidedly male.

"Bobby Lee?" John asked.

Jenny looked up at the large Indian and shook her head in wonder. "Well, it ain't Chuck Berry. Look, you don't have the time." Jenny touched her own cheek. "And my Jenny girl doesn't, and believe me, that's the only reason I'm turning into Gary Cooper here."

"What are you—"

"Shut up, man. Listen, you tell Jenny I never meant no harm. I loved her and that's why I chose her. That's why I stayed and that's why I made her life hell. This is my makeup to her. You'll know when to run, Tonto. Now get her ready to go, get to your basement, and kill this fucking thing. It gives ghosts a bad fucking name."

Jennifer fell forward into John's arms. She moaned and started to come around almost immediately. She had tears in her eyes, as if she knew exactly what her personal ghost was going to do for her.

John looked up at the exact moment that Leonard Sickles was pushed out of the way by an unseen force. Leonard hit the Persian rug on his back and watched as a sparkling wave of light shot through the exposed hole in the large door. Suddenly the beast roared in anger and the pounding stopped. The only sound in the ballroom was the crying coming from Wallace Lindemann at the back of the bar.

The doorway on the left side slowly opened. Leonard ran, with John carrying Jennifer close behind.

Bobby Lee McKinnon was giving them the time they needed.

Harris Dalton and the fifteen technicians, assistant directors, and producers split into groups, hoping to keep the thing they had sought earlier in the television special out of the production van. All of the enthusiasm they had shown in the beginning had vanished now that the scenario facing them was real. If the thing now punching five- and six-foot dents into the trailer's steel frame got inside, they would be devoured. All of them knew it.

"I think it's drawing power from our electronics. What if we get outside somehow and kill the generator?" Nancy, his assistant director, asked as she picked herself off the carpeted deck.

"Okay, I'm game. Do you want me to open the door and you just squeeze by whatever the fuck it is that's out there and make a run for the genny?!" Harris shouted. He watched a corner of the steel door pull outward from the trailer's frame.

"Oh, man, look at that," Nancy said. There was no way past the thing that was outside.

A large flash of lightning illuminated the grounds and they saw a large arm, mist-shrouded and black, reach in and take a swipe at the closest technician, striking him in the chest and sending him flying. Harris reached for the phone and placed it to his ear, trying desperately to punch in the numbers for New York. As the tones sounded, he heard laughter through the phone line. *"They're mine . . . they're mine . . . they are MINE!"*

The corner of the large door peeled down from the hinge that held it in place.

"Oh, crap," Harris said.

When the door to the sewing room bent inward, Gabriel knew that the entity had discovered their whereabouts. Each person took a step back from the discovery inside the closet that had unnerved them all. Gabe turned the storm lamp toward the open closet one last time to absorb what he was seeing.

The door was slammed again. Damian Jackson saw to his horror that the lock was unlatched. He dove for the door and tried desperately to slam the lock home with his good hand, but the door bent inward with such force that the wood cracked and splintered. Julie saw what he was trying to do and reached for the lock herself, finally getting a hold on it and ramming it home. The beast outside seemed enraged that Gabriel and the others had managed to penetrate its inner sanctum. The pounding and thrashing became more intense, slinging splinters of wood off the cracked door into the interior of the sewing room.

Gabriel moved to the closet and ran his hand over the garment at the front. It looked to be a bodysuit of some kind. Made of white cloth, it was knee-length and ended at the collar. To his horror, it was complete with breasts—cloth, to be sure, but full and ample breasts. And it had many companions. Some were heavier than others, but all came equipped with breasts. Gabriel quickly counted twenty bodysuits, each one meticulously hand-sewn. Worn underneath a dress, no one would be able to tell that they were false forms for a woman who wasn't a real woman at all.

"It's all fitting together." Gabriel hurried from the open closet to the door. He held the lamp high. Jackson, George, and Peterson had their weight firmly planted against the wood, trying to keep the entity at bay.

"We know"—Gabriel shouted—"we know who you are. We know why you weren't in any of the pictures of your family. You weren't one of the girls; you're the son, Mrs. Lindemann!"

The beating against the door stopped. A screech followed, shattering the standing mirror closest to the door.

"You were born a boy. You became a woman!"

The scream of rage came again and the entity came at the door with its full force behind it. The door bent, cracked halfway up, and sent Damian Jackson flying back into the room. George and Lionel Peterson were thrown to the floor. The door was there for the taking, and the entity took full advantage of it.

As John, Jennifer, and Leonard ran through the smashed door to the right and the door that Bobby Lee McKinnon had opened to the left, a battle was taking place in the living room. Bobby Lee, a sparkling, shimmering version of him, was in the air, on the back of the dark mass that had been attacking the ballroom. Jennifer stopped and gaped in wonder as the black entity tried desperately to dislodge the pest that had planted itself on its back, roaring in anger and shock that an entity it had no knowledge of was stopping it from its goal.

"Go!" came Bobby Lee's voice, tired and frightened. The swirling black mass finally managed to rake its dark claws across his shimmering form, sending him flying from its back. The black entity charged at the downed ghost of the former musician.

Jennifer screamed but John pulled her away. The swirling and pulsating mass attacked to kill. Leonard helped John and actually lifted Jenny off her feet, sprinting through the dark toward the kitchen. They slammed into the swinging doors without noticing the smashed front doors or the storm outside. They failed to hear the screaming of those trapped in the barn and the production van. John lost his breath as he slammed into the door at the far end of the kitchen. Jenny and Leonard couldn't stop their momentum and slammed into his back as he tried to open the basement door. Finally he pushed them out of the way and opened the door. The blackness of the stairwell opened up before them.

"Inside—hurry!" John cried out.

Jenny went first and then Leonard, just as a man's scream was heard from the living room. John knew that Bobby Lee was done for. He had given his false afterlife for them, and it wouldn't go to waste. John entered the stairwell and slammed the door closed, locking it from the inside.

Leonard and Jenny stumbled down the dark steps. John started down behind them, knowing full well that if he lost his footing he would break every bone in his body on the concrete floor below. As he forced himself to slow down, he heard the smashing of the door far above him. The entity was on its way down to stop him from doing what had to be done.

John hit the turn on the stairwell just as Jenny and Leonard hit the bottom. Lonetree took a chance and started taking the invisible stairs two at a time, nearly breaking his ankle on the last step before touching firm, flat concrete.

"The trapdoor, we have to open it!"

Jenny was crying but still trying to function. She ran toward where she remembered the door to be. Her foot kicked something on the floor and then suddenly a bright beam of light illuminated the floor as the flashlight spun in a circle. Jennifer picked it up, not knowing it was the same flashlight that Kelly had been holding when she was attacked just thirty minutes before. She located the subbasement trapdoor and then sighed.

"The lock's been removed and then bent back into position. We'll never get it open!"

As John and Leonard joined Jenny at the trapdoor, it started to rattle in its frame. The concrete cracked around it and the door actually bent outward, rattling violently. Jenny could swear she heard voices of desperation from the other side.

"Jesus, it's already in there!" Leonard said as he backed away.

"No, but something is that can help us, I think," John said. He ran to the far wall and one of the old wood stoves that lined it. "Help me. Hurry!" He pushed against the quarter-ton stove.

Leonard and Jenny immediately saw what he was attempting. They joined him and started pushing the wrought-iron stove toward the trapdoor. John tilted the heavy stove on end and flipped it over onto the thin, wide door. The weight disintegrated the trapdoor and the stove hurtled down, smashing and breaking the wooden steps as it fell to the deepest part of the house.

Above them they heard the black entity storming down the stairs, cracking the wooden steps as it came.

Suddenly the basement filled with light. Shades of colors never thought imaginable emanated from the dirt-lined sub-basement, accompanied by the gentle smell of young girls. Wisps of curling streamers came out of the hole and they all heard the screams of torment. The room filled with the sound of women screaming their horror at what had happened to them.

"Who are they?" Jenny asked. She ducked as several of the tendrils whisked by her head.

"Mothers . . . they're mothers," John said, as if in a daze.

The entity coming down the stairs had stopped and was screaming in outrage as the real secret of Summer Place spilled out of the bowels of the house. The swirling, multi-colored tendrils of spirits that had been tormented for close to a hundred years hung momentarily in the air around John, Jenny, and Leonard. Then, with the roar of outrage from the stairs sounding again and the sound of the beast retreating,

the tendrils of rainbow-colored spirits screamed their own indignity and shot forward and up the stairs.

"Get her," John said, as if to himself.

The entity was caught as it reached the doorway to the basement. Lightning flashed throughout the house as tendrils of
color struck the beast. It roared with pain. The tendrils
curled in and out, around and through the black mass, and
every time the beast screamed, it weakened. The ghosts of
the women who had met their end at Summer Place vented
their revenge. They split apart, scattering throughout the
house.

The black mass smashed through the door. It lifted Gabriel
high into the air, closing around his throat and squeezing
the air out of him. He clawed at his throat, fighting to breathe,
but broke one hand free and waved the others out of the
room.

Damian pushed Julie, George, and Peterson out the doorway. He was about to turn and help Gabriel when a powerful
wind slammed into him and knocked him down. Gabriel was
thrown hard into the wall. His body slid down and thumped
onto the carpet. Jackson went to him and started pulling the
professor out by the arm. The multicolored wisps of smoke
were all over the black mass, which was screaming out in
pain. Parts of it were being torn free to vanish like smoke in
the wind. Jackson finally managed to get Gabriel's still form
out of the room just as the beast roared in newfound pain.
Then as suddenly as their rescuers had appeared, they vanished. The black mass had vanished also. The air warmed,
until Jackson could no longer see his breath.

Gabriel moaned and tried to sit up.

"Take it easy, Professor. You have two broken legs."

Gabriel opened his eyes and looked up at Jackson. "Now
tell me I don't know how to throw a Halloween party."

Jackson smiled for the first time in what seemed like many
years. He patted Kennedy on the shoulder and sat down

beside him. "I think I'll skip your next party. I'm way too old for this shit."

Outside, the night became silent with the exception of the falling rain striking the production trailer's smashed and battered exterior. Harris Dalton picked himself up off the floor and looked around as the power came back on. The others in the trailer were all right—they slowly raised their heads.

"Is it . . . is it over?" Nancy asked.

Harris didn't answer. He stood in stunned silence as the night returned to normal. Lights were flashing on the phone terminal. He took a deep breath and reached for the cracked instrument, then pushed one of the flashing buttons.

"Dalton," he said as calmly as he could.

"Damn it, man, where have you been? We've been showing nothing but dead air for the past twenty minutes!"

Harris pushed the main screen button, bringing online the camera that lay on its side in the rain. The view showed the smashed front doors of Summer Place, and to Dalton's horror, several people lying on the wet ground. To his relief, several of them were moving, starting to pick themselves up.

"What the hell happened out there?" Feuerstein raged.

Harris looked at the men and women looking at him. They were all flushed, and most were shaking badly. He shook his head and looked away, placing the phone back to his ear.

"Before I tell you what you can do with your special, Feuerstein, I'll say this, and I think I speak for the rest of my crew: I quit. Now, you have a happy Halloween, you son of a bitch!"

John looked down into the hole that was the subbasement. Jenny knew what he was going to do and reached out with a shaking hand to stop him. He smiled and touched her arm.

"There's nothing down there that can hurt us. We have to look for Kelly and Sanborn. They could be hurt down there."

Jenny whimpered but let go of John's arm. Leonard came

over when Lonetree looked his way and placed his arm around Jennifer. He nodded that John should go.

Lonetree shined the light around the darkness below and saw that he could shimmy his way down the broken staircase where the stove hadn't demolished it.

After three minutes and almost falling to his death five times, Lonetree hit the dirt floor of the subbasement. He shined the small penlight around and saw the stove which he had used to free the trapped entities. Then he froze as he saw some of the barren earth move to his left. A hand pushed its way through the dirt. He grasped it and pulled. Kelly Delaphoy came free of the soil with a gasp, trying desperately to breathe. John left her lying on the hard-packed floor as he searched for Jason Sanborn. It didn't take long—he heard the associate producer moan as he too broke free of the spot where the black mass had buried him alive.

Kelly was spitting dirt out of her mouth and crying. John assisted Sanborn to the wall and helped him to sit.

John looked around as they recovered from their premature burial, and he noticed the designs on the wall. Pentancles and other demonic designs were etched into the hard earth walls beneath Summer Place.

"God almighty."

EPILOGUE

*. . . and whatever walked
there, walked alone.*
—SHIRLEY JACKSON, *The Haunting of Hill House*

Kelly paid for the meeting room at the Waldorf-Astoria with the severance pay she had been issued the week before. At the table were eight people, four of whom were now happily unemployed.

George Cordero, Leonard Sickles, Harris Dalton, Kelly Delaphoy, Jennifer Tilden, Jason Sanborn, Damian Jackson, and Julie Reilly spoke in hushed voices, catching up on what they'd each been doing over the two months since Halloween night at Summer Place.

Wallace Lindemann had committed himself to a hospital in Westchester County, New York, for treatment of alcoholism and a possible schizophrenic condition brought on by his stay in his only investment left in the world. As for Lionel Peterson, he had moved to become head of Fox News, where, as Julie Reilly put it, absolutely no one would ever take him seriously again. Julie, Kelly, and Jason had been released from their contracts by the network—the company was "moving in another direction" with reality television. Julie had not been offered the anchor chair for the *Nightly News,* and that had forced her out, along with *Hunters of the Paranor-*

mal. Damian Jackson had been forced to accept early retirement from the Pennsylvania State Police, on the grounds that he had been overworked to the point that his reports no longer made sense. As for the network, it was being sued by every one of the sponsors that had bought into the prime-time Halloween special—a debacle that had forced the aging CEO to step down (with a full golden parachute, of course).

The door opened and everyone turned to see Gabriel Kennedy being wheeled into the meeting room, with John Lonetree pushing him along. Gabriel was parked at the head of the table, and then John took a seat next to Jennifer. She leaned over and kissed him. Jenny was resplendent in a bright yellow dress, and her weight had come back strong. Her life had totally turned around. She could even listen to "oldies but goodies" stations again without feeling bad over Bobby Lee McKinnon and his sacrifice for her. She smiled at Lonetree and leaned back in her chair.

Gabriel took in all of the faces around the table. He tossed a large folder onto the table, and once again looked from face to face.

"John, would you like to start? Then I'll give you the police findings."

Lonetree squeezed Jenny's hand and then slowly stood.

"The dreamwalk is where the story starts and ends. When I was under, I was able to see the very beginning—the creation of Elena Lindemann, if you will. In all actuality, Elena Vilnikov was born Vasily Gregory Vilnikov in 1881—the only son of Russian parents who were distant relatives of the Russian imperial family, the Romanovs. Vasily had twin sisters, who were four years younger. The father doted on the girls, to Vasily's severe detriment. The boy was ignored, ridiculed, when all he wanted in life was to be loved. As you may remember from Leonard's photographs, there were no girls that matched Elena's age in the family, only the boy and the two younger sisters. Vasily had a warped impression of just what his father hated about him. That was the spark, we think, that ignited Vasily's plan to become what he knew his father loved: a girl."

John paused for a drink of water and looked toward Gabriel, who nodded his encouragement.

"During the dreamwalk, I witnessed Vasily's turning point. He burned his father and his sisters to death in their house. He escaped with his mother, who we may assume covered up for him until the day she died, leaving the boy alone in the world and free to become anyone he wanted. We can only assume he had launched into a homosexual affair with F. E. Lindemann at some point. At what point Frederic was talked into actually marrying and allowing his lover to become a full-time woman . . . that's only conjecture."

"We do have proof—the bodysuits in the sewing room, sewn by Vasily's meticulous hands," Gabriel reminded everyone.

"As for the children of Elena and F. E. Lindemann," John continued. "Now, Vasily obviously couldn't have children. So they created changelings. Children were stolen from their mothers at birth—or were cut directly from their mothers' wombs. There were no end of immigrant mothers, pregnant and seeking help. The Lindemanns were handily positioned, taking in those pregnant immigrants. Alone in a new world, they would never be missed. To outward appearances, it looked generous, assisting those lonely women by providing them work and lodging."

"You mean to say that none of the Lindemanns' eight children were their own?" Damian interjected. "That they were—"

"Changelings," John said.

"The sons of bitches."

"Yes," John agreed. "One of those young women was the sister of the German opera star Gwyneth Gerhardt. Gwyneth came looking for the girl after she got pregnant and ran off to America. She tracked her to Summer Place and suspected something wasn't right. I witnessed her death when she got too close to the truth."

"The trapped spirits in the subbasement?" Julie Reilly asked.

"Yes. They were the mothers of the changelings. They were brought to Summer Place and buried in the subbasement, along with twenty-two other women whose births weren't successful."

"My God," Jennifer breathed.

"But the hauntings supposedly started long before the death of Vasily—er, uh, Elena," Kelly countered.

"That is more speculation," Gabriel said as John took his seat. "I finally had a talk with the silent movie star's companion, a lesbian who had a long-standing affair with her. She finally admitted that Vidora Samuels told her she had been raped by a man. Now, we can speculate that it may have been F. E. Lindemann who had committed that crime, or it could have been Vasily. The actress never could identify her attacker, so she just said there was no one there—that was how the haunted house stories began. We can presume the same story goes for the gossip columnist. But since her assault was attempted in broad daylight, she may have seen her attacker."

"So why not tell the police?" Julie asked.

"Because, we have since learned, the newspapers she wrote for were mostly owned in silent partnership by F. E. Lindemann."

"Shit. They skipped through life without a care in the world. But their own children, they seemed to have been cursed, themselves," Jennifer said.

"You bet they were," Gabriel said. "Not one of them died of the causes listed on their gravestones. As a matter of fact, there isn't one body in any of those graves."

That sent everyone to asking questions all at once, but Gabriel was patient and let the voices around the table calm before he continued.

"The children were each lured home one at a time and killed by their parents."

"What . . . what for?" Jason Sanborn asked, feeling sicker the more he heard.

"Who knows? Maybe because they were indeed change-lings, maybe because Elena couldn't call them her own, or maybe just because they weren't babies any longer. The one thing we do know for sure is that all eight of the bodies were buried right alongside their birth mothers in the subbasement. That has been confirmed through DNA testing. Altogether, we are looking at one of the first substantiated cases of a brutal serial killer who was into devil worship on a major scale. With the eight changelings, there were thirty-one bodies unearthed under Summer Place."

"I think," John said as he stared at the table, "that Elena, or Vasily, was so evil that his power kept growing even after his death. Hell, maybe we'll never know how the entity was really created. But everyone here must understand: where there is one, there is another, and another."

Everyone talked for another half hour and then Gabriel cleared his throat. He picked up the folder he had placed on the table when he entered the room.

"This is from Lord Henry Wilcox in the House of Lords in Great Britain. He has requested our services, naming each and every one of us specifically. It seems he has some trouble on his estate in Scotland. Several people have disappeared, and he wants us to investigate. The police and Scotland Yard have come up with no viable answers. Although I initially turned him down, he has become quite the persistent gentle-man. He has placed an offer of one million dollars' compen-sation for each member of . . . well, each of us, to find out what is stalking his estate."

The room was quiet, and Gabriel waited for the refusals to spill forth with vehemence that would be well deserved. Instead, each person looked to the next.

"I'm out of work, so a million dollars looks pretty damn good to me right about now," Julie said.

"I hear that," Kelly Delaphoy agreed.

"Are you people nuts? Wasn't Summer Place whacked enough for you?" Leonard asked, rising to his feet.

George Cordero placed his hand on Leonard's and pulled him back into his chair.

"That translates into: When do we go?" George smiled at Leonard, who only grimaced.

"Detective Jackson, what do you say?" Gabriel asked the large man to his right.

"That's former detective Jackson. And just to let you know, I didn't save as much money as I should have. So, I agree. When do we go?"

It was agreed. They would do just one more investigation to get everyone back on their feet again.

As men and women started gathering their things, it was John Lonetree, with Jenny on his arm, who asked the question.

"By the way, Gabe, what did Lord Wilcox say? You stopped at 'each member of.'"

Gabriel hesitated, then smiled. "Why, it was that stupid name that Julie called us during that damned Halloween special."

"I don't remember," John said. "I was a little preoccupied at the time."

Most in the room rolled their eyes, but it was Gabriel who reminded John what they had been nicknamed during that long, dark, and very stormy night in Pennsylvania.

"Each member of the team known as . . . *the Supernaturals.*"